The Boat

When Eileen moved to the remote sanctuary of the cottage seeking only a peaceful, quiet place to rebuild her life, she had no inclination the property, long abandoned, would hold so many secrets. She was also unaware they would create the amount of intrigue and mayhem they did.

When she received a phone call inquiring how she was doing, her first thought said it all.

How would you tell someone, "Oh by the way. I've been shot at, killed a man, had my house invaded with the law, Feds, DEA and anyone else with a badge. There were agents with titles only pronounced in acronyms.

"Then the house was blown up along with my Jeep. But, not to worry—the dogs and I are okay." Sounded flippant, even then in the mental recounting. She might also add: it still scared the living hell out of her.

The Boat

H. Wakefield

A Wings ePress, Inc.

Mystery Novel

Wings ePress, Inc.

Edited by: Jeanne Smith
Copy Edited by: Joan C. Powell
Executive Editor: Jeanne Smith
Cover Artist: BJ Haynes

All rights reserved

Wings ePress Books
www.books-by-wings-epress.com

Copyright © 2016 by H. Wakefield
ISBN 978-1-61309-719-9

Published In the United States Of America

Wings ePress Inc.
3000 N. Rock Road
Newton, KS   67114

Dedication

To all my friends and family who made this possible.
I am grateful for all of your assistance and support.

One

It was early morning as I stood on my porch surrounded by police, wardens, sheriffs, and other strangers. Some called themselves agents. All were showing badges and talking way too fast. This, after a very long, and very bad, night was enough to give me a momentary scare for a good reason. The man I'd killed was still lying on my beach, right where he dropped when I shot him.

One of the men detached himself from the group and marched over to where I stood. Without preamble or introductions, he barked, using his gruff, *no nonsense* tone, "Okay, where is this Biter? I need answers and I need 'em *now*.

Hell of a great cop… he couldn't even get my name right. "Who's responsible for this? I need information immediately!"

I *was* upset; however I wouldn't allow him or anyone to browbeat or bully me. During my sixty-seven years, I had endured more than my share of loss and abuse…physical, financial, and mental. This man wouldn't become an exception to the rule. "I would say I must have been partly responsible. I shot him. The other part of the blame was his. He was trespassing on posted property. More importantly, he shot at me first. I'm Eileen Byther…do I need to *spell* it for you? This is my home."

I'd moved to this remote coastal town with my dogs to get away from strife and people. I had needed a safe and quiet place to heal while rebuilding what would be left of my life. I didn't even like to trek into town with its five to six hundred people if I could avoid it. Once a month I reluctantly went to the post office for my mail. I used a hot spot for my internet and cell phone. Those were my only connections to the world, which, frankly, held no further interest for me. I did most of my shopping, when necessary, in a larger town known as, *the city,* miles away. When the trip was necessary, I drove over back roads, bought what I needed, and returned home, without ever setting a foot in the town.

My children understood my hermitage. They all had very busy and productive lives of their own. They kept in touch with me through e-mail and phone calls, wishing me well. As far as I was concerned, they would *never* get wind of this incident.

My only surviving sister, Kate, lived in Virginia. She had managed to create a life for herself after an abusive relationship forced her to move. She'd developed a new and lucrative career doing repossessions for banks. She also volunteered with a shelter that assisted women who were fleeing from abuse. We didn't talk often, keeping in touch with e-mail occasionally. She would never hear of this debacle either.

I had no idea who any of these people were. I could identify what the ones in uniforms were… the others, no clue, nor did I care.

Two

However, first let me try to explain how and why I arrived here. Then perhaps you'll understand, or maybe not. I feel I should give you fair warning because this went from bad to unbelievably horrible in a brief span of time.

I'd purchased this cottage some time ago. I didn't know why at the time, but for most of my life I'd bought and sold real estate. I'd heard about the property through some folks in a passing conversation while traveling through a town along the Maine coast.

I'd driven to the property which local folks had declared a *dead issue*. They'd told me everyone who ever lived there had died.

Typical of Mainers, they also neglected to mention the folks who inhabited the cottage came there only for summers, and were elderly. Most were well into the end years of their lives when they died.

Several generations had shared the cottage until there were no surviving family members; it then reverted to the town for unpaid taxes. Town officers wanted it off their books.

My first glimpse of the cottage came after a very tenuous and rough drive over what the natives would call a *trace*, perhaps because there was only a trace of where an old road might have been long ago. The drive had been a challenge for my ancient Jeep, a Grand Wagoneer, that wasn't so grand anymore.

After the slow, bumpy, and muddy trek into the property, my dogs Seaweed, an inherited old Sheltie, and Shadow, my small Rottweiler, and I were free to explore.

The first breath of the salt-laden air had stirred my heart and soul with the nostalgia of a long ago childhood spent on an island.

I saw a typical, gabled, pointy-roofed, story-and-a half building with a wrap-around porch shingled in the decorative style of some quaint long-ago time. It remained true to the period, with an abundance of gingerbread trim.

The cottage was perched high on a rocky point surrounded by a thatchy-grass yard edged with ledge leading either to, or from, the ocean.

The small sandy beach appeared contained within the arms of the rocks as they curved around it on each side forming a calm pool. At a glance, it was hard to determine if the cottage was gazing out to sea or guarding the land. Either way it felt safe, inviting, and comfortable.

I had expected to see a tumbledown shack. Instead, there was an artifact from the past.

The yellow paint on the old cottage was peeling while the white trim paint had blistered. The porch steps were dubious, while the porch appeared like no one, except perhaps a field mouse, had crossed its weathered boards for many years.

I walked around the building, taking note of the promise the project held. I smiled at this observation from a person who, in her day, bought some odd and sometime derelict buildings for renovation and resale. I had done this using the guise of a hobby. Translated, this *hobby* meant a lot of hard work for satisfaction and extra money.

I'd not seen a foundation or even if there was one because of all the old grass against the building.

The roof didn't looked great, but there were no gaping holes apparent. It was an old roof with patches of moss growing here and there. There was evidence left by the sea gulls of their use of the ridge for a lookout post.

For the age of the cottage, the chimney seemed fair, standing tall and straight with probably no mortar left. It was still there, nonetheless. Overall, it looked good to me.

I returned to the porch for a peek in the windows. I wanted a glimpse of the interior. I stepped gingerly as I moved, being pleased at how secure it felt, in spite of the appearance. The windows were large with four panes of glass, without screens or storms, to obscure my view. I peeked, no, I *pressed* my face to the window; the inside was furnished in a style in time somehow lost to us.

Although there was electricity to the building, there were kerosene lamps on the wall with one on the stand in the front room. I assumed it was because, with wind and storms, the power was at best inconsistent.

I could almost smell the wonderful, dusty mustiness. Ahhh, that was so good!

As I continued around the corner of the porch, I looked into another window. This was a small bedroom with an iron bed covered by a patchwork quilt. The bureau stood tall with an old oval mirror held in upright arms. There, again, was an oil lamp on the bedside stand. In the corner sat a white iron washstand with the pitcher and washbowl. There was a braided rag rug on the floor. The only other thing in the room was a very inviting wooden rocker. It had an afghan laid over the back and a pad on the seat. It was so peaceful and undisturbed. I'd almost expected to see an old dowager come and sit down.

I found an ancient, worn, wicker rocker on the side of the porch along with a pair of rotting wooden Adirondack chairs near another set of steps leading down to the grass. The second steps were not in good shape, so I didn't venture down them.

Instead, I pulled the rocker around to the front of the cottage and sat gently on the chair. It held; how nice was that for a welcome?

I had found an old home with good bones and great prospects. The property and I shared many similarities: we were both older, changed by time, but still resilient.

I could see where birds had made their nests over the years in the overhead rafters under the porch roof. The railings seemed to be intact. As far as I could see all the balusters were there.

The cottage seemed frozen in time. Considering the amount of vandalism that was rampant everywhere, I couldn't understand how it had withstood those worldly problems.

I felt blessed to have been allowed the opportunity of sitting there looking out across the bay to a small island beyond. The dogs were lying comfortably beside me after their bounding inspection of the shore.

It had begun to rain softly. I listened, marveling at how wonderful it sounded as it hit the roof then dripped off onto the ground below… the smell was exquisite. The property was so much more than I'd anticipated. The ocean lapped gently at the rocks, combining smells of the shower as it moved slowly away.

I'd been transfixed in a space where time and troubles didn't exist.

I carefully walked to the back of the cottage, then climbed up onto the substantial granite ledge. The ledge rounded up then dropped sharply onto the rocks and sea below.

I checked the roof from that angle, noticing what appeared to be a vent pipe for plumbing. Could it be over time they'd installed plumbing in the building? If so, I assumed there must have been an attempt, at some point, to install a septic tank.

The well had been an easy find. I nearly fell into it because it was no longer covered. The hand-dug well appeared to have been there for many years. Surprisingly, it was quite large and deep with a substantial amount of water showing. I mused at the novelty of a good fresh water supply so close to the ocean.

The property seemed well worth a bid. I returned to the town office and made a shamefully low bid I knew could be covered with the sale of a CD I owned.

To my astonishment, the next week I received a notice; the town was ready to execute a quitclaim deed on the property. They requested I send them a check, and no, it wouldn't be necessary for me to return to complete the transaction.

However, they did make note: I should be certain to maintain all of the tax payments as they became due. If taxes again became overdue, the cottage would go back on the auction block.

That wasn't a real *friendly town.*

I sent the check. They sent the deed. I recorded it. The cottage was mine.

It had been so peaceful and quiet there I could have sat and listened to those comforting sounds and smells forever. Perhaps someday I would make it happen. The dogs and I would go there, open the cottage, and stay for a few days. It was my dream.

I managed to return only once for a couple hours after I purchased it, due to a busy and often chaotic schedule. I'd explored the interior while arranging for the well to be covered, road repaired, and other small things done.

There were open rooms downstairs consisting of the living room with a stone fireplace. There was a bedroom off the end near the fireplace and a dining area on the end by the kitchen.

The kitchen contained an old wood-gas combination stove and a relic of a refrigerator.

There were two bedrooms upstairs. To my delight, there was a very primitive bath on the second floor.

All of the camp furniture remained, along with abundant dust everywhere. It smelled good to me; just as times spent in old attics… that particular smell you get only from antiquity and/or solitude.

While there, I managed time to sit on the porch for about an hour. I just enjoyed the smell and sounds of the cove.

I didn't ever intend to sell the cottage although I knew I could, instantly. I'd found a jewel; it was truly a gift from God. It was exactly what I needed.

Three

On my return a year later, the cove was still and calm. The old cottage sat proud, strong, and secure on its rocky base.

That had been more than I could say about myself. Finding out at sixty-seven I no longer had a marriage, home, employment, very little money saved, and a bruised ego was almost too much to bear. I was getting older and I'd always been a proud person. I was struggling desperately to put myself and the remainder of my life back together. I stood quietly, just taking comfort from the proud stance of the old cottage. There was a message there.

The storm-battered exterior of the old cedar shingles had weathered well. There were still dabs of pale yellow paint clinging in curled fragments. The old, once white, trim paint was almost completely gone due to the wind and time.

The road into the cottage was just a bit worse than on my last trip, even with the repairs I'd requested. It didn't appear as though anyone had tried to navigate the road recently. Most likely, because when a driver came off the dirt road it connected to, it appeared to be just an old abandoned, very muddy logging road through an alder swamp.

Even with the old Jeep, it had been a chore to reach a parking spot near the base of the ledge.

My motto in life is *when the going gets tough, the tough get going*. Well, I was going. I had started over many times in my life. I could and would do it again.

I arrived in the early spring. It had been good timing, even if it was not by my choice, but by circumstance.

The loss of the marriage, or the charade, was a blessing in disguise. It had been short and bad from the beginning. I'd wanted someone to love me, thinking I was special. He wanted someone to front his new business venture. Long story short, I had the funds; he had the line.

The resulting failure of our business was one of many self-induced monetary fiascos in his lifetime. A fact I learned too late. There was no longer a need for the guise of marriage.

There had been no way to recoup my loss financially. I came away with my cottage, the old Jeep, and my dogs, along with an increase of stubborn and a more resolved attitude.

I'd been single for a very long time prior to the marriage. I knew I was more than competent to handle the task; after all, I had lived comfortably while managing to raise three great adults.

For me, being single again was a weight lifted off my mind. I was free!

I loaded my Jeep, with all I could stuff into it, took the two dogs and left. We moved to the only place I had, my cottage.

I'm sure we were quite an interesting sight. Not a problem… we were there to settle in and make it our home. This task would require lots of cleaning, airing out and speculation about renovating. I needed to begin living again.

During my second week there we survived a night of horrific gales. I thought the cottage would certainly fall off the ledge into the ocean.

When I looked out of the kitchen window while fixing coffee, I saw a small white boat had washed ashore into the cove. It was lying on its side at the shoreline. It looked as though someone had simply discarded it. The boat seemed content to rest there.

Large mug of hot coffee in hand, followed by my faithful, frolicking buddies Seaweed and Shadow, we set off with great anticipation to explore what the storm had delivered. There were old lobster buoys, loads of kelp which surprised me. Although, often we would get a wash of seaweed, we seldom got any kelp on the shore after a rough tide. There were other pieces of storm debris, but my primary interest was the boat.

I wanted a boat from the day we moved there. I had known I couldn't afford the expense. Here was a boat! It wasn't a great one, but a *boat*!

It was an old boat. I found the design very appealing. It was similar to a pea pod with a small half teardrop stern in a curved form fitting the sides of the boat. There were three seats; the middle one was good size while the other two were smaller.

As I checked the boat over more carefully, it appeared it hadn't been in the water for a long time. It was in serious need of some repairs and caulking to keep it afloat.

With wooden boats, it's necessary to apply an application of caulking material to the seams. The material was generally made of cotton fiber, applied using the caulking iron, which resembled a blunt, wide-bladed chisel used with a wooden mallet.

The boat had no identification. It had no name or numbers of registration.

It did have oars still clamped into wooden holders along the inside of the gunwales. Rather a nice touch, I noted.

There was a large block in the floor forward with a round hole corresponding with the hole in the front seat. I didn't know why it was there. I filed the info into my brain for a later discussion with myself.

It hadn't been as waterlogged as I would've anticipated. Therefore, it couldn't have been in the water for a long period of time, which seemed strange to me.

The next chore was to get it higher on the beach away from the tide line. Thank God it had come ashore on a high, driving tide. If it would've sunk in the cove where the water was deeper, I probably couldn't have rescued it.

As the day progressed, I managed to devise a method to get the boat moved. I used the Jeep, some small logs, and a combination of ropes and chains I'd found in the old shed to pull the boat up onto the edge of the shoreline. Once I had it onto the sea grass, I rolled it over on blocks. Then I could think about working on the bottom.

Being a project person, overall it had been a good day's work. It made me happy. Actually, I was happier that afternoon than I'd been in a long, long time.

On the way back to the cottage, the dogs were digging in the tide-line. They seemed very interested in something. I gleefully went to explore with them. Half buried in the sand and seaweed was what looked like a large, canvas square.

I scavenged and salvaged everything I could, so I eagerly assisted in the dig. It was a small mast with the canvas rolled around it, still partially lashed with rotting rope.

Mystery solved about the block with the hole. This belonged to the boat. Now, if I could find the pin, which held it firmly into the block, I was golden. We searched but without any luck.

OK! I did the math…boat, sail, mast, no pin. Not a big deal…I would make one out of something.

I laughed. I had always wanted to learn to sail. Now, I had a *sailboat*! How good is God?

Even better than I knew or could imagine. While we were walking to the far side of the cove later in the evening at low tide, I saw what appeared to be some odd driftwood. With renewed interest in our post-storm salvage project, we went to investigate.

It was not driftwood, but a wooden handle or long lever to something, so we dug it out. Low and behold! There was the rudder with a tiller arm attached. It was in rough shape but I knew I could repair it. This was how I would steer the boat.

I hoped no one would come to claim the old boat; I really liked it. There was something about the shape and style of the boat being somewhat unusual, but yet somehow very familiar. I would have to research it in a library or online. One thing I knew… it was old. I was familiar with the laws regarding salvage. The craft had no name or numbers or other identifying information; it was mine.

I had an extensive knowledge of boats, having always been around the ocean. I'd grown up on an island and then been involved with working boats as an adult in one of my other careers.

Over the duration of my life, I'd been fortunate enough to do many different things. Some good, some not so good, but they were all interesting. The knowledge gained had been useful repeatedly.

I often thought the reason folks didn't go anywhere interesting in life was because they just didn't try; often quitting too soon. That's what life is, just situations. You either make them work for you or let them defeat you. There were many times in my life, this one included, when I could have just quit, but I guess I didn't quite know how. Perhaps pride got in the way. I just couldn't or wouldn't quit.

I worked so hard to get the cottage comfortable enough to spend the winter there without a central heating source. Presently, I only had the old wood stove in the kitchen and the fireplace. There hadn't been any insulation in this ark of a building.

The basement was a very small, low, cement block area under the center of the cottage. It enclosed the water and sewer lines and afforded a minimal storage space. There hadn't been any insulation to protect the pipes from freezing.

The cottage had been used in the summers and was never been designed for year-round living.

I completed the insulation as the first necessary task. Without insulation, we couldn't spend the winter there.

The redeeming feature was, between the outside wall and the inside pine boards, there were no fire stops to interfere with the placement of rolled insulation. I'd very carefully removed the pine boards, applied the insulation, and then replaced the interior boarding.

The old pine boards had the wonderful coloring, the product of time; it was worth the effort to reuse them.

To add to the angst of the labor, when I called the lumberyard requesting a delivery of materials, they said they'd only come so far down my drive. They told me it was due to what they called *the condition of the trace*. Still, they'd take this same truck to a new construction site, burying it to the axles in mud while thinking they were cool.

Oh well, the joys of doing business as a *woman...* in a rural area time passed by some 200 years before... never to return; doing so with no regrets.

Days went by and I continued to work on the winterization of the cottage and the boat. Working on the boat seemed so relaxing it wasn't work. I had caulked the seams along the keel, sanded and painted the bottom. It didn't look great, although it did look a lot better than when it arrived. I named the boat, *Survivor* and carefully painted the name on her stern. The boat had become a welcomed distraction!

Finally, I rolled the boat back over, ready to re-float it. It had been much easier to haul the boat up onto land than to put it back into the water. In the Down East coastal area, the tides can range from 15 to 21 feet. I figured and fussed until I worked out a roller system with the same logs I'd used to get it on shore.

It was a three-day operation but finally I succeeded in refloating the boat. I was so proud!

Now, if it didn't leak too badly or sink I could have fun going fishing. It leaked some. I was hopeful the wood would swell, helping me out… also I was sure I could bail.

I fixed a mooring for her. We were in business. I chided myself, *if going fishing, rowing and sailing …who knew what could be next?*

I was so excited! After all the hard work of winterizing the cottage, I at last had a fun project. Even if I'd have to bail to stay afloat, I'd only take her out in the cove for the maiden voyage. I knew if my bailing wasn't adequate, the dogs and I could swim for shore, towing the boat behind us. We all, the dogs and I, swam frequently, so I knew we could do it.

I found an old enamel pot, already repaired in the tool shed/old privy which would work perfectly for keeping the boat afloat. I laughed when I looked at the patch-up; the job had been crudely done, but done just the same. They had used something resembling old washers, a piece of rubber, and a screw. I was not sure why or how, but it worked.

I just needed to see how good I would be at bailing. This would be a great practical application if it worked.

Gee whiz! I realized my sense of humor had returned.

I made a quick trip to town, picked up some fishing line, leads, hooks, and jigs, nothing fancy; just small hand-lines. No need for bait…there was a bed of mussels on the rocks. I had grown up fishing for mackerel and pollock. I was ready.

We pulled the boat in to shore. Seaweed, Shadow and I boarded our craft, rowing out a ways to where I thought we might find a fish to tease me. I hadn't tried the sail yet and I wouldn't, until I was certain about how much the boat would leak.

I was so anxious to check out the leaking I hadn't minded rowing. The design of the little boat made rowing easy; it seemed anxious to go.

As a child on the island, I would *borrow* a boat with my brother any chance we got; I loved to row and fish. I felt like a kid again!

I let the boat drift while I baited the hook with a mussel. My life improved rapidly. I felt like *me* again, almost.

I had just begun fishing when I had my first nibble. Just like riding a bike…you never forget how to do it. I pulled in a beautiful, shiny mackerel. This was my supper!

I rowed and fished for over an hour with a minimal amount of bailing, considering. We returned to the mooring with supper in hand and a smile on my face.

That was the last day of peace for a long and difficult time.

Four

They, the gang of men, were milling around trying to put together what had happened. Other than the first question about who I was, even though I was the *star* of the show, they were not talking to me.

Had I really created this whole mess?

This is what happened if you take protecting your property into your own hands, with a gun. I knew and understood guns, having learned to shoot as a child with my father. I had done some competitive shooting as an adult. I was also very aware of the rights of citizens to defend themselves and their property against invaders who were using deadly force. I was damn sure going to stand my ground.

What should I have done? After I called the police on my cell, it'd taken them three hours to show up. That was progress, I guess.

Finally, the agent separated himself from the pack. He was coming my way. His voice was still gruff when he said, "We need to talk."

I was drinking a cup of very black coffee. I needed it because it had been a very long and violent night.

At my age, I needed my sleep, to be alert and somewhat nice on demand.

Introduction made: "I'm agent Henry Brown, call me Hank."

I guessed him to be in his late sixties, slightly overweight, and not terribly physical. He wasn't paunchy. He was not a Maine native and clearly here under duress. I guessed his height was just short of six feet with a fair head of graying hair and a salt-and-pepper mustache. He had strange blue/green eyes which seemed older than time. He was dressed in a pair of casual chino pants, open-necked polo shirt, and a poorly cut sport jacket. I noticed he was wearing the standard never-shine black cop shoes.

He went straight to the point. "I need to talk with you regarding what transpired here. Do you have any more coffee? Please, it was a long trip and I need a cup."

I thought if he wanted to drink this three-hour old coffee, he was beyond desperate. This was not my problem.

"Sure, its old, but you're welcome to a cup. Come on in." Showing him to the pot and a mug was easy.

He was doing the usual *cop inventory* as he walked in, mentally assessing everything. He had some competition as my dogs had him in their sights.

Hank asked, "Do you want to talk in here or outside?"

"Doesn't matter to me, let's just get done so everyone can get out of here as quickly as possible?"

He took a sip, nodded. "Tell me what happened."

Interestingly, this was the first time anyone had bothered to ask, so I told him, "I'm a light sleeper, and so are the dogs. As neither of them are barkers, they alert me with a nudge and a low growl if something's wrong. We hadn't been in bed long when they began acting anxious. I listened, but didn't hear anything out of the ordinary. I trust them. They have far better hearing than I do. I got up, and looked out of the window, without touching the curtain.

"There was a quarter-moon with lots of stars. I checked the parking area. I didn't see anything. Then, a movement down by the cove caught my eye. At first, I thought it had been my imagination. I saw two people down by the water. I knew they were trying to steal my boat! I was *pissed*! If it had been the legitimate owner of the boat, they would not be arriving in the middle of the night to retrieve it. Yanking on my robe, I grabbed my 30-30 rifle and ran down the stairs.

"I started to open the door a crack then hesitated and dropped to my knees. I told the dogs to stay, checked the rifle to be certain it was loaded then jacked a round into the chamber. I carefully opened the door and crawled out onto the porch.

"One of them was walking up toward the tree-line while the other was trying to do something on the shore. The person by the water was too far away from me to tell what he was trying to do. The other person wasn't far from where I'd tied the mooring line.

"I yelled, 'STOP! HANDS ON YOUR HEADS OR I'LL SHOOT'! It never entered my head they'd be carrying guns. Let alone shoot at me. However, I knew I was fast enough, if necessary, to cover them both. I knew they could hear me because I heard one of them say, 'Shit, let's get the hell outta here.' I couldn't make out other conversation.

"Then the jerk up by the tree-line fired a shot at me. It struck the cottage and I returned fire. I was angry! How dare they? He began running toward the water yelling to the other one while he shot again. He missed the cottage that time and hit the rocks by the front porch.

"I got serious, took a good aim, and returned fire, hitting him.

"The other one jumped into the water and was gone. A few moments later, I heard an outboard motor running hard, then slowed before it sped away.

"They never came back for the one on the beach. I called the police. I took the dogs, my rifle, and the flashlight and walked down. He was already dead.

"The tide was going out so I left him there without touching him; or the crate, or whatever it was on the shore. I watched the scene, but no one returned for him, or the box.

"After three hours, you, along with the rest of the troops, arrived. I'm sorry he's dead. I was not going to let him steal my boat. It's mine! It came ashore in a blow and I saved it! I repaired it, named it and I will be *damned* if anyone is going to take it away from me."

Hank sat there silently for a long time and just looked at me. What, I wondered, was he thinking. After a long pause he finally spoke. "He wasn't trying to steal your boat."

My turn, "Then what in hell was he doing coming ashore to take a damn leak? He was armed to the teeth."

At that, I got a big belly laugh out of him. He helped himself to another shot of awful coffee.

I felt guilty.

I got up and prepared a new pot. I didn't want to be responsible for killing an agent. He stood, filling his cup with fresh coffee.

Interestingly, I noticed the dogs had lain down and were no longer watching him so intently.

I inquired of him, "So, what was in the box sitting on the shore?"

Hank considered the question for a long time. Then, nodding to himself, as if agreeing to something only he knew, he simply said quietly, "There were some small arms, munitions, rockets, and small bombs."

My mouth dropped open. "Don't you think that was overkill to steal a boat?"

This time he threw his head back and laughed aloud. "They were not trying to steal the boat," he repeated.

Again I inquired, "What were they doing?"

Heavy-handed knocks on the door interrupted him. Hank stepped outside. After a great deal of talk, with hand gestures, he returned.

He sat in his chair, looked longingly at the coffee pot then to me. I am old, and admittedly short on social graces, but I understood the look. I get it all the time from my dogs when they want something. I got up and filled his cup, again.

I waited while he continued with the internal arguing with himself; he nodded, and then asked, "How long have you lived here?"

I explained I'd purchased the property about three and a half years ago. However, I just started living there the past couple of months. "Why is that important?"

Hank's next question was, "How long had it been empty before you moved in?"

To be honest, I'd no idea of the years it was abandoned and told him so.

I was puzzled about what it had to do with this mess. Hank said, "I think you should plan on leaving now and staying away until this is finished."

I must have looked like the village idiot to him. My jaw was agape with nothing coming out of my mouth but a noise; even I didn't know what it meant.

My temper had begun to roil. It came from the bottom of my feet to the very last hair on my graying head. I hadn't been angry in a very long time, thanks to living alone and avoiding people. However, my temper still had a way of knowing how to surface. I was *boiling mad*. I honestly think I was madder than I'd ever been. Many times in my life, I'd thanked my temper and tenacity for my survival.

I finally managed to grind out, "Are you nuts? No one, not you or anyone else is going to **ever** tell me to leave my own home again."

Hank stayed calm, and stated in a very quiet voice, as if he were indeed trying to talk to a village idiot. "It isn't safe for you to stay here. They *will* be back."

I still couldn't grasp anything reasonable. "*Who* will be back and *why*? Either level with me, or go stand outside with the rest of the damn crowd."

Truly, it was a crowd. I just wanted all of them to get to hell out of here and leave my property and me in peace.

"Are you going to charge me with shooting him?" I figured it was a fair question. I hadn't gotten an answer.

There was another knock on the door… this resulted in an additional conference. To which they didn't consult me nor was I invited to attend. The secret conversation ended with everybody walking down to the tree line to stand with the men gathered there.

As I watched from the kitchen window, there were men carrying what looked like oversized black plastic construction bags over their arms. Two others were carrying shovels.

What were they doing? Well, whether they liked it or not; it was still my property! I pulled on short boots, left the dogs inside and went down to see. If they were digging a garden, I didn't want one there. I figured they needed some directing.

Big mistake! They hadn't seen me coming until I was right behind them; then it was too late. They were shoveling what looked like bones into the bags. On the other side, they were unearthing more of the same crates found on the shore last night. Where they were extracting the bones, there seemed to be a great deal of white powder. Humm, do you suppose lime, I wondered; how long had this been there? Why hadn't I noticed this area before?

All good questions but, from the look on their faces, I wouldn't be getting answers anytime soon. Hank turned, spotting me and almost shouted, "Get back in the house and stay there!"

"Not until someone tells me, with a great deal of clarity, what in hell is going on."

I must confess, something resembling a stare-down was what followed. Hank walked over, took my arm by the elbow and propelled me back to the house. He didn't hurt me. I knew he was serious about the process.

After he'd returned me to the house, he'd given me a stern look. "Stay! I'll be back."

I had stayed. I waited impatiently for what seemed like forever.

I had a moment of great clarity; I could lose my home and/or go to jail. My mind wandered back to review all of the effort I had expended in winterizing the house. Just to manage a winter here had been a Herculean task.

What would I do about my dogs? We only had each other.

My mind cleared. I went from *fear to fight* in an eye-blink. *There wasn't any way I was ever going to be forced to vacate my home, not by anyone or anything!*

When he returned, he was gruff. "Get packed, you're leaving now." I was resolute.

I guessed he couldn't have had a great record of accomplishment with women in relationships. He thought because he'd spoken I'd jump.

"Never happening. I jumped for the very last time, a long time ago. I live here. This is my home. I'm not leaving. Clean up your mess out there and then leave. If you're going to charge me with something because I protected my property and myself, go for it. In the meantime, remember to remove the slug from my wall as evidence. When am I going to know what the mess down there is about?"

The conversation resulted in a big huff of exhaled air, along with the reddening of his face. I'd seen a flash of what I detected as real serious anger in his eyes. He made an abrupt about-face, then slammed out of the door. While I watched from the window, he fairly stomped his way back to the pack of onlookers with his cell phone jammed to his ear. I got the overall impression he was upset, too damn bad for him. I wasn't going to allow him or anybody else to evict me from my home.

In retrospect, if I'd just buried the corpse on the beach in the same spot where they were digging, and called it good, it would've been done. Then I could've carried on with life in the cove, all peaceful and quiet. Why couldn't everyone just mind their business and just leave me alone?

While I was still watching the meeting from the window, there was a loud, noisy motor sound down in the driveway by my car. Someone had arrived bringing a large, ugly looking ATV. They were in the process of maneuvering it down to the beach toward the group of men. I was *ripping mad* again. I've always hated those damn things. ATVs were loud, smelly destroyers of the terrain. They were continually damaging the beaches, tearing up the dune grasses and plants. In general, they've raised the dickens with the ecology. I had no idea who brought the thing to this picnic.

They'd begun to load stuff into the rear of the ATV. There was too much head-shaking going on.

Oddly, other than putting him into a body bag, the man I shot was still lying on the sand. Perhaps they had even forgotten about him. I assumed he was the reason they'd come in the first place. *I'm just a silly old woman; what do I know?*

More talking, a lot more gesturing towards the cottage. Then Hank emerged from the pack and returned to the porch. He looked like he'd just drawn the short straw on a bad situation. He didn't look at all happy. Too damn bad… that was his problem, not mine.

The first words out of his mouth were, "Is the rifle the only firearm you have?"

I'm honest to a fault so I told him. "No, I have a 12 gauge shot gun, a .38 Colt Detective Special, and a .22 Browning automatic handgun. Why?"

His next question was a series of inquiries "Have you ever shot anyone before? How long did you think about pulling the trigger? Did you think you'd hit him?"

Well, wasn't he just full of stupid questions? "Nope; never shot a person before. The first shot came after I told them to stop and he fired at me. When he shot at me the second time, it was pure instinct. He'd shot at me twice. I improved my aim and fired. I didn't intend to kill him. I just wanted to stop him.

"Now, to answer your other question, of course I thought I'd hit him. An expert instructed me long ago, if you pulled a gun, you needed to be prepared to use it, or have it used on you. Nobody will ever victimize me again. Are you planning on taking my guns?"

His answer surprised me. He didn't even hesitate for a breath, "Not a chance."

We sat quietly for a few minutes, then he asked softly, "You really won't leave unless we physically carry you off the property, will you?"

I didn't delay for a second before I answered him, "Nope."

"I was afraid that would be your answer. How many bedrooms do you have here? Do you have indoor plumbing? Can you cook? How much food do you keep on hand?" As he was asking this silly jargon, his eyes had begun to crinkle at the edges. He didn't look quite as fierce.

No matter, I wasn't biting. I'd fed the last male visitor to my home a long time ago, creating a hell on earth for myself. Now, the only man I'd ever feed again was my son. How, I wondered, was I ever going to couch that in proper language? I wanted to convey my stance without sounding like a jerk myself.

I thought, *Oh, Eileen, just go for it.* "I have three bedrooms, along with an ancient bathroom. I'm a great cook for the dogs and me. I only store staples, eating mostly seafood I dig or catch. I'm not interested in entertaining visitors at all."

Good and to the point, I thought.

We were back to the staring contest. "Well, like it or not, if you refuse to leave, then you *will* have company. End of the discussion.

"This is a serious crime scene. They'll return. They've been coming here for quite some time. Those supplies buried above the shoreline were just the tip of an iceberg. That's not even considering how many remains are buried there. Because the cottage and the cove were obscure and vacant for so long, it was ideal for their purposes. Until we catch them, you'll have company. End of the story.

"If that annoys you, the government can take the property and evict you without recourse. That's how serious this is. So do you stay or go? This is entirely up to you."

I knew when my back was against the wall, and it was. "I can't leave. This is all I have left." Even to my cynical ears, it sounded pathetic. I'd never liked *pathetic…* on any level. However, the truth was the truth.

To say we formed an alliance would be a lie. Perhaps we could've called it a passive aggressive stance.

I would have to admit they were generous with the food provisions they supplied. I wouldn't need to go shopping again for another year.

There was an added bonus along with the food. I wanted to mention this along with some mirth, on my part. When the first load of food arrived, I asked Hank where he intended to store it. Without missing a beat, as if he were again speaking with an idiot, he snapped, "In the fridge, of course."

I quietly pointed to the ancient fridge, telling him to *store it*. A much nicer approach than to *stuff it*, I thought. Hank's mouth dropped open. So now who looks like the village idiot? He had provided my laugh for the month.

He went out of the door, yelling to I guess whoever would listen. He made his way to the truck delivering the supplies. Within two hours, they returned and unloaded a brand new refrigerator. With a great deal of jockeying, they managed to get the old one out, and the new one in. Those men even set it up, putting the food away in the process. I appreciated their assistance.

I lived on a very limited budget; this would be a blessing, if there were one to come from this mess.

They continued to dig in the bank, crating stuff. There wasn't any chance I'd ever get the opportunity to see any of the results. Truthfully, I didn't know if I really wanted to see or know. Hank wouldn't tell me anything other than, "We have this under control."

I didn't believe him for one second. Part of my distrust was influenced by truth. Even though the men left each day, Hank continued his ever-watchful surveillance of the area.

Late one afternoon, I managed to wander off without Hank in my back pocket. I strolled up the trace, which by then resembled a super-mud-highway compared to what it had been. It was wider and muddier, resembling the mighty-monster-mud-runs the natives loved so much. To me, it was a disgusting mess. The larger vehicles traveling in and out had wrecked the road beyond any repair I'd ever be able to afford. I was damned discouraged.

I encountered two men dressed in dark camouflage gear. I surprised them, it was apparent, but only slightly less than they surprised me. I had no idea anyone was camping out there other than Hank.

I had to say they were rapid on their responses because Hank arrived on a dead run. Humm. I didn't know he was even capable of moving so fast, or for so long.

Oh my, appearances were deceiving.

Hank quickly escorted me back to the cottage. He informed me clearly it was where I was to stay. That would be the status, unless or until he gave me permission to do otherwise.

I was immediately dismissed when I inquired about the patrol in the swamp and told, "It's nothing for you to be concerned about."

Did I mention I hated dismissive men? I may need to rephrase—just saying, I hate men. They have all the tact of a socially radical porcupine with late stage rabies.

The unholy alliance lasted another two weeks. Meanwhile, they finished whatever they were trying to do and left. All without incident, I quickly pointed out to Hank on several occasions.

Finally, the day came when they were gone, or should I say they just stopped arriving each morning at dawn.

Hank, however, seemed reluctant to leave. "Well, I guess the time has come when I'm going to be recalled. I know you didn't appreciate my being here. I will admit, in spite of it, you have been kind and considerate. You shared your space and cooked great meals. It will take me a month to lose the weight I've gained.

"I'll miss sitting on the porch to watch the sun rise with the dogs listening to the throb of the lobster boats at work pulling traps. As an adult I never owned a dog, and didn't know how much they could add to a life. Thanks for sharing them with me." I was dumbfounded.

For all the time he'd been there, he hadn't been much of a conversationalist. I surmised it was in part due to his job, isolation, and circumstances. "I know you have tried to protect me even though I felt it unnecessary. I appreciate your efforts. Now you can get back to your real life. I'm certain being stuck out here in the middle of nowhere with a grouchy old lady was not your first choice of an assignment."

Hank's reaction was priceless! He threw back his head and just belly-laughed until I could see tears on his cheeks. Glad to be entertaining.

Still laughing, he walked down to the parking area, bag in hand. I heard a vehicle approaching. Just as the car arrived, Hank turned around. He stopped, tossed his bag onto the back seat, spoke to the driver, then strode back to the foot of the porch.

Looking up at me, he stood very quietly and spoke so softly I could barely make out his words. He said, "Eileen, this could cost me my job; however, I feel you need to know. This wasn't a casual problem here on your beach." After a long hesitation he added, "We knew contraband was coming ashore in this area, but we thought they were bringing it in on boats. We were never able to find them. They'll most likely come back here in time to see if they can recover anything we missed. There's a possibility we didn't find it all. If anything strange happens or someone comes you don't know, call the cell number on my card. Also, keep the shotgun handy. These people will be playing for keeps. You cost them a lot of money and equipment. I'm sorry my team didn't tell you what was going on. I wasn't in charge of that facet of the operation. I admire your guts and want you to know I did enjoy being here. Take care of yourself and the dogs. I'll miss all of you." With those last words, he turned and was gone.

Five

At last, my home and the cove were mine again. To celebrate I planned to go sailing and fishing for my dinner. I was so happy to have my space back I could have sung out a happy song, doing the snoopy dance. Even the dogs felt my relief. They were chasing around and sounding their happy barks.

Life was good again. Now I had to regain the rhythm of my life and continue my work on the cottage. How had things gotten so crazy so fast?

Thankfully, after a few quiet and peaceful days, life was beginning to return to normal.

I was thinking this as I stood in my favorite place on the large ledge, at the seaward side of the cottage, watching the ocean. The ocean had churned up good-sized whitecaps in the stiff wind. I enjoyed the contrast to my quiet little cove where my boat rested on the mooring. I had planned, if the wind tacked off early in the evening, to go for a short row while I dropped a line. A fresh fish would taste good. It would also reassure me that normalcy had returned to my life.

Six

I heard the vehicle coming down the trace long before I saw it. The dogs had also heard it. They didn't enjoy strangers any more than I did; therefore, they were running and barking. I hadn't met anyone local, so to me everyone was a stranger. I'd had my fill of strangers in the past few weeks.

I made a quick trip to the front door and picked up my shotgun. My timing was perfect. I arrived at the parking area just as the man stepped out of his car.

He stood in front of it, waiting for my arrival. He quickly introduced himself. "I'm Ben Hayward, my son and I own a boat yard down the coast from you. I've come on business. I understand you've had some problems here lately. I can understand why you wouldn't be keen about a stranger driving onto your property. However, as I didn't know of any other way to contact you, I felt I needed to come in person."

He was a big man. I estimated he was my age or better. He looked fit, even for a large person.

The dogs were standing at attention in front of him. He was intelligent enough to know better than to walk forward.

"State your business. Make it fast. I'm not in any mood to entertain more idle chatter or have any more idiots on my property." Well, that was clear and to the point, I guessed.

He replied, "I came because I understood there was a small fracas here a few days ago. In addition, part of it was a misunderstanding about a small boat. Over the years, I've developed a passion for either restoring or replicating some of the older boats no longer in existence. I've come to retrieve it. I'm more than willing to pay you for your trouble."

When he'd stopped speaking, either to catch his breath, or because I hadn't responded to his diatribe, I figured the time had come to stop the show for good.

"You're here about my boat, aren't you?"

His reply left no doubt. "Yes, I think it's the one I lost several weeks ago in the bad blow we had. It's a very old boat. The craft was a design I'm extremely interested in. May I see the boat?"

My reply was instant, "No. The boat is not yours. It's *mine*. It washed ashore here and sank in my cove. I retrieved it, repaired it, and the laws of salvage remain intact. There were no numbers, names, or identifying information on the craft.

"So, no, you can't have it. Now get back into your car, get off my property, and *do not* return. Have I made myself clear?"

His protest, under different circumstances, would have been comic. My sense of humor, however, had been broken beyond repair.

Furthermore, he couldn't seem to understand English.

He persisted. "I guess I didn't make myself clear to you. It *is* my boat and I *intend* to retrieve it."

Although he had controlled his voice, I could see from his body language he was rapidly becoming agitated. The last thing I wanted to deal with was another irate man.

I shifted the shotgun slightly and Shadow emitted her low warning growl. It was time to end this sideshow.

I must not have been as clear as I thought. I tried again. My patience was exhausted. "I would rather shoot you, here and now, than give up the boat. The choice is yours…do I shoot you, or do you go pester someone else who's impressed with you? The boat is mine. It stays here. *That* is the end of this discussion."

He blustered then huffed; redness rose in his cheeks. He hadn't made any move to return to his car, so I figured perhaps he needed some extra encouragement.

I guess if an outsider had been watching, it would have seemed humorous. He was a large man trying to reason with a short, small, older woman with a long gray braid who held a shotgun on her arm and was witnessed by two dogs.

I moved the shotgun up into the crook of my arm while commanding the dogs to back up. At times like this, I find the dogs hysterical. I had no idea what they were thinking or what they really would do. Standing at attention, both had retreated until they were even with me.

Mr. Ben was thinking this gesture over. Nodded his head, he pulled the oldest line in the book out for a replay. "I'll be back."

My parting reply had been simple. "Don't bother."

He backed the Expedition slowly and skillfully, I might add; out of the trace. I knew this wouldn't be the last I'd see of him.

I expected the sheriff's arrival within the hour. Ben was a man used to getting what he wanted.

He wanted my boat. I was *never* going to give him *Survivor.* She was mine and I fully intended to defend my rights to her.

The weather was hanging low and feeling mean when I awaken in the morning, never a good sign on the coast. I knew we were in for a good blow and most likely a pounding rain. I drank my coffee standing on the porch watching the clouds and the water. Both were that dark grey that bodes no good.

I stood sipping the coffee, and assessing the weather situation and realized it would be necessary to bring the boat in from the mooring. Even in a sheltered cove, I could still get substantial sea swells and surges.

Never an easy task, but I knew it had to be completed. It would be impossible to haul it on-shore with the Jeep, due to the recent excavations by Hank's crew. Unfortunately, when the men left, it was just too soft to use the old Jeep without being stuck. I wouldn't risk that.

I gathered the tools along with the come-a-long I had purchased at a used junk shop, and some heavy rope. The come-a-long was a heavy duty one and the rope weighed about the same. I loaded the big old wheelbarrow, my go-to tool, and pushed it to the beach. With the tools assembled, I retrieved the logs used when I first pulled the boat on shore. They were not easy to move. I took my time. I worked them slowly down to the edge of the water, spacing them to use as rollers.

I needed to get the come-a-long attached to a tree with enough girth to haul the boat. I also prayed the rope would have enough length for the job. The tree was farther away than I'd guessed. Nothing to do but lay out the line and hope it was enough, not quite. Damn!

I remembered the old piece of logging chain in the shed I'd used the first time. I mused to myself at what folks leave behind. I began the hunt and sure enough, I found it in an old rusty washtub in the corner. God only knew how long it had been there before I'd used it to haul the boat the first time. I needed to get it to the beach. It was so long and heavy I couldn't lift and carry it. I just dragged it out. What a great hunk of chain!

I attached it around the tree, set the come-a-long on a block of wood out of the sand, and began the task of bringing the boat in. I wasn't sure if having the tide going out instead of coming in was an asset but it was what I had to work with.

The wind had been increasing steadily. I wished I'd listened to the weather report last night or this morning. I hadn't.

I really hadn't cared anymore what was going on in the world.

I know, shame on me. With this storm, I might pay a high price for my lack of interest.

I brought the boat onto the sand, attaching the prow line to the towrope. I ran up the beach and began to work the come-a-long. I hoped and prayed I hadn't wasted my fifteen dollars when I had purchased it. I'd oiled and cleaned it before storing it in the shed. Decisive moment… would it work or not?

I turned the lever slowly. Ever so slowly, the boat moved forward up onto the first roller I had sunk into the wet sand. I'd been unsure if the placement of the come-a-long was correct. Would there be enough elevation where the crank was to encourage the boat to make the next log okay? Very carefully, I cranked. All the while watching, and then stopping to run down and check that I hadn't damaged the hull. I was doing all right, so far so good.

I needed to build a cradle to do this, just not today. The boat came to me in a storm. I didn't want to lose it to a storm.

Time passed. The work was hard and slow. I'd moved the logs three times to position the boat where I felt it would be safe. I knew it would be difficult to get back into the water after the storm passed.

I'd worked so hard for so long, I didn't realize how foul the weather had gotten. I covered the come-a-long with a small tarp the crew left in the tree line and anchored it with stones. It was the best I could do.

With the shed closed up, and the Jeep checked for open windows, I made my way to the porch to rest for a minute.

When I let the dogs out of the house, they stopped, put their noses in the air, sniffed, then came and sat at my feet. How strange. I wondered if while I'd been moving the boat they'd turned on the radio and knew something I didn't.

I checked the outside of the house looking for anything that could blow away or break a window. I moved the big wooden Adirondack chairs to the shed with the trusty wheelbarrow.

The chairs were old and heavy. I seemed to be seeing a pattern evolving here; everything is old, heavy, and difficult to move. Must be me. *Wonder when that happened.*

Standing on the edge of the rocks and looking out across the sea, I'd seen mammoth waves forming off shore. The waves rolled like oil into the rocks, throwing spray into the air.

Thank God it was low tide. How bad, I wondered, was this going to be when the tide was high? It seemed like the wind had increased by the minute.

This was definitely going to be an *Evangeline* moment, with the waves breaking on the stern and rockbound coast. I remembered reading that Henry Wadsworth Longfellow poem as a child and loving how he described the sea during a storm.

There had been nothing else to do but get inside before the rain I could see off in the distance arrived. No point in being soaked before it was necessary.

I needed to get water stored because I was certain I'd lose the power. When I get rich, (my favorite just-for-me joke), I will buy a generator for the cottage. Then on cold snowy nights or during hurricanes I would sit in comfort while I read or painted.

It was always nice to have dreams of days to come; it made the bad days easier to deal with.

Seven

As much as I hated the trip to town to get the mail, I needed to go. I had not gathered my mail for some time and if we lost the power it could be days before it would be restored. I wasn't a paranoid person. I just liked my privacy, of which there had been far too little lately. However, when you live in a small town, in a rural area you are fodder for gossip. I wasn't stupid, nor did I get this old, by not dying young.

When I went to the post office, I always parked my vehicle so I would be able to grab my mail and be out of the door before I was asked if everything was peaceful out my way. If asked, I'd nod, no verbal answer required. Then get out of town.

I managed to make it out of the door and literally ran into Ben, nearly knocking us both down.

I mumbled, "Sorry." Then kept going.

Ben was faster on his feet than I would have expected.

Before I could duck into the Jeep, he was there. I couldn't get the door opened.

"How does one get in touch with you?" he asked.

"They don't." I knew it sounded curt; however, the conversation was over, as far as I was concerned.

Ben, however, had a different idea. He reached into his inside pocket, pulled out a card and a stub of a pencil. He scribbled something on the back and passed it to me.

His next words surprised me. "There's something strange going on off shore. The men on the boats have been talking about stuff that's not right. If you have a problem call the number on the back of the card; this phone is *always* with me.

"You already know the police won't arrive for hours, if they even bother to show up at all. By the way, be careful and pay attention to anything out of the ordinary." With that, he walked off.

How strange was that? It seemed odd, a man I was ready to shoot recently would be concerned enough to give me his phone number. I stuck the card in my jacket pocket, filled the Jeep with gas, and sped for home.

That night the wind howled while the rain pelted the cottage. The windows shook and rattled. The panes of glass sounded as if they'd fall out. They might be completely sucked out of their frames and lost to the storm. It was relentless. Along about first light it seemed to have blown itself out and kind of faded away. I was thankful the cottage was still in one piece.

Here on the coast, the weather is strange and always changing. Yesterday's gale would have blown the bunnies out of the woods. Today the sun was warm, and the wind calm, inviting me to come out and play.

Play I did. I re-launched *Survivor*. The difficult work was well worth the effort. Fall boating, to me, is the best. I intended to use the boat until I needed to beach her for the winter.

Soon it would be my first winter here. I had stockpiled wood for the fireplace and the kitchen stove, and installed some of the old wooden storm windows I'd found in the shed. It had taken days to take the glass out, re-glaze, and paint them. I was grateful they had been there. I didn't have funds to put new storms on. I used the ones I had on the north side and a couple on the east side. I needed to go to the salvage place a couple of towns away and see if I could find enough windows to do the rest of the house.

The beauty of the house being an older structure was most folks had replaced the wooden storms with aluminum replacement windows. I knew I could salvage enough to finish all of the windows.

The weather was getting nippy even with the stilted sun. There was what they call a *mackerel* sky. It seemed evening had come early because of the overcast.

I stood on the porch letting the dogs enjoy their evening romp. I noticed it was much cooler. There was a clearing sky filling with stars, but no moon. Strangely, here by the water, with no artificial lighting, the stars gave off quite a bit of illumination.

It was time to stop for the day. I was tired. I didn't even have enough energy to read.

We retired for the night and soon were all tucked into bed, sound asleep.

Eight

Shadow poked me with her nose, emitting the soft growl which notified me of trouble. I am usually a very light sleeper but tonight I had trouble rousing myself. Her second growl was loud and *urgent*. This was the get-up-now growl! I bolted out of bed, checked the window, and looked toward the cove. In a flash, I remembered vividly the last mess.

I didn't see anything. Shadow continued growling. I pulled on my jeans and sweatshirt and stuffed my feet into my sneakers. Carefully I started down the stairs, then changed my mind. I slipped back to the bed and retrieved the small .38 Colt Detective Special I kept between the mattress and the box spring. I stuck it into the waistband of my jeans. I checked to ensure my 30-30 rifle was by the door as well as my 12-gauge shotgun. I grabbed my jacket off the peg on the wall, crammed extra shells into the pockets for the shotgun and rifle. The dogs stood at the ready, waiting to see what I would do.

The starlight outside gave enough illumination in the house so I didn't need a night light. On the kitchen table, I'd seen the shape of the card Hank had given me. For some unknown reason, I put it into my pocket along with my cell.

Behind me, the dogs were still growling. Thank God, they're not barkers. Whoever was out there would've known I was aware of them.

I looked out of the kitchen windows; I saw the cove, the driveway, and the spot where I parked my Jeep. So far, I saw nothing out of the ordinary but I knew *something* was spooking the dogs.

I knew the terrain around this house like the back of my hand. I had explored it often. I loved walking on the rocks and finding new places to sit, paint, read, watch and listen to the ocean.

I also knew from those explorations the only way someone could approach the cottage was from the road or the cove. Even for an experienced climber, the trek over the rocks would be extremely dangerous, even in daylight.

I didn't want to go outside until I knew what I was dealing with. So far, other than the constant growls of the dogs, there was nothing. *What is going on out there?*

It didn't take too long to get the answer to my question. I heard a noise I didn't quickly recognize, just sort of a *whoosh.*

The Jeep exploded. Somehow, I knew the sound I'd heard was a rocket launcher. Oh. This is what's happening! I'm having a war. No one sent me an invitation. Shit, this isn't going to be good, for sure!

I ran into the living room, hushing the dogs. I dropped to the floor, yanked the scatter rug back, and opened the trap door.

It led to the space below the cottage which housed the water pump and the septic lines. It was small and very tight. A padlock on the exterior locks the door from the crawl space to the outside. I put the dogs down there, along with my rifle and shotgun. When I closed the trap door, I prayed the dogs would be quiet. I grabbed the key to the lock from the key hook along with my purse hanging there. I opened the window with as little noise as possible. I was thankful I hadn't put a storm window on it. I climbed out, dropping to the ground. I was fumbling with the key for the lock just as I heard another *thrump* as the rocket launcher fired again. Door open, dogs out, guns retrieved. That's when all hell broke loose!

Force of habit, I closed the door and snapped the padlock.

The rocket hit the upstairs bedroom window. Hunkering down, keeping the dogs close, I stumbled over the rocks on the back path leading to the big ledge.

The house was old and began to burn rapidly.

I hated those bastards, whoever they were. I really wanted to turn around and kill all of them.

Lucky for them, I had to save the dogs. We skidded and slid down the rocks and around to the big cave. Not really a cave, but hollow and above the high water line so it was dry.

The house was really burning and they were firing rounds at it from high-powered automatic weapons. *It was total overkill.*

I plunked Seaweed down with a pat. The poor old girl was shaking all over. Shadow wanted to go take care of business. I knew we couldn't begin to compete with either firepower or stamina. I had no idea of how many were out there, or why.

I pulled out my cell and dialed 911, getting the usual, "Nine-one-one what is your emergency?" I gave her a quick synopsis of the problem; she told me to stay on the line.

"I'm on a cell with limited coverage *I can't stay on the line*." Her reply set my teeth on edge.

"If you do not remain on the line, I cannot assist you." I had no recourse. I ended the call.

I reached in my pocket and found what I thought was Hank's card, but when I got it, where I could see from the dim light of the cell phone, it was Ben's. Oh, what the hell, can this get any worse than it is? I dialed the number he'd scrawled on the back. One ring, two rings, three rings… I was certain it would go to voice mail on the next ring. By some miracle, a sleepy, gruff male voice answered. *Thank you, God.* "Ben, this is Eileen down at the Breen house. I got trouble. Someone has blown up my Jeep. They're using a grenade launcher to blow up the cottage. Now they're on foot looking for me with automatic weapons. I called nine-one-one but they're not going to do anything for me. I need help and I need it now!"

The only response to my load of unpleasantness was, "We are on our way. Stay hidden. Wherever you are, don't move. I have your number. When it's safe, I'll call you. Are the dogs with you...oh never mind, stupid question. If you need to, shoot to kill...my money's on you."

The dogs and I were crouched as far back in the cleft of the rock as we could get. Keeping the frightened pups quiet would be a chore. They seemed to sense the need for silence. I could see beams from a high-powered light swinging around in the air over our heads. I could hear voices, but couldn't make out what they were saying. My beloved cottage was burning and the noise was fierce. *Why,* I asked myself again, for the hundredth time, why?

They were close. I made out a male voice, not a Maine native. "Do you see anything?"

The person who responded was a native, "Naw, I think we cooked the bitch and those hounds, serves 'em right. We need to get out of here before someone sees the fire, although in this shit hole I doubt if anyone would care."

I had been so tempted to crawl out of my hidey-hole and blast them both. However, I knew better. That act of stupidity would have resulted in instant death. Common sense prevailed; I stayed hidden.

I had no idea how many men were up there, but more than just those two, I was certain.

My priority was to take care of my dogs. I couldn't if I died.

I heard the whine of an incredibly high-powered boat engine. I couldn't identify it. It sounded like the boats I've heard at the Jonesport boat races when they race up across the Reach for the Fourth of July celebration.

It couldn't be the intruders. They didn't have enough time to return to the beach. There is more than one of those boats out there. Where are they coming from? I was certain it wasn't a police boat, or the coast guard, certainly not a fireboat. What was it and how many?

I also heard at least one very large truck coming down the trace. Who could it be? I was terrified and isolated. I didn't want to leave the dogs nor the safety of the cave, but I wanted to know what was going on. The dogs won again. I hunkered.

I pulled out Hank's card and dialed his number. He answered on the second ring. He's not sharp, but he was at least trying. "Hank here, this better be important or I will hang you by your balls."

I spoke as quietly as possible. "Hank, its Eileen, I have trouble. They blew up the Jeep and the house. The dogs and I are hiding in the rocks. There are at least two or more of them. They have grenade or rocket launchers and automatic weapons. One of them is not a Mainer. I can't tell where he's from. One of them is a Mainer. I don't know where or who anyone is. Don't try to call me back…it will alert them and I don't want to be discovered; it's not safe. I called nine-one-one. They told me it was necessary to remain on the line or they couldn't assist me. I couldn't remain on the line because of the circumstances. I called a local. I've heard a lot of boats and a very heavy truck. I'm not coming out of hiding until I have to. You were right; they did come back. Thank you for trying. I'll contact you again if I get out of this mess. Do not call me back; it will alert them to where I'm hiding."

I heard gunfire, a *lot* of gunfire. I heard the launcher go off again. I didn't hear an explosion. Did it go into the water? It sounded like a war up there. There were bullets bouncing around the rocks. I huddled back as far as possible, holding the dogs close so they wouldn't move.

Again, I heard more gunfire, then screaming, awful screaming. I'd never heard a noise like that. I was beyond scared. I was petrified. The dogs huddled closer as if to protect me. They were so brave and I was so frightened. I wanted to cry. Somehow, over the years I'd forgotten how.

People tell you when you're drowning your life flashes before your eyes and I think it's true…no matter how or when imminent death rears its ugly head. Dear God, I prayed, please don't let the dogs get hurt or anyone who is innocent be harmed.

The screaming was still going on. No! Let this mess stop, please! Quiet! Will it last?

I heard Hank shouting. Damn, I didn't disconnect. He was frantic. "I'm okay and I have no idea what is going on up there. I'm also smart enough not to pop my head up. I'll contact you when I know more." This time I disconnected.

I wondered how men go to war and live this every day for months at a time. They must possess extraordinary courage.

I heard a siren. At any other time, it would be a relief. Right then, in the quiet aftermath of this conflict, with the house still crackling from the fire, it seemed like comic relief. I nearly forgot I was hiding for my life and laughed aloud.

A loud speaker blasted, *"This is the police…put your hands up and come forward."*

Was this a joke? Had I experienced a bad nightmare? Perhaps I would awaken soon. Nope, it wasn't a dream. I could see flashing blue lights. Sorry, I was still not coming out. I thought I would stay here with the dogs for the rest of my life, however long it may be.

My phone rang the little song telling me I had a call. Reflexes were still good. I said, "Hello." Just as normal as can be. I was amazed with myself.

"Eileen, this is Ben. Where are you? Can you and the dogs make it up to where the shed was?"

My response was, as always, slightly caustic. "Of course, we'll come right along."

I was terrified of what I would find when I climbed up onto the ledge. I needed to stay strong for the dogs and myself.

I gathered up the rifle and shotgun under one arm. I held Seaweed under the other. Shadow followed on my heels. We climbed up, out of the jumble of rocks.

Thank God I'd worn my sneakers! The stones were slippery and very steep. When I was going down, I'd been so concerned about getting to safety I hadn't noticed how dicey the descent was!

We arrived at the grassy area on top of the ledge. I carefully put Seaweed down on the ground and gave her a pat. She was still shaking. I was worried about her. She's old, and not too well. Any stress wouldn't be good for her. Shadow licked her face to tell her everything was going to be all right. Perhaps I should sit and let Shadow lick me as well.

I wondered if life would ever be *all right* again.

I squared my shoulders and walked on. The decisive moment was here and now; was this going to be survivable? I answered myself… *you're still alive, and so are the dogs.*

The burning hulk of the Jeep was testimony to the munitions used, whatever they were. I'd loved the car.

The house was falling in on itself. After all these years withstanding storms and its age… to die like this. I was beyond sad. This was going to be my *forever home.* Now I was homeless.

Still, I kept walking with my ever-faithful pals beside me. I didn't recall the parking area being so far from the ledge. Do you suppose the blast moved it? *I am beginning to worry my mind is playing tricks on me. I have to get a grip!*

For a moment, I just stood and stared at the devastation. I smelled the stench of fire combined with death. It stung my nostrils. I glanced down at my dogs, realizing they *are my family.* All I have left!

Somewhere, in the most primal part of my being, I began to feel a rage I couldn't quench. My only sorrow was that whoever "they" were, lying on the ground dead, I couldn't kill them again. I knew I had to handle the rage or it would do one of two things: kill me or make me tougher. *I knew I would not die for those bastards.*

As I approached where I used to park my now-dead Jeep, there stood a group of men in the clearing. One separated himself from the others and walked my way…it was Ben. I had nothing to say. For once in my life, I was at a total loss for words. The most I could do was nod my head. He nodded. Words wouldn't work then for anyone.

There were spotlights being set up to flood the area. I heard a generator running. As each one was illuminated, it became progressively worse. I'd been right; it sounded like a war zone. Now it looked like one. There were dead, at least I thought they were dead, bodies lying at strange angles. In the last flickering light from the burning house, they looked demonic. It was a scene straight out of *Dante's Inferno*. Somehow, I was certain they were demons, or at least demon possessed. Otherwise, why would they have done this?

I was unsure if anyone could, or would, tell me what happened or why.

The best part of this horrific scene, if there could be one… *Survivor* was still riding high on her mooring as if nothing had happened.

A tear stole down my cheek. God spared the dogs, my boat, and me. It would somehow be okay. For this moment, however, I felt like Job.

I was a sad sight. A tired old woman clutching a rifle and a shotgun under one arm, a purse slung across her body with two very frightened but stoic dogs sitting at her feet. This was the first time I'd ever felt *old*. It frightened me.

The state trooper was walking in my direction. This should be an interview for the ages. He strutted to within a foot of me. It was too close for Shadow's comfort level with a stranger. She stood at attention and let out a loud growl. The trooper stopped. "You need to put the dog on a leash."

I burst into laughter. I couldn't contain myself. He was unimpressed and squared off.

"Yes sir! I'll run right into the house and get a leash, just for your comfort. You, sir, are an idiot! Sorry, but I don't think you have a very good grasp of this situation. Please take a step back and she'll stop growling. She believes you're too close to me." To my amazement, he did; she stopped. Proper boundaries were established.

Oops! I guessed wrong with that assumption. Ben stepped between the trooper and me. He is much larger than I remembered. I couldn't see the trooper around him, over him, or beside him. I could hear him, though. "Trooper you need to re-group. The first thing you need to do is apologize to this woman for your deplorable behavior. This was her home. These thugs also destroyed her car, and decimated the area.

"From the looks of this, do you think *maybe* they could have been trying to kill her?" Ben stepped back beside me.

The trooper, looking shamed, muttered, "I'm sorry for my approach. To tell you the truth, this is outside of anything I've ever encountered. I called for backup and others are coming. The only thing I was told is not to touch nothing. The Feds are on the way."

The next words out of his mouth proved I was right…he was an idiot. "I'll need to take those guns you're carrying; this is a crime scene, after all."

My reply was simple. "No, you're not taking *anything*. Now stand down and leave me alone before I say something I will certainly regret." To my astonishment, he walked away, even if he was muttering.

I needed to sit. Heading for the rocks by the cove, I began to shake like a leaf in a fall gale. I knew it was only a matter of minutes before I'd keel over.

As I neared the rocks, Shadow began growling in earnest. It was a low deadly growl, a sound I'd never heard from her.

Lying in the shadow of a large rock was a man covered with blood. He was still moving, looking mean as a snake.

"Ben, come quick!" was all that escaped from my mouth. The man lunged at the same time Shadow leaped at him. Thankfully, he was injured and weakened to some degree. When she sprang, she took him down.

Ben rushed up, taking in the scene. In a second, he had a .45 automatic pistol in his hand and said, "Call the dog off."

Shadow came at once and stood at attention. However, her eyes never left the men.

"Can you get the trooper?" Ben asked me. I thought I could, maybe. I nodded; keeling over would have to wait in line.

I hurried to where the trooper stood with his back to me. I grasped his arm, turning him to face the shore. "Didn't you hear the commotion with the dog barking and my hollering? Are you deaf as well as a greenhorn? Ben has one of the men who just tried, yet again, to kill my dog and me while you're standing here gazing into space. Get the hell down there and do something useful. Perhaps you will finally figure out who the bad guys are and stop harassing the victim."

I needed a place to stop. Even on autopilot I knew I was about to be violently sick. I walked to the edge of the sand, and vomited until I was sure I would never need to again.

When I looked back a few feet, there sat the dogs. Seaweed was licking Shadow as if she were trying to tell her, "Good job, you brave friend."

Ben came to me saying, "The dude is cuffed; he's no longer a problem."

"Thank you again." It was all I managed to say.

Ben's cell rang; his face tensed. He listened, and then growled, "Are all of you okay?"

He paused, listening, and then snapped, "No shit! What happened?" followed by a long *listening* pause. His face showed even *more* concern.

"I don't *give* a damn about the damage! Did the Coast Guard ever show up?" Ben listened intently, his face wrought with concern, his eyes squinted as if to help him hear. Ben waited out an even longer pause. Then he yelled, "You did *WHAT*?" Again he waited for another long pause, and then spoke softly and dangerously, "*You*, my son, are an idiot. I told you to be careful! I said; find the damn boat and call the Coast Guard. Why in hell did you engage a bunch of drug and gunrunners? Then you *boarded* their boat? You are nuts!"

Following a short pause, Ben's face softened and he chuckled.

"Oh, I see. Just because they shot a hole in *your* boat, you needed to take care of business. Where are they now if the Coast Guard hasn't arrived?

"How are they tied up, if I may ask?" He listened for a second, nodded, and then grinned. "Yup, you tied them with rope, wrapped them in camouflage netting, and then hung them from the rigging. I would say it certainly should keep them in place.

"Are you sure you and the others are all right?

"If this was the most fun you've had since you left the Seals, you're one sick dude who needs to go to the city more often.

"No, we're okay here. I'm not sure of the body count yet. I must be losing my touch; one of them was still alive. The buildings are a total loss along with the auto. They finally sent a trooper, but a really green one. He doesn't know what to do. He told me the Feds are on their way.

"Are you going to tow the boat or wait for the Coast Guard? When the Feds get here, I'll tell them to contact the Coast Guard. If they get there before the call comes, please fill them in so they won't do something stupid like arrest you guys.

"Call if you need me. By the way, good job, son, I want to know how you found the boat. I'll talk with you shortly."

Ben looked over at me, nodded, and patted me on the shoulder with a half smile. "It'll be okay in time, don't worry."

I wished I could believe him. I had always said I wished at times that someone would tell me it would be all right, even if the person were lying. This was one of those times.

The sound of a helicopter trying to find a landing place interrupted everything. Everyone was listening to the sound of the engine while watching the landing lights. The lights of the craft dropped behind the tree line and the engines silenced. They must have landed on the road; it was the only flat, sort of open area.

Before long, Hank and his gang arrived, good old Hank. I heard him bellowing before he even got near the scene. Someday, he would give himself a stroke if he couldn't learn to calm down.

It had already been a long, terrible night. I knew things were going to escalate, making it even worse.

Before Hank reached me, Ben grabbed his arm; beginning a discussion with him. I only heard snatches of the information. Hank tried to shake off Ben's hand. I couldn't understand all of the conversation. I heard enough, though, to know Ben was trying to relay information from the conversations he'd had with Eric.

Hank yanked out his phone and began talking heatedly, gesturing wildly with his free hand, all the while glaring at me.

This *must* be my fault, as usual, from the look I was getting.

When he stopped yelling, listening to whoever was on the phone, there was dead silence. A look of total disbelief spread quickly over Hank's face. You could have heard a pine needle drop.

I heard loud and clear, "You have got to be kidding me. *We couldn't* find them; the Coast Guard *couldn't find* them *and* then some local-yokel *lobstermen* in a God forsaken town captured them? They found the boat, a load of arms, and how much heroin?"

"I need to get a different profession!"

He followed that up with, "Yes! Keep me posted!"

"Wait, you need to keep this under wraps and out of the press. I don't care who you say told you to. You can say it was anybody, even the President, for all I care! Just lock it down NOW! If one word of this gets any airtime, you will be swabbing decks in the bowels of a vessel for the rest of your time in service. *Am I clear*?"

Hank was wild, which was obvious. Why, as usual, I hadn't a clue. Nor at this point did I give a damn. It had to be a male ego thing.

We had the crooks. They couldn't find or catch them. The locals had apparently succeeded where Hank's crew had failed. I was grateful and frankly stunned as to why Hank was not. I figured, at this moment, it sucked to be Hank, and too damn bad for his ego!

I didn't care; my entire life and most of my possessions were gone. That fact was more important to me than his sense of self-worth.

Ben started to walk away when he glanced back at Hank who had his head thrust forward, stomping toward me. Without hesitation, Ben turned on his heel, matching strides with Hank.

Now there were two very angry men headed on a collision course for me. Had I not been so exhausted I would have fled to somewhere else.

Shadow changed her sitting place. She was right in front of me. Poor old Seaweed didn't move. If I had trusted I wouldn't fall over, I would've scooped her up and held her.

I don't think Hank realized he had an escort until he bellowed, "Damn it, woman, I told you they would be back, this was not a game. Now I'm telling you..." that was as far as he got before Ben swung Hank around to face him.

It was apparent Ben was very angry. He kept his voice controlled and low, but the force was there.

Maybe threatening to shoot him days ago hadn't been a smart move on my part. Later I would apologize for my threat.

However, Ben still cannot have *Survivor*.

Carefully, Ben spoke to Hank as one would explain something to a limited child of about two. "Have you even bothered to look around here yet? Just in case you didn't happen to notice, I would like to point out to you some facts. They burned her house and destroyed her car. Dead bodies litter the cove. Somehow, all you can do is yell and vent at a woman who is lucky to be alive. She is barely standing on her own strength. Although, I admit I have no clue how. We found the offshore vessel loaded with arms and drugs. All this accomplished with no assistance from your group.

"If you still find it necessary to vent, let's you and me take a walk. You can yell all you want, until I get sick of your pompous attitude and flatten you on the spot. Now, either you lighten up and be respectful or walk away until you can."

Wow, I am impressed! I do not impress easily.

Hank simply hung his head, mumbled, "I'm sorry for acting like a jerk. You sir, have no idea of how much time and energy we have expended to catch this gang. Then to be blind-sided seems so weird.

"We appreciate your help, don't take me wrong. To be very honest with you, we were not even close to any solution.

"I figured they'd sneak back ashore here, but not to do this, or I would have moved her out regardless of the mayhem it would have caused. I'd have put her in a safe house. Now I don't know what will happen here. The head and horns of the outfit will be here in the next load."

Ben's phone rang. "Yes, oh they finally arrived. Good. They wanted you to do what? No way; round up the boys and get back to shore …they can mop up their own mess.

"I know, I guess our assistance was a nuisance to the whole damned group involved in this.

"Can you manage to get the boat back to the yard? Okay, I'll be there shortly.

"Please go over to the loft and turn on the lights and the heat. I'll be bringing someone with me."

Hank had been listening intently. "If you're thinking about taking Eileen with you, it is not going to happen. She is a Federal witness and she will be billeted where I say."

Humor always returns to me at the oddest times; both Ben and I spoke at the same time "Bullshit." I began to laugh. I couldn't have stopped even if I'd tried.

Nine

Ben carefully removed the two guns from my arm. I'd forgotten I was still holding them. He gently placed his arm around my shoulders. Then speaking softly, he told the dogs to come. We walked away.

I was way beyond *out of it*. Ben led us quietly to the cove. There, riding at the edge of the water, was a black Zodiac. I hadn't noticed the skiff; it blended perfectly into the background.

Ben lifted Seaweed off her shaky little legs. He placed her carefully on the floor of the craft. Then he assisted me to board. Shadow just leapt in as if she went for a ride in that thing every day of her life.

In my next life, I want to come back as a dog just like her.

Ben plucked the small mushroom anchor from the sand, spun the boat, stepping with ease into the stern.

There wasn't any conversation between Ben and me. I was finished. I knew it. My spirit had taken a time out. I allowed it.

The motor, to my surprise, was battery operated. We glided quietly out of the cove. The only sound was the water sluicing along the boat.

Outside the rocky point, sitting off a short distance, riding quietly on the water was a larger boat. It looked like one of the cigar boats they race. How out of place it seemed in this fishing boat community! Even when exhausted, with my senses nearly shut down, I marveled my mind was still able to register information.

Ben came alongside and whistled once. Men appeared as if from nowhere. "I'm going to continue on with the Zodiac. It'll take longer, but I don't want my guests disturbed any more than they are.

"Allow me a good head-start then go to the boat-yard. If I need you to return for a tow, I'll call on the phone.

"Be careful, the boys are all heading back. Eric took a hit. I don't know the extent of the damages. I'm not certain how fast he can cruise.

"Keep your eyes open just in case the whole gang was not on board the vessel they caught. They're mad and really out for blood now.

"Call me if you see anything unusual, no matter what it is. Okay?"

The peace and quiet of being on the water was a Godsend to me. I watched the glow of the phosphorus as the propeller churned in the dark water. This was something I hadn't seen for years and it calmed my soul.

Neither Ben nor I spoke.

The entire night had been a terrible, horrific, and chaotic time.

I heard the sound of Ben's big boat when they started the engines. Before it even moved, the sound vibrated off the water. I recognized that sound. It was the same as the one I'd heard while hiding in the cave. What a powerful engine or engines it must have.

We slid quietly over the water accompanied by the roar of the other boat in the distance.

We arrived at a rocky point of land jutting out into the ocean. Ben went on the inside and followed it around to the end. It appeared to be a natural breakwater.

The other boat had passed us long ago. I couldn't hear it anymore. As we rounded the point of land, I could hear other boats. They sounded quite far away. There were lights on the shore. It appeared to be a large facility, judging from the illuminated areas.

Ben brought the Zodiac alongside the float with a comfort level only coming from always living on the water and using watercrafts.

Men arrived as if they'd choreographed this dance forever. They quickly berthed our boat.

Ben passed the rifle and shotgun to one fellow who, without a word, checked to see if they were loaded. He emptied both, and then placed them in a tote along with the ammo.

Ben carefully picked up Seaweed and passed her to another man while giving him a caution, "Careful, just hold her. She's old and exhausted."

Shadow was not leaving me. She sat until I gave her a hand command to dismount. Jumping to the float, she stood waiting for me.

I hoped I could stand and get out of the boat without embarrassing myself. I wasn't sure, but I tried, almost managing to get up by myself. Ben reached over and steadied me. With his assistance, along with the man on the float, I got out. I stood on my own, but just barely. I wobbled. Thankfully, the man hung onto me or I would've fallen into the water. Ben easily stepped out of the boat onto the float, took my arm, and together we made our way up the gangway.

There was an open golf cart waiting. We loaded into it without a word; the tote was set carefully into the back. We moved off slowly. Where to, I had no idea; nor did I care.

For once in my life, I knew I wasn't in charge. It seemed, for the moment, to be okay.

Ben stopped in front of a very large building with the top floor windows all aglow. There were more men, perhaps the same ones. I couldn't tell. Was this an army installation or something? I hadn't known there were this many people living in this town, let alone in one place not very far from where I lived.

My mind skidded to a halt. *Did I still live there/here? Could I do this?* As of that very second, I didn't know how.

I truly had nothing except what I had on, a purse, two dogs, three guns and yes, a boat. My inventory taken, I turned my brain off.

Ben had been speaking to me. I hadn't heard him. I was shutting down. This was not good. He tried again. This time I tried to listen. Ben asked, "Can you manage a few stairs or do you need the lift activated?"

I tried to nod a yes. To which choice I didn't know. I needed to pay attention. I tried again "Stairs okay." *I hope.*

How stupid I must seem. It no longer mattered; it was all I had left.

Ten

Gentle hands picked Seaweed up. Shadow hopped out, making a subtle noise, alerting me she needed to go. She looked up at Seaweed then to me. "The dogs need to have a short walk. I'll take them."

It'd been good; old habits kick in just when you need them. I took Seaweed, putting her down on the ground. The three of us walked over to where it was grassy. They're good dogs, those two! They walked onto the grass, did their thing, returned as if we always did this, right here at this time of the night.

By the time I returned to the golf cart, I was functioning better. At least that was my assumption.

Ben led the way up a flight of stairs to a landing. When he opened the door, I was shocked. What a lovely space. It was all natural wood but very well finished. It was warm. I hadn't realized how chilled I'd been.

Ben spoke in a kindly manner, "Eileen, you'll find everything you need here. Nobody will disturb you. Take a warm bath, try to relax, and if you need anything, call my cell.

"I'm going to see if I can get a few hours of sleep before the idiots arrive, as I am certain they will.

"I'll talk with you later. Have a good night, what's left of it.

"I had Eric leave you some dog food in the kitchen. It's probably not what they're used to but it will feed them until we can get their brand." With that, he closed the door and descended the stairs.

I locked the door. Only then did I realize I was still carrying the revolver in my waistband.

When I glanced around the apartment, I noticed it was small but very nicely arranged. Even in my wrecked state of mind, I appreciated it. In front of me was a small, fully equipped kitchen with a table and four chairs tucked off to the side.

On the counter sat a small bag of dog kibble. I gave both dogs a sample for being good.

At the entry to the room there was a small, comfortable sitting area, with a couch, matching chairs, and an entertainment center with a flat screen television. The floors were wood, all nicely polished with large area rugs.

A very handsome freestanding gas fireplace burned quietly, emitting a nice warm glow, heating the room.

The bedroom suite was located on the right-hand side of a short hall. I opened the door, revealing a large bed, two bureaus, and a comfortable chair.

When I opened the bathroom door, there was a large jetted tub, separate shower, and blessed be, a washer-dryer stack.

I took Ben's advice and began to draw a bath.

I was a wreck physically, personally and mentally.

I found a big, soft terry robe hanging on the door. It smelled so good and clean. *I smelled of smoke, dirt, and fear.*

While the water ran, I checked out the vanity, finding a supply of new toothbrushes, toothpaste, lotions, shaving cream, razors, after-shave, aspirin, and Advil.

This was nicer than most hotels I'd visited, some nice ones, when I had a *real* life.

When the bath was ready, I added bath salts, stripped, and tossed the clothes into the washer. I prayed I wouldn't run their well dry or overload the septic system in my quest to get rid of the stench from the night.

As I climbed into the tub, the dogs came, taking up positions on the bath mat. Then, they quickly fell asleep.

I tried to shut off my mind, relax, and float in the tub. Still, the events of the night swirled in and out. I knew if I didn't get this to stop, it would drive me crazy. Then they would've won. *No, I won't ever let it happen.*

I completed the bath along with washing my hair and then wrapped myself in the wonderful terry robe. I tossed my clothes into the dryer. At least, I didn't have to decide what to wear tomorrow, or today. I had what I had.

I turned down the bed, slipped between the sheets, still wearing the robe. I knew I would never sleep.

When I finally awoke, becoming aware of life, on this planet, the room was sun-filled and brilliant with light. Both dogs were staring at me as though I'd just landed from the moon.

Where was I?

Then it began to filter in, thankfully in a very slow, seeping awareness. I was reluctant to get out of the warm, safe cocoon of a nest to face what was coming.

I'm usually an early riser. I love seeing the sunrise. I like to enjoy every moment of God's glory. Down East, it appears the sun rises out of the water, shedding warmth and light over the earth. I'd certainly missed the sunrise this morning.

I checked the dryer. My clothes were clean, dry and smelled good. Once dressed, I found the makings for coffee in the cupboard. I set a pot to brew.

Then it was the dogs' time. They were ready to be up and let out. I tried to be careful and quiet. I had no idea what the folks here had endured last night or what their lifestyle was.

The dogs did their sniff test for pee spots, finished their thing and returned to me without any hint of exploring.

Back inside, I fed them, refilled the bowls with water, and then it was coffee time.

The first sip was heavenly! Then, my mind kicked into high gear. What was I going to do?

I am a practical person, if nothing else. I thought I would drink this good coffee, thank God for the day and then I'd get on with the tasks of the day. Decision made. I drank my coffee.

I knew it was necessary to stay calm and focused. Find out what I had left, if anything. Then I needed to make a plan for going forward, and lastly, execute the plan. *Eileen, that is great advice.*

I would've told anyone else the same thing, if this experience or another life crisis had occurred in his or her life. Only problem is, *this is MY life crisis.*

I was enjoying my second cup of coffee while doing this desperate mental exercise when the dogs alerted me someone was arriving.

The soft knock on the door required me to stand and begin to show up in this game called life.

I opened the door to Ben who was carrying a tray full of food. "Bearing gifts for guests," he told me as he made his way to the counter. Smelled good; I could smell bacon. The joke is, I love bacon, but seldom bought any.

He reached into the cupboard retrieving two plates, a cup, silverware, napkins along with salt and pepper. I was amazed!

Ben invited me to join him for breakfast. "Come eat while it's hot. You're going to need this for today." He poured himself a cup of coffee while refilling my mug. Suddenly, I realized I was starving, although I hadn't even thought of food, except for the dogs, until I smelled the bacon. What can I say …I'm easy.

The food was great… scrambled eggs, home fries, bacon, and homemade muffins. I ate as if it were my last meal.

Ben slipped the dogs a piece of bacon. They loved him, the traitors! He broke the silence with "They've already been on the phone this morning demanding I deliver you at once. I told them we would be there if and when—if you wanted to and when we got ready. I hoped it would meet with your approval."

This was the right time to apologize for telling him I wanted to shoot him. "Ben, I'm sorry I threatened to shoot you the other day."

His reaction was a slow grin. "Eileen, at the time you told me I really didn't believe you had the moxie to shoot me. After last night, I'm much better informed. I wouldn't try you again, okay. By the way, that's a nice piece lying on the counter."

I'd forgotten I left the .38 there last night…sloppy housekeeping. We finished the meal, stacked the dishes into the sink, and then readied ourselves for the onslaught of the day.

Ben spoke softly. "Before we go, I want to show you something you may enjoy seeing. This is my *art* gallery of sorts." We walked down the stairs to the ground level of the building. It was larger than I thought and really well constructed with steel beams and trusses. A great work space.

Ben led the way through a door at the end of the shop area into a space filled with small boats on sawhorses. Drawings and blueprints covered the walls, along with photos from every era of small boats. "This is where I spend most of my time. I like to restore and replicate old designs dating back to times gone by."

I was impressed with the small hulls and the workmanship each one represented. I loved the smell of the shop. The scent of freshly worked pine was overwhelming. Only woodworking produces this unique smell. "They are lovely…you do nice work."

Ben nodded then quietly added, "I would never wreck a boat. I only restore them to copy the design. You can't find blueprints for most of the home-built crafts they sailed long ago. I have to find one, in whatever shape it's in, then carefully measure and tweak it till it's perfect."

Eleven

Ben's phone rang. I figured our day was about to begin. "Eileen, if you're up to it, they want us to come to the cove."

I nodded. I couldn't find any reason to delay further, except I didn't want to go. I wanted this to be a bad nightmare. Then I would wake up with everything normal again.

When I got into Ben's truck, I noticed the tote with my rifle and shotgun in it sitting on the back seat.

Ben had carefully picked up Seaweed and placed her on the front seat. Shadow had jumped into the back. She stood, as always, with her hind feet on the floor and her front feet on the console. I called it her *command post*.

I knew I wasn't ready, but this was real life. I needed to pull on my big girl, all grown-up panties and get with it.

Most things in life just *seem* to happen; not according to any plan or scheme, they just occur when you're busy with life. Good, bad, or indifferent, I needed to make the best of them.

I felt more like myself, thanks to the full stomach and clean clothes. When I left the apartment, I'd slipped the Colt revolver into my purse. It had been sort of an after-thought. With the direction my life had gone recently, I might need it. Better safe than sorry or dead…dead was fast becoming more relevant.

When we reached my road, it appeared to be a command post with an armed guard standing watch. The guard was in full military get-up, standing back just inside the trees, out of sight from the main road. Ben slowed the truck, waved, and then drove on. The road was a horrible mess. All of the traffic in and out had trashed it completely.

Groups of men clustered around three black SUVs. They'd parked next to the twisted hulk of my Jeep just lying there in death. How sad… it had been a great vehicle. I'd loved the poor old thing. What a contrast! I'd once thought the Jeep, and I would grow old together, and now it was gone. How rapidly situations change our lives, thoughts, and goals.

The remnants of the cottage stood stark against the sky. The chimney and a couple of pieces of charred studding were the only things upright. My stomach churned. I could feel tears burning in my throat. I was profoundly saddened. It looked much worse than I'd remembered from last night. It had been my home. I'd been happy there.

The minute we drove in, they began marching towards us like a swarm of gnats on a hot, sticky July day. They were equally as unwelcome in my space.

Ben asked, "Eileen do you want to leave the dogs in the truck?"

I immediately thought, *what a nice gesture. Most folks worried about a dog shedding hair or eating the seats or something.*

I was touched. "If you don't mind, and if she doesn't, I'll leave Seaweed here to rest. Shadow won't stay if I go, but she'll be okay."

We exited the truck, just barely stepping on the ground, when Hank began his rant with, "Well, Byther, where have you been? I need some answers. I look like an idiot to my bosses."

My reply, "Then, Hank, it sucks to be you. A man can only look like what he portrays, so don't try to blame me for your short-fall."

I swore I heard a snicker from Ben.

Hank was not happy. He wasn't about to get any happier with me.

"You're going to take a number and stand in line; this is still my property. There are things that are more important with a higher priority that need attention first. I want to figure out what my priorities should be. Do I make myself clear?"

I always was a person who enjoyed the times a blusterer was required to quit earlier than they thought they should. They appear to deflate in front of your eyes.

I walked slowly, literally dragging my feet, toward the ruins of my home. I heard the dead silence. Everyone there was waiting for me to get all *girly,* bawl and carry on. It was never going to happen. My emotion was pure hatred and anger. Why had this happened? Who'd done this? I wanted some answers.

To hell with them …I would never allow myself be remembered as the local wuss! I snapped my head up, squared my shoulders, and strode forward. There were too many things needing attention and I intended to accomplish as much as I possibly could.

The floor hadn't caved in as I'd expected. I approached the door to the small basement area. I'd closed and locked it last night when I fled. Why I still didn't know; habit, I guess. The door remained closed. I unlocked it, then gently pushed it open, fearing what damage I'd encounter. The space smelled of smoke. Otherwise, it seemed to be unharmed.

It appeared the well pump was also undamaged. This was a small victory! Still, I was grateful.

I crouched down and stepped inside to reach the small storage area; everything seemed to be intact. It was obvious the fire had burned up and consumed the structure, but had not burned through the floor in this section.

My safe box was there. I retrieved it. I knew I'd need the paperwork to begin to resurrect this mess. I took what I thought would be needed. I stepped back outside, relocking the door.

Ben took the box from me; carrying it to his truck. He placed it on the back seat. I watched him as he sneaked a quick pat to Seaweed on his way out. She needed that. Perhaps he did also.

I walked back to Hank and his gang. I was as ready as I would ever be. Ben joined us.

Hank wasn't happy to have him there. Too damned bad for him; I wanted Ben there.

In truth, Ben knew more about what happened than I did. I would've thought they'd be all over him with questions. I wondered if it were that 'man thing' called *ego*.

Hank began with his usual lack of tact. "What happened here last night? You called me and said they had returned. Who had returned? What'd they want? Where'd they come from? How'd they get here? What time was it? Are you going to tell us or just go off again?"

That did it! "Hank, I want you to back off and stop harassing me. I'm damned tired of the constant ass chewing you constantly dish out. Besides, your delivery stinks!"

Taking a very deep breath while I tried to remind myself I was still a woman with some manners, perhaps, maybe, "You can see with your own eyes what went on here. I've no idea who they were. You do. I've no idea where they came from this time, any more than I did the last time. I assume they came by boat. Most people don't go swimming with grenade launchers and automatic weapons.

"As to what time; check your damned phone. I called you while it was underway."

"Now, speaking of just going off, if you and your cronies had done your jobs properly in the first place, they would've all been arrested. Then, none of this would've happened.

"Instead of thanking folks who risked their lives and equipment, you act like they invaded your private space and you're pissed. Now, unless you can add anything relevant to this situation, I have things needing immediate attention. I need to return to my life.

"Also, I expect you and your band of merry men to repair my driveway. You've hacked it up even more than the last time you invaded my place.

"You have exactly fifteen minutes to ask, or do, anything which requires my attention. Afterwards, I'm out of here."

I rather laughed inside. I already knew, with this group, it'd take those men most of the allowed time to get their jaws closed.

Hank was red as a beet. I thought, not for the first time, he was definitely stroke material.

A tall, thin, middle aged man separated himself from the group and moved forward. He appeared to be more in command of himself, and the situation, than Hank.

He came forward, extending his hand. "I'm Hogan, Les Hogan. I'm pleased to meet you. Although profoundly sorry for what's happened here. I can assure you; we appreciated *all* of the assistance rendered last night."

"Any damages to property and equipment will be reimbursed liberally. Including, I believe, one of your boats, Mr. Hayward."

"I trust there were no personal injuries to any of the men involved. I would like very much to speak with your son regarding the capture of the boat off shore."

At last, a person who could assess and repair while appreciating the devastation. I was impressed.

Apparently, so was Ben.

Ben pulled out his cell, pushed a button, spoke briefly, then asked Les, "Where would you like to meet and when? Eric is available now. Do you want him to come here?"

Les nodded in assent; the call ended. I left to allow them to chat between themselves.

I walked to the ledge, surprised at the lack of debris left from the fire. It was mostly ash, burned timbers, with the old iron bedstead from upstairs still upright, but now sitting on the first floor. It sat there beside its mate, which had been in the first floor bedroom. The kitchen stove still stood, covered in soot and ash while the new fridge was a twisted mess. The old iron sink sat on the floor. I had planned, during the winter, to build a nice cabinet for it. It was too late now.

I looked over at *Survivor*. She looked a little low in the water. I needed to pull her in and bail the water out. It'd been a few days, and even with my best efforts, she still leaked a little. This was another one of my proposed winter projects.

I thought, not for the first time, *Eileen, how are you going to fix this situation?* I truly didn't know. I was certain I could and somehow I would. I always had.

Shadow sat quietly at my feet, looking desperately sad. I wondered if dogs understood things like we humans can. To what extent did they understand? I was certain she knew our home was gone.

I walked on toward the cove and began to pull the boat in. I was always better when I was doing something.

The men seemed to be content to chat amongst themselves. However, I was more than happy to be relieved from joining the burdensome conversation.

While I was tugging on the mooring line bringing the boat in to shore, I heard a high-powered vehicle coming down the trace. It came to a stop beside Ben's truck.

The man who emerged was a total replica of Ben, just younger. He nodded to his dad, acknowledged the other men, and then walked on toward me. He walked in the same no nonsense way his father did. He stuck out his hand for a shake, "Hi, I'm Eric, pleased to meet you, sorry for the circumstances. Here, let me give you a hand. Needed a little bailing, I would gather."

My jaw was ajar. He took the mooring line, pulled with ease until the boat was well up onto the sand.

"Wow! You really do know how to do this easier than I could. I get it up enough to beach it. I then get aboard without wet feet. It always required a lot more pulling. Thank you.

"Eric, I want to thank you for all of your assistance last night. I owe you folks a lot. You go play with the crowd. I'll bail the boat."

He laughed. "The reason I could get it higher on the beach is because I'm a lot taller than you. The only reason you want to stay and bail is you'll accomplish something. Talking with them will be a total waste of my time. I'll swap with you."

My turn to smile. "Nope, I already did my fast five minutes. I am, as they say Down East, *well and truly* done with them."

Eric returned to the group of men where they chatted. Les appeared to be the leader. Sounds of laughter floated on the air. Seemingly, a lighter mood was prevailing.

I bailed *Survivor* while Shadow sat on the prow seat and watched both the merry men and me. Task completed.

Soon, I would need to pull and cover her for the winter. It was a good job to focus on. It'd keep me from falling into despair over the rest of the mess. Shadow jumped down as I pushed *Survivor* off. I used the reversing pulley line to put her back out on the mooring.

I must have finished at the right time because the merry men were approaching.

Ben and Eric were standing next to their trucks talking and nodding. Eric slapped a good-natured pat on his dad and strode to his truck. With a mighty roar, it started and he drove slowly up the trace.

Ben was walking on a course to reach the congregating group. They seemed to surround me. I was out-numbered. My back was to the water, they were on the shoreline above me. They seemed to tower over me. My being just a bit over five feet tall was not an advantage. Perhaps I'd better pull the boat back in. Then I'll deliver a sermon to them, as Jesus did when the crowds had invaded His space. *I thought, good to know that I haven't lost all my sense of humor. Go Eileen.*

I needed to change the dynamics; I wouldn't ever admit it to them, but they challenged my comfort level.

I climbed upon my favorite 'coffee and at times wine drinking' rock. It is also what I call my *counseling* rock. I talk to God often sitting there. I've made some of my best decisions while sitting and sipping there.

Les stepped forward and began the conversation, "Eileen, I know this has created one hell of a mess in your life. I have some solutions. I'd like to discuss them with you. Would this be a good time?"

I hadn't thought there would ever be a *good time* so I guessed I should hear him out.

Ben stepped forward and addressed Les directly, "Can we move this to a better location; like perhaps my place?"

Les nodded agreement. Like sheep, the merry men returned to the black vehicles they'd driven here.

Ben and I, with Shadow on our heels, loaded into his truck.

No wonder the drive was such a mess; it had become a super highway of sorts. Next thing I knew, they'd pave it and install stoplights.

Twelve

We were silent for a few moments, then Ben cautioned me, "Eileen, I don't want to interfere, but do a lot of listening and no agreeing until you have *exactly* what you want. These people are in a pickle and they know it.

"I'd put more credence in what Les had to say than Hank. I don't think Hank is a bad fellow, but he's lost on this case. I'm not sure why. Just be careful and make sure you know what you want for yourself."

As always, good counsel was never lost on me. I appreciated Ben's input. I'd become even sadder by the day for wanting to shoot him. I was wrong. However, I'm still not sorry enough to give him *Survivor*.

When we arrived at Ben's property, he parked in front of the big building with the apartment above. He took out the strong box along with the tote and placed them by the door.

I took Seaweed for a short walk with Shadow. They both seemed to like being here, away from the mess. They did their business and even managed a short romp with some yipping I call their *play song*.

When I returned to the building, Ben had moved the things inside the door. It appeared Les was busy instructing the merry men in something. They returned to their cars.

Hank was sulking. I could tell because I'd seen the look before. Ben carried my things up the stairs. He was on his way back out to his truck when I reached the door.

I spoke before he could leave. "Please stay, if you can spare the time. I'm not comfortable with a one-on-one without a witness."

He followed us back up the stairs.

I made coffee and we all sat around the small table.

I was unsure of what would happen. I'd been certain of one thing: I was going to listen hard. I would not speak until I'd heard everything Les had to say.

Les got directly to the point. He didn't seemed to mind Ben's presence there, which slightly quieted my paranoia.

I thought, *how strange, we're going to have a meeting, yet not one of us has a pad of paper or a pen.*

Les seemed unfazed by the absence of note taking. He began at once. "Are you wanting to retain the property on the point? Would it be your plan to rebuild there? It's a no-brainer that you need transportation, temporary housing, clothing and other personal items.

"The proposal I'm offering is this: we'll provide you with funds to purchase a vehicle, clothing and provide a housing allowance. We'll rebuild the road, clean up the mess from the fire, and remove the wrecked car. Now, let's discuss the house. I'll provide you with the funds to rebuild. I can't authorize an excessive amount for an elaborate structure. However, it will certainly be a much better structure for a permanent home than the cottage you lost."

I was stunned. I never expected that. "What's the catch? I've maintained a small policy on the cottage. Considering the circumstance, I doubt they'll pay it. The car was only insured for liability."

Les was ready for my questions. "The catch is this: no matter what, it *NEVER* happened. This is imperative. Do you understand? Have you seen any news today or listened to the radio?"

I shook my head no.

Les continued, "I didn't think so. There was nothing on the news about this, at all. It must remain this way for security reasons. This mess isn't over by a long shot."

My reaction to the statement shocked me. I'd begun to shake. Not over! I don't think I could go through it again. I moved here for peace and quiet to live out my life in a calm manner without strife. "What you've just explained to me is if I rebuild, they, whoever they are, will destroy it again?

"What'd I ever do to anyone to create such hate? I don't even know who these people are. How did they know me? Do you even know the answer to any of this? Les, can you tell me honestly why there were no fire trucks there last night?

"Also, when the first incident occurred, how was it the sheriff and game wardens didn't even speak to me?"

Les sat and pondered his answer very carefully, "This had nothing to do with you, Eileen. You're a victim who just happened to be in the wrong place at the wrong time. This scrap was truly between the forces of evil, something you couldn't even imagine. I checked your background thoroughly before coming here. You must be part cat. I don't know how you've survived this long, let alone last night.

"Lady, you've got some real grit. Hank was wrong when he let you stay the first time. However, if you hadn't stayed, we wouldn't be where we are in this investigation. Without your call to Ben, we would never, ever, have gotten this far."

Les continued on. "This can't get out to the public, which was the reason there were no volunteer fire fighters. The 'first incident,' as you called it, was taken care of with the local law by letting them know the Feds were in charge.

"We've been working with them for some time trying to solve and resolve this problem. The greatest thing about this town is people will talk, speculate, and then move on. They'll forget all about what happened and you."

My turn. "I want to know how you handled the trooper who was there last night. He knew what the aftermath was. He would certainly discuss it with his superiors, wife, girlfriend, whoever..."

My statement garnered a slight smile from Les. "No, he won't ever mention it. By some stroke of fate, when he called for back-up last night, our man working with the state police was on duty. He got the call and took care of the patch to us. Early this morning, the trooper, much to his glee, became the newest member of our team. He is on his way to Virginia for intensive training. According to him, it was the best call he ever got."

I needed to ask, "What will the fallout be to me personally? Will I always need to be looking over my shoulder? What will be the restrictions?"

Les leaned forward and was earnest in his answer. "You can take what I offered you, stay here as you have indicated you want to, or I can put you somewhere in a safe house with a new identity. The new identity and safe house would mean no contact with family or friends. It's your choice, not mine. I'll do whatever you want.

"The problem is this: I need your answer now, in order to close this part and move on to the rest of the mess. Take a few minutes and think about it. Knowing your past, I realize this is something you've done several times, mostly with good results."

Les turned his attention to Ben. "What do you think they were planning on doing with the kegs of heroin they had in netting all tied together? They also had crates of munitions trussed up in the same manner."

I knew the answer to that. I spoke up, "They were going to set the gear on the bottom with a low float-line and GPS co-ordinates. They would then use a zodiac like Ben's to hook the line and pull them aboard. They couldn't use a lobster buoy to mark the spot because a strange buoy would start a lobster war with the locals.

"The first time they came ashore in the cove, they had crates of the munitions. I don't know if they had drugs, but I think they did. I didn't hear them come in. The dogs let me know. I thought it was someone trying to steal my boat.

"I sure screwed up when I shot the guy. My life changed so much. I was looking for a quiet retirement, sitting on the rocks painting, fishing, and living on my social security.

"By the way, if I took the funding you offered, would it affect my social security, income tax, scrutiny from any other Federal or State concerns?"

I thought Les and Ben were going to laugh themselves foolish over my questions. Finally, Les gathered himself so he could speak, "No, no, no, and no."

Les continued, "I need to know how you figured out how they would retrieve the booty."

Silly man…if he'd checked my background, he would have known I not only worked on a commercial fishing boat, I'd later been the settlement house for several large commercial fishing boats out of Portland.

It had been an interesting assignment. I micro-managed the crewing needs with workers, kept the equipment bills and supplies paid, along with paying shares to the crews.

I remembered the crew losing drags if a cable snapped when they would get hung-up on the bottom while dragging for fish. The crew would then use a dragline with the GPS co-ordinates to retrieve them with good results.

"You did the background check; you figure it out, Les. After all, you're the professional. I'm just the *little old crazy woman* in this group.

"Will you repair Eric's boat and compensate the guys who assisted in the capture last night or is it none of my business, about *what never happened?"*

Les assured me he had already squared it with Eric and the boys. He was waiting for my answer about what I wanted to do.

It seemed as if Ben was quite interested in what I was planning as well. I needed Ben's input into this regarding the rebuilding. I knew he would understand my concerns.

Directness has always been my strong suit so I asked, "Ben, what do you think about rebuilding on the point?" I loved the placement of the cottage out on the rocks. The structure had remained there for a good many years. Good carpenters certainly built it.

"You know the area. What are the chances of getting a pre-built in there and how strong do you think they are? What about a foam and reinforced concrete application for the house, then with wood sheathing and a cedar shingled exterior. I am open to ideas. You know the extreme winds and weather we have here."

As always, Ben gave a thoughtful answer, "Let's do some research. Les, what's the budget going to be to replace the cottage? Available funds would be a starting point."

I'm direct, just not *that* direct. I appreciated Ben's inquiry.

Les made an inquisitive gesture by lifting one eyebrow, then a slight shrug of his shoulders before he answered. "Eileen, I'm going to deposit a set amount into a bank account in your name. You can draw against it as you please. You can transfer the funds into your current account or set up a new one for the construction. It won't make any difference to us how you do it. I'll authorize five hundred thousand dollars deposited before I leave this room. I'll give you a printout of the account numbers and passwords necessary to access it. It'll be at your discretion regarding how or what you spend on anything. This is your tax dollars at work. How's that for a change?"

When I recovered, I only uttered a quick, "Outstanding!"

Ben smiled.

Les excused himself and went to his car, returning with a briefcase. He retrieved his laptop, a small portable printer and began working. Twenty minutes later, he passed me a printed sheet with account numbers, amounts, passwords, and transfer information.

He then passed Ben a similar sheet. Ben accepted with a slow, slight grin.

Les continued typing. He printed another sheet and passed it to Ben. "That one is for Eric.

"By the way, I met him when we were Seals together, then we both worked for the agency; he's a great guy. He saved my life once. I've never forgotten…another situation *which never happened*. I hadn't expected to see him again. I knew he was still with the service, but in a different capacity.

"Life has a funny way of recycling things when you least expect them. Eric explained to me how he's been working undercover with the Department on this case for some time. All the information he'd been given was what we knew. We thought it was being transported boat-to-boat. He had the mandatory communication equipment all set up."

Les turned his attention to me, "By the way, Eileen, if it meets with your approval, Ben has asked if you could remain here until the house is restored. We've agreed on a figure and I've included the payment in Ben's settlement.

"Now, I need to get out of here. I need to deal with the rest of this situation. If I hear of anything else in this area, I'll be in touch with both of you through Eric.

"Good luck with the reconstruction. If I'm ever up this way again, I'll check in with you. You can tell folks I'm a Fuller Brush salesman." With a big grin and a handshake, he was out of the door and gone.

I just sat there staring at the paper in my hand. I shook my head and looked over at Ben. He looked about as shocked as I was.

Thirteen

I said, "What I wouldn't give for a good glass of wine, some crackers, cheese, and a rock to sit on and just listen to the waves."

Ben's reaction was strange. He got up and left abruptly without a word. Had I insulted him, hurt his feelings? He was a strange person.

I looked out of the window at the water. What was I going to do about putting my life back together? I needed a pad of paper, a pen, and a plan.

This brought a pang of sadness to me. Old memories often die a prolonged death. Maybe they don't die…they get stored in places in the brain until something kick-starts them.

When my oldest two children were little, we lived in a two-family house. The day after Christmas, the upstairs tenant started a fire, which nearly destroyed the house. Even though it had been an accident, it was tragic. In my mind, I could still see the Christmas tree, our opened presents under it covered with real icicles where the firefighters had extinguished the fire. I'd been able to stand in our living room and see the sky through the roof.

I'd made it through that and many, many other adversities over the years. I knew I could do this.

I looked through the drawers of the kitchen cabinets—bingo! A pad of paper and pencils…I was in business. Moving to the living room, I sat in the big rocker-recliner. I was great at list making. Somehow, it was soothing to me. It made me feel more in control.

I needed wheels first. Maybe second. I needed clothes, dog food, and then wheels. I also needed a laptop and a printer to replace my old faithful ones. Once I started, the list began to take shape.

There was a soft knock on the door. When I opened it, a man greeted me holding a picnic basket, wearing a big grin. He had a blanket over his arm. Ben's question was easy, "Your rock or mine?"

We walked down to a great flat rock in the shelter of the shrubs allowing us a fantastic ocean view. The late afternoon sun was still warm on our backs. Ben spread the blanket carefully, then placed the basket on it.

We sat, as if by command, with Shadow joining us, also in a prim sit.

Poor old Seaweed had seemed content to stay on the bed and sleep. She'd earned the privilege.

Ben extracted two stemmed wine glasses, a bottle of white wine along with a bottle of red. He laughed, "I know nothing about wine so I raided Eric's cabinet. I've no idea if these are good, bad, or indifferent. He could've made them in his bathtub for all I know." We laughed like kids.

It was nice to laugh again for a change.

Ben unearthed cheese, crackers, paper plates, and napkins. He suddenly looked into the basket and hung his head. "I didn't remember a knife to cut the cheese." I saw the idea dawn on his face before he moved for his pocketknife. "Will this be all right?" He cut cheese; we sipped and munched for a few peaceful, almost normal, moments.

Then his cell rang.

"It's Eric …I need to take it." Ben's face darkened. His fun-voice became a growl, "Where are you?" Ben paused to listen.

"Okay we're on our way. I can hear Dan leaving the yard right now."

Ben relayed the important part of the call. "Eric was out testing one of the boats. When he went by the cove there was someone there. He thinks it was a bunch of teens. There wasn't any reason for anyone to be there. He called Dan first, then me. Let's go see what's going on." We jumped up and made a beeline for his truck with Shadow on our heels.

Just as we were entering the drive, a.k.a. *swamp-hole,* we met a beat-up old truck coming out. Ben swung his truck sideways so they couldn't pass. There were three frightened teens huddled in the truck.

Ben bellowed; "What in hell are you guys doing here? You're smart enough to be where you don't belong, but from the looks of you, nobody could read the sign at the end of the lane! What're you up to? I want answers. I want them now or I'm calling the law along with your parents." He held his phone in his hand for them to see.

One of the acne-scarred youths stuttered, "Nothing, sir. We just wanted to see what happened out here. We didn't touch anything, honest. Please don't turn us in or call our parents. They'll ground us forever. We'll never come out here again, we promise."

Ben gave them a fearsome, evil look as a backup to his threat. Then he moved his truck so they could leave. Boy, did they go! Tires spinning, mud flying, they were gone.

Ben drove down the rest of the driveway slowly, with some respect for his poor truck.

We saw Dan standing on the rocks. He was signaling to Eric, who was waiting offshore in the boat, that everything was all right. Dan waved, nodded to Ben, and hoisted himself back into his monster of a truck and left.

Survivor still sat untouched on her mooring like all was well in the cove. I looked at Ben and said, "I shouldn't leave her here. The temptation is too great. Someone *will* steal her."

Ben sat, staring at the boat for a nano second, then grinned like a kid. He asked, with a sidelong glance, "How brave are you?" Then he laughed aloud. "*That* was a really stupid question; ignore it. Come on, let's play."

We climbed out of his truck and walked to the cove. Ben pulled on *Survivor's* mooring line in smooth, sure pulls. When he had the prow beached, he gestured for me to get aboard. Shadow hadn't waited for an invite. She popped onto the prow seat.

"Can you sail this or do you just row?" Ben asked as he loosed the line and jumped aboard. For a man of his age and size, he was in good shape.

"I rowed because I haven't really mastered the art of sailing. Sailing was going to be my fun project for fall, after my work was finished. Ben, do you know what the weight limit for this craft is?"

His answer was professional. "How much free-board do we have?"

I put my hand over the side to check. "We haven't sunk yet, so I'm guessing that's enough." I figured one professional answer deserved a like reply.

I sat on the middle seat, closest to the mast with the sail wound tightly around it. It was still tied very carefully; like a trussed duck.

I told Ben, "Do not laugh…the boat came ashore in pieces with no instruction manual. I did the best I could."

I began to untie the rigging, and then passed Ben the tiller. He fitted it over the stern in the slots, which held it tight.

I had a sudden thought. "Ben, you do know how to sail, don't you?"

All I got in return was a heartfelt chuckle.

There was, of course, water in the boat, so I retrieved my handy bailer, and began to bail.

We were moving, although there didn't appear to be any wind. We began to move smoothly and rapidly out of the cove. I was so excited I forgot we could sink. We had no life jackets on board the craft. Oh, what the hell…I bailed and enjoyed.

Life is full of risks. Therefore, enjoy it…you could be dead tomorrow by this time.

We were just swinging toward Ben's point when we saw Eric in a boat heading toward us. Some distance off, he slowed almost to a stop and yelled over, "What in hell are you two idiots doing?"

I called back, "He's sailing and I'm bailing." He just laughed like crazy. "Do you need a tow? Do you looney-toons have any life vests?"

Ben called back, "If she can bail fast and long enough while the breeze holds, I think we'll be okay. Do you have any inflatable jackets on board with you? If you do, toss us a couple…make it three, one for Shadow also."

Eric was really a great sailor and knew his boat well. He came alongside us without a ripple and tossed the three vests into the boat; then glided away. "Call me if you need a tow. I won't go in till you children are safe." There was lots of laughter in his voice when he delivered the last statement.

We bailed and sailed in silence, enjoying the peaceful sounds of the water as it rushed along the sides of the small craft. I'd known it would be fun to sail this little boat. I just didn't know how *much* fun.

Ben did indeed know how to sail.

Shadow sat tall in the prow watching everything. She loved the water, boats, swimming, kayaking, and going fishing. Digging clams was her all-time favorite.

We made it to Ben's float without incident. We furled and tied the sail; then he secured the rudder.

Now that I could see her from the apartment window, I knew *Survivor* would be safe.

As we walked up to the apartment, we made a side trip to the rock where our picnic had been. The ants and the sea gulls had found the cheese and crackers. The wine was still intact. We toasted our first sailing venture.

Then we needed to get Ben's truck.

Dan strolled over and offered us a ride in his monster. Oh well, why not, we'd done everything else today. We climbed up and into that monstrous truck. Dan tore down the road at seemingly breakneck speed. What a ride!

It was a relief to get into Ben's truck, put on seat belts, and drive as our age dictated we should.

Fourteen

Ben offered, "Tomorrow we need to go shopping somewhere in civilization. Have you thought about what you are going to buy for a vehicle? I know you have some definite ideas about certain things. I'm hoping you'll consider something substantial and safe.

"You would probably like to buy some clothing first, wouldn't you?" Ben was carefully threading his way up the trace. It was getting worse with all the traffic.

"Ben, who would you hire to repair the driveway? You must know someone you'd recommend. I'd like to have the drive widened, leveled, and have culverts installed. The contractor will need to add stone to the base. If they can get the elevation and slope corrected, they can surface it with a good rough gravel finish."

I'd already designed the drive in my mind. My thought was simple. I wanted the drive to curve in such a way that when someone drove onto the property, the house would not be visible until after they'd executed the final turn.

Ben laughed. "You're more interested in getting a *driveway* in than going *shopping*? I should have known."

"When we get back to the shop, I'll call old Woodie. He's a piece of work, but a real pro at these things. He'll treat you right on price and time. He's a little rough around the edges so don't get offended."

Ben offered, "Would you rather go shopping for the vehicle by yourself? If so, you're welcome to take one of the cars at the yard. Have you considered what you want?"

Ben seemed fine, whether or not I wanted his advice.

I wasn't sure how I felt. I'd lived alone most of my life and with no need to consult advisors, I made my own decisions.

In retrospect, the times I'd gotten into trouble were when I thought someone else knew better. Those were the times when I really got blindsided…never again, ever.

Ben didn't seem to have an agenda; so far, he'd not raised any concerns on my radar.

"I'll see what tomorrow brings, if that's okay with you. I don't want to continue to monopolize all your time. I know you have things to do." We rode in comfortable silence back to the shop.

True to his word, Ben called Woodie. "He'll meet us there at first light. I will add this…he is serious about meeting at daybreak, most likely five. He works daylight to dark without stopping for anything, but he is good. He built all the roads in the boat yard and you can see they get heavy use. I've never had any issues with them. The original roads here were just like your trace when I started. He'll stand behind his work; checking it in early spring to see if you need any additional fills or compaction."

Fifteen

Ben walked to his drafting table where he flipped up a clean sheet on his large pad. He began to sketch. *Damn!* He was fast and *good*! In a matter of minutes, he had *Survivor* sketched out on the paper. "How much does Shadow weigh? How much do you weigh?" He was so lost in his sketch he seemed not to notice I hadn't answered him. He turned his head, seeking information. He looked so earnest I knew he was working something out in his mind to do with the boat, so I wasn't offended.

"Shadow weighs about seventy pounds and I weigh about one hundred and thirty. Why?"

Ben's reply was reflective of his observations while we'd sailed. "When we were sailing, I was fascinated with the way the boat was responding. It had something to do with the displacement of weight. I needed to calculate the weight of all on board to figure it out. I weigh about two hundred and twenty, so it's fairly even. You kept it bailed so there wouldn't have been much weight in the residual water in the bottom... hummm."

Ben was musing while he figured on the bottom of the sheet. I added my two cents. "How about the weight of the mast and the canvas? Wouldn't that need to be factored into the equations?"

A large, spontaneous grin spread across Ben's face. "You're a good observer. Yes, it would make a difference. I'd guess about forty pounds for the mast and canvas."

"That was one of the slickest small sailing boats I've ever piloted. Eileen, how did you fix the leaks when it first washed ashore?"

Easy answer. "I caulked her with cotton caulking using an iron and a wooden mallet I made so I wouldn't harm the planking. She needed more work on the bottom. I didn't know how much she would leak until I re-floated her. She was going to be one of my winter projects. I planned to tarp her on horses so I could work on the warmer days. I wanted to add more caulking, sand her down to bare wood, prime and paint her. I've always loved to row. I found, with the two dogs and myself, I could move along nicely. I have eaten lots of fish, thanks to that little craft."

Ben nodded, then spoke very carefully. "What would you say if we brought her into the shop where you could work on her this winter? While you worked, it would be warm and dry. There's a new and better caulking fiber you might want to try. There are all kinds of sanders here you could use. With the vacuum system on, you can sand without a mask. I'm sure some of the old paint is lead based."

I was surprised at the offer, but wary. "If I put her in your shop, are you not going to let me take her home?"

Ben was hurt. I could see the sadness in his eyes. I was sorry, but I needed to ask.

"Eileen, I would *never* take the boat away from you. You've lost enough in your lifetime. That's apparent. I'm not a mean person nor would I ever harm you. I hope you'll always know that."

He continued, "While she's here, what do you say about doing a project together? Let's measure, make technical drawings, and see if we can replicate her. We would use the new materials available, and then we'd both have one. Who knows, if it works, we could build and sell them to only true believers. We'd call it the *Survivor Line*. I always knew there was a market for this size. If I could reproduce her quality of sailing, we would have a winner. Think about it."

Ben gave me a slightly woeful look. "Like you didn't have enough to think about right now, huh? Sorry, I didn't mean to crowd you."

I grinned because I'd caught Ben's enthusiasm. "I like the idea lots!"

It would be a nice break to think about something positive, certainly more invigorating than dwelling on crisis management and mayhem.

I went upstairs to the apartment to feed the dogs and take them for a walk.

I needed to take some time to ponder Ben's offer. As long as I could remember, I've always had a good mind with the ability to process several things at one time. I did my best mental work when I have several different projects going on. I certainly have an abundance and variety to decipher now.

I reflected on the fact it had only been a day since I thought I wouldn't live through the invasion, the loss of my home and the car. In the same time span, I'd received funding for reconstruction of the home along with replacement monies for a vehicle.

I liked the thought of the offer to join with Ben building and selling boats.

Sixteen

Seaweed finally seemed more like her old self. I could see Shadow was taking care of her. They trotted off down the road together in the playful jog they have. It always made my heart happy to watch them. They were so different. Shadow was strong and stocky, while Seaweed was small-boned and delicate. It was good to see they were going to be all right.

Returning from our walk, we met a car coming in on the road. I called the dogs to me and put them on the sit/stay command off the roadway. The large car hadn't slowed at all. The woman driving seemed not to have noticed us. Oh well, we'd seen her, so all was well. It was odd to see a car driving so fast here in the boatyard. Even Dan puttered in and out with his *shake-rattle-and-roll* truck.

When we arrived back at the shop, we climbed the stairs leading to the apartment and found a note on the door inviting me to dinner at the main house.

Suddenly, I realized I was starving. Then it dawned on me. Other than breakfast, the crackers, and cheese we'd hardly eaten, I hadn't eaten all day. I searched both the cupboards and refrigerator where I found some crackers and cheese. I needed to add food to my shopping list. Wonder of wonders, I found a small diet Coke in the cupboard... my favorite!

My world became great right then. I thanked God for the bounty while stuffing my face. How good it tasted! I would make it until dinner. I needed to go shopping tomorrow.

I scrubbed up, dusted off my attire... gee whiz... easy decision as to what I will wear to dinner. The only thing I own.

With Seaweed settled on her favorite spot, a towel placed on the bed, Shadow and I strolled to the big house at the end of the point.

I pulled the cord for the doorbell and was pleasantly surprised when it set off a series of bells making a nice nautical sound befitting the placement of the home. The house looked out over the water on three sides.

Eric opened the door with a welcoming smile and ushered me into a gorgeous, light-filled room. The entire front of the house was windowed for light and view. It was perfect. "How lovely… the placement of your home is perfect. Were you the builder?"

With the grin I had seen so often, he told me the history of the structure. He and his dad built the house together. They'd started when he was a teen, making some modifications as he got older and his life changed. They had built the newer middle section of the dwelling when he returned from the service. He knew this was where he wanted to live for the rest of his life.

They added the wing when he married his wife, Belle, and started their family with her two young children.

He explained, "My family's not presently at home."

Eric escorted me into the dining room, where Ben and a woman were already seated, sipping glasses of wine.

Eric introduced me to Nina. She was a tall, large woman who was well dressed, with a hairdo out of the seventies. I would have guessed that in her younger days she'd been pretty. I estimated her age to be about the same as mine.

"I'm pleased to meet you." It was all I got out before she took over the conversation. Hmm, large and definitely in charge would be my opinion.

I sat, taking the glass of white wine Ben had poured for me. It was a great Riesling, one of my favorites.

Nina talked on, regaling us with tales of her travels, from which she had just returned. She was a good orator. I noticed she liked to reach over and pat Ben's arm for emphasis. She had done that on several occasions during her discourse.

Ben seemed uncomfortable while being extremely quiet.

Eric managed to get a few words in from time to time.

However, Nina must have felt it was her role in life to educate us. This point was clear as she talked on about the cultures, dress, occupations, attitudes, and politics of each country she'd recently visited.

The odd thing I noticed, she never took a break to inquire about either anyone or anything. Seemingly, she and Ben shared some history. I got the impression she had been here frequently and she knew both Eric and Ben well.

I was just happy to sit in a lovely home, eat a delicious, well-prepared meal along with a glass of excellent wine. I was a simple person who enjoyed simple things, especially after the last couple of days.

A middle-aged woman, who was obviously the person who had done the cooking, served dinner nicely. The meal was delicious and well presented. I ate and enjoyed every bite. Finally, the coffee and dessert arrived. However, there was no break in the constant chatter from Nina. It seemed as though she never stopped. Nor I noticed, did the patting of Ben's arm.

I could see his distress was increasing as well. Eric also seemed ill at ease. These were interesting dynamics. This from two men whom I always thought of as being very comfortable in their own skins; it left me wondering why.

I finished my coffee, thanked Eric for dinner, said good-bye to Nina and Ben.

Ben stood. "I'll walk you back to the shop."

Nina spoke up quickly, "Are you parked down at the shop? I didn't notice a car down there when I came in. For *Heaven's sake*, Ben, it is just a short stroll down the road. If Eileen got here, I'm sure she can find her way back."

I smiled. "Ben, I'm fine to walk back. Shadow has waited on the porch to escort me. You have a guest. Please, give my compliments to the cook… the dinner was a real treat. I can see myself out. Thank you, Eric, this was special."

I was out the door, happy to have escaped any more chatter from Nina.

Shadow and I enjoyed the evening stroll back. I was not a person who enjoyed *chatter*. Although I have always loved hearing a good tale told with finesse, I find it downright boring when someone talked just to have control of the floor.

The evening air had a hint of fall with the wonderful smell of fir and salt air. It was a scent indigenous only to the Down East coast of Maine. Each season has a different aroma to enjoy. Soon it would be snow and balsam.

I gathered Seaweed from the bed and the three of us took our nightly walk. The gravel roads of the boat yard were in excellent shape for walking, being mostly flat, because the ground was old blueberry land. The low bush blueberries grew in abundance in this area of the state. The berries would grow right to the edge of the rocky coast.

With starlight and the soft glow from the large lights used to illuminate the boat yard, visibility was not an issue. The dogs and I strolled for a bit then returned to the shop. With part of our evening finished, we were ready for bed.

I'd just wrapped the robe around me, missing again my personal things. I always took those common items and actions for granted. I read my Bible and devotional each night. Sometimes I would write in the journal or just read a magazine. I loved to read in bed.

I heard the door to the shop downstairs open. Shadow was on alert. Then I heard angry voices floating up the stairway. It was Ben and Eric. Eric said something I couldn't hear distinctly but there was no question what Ben's reply was. "I don't give a damn what you think. I cannot stand that damn woman, period."

The outside door closed with a slam. I'd no idea who had left or if both of them were gone.

My feelings were hurt. What had I done? How had I infuriated Ben? I thought I'd been polite and gracious throughout dinner. Perhaps he was just tired of babysitting me.

I lay in bed awake for a long time. I knew my emotions were running close to the surface. They were rubbed-raw with the events that had happened. Then a great sense of loss seemed to spread over me. It was such a dark feeling I became terribly frightened. I sat upright in the dark and pulled the dogs close to me for comfort. I knew I couldn't allow any emotion that strong or negative to take root mentally. I chastised myself. *Eileen, you are a stronger person than this.* I also knew I didn't want to be a burden to anyone.

Seventeen

Thankfully, my solid resolve kicked in. I set the alarm on my phone. It would give me enough time to walk to my trace for the meeting with Woodie. I needed to get the construction of the driveway underway. It was imperative to be in, or on, my own space. I'd leave Seaweed here; taking Shadow with me, I would hike down to the property.

Morning, for me, came early. Thank God I was a morning person. With coffee made, dogs fed and walked, Shadow and I started on our journey.

It was still dark. It usually is in far Eastern Maine that time of day. The great thing about being so far east is when the sun comes up, it *comes up*, and daylight is almost immediate. We were nearly to the trace when dawn first streaked the sky with brilliant colors.

I could hear a truck approaching slowly and knew I was at least on time.

When Woodie stepped down from his battered old truck, I snickered to myself. He was a big grizzled man with a full head of wild, long hair and a shaggy full beard. He must have been six and a half feet tall and broad. As they would say Down East, *he was a big-un*.

As he walked toward me, Shadow seemed to be trying to make up her mind if he was good, bad or what. Finally, she must have concluded he was all right because she sat beside my leg. If she were unsure, she would've sat in front of my foot. If she really doesn't like or trust a person, she'll stand, block-up her body to make herself appear larger than she really is.

Woodie said, "You must be the little lady Ben told me about." Shadow's tail-nub began to wag. She had decided he was okay.

"Yes, I'm Eileen, thank you for coming. Ben spoke highly of you and your abilities.

"As you can see, this is quite a project. Can I show you what my ideas are? I'll need the drive to be substantial so it can support cement trucks and delivery vehicles. I would like you to raise the grade, put in culverts, and create a drain basin to keep the water level down. I'd also like the drive to have some curve to it so folks can't see the home or garage when starting down the drive or passing by. I'm going to install a large, metal gate out here when I'm finished with the rebuilding. Can you do that?"

I learned long ago when talking to Down Easters I had to determine two things: if they could and if they would. Now I knew he could, but would he?

I knew he was a true Down Easter by his accent and mannerisms. I had always enjoyed working with the natives in this portion of the state. They are extremely talented, with a great work ethic.

Woodie answered with the classic, "Ayuh, not a problem. Let's walk down and take a look."

We had just started walking down the drive when Ben came tearing up in his truck. We hesitated, waiting. Woodie waved then just stared at Ben. "Mornin,' Ben. You get up on the wrong side of the bed?"

Ben did look out of sorts. I couldn't guess if he were worried, mad or both. He was really in a snit for sure. When he reached us, his first words confirmed it…he was both.

"Where were you? I couldn't find you. Finally, I called your cell and it went to voice mail so I took the liberty of going into the apartment to check on you. When I found Seaweed sleeping and Shadow gone, I surmised you'd walked here. You knew I'd pick you up. *What were you thinking?*"

Okay, time to set this straight.

"Ben, I don't expect you to hand-hold me. We made the appointment with Woodie for my job so I came here to meet him. You have a life and things you need to do. I've appreciated your assistance but I have also monopolized way too much of your time already."

I turned from Ben and walked after Woodie. It was of the upmost importance the construction be completed in the manner I wanted. The job required a thorough discussion with the contractor.

As I walked down the drive to catch up with Woodie, I heard Ben's truck spin around and take off. Had I been too abrupt? I didn't think so. He'd stated last night he *was sick of that damn woman.* Now he would be off the hook. There was a road to build, a house to erect and my life to put back together; I was ready to be moving along.

Woodie knew his business. He assessed the terrain, making comments about which was the best way to approach the rebuilding as we walked.

When we rounded the bend at the end of the drive and he faced the wreckage of the burned-out shell of the house strewn on the rocks, he stopped. Then he seemed to ponder, looked back at the drive, nodded, and then walked up onto the rocks for a closer examination. "Have you talked to anyone about removing the debris?"

I shook my head, "No. Not yet."

I knew I needed to get the site cleared and cleaned before I could even think about re-building. I knew that unless and until the driveway was re-built, we couldn't get trucks or equipment in to clear it.

I thought Woodie and I were in accord in our thinking. He asked, "Why don't I take this mess and bury it under the new drive? Even though it's fire-damaged, I can still use it to make riprap for the base, then you won't have to haul it out. I can get most of this with my big picker I use for logging. I'll have my men clean everything so the site will be ready for reconstruction. How does that sound to you?"

Easy answer from me. "It sounds like the angels are singing."

Woodie and I talked price and time. He understood exactly what I wanted. He'd begin today by moving his equipment into place.

I was satisfied. This would be a good beginning.

Now I needed to obtain transportation and temporary housing. I already had a plan forming in my mind as I walked back up the drive. I thought when the drive was usable and solid enough to support it, I would set a small travel trailer for living space while I worked on getting the house done.

Lying awake last night, I'd figured out how to get water and power to a camper. If I used a portable dump cart for waste disposal, I could use my existing septic system. In my other lifetimes, I'd owned recreational vehicles and travel trailers.

I was feeling better than I had since this disaster happened. I always did better on my own with a plan I felt I could control.

When I arrived at the drive's end, Ben was waiting in his Excursion. To say his face could've held a day's rain wouldn't have been an exaggeration. He stepped out, opened the back for Shadow. The traitor jumped in and sat down. Ben closed the rear and opened the passenger door. Like Shadow, I got in.

He passed me a cup of hot coffee in a travel mug and began to drive slowly down a dirt road I had noticed but never bothered to explore. It went through a beautiful, mature stand of firs then onto a large open blueberry field. The leaves on the blueberry bushes were already the brilliant crimson they turned in early fall. I noticed this field still had the glacial-till rocks that are so prevalent on the blueberry fields in the Down East area. This meant someone needed to have the field hand-harvested.

This used to be traditional for this area, although most growers had progressed to mechanical harvesting. Removing the rocks allowed the mechanical harvesters to work, eliminating the seasonal raking jobs so many natives depended upon.

Although this was a dirt road, it appeared to be in good shape; most likely due to the fact it was also all fine gravel where blueberries grew. It was a very silent drive.

When we reached the end of the road, there was a small weathered cottage sitting on the rocks overlooking the shore. There was also a small detached two-car garage. An American flag was flying on a very tall, substantial flagpole. This was Americana at its very best!

In my last life, I would have taken out my camera and snapped photos. My instincts told me this was not a photo shoot.

Ben had something on his mind. I was about to find out what, when, who, and where.

He didn't waste any time in his delivery. "I'm a really numb man. I couldn't begin to figure out what in hell was wrong with you this morning.

"Eileen, I see you as the most solid woman I've ever known. I swallowed my stubborn pride and asked the only person I know…who has a good head on his shoulders, thanks to his mother. I asked Eric what was wrong. He told me my big mouth had gotten my chicken-ass in a sling.

"When he recounted my tantrum of last night in the shop, he was sure you thought I meant you. I'm sorry for making you think that.

When you get to know me better, you'll understand I have few, if any, filters. When I think it, I say it.

"Nina drives me nuts. She and her husband Paul were folks my wife and I, when she was alive, chummed around with some. Paul loved the water and boats and so did I. Nina and my wife liked to shop and travel, so they did. It was a great solution, giving Paul and me a break to do what we liked. It also worked well for the women.

"After my wife passed, Paul had cancer and in a very short time he died also. For some reason or other, Nina thinks, or did think, until last night, I was going to become her *escort du jour*. After you left last night, she started laying out plans for us... can you believe that... for us. Nina and I would do this, go there, and travel to this place. She went on and on *ad nauseam*.

"I hit the roof and explained I had no interest or intentions of joining her in any of her damn plans. Although I respected how, in our former lives as married couples, we'd enjoyed a friendship. The pair-of-couples part of our lives was gone and done.

"I informed her I have a life and she's not part of it, period. When she asked me if the *poor dinner guest*, referring to you, was part of my new life, I lost it. That was when I came to the shop. Eric was trying to calm me down so as he put it, *I wouldn't stroke out*.

"In the process, I felt he was talking to me like I was a bad kid for being rude to Nina. That was what you heard.

"I do need to add one thing... other than your threatening to shoot me, I have enjoyed this time immensely. I feel alive again, thanks to you. So can we at least be friends?"

Wow, for a man of few words, this must have been a year's supply. Ben was clear, concise, and concerned about how I felt. I appreciated that.

"Ben, thank you for sharing this information with me. I was aware Nina had more than a proprietary interest, real or imagined, in your relationship. I also knew you were very uncomfortable with her touching you. I'm sure my being there didn't add any value to the situation. For what it's worth, I'm sorry.

"I very much enjoy you as a friend and appreciate all you and Eric have done for me. I've lived alone for most of my life and know some of my independent ways are offensive. I never wanted to create a problem or be a burden to anyone, least of all to folks who have been extremely kind and helpful, going way beyond the call of duty."

This seemed to be the right time to share my thoughts about moving with Ben. "I've been thinking about purchasing a travel trailer I can set on the lot when Woodie finishes the clearing and the drive. I wouldn't be sponging off your hospitality. I would also be on site for monitoring the construction of the house."

Ben looked horrified. When a big man looks like that, it's almost comic. In addition, thankfully I suppressed my personal pleasure at being quick to hide the impending grin.

Eighteen

Ben's cell rang with an odd ring. He answered without even glancing at the caller ID. "Be right there. Where are you? Okay. Yes to that."

He was distracted as he swung the car around and drove as rapidly as the dirt road would allow.

I had no clue about what was wrong. He would either share or not. If not, it was none of my business, so I wouldn't pry. His jaw was set and his focus was in getting to wherever he needed to be, *quickly*.

We swung onto his road with dirt flying from the abrupt, high-speed turn. The big bus of a car handled well and Ben was a competent driver. We arrived at the shop in a cloud of dust.

Ben yanked open the back door for Shadow as he said in an urgent voice, "Eileen, come on; this is about you."

What now, I wondered. We entered the shop, going directly to the left side, not to where the drafting tables were, and entered a room. I hadn't noticed it when I'd been in the shop before. This was most likely because the pine interior of the entrance blended perfectly as just part of the main wall.

It was a small private office. It was without windows, containing a utilitarian desk with a large chair behind the desk, where Eric sat. There were four smaller chairs sitting in front of the desk. The

104

biggest surprise was the bank of computers along with what appeared to be highly technical radio equipment on the side wall. I knew in an eye-blink this wasn't equipment necessary for running a boat yard, no matter how large.

I was instantly uncomfortable. When my radar gets to this stage of alert, I become *very* cautious.

Ben closed the door and locked it. He nodded to Eric. Ben offered me a chair then sat in the one beside me with both of us facing Eric. Shadow, sensing my anxiety, sat beside me leaning against my leg.

This was a definite power shift. *Why*?

Eric didn't hesitate to say, "Sorry to interrupt your day, guys; this is important. I need to explain something to you, Eileen. Although they instructed me not to, I think, with what I now understand, you should have this information as well; it involves you personally.

"I've been working with the Feds on this case. As you may have surmised, when I left the service I kept all my clearances. So from time to time, they call me in. This case, however, found me.

"I talked to the Zodiac rep yesterday and he fitted in a piece of the puzzle for me. Dad, since you ordered the electrically set-up Zodiac you purchased four months ago, there have been three others ordered and delivered. This is unusual in the area, because of the expense.

"One of them was sold to Bart in the village. When he took over his father's garage, he was struggling just to maintain the business. I know there wasn't a mortgage on the property. How did Bart pay for the boat… cash, and why would he want it? That's just the tip of this mess.

Eric checked a sheet on his desk then looked directly at me. "When the first problem happened in the cove and you shot the invader, how many men were there?"

"I only saw two. The one I shot was closer to the tree line at first. The other person was about half the distance away and moving up the beach toward him.

"When I hollered, the one closest to the water bolted back toward the shore. The other one shot at me. He had an automatic weapon. After the first shot, he was running while firing like a crazy person. Then he stopped, taking better aim, and fired again, hitting the cottage next to me. I aimed and shot him. The other one was in the water heading out of the cove, or that was what I assumed. Why do you ask? I told the army who invaded my place all this information."

Eric paused and studied me for a brief moment. "Could you recognize the one who got away if you saw him?"

"Goodness no…it was dark. They had on wet suits or something black. Considering the distance, even if it had been light, I'm not sure I would've gotten any of their facial features.

"You know, thinking this over, the man…may have been a person from this area. I'm saying he had a very distinct Down East accent. I recognized it when he hollered, "Shit! Let's get the hell outta here!"and his voice sounded low and raspy. Do you know what I mean?"

"Eileen, this is the problem. Whoever it was thinks you can identify him. The reason they trashed the property, based on the information I received this morning from Les, is they're not finished with you.

"You need to stay close to here and keep Shadow with you all the time.

"Dad, I want you to stay armed with your pistol and be careful. Eileen, do you still have your handgun? If so, carry it, even though you don't have a permit to carry concealed. If you get into a situation, use it. I'll trust your judgment. This is going to get very dicey, very quickly.

"Les, although reluctantly, agreed you should be warned. I must tell you, Eileen, he wanted you removed to a safe house. I hope I didn't overstep my bounds when I told him you wouldn't leave.

"We need to put together a plan to catch this guy. He has a lot riding on not being ID'd. This was a very large operation with some local involvement. There's a lot of money and power at stake and they're not going to quit easily."

Eric continued after a slight hesitation. "The Feds traced the munitions found on the boat we stopped, along with the ones taken from your cove. The stash of munitions was from a very large heist taken from supposedly a very secure munitions storage area.

"The heroin came from another source, equally secure. Les thought the source was from some very large drug raids on trafficking routes. Because they were never in the news, the public had no knowledge of them.

"We now know these are all inside jobs. The Feds are trying to identify the person or persons responsible. According to Les, they thought this part of the operation happened only in small batches. Then it was buried along the coast in different locations for future sales.

"The Feds had always thought the drugs were coming ashore in boats. However, they couldn't find any contraband when they boarded crafts in this area.

"The boat we boarded and seized the other night was specially built for this operation. It didn't show on the radar and if I hadn't nearly rammed it, I would never have found it.

"I surprised them as much as they surprised me. When they recovered, they shot my boat with a rocket launcher. The fact they had no training with the weapons saved our lives. We would've all been goners.

"I've got to admit, once I saw it, the vessel was the ugliest craft I'd ever seen. Once I got aboard, I found they'd covered it in a camouflage netting, also military gear. Similar netting is available in sporting goods stores for duck and goose hunting, just not in that size or density.

"All of the information I've given you folks has to stay in this room. Understand?"

Ben seemed to be thinking this over carefully. He had a grave expression on his face. When he spoke, his concern was apparent. "Do you think it will ever be over, Eric? Eileen is in hiding; your family is living in isolation while they're still looking for a way to get rid of what they think is an eyewitness.

"Does anyone around here have any idea how involved in this mess you are?"

I could see Eric was trying to calm his dad's fears.

"Nobody we are aware of, yet.

"Trust me. I'm armed and being very vigilant. I know how dangerous this can get.

"I think at the moment, the local who is involved is the first danger. The next is whether they'll send in a backup to do the actual killing. We're also concerned they'll get rid of the local and supposed eyewitness. It's up in the air. Perhaps they will simply eradicate the local person and walk away.

"They can't afford many more mistakes because we're a whisker away from rounding up a bunch of them.

"This certainly has to be creating more pressure at the local level. At this point, we don't know what they'll do or who they are.

"I must confess being in a war situation is much easier because you know who the enemy really is. I'm skeptical we'll even know *whom* until they make another move so we seize them.

"This is why I'm telling you both to be wary of *everyone*. Les has relayed to me the Feds are thinking this was just one of many stash-spots.

"We theorize the heroin is being sold to raise funds for recruiting and distribution, while the munitions are being sold and stockpiled for a possible multi-strike terrorist plot. These people are dangerous.

"Until we have a break on who the insiders are, we're treading water. They've checked the serial numbers on some of the munitions. They know the approximate dates the thieves hit which storage facilities. Some date back a couple of years, yet some of the munitions, like the box on the beach, were very recent acquisitions.

"There have been at least three high-security facilities identified just from the batch we found here. The Feds are still working on the load from the boat."

Eric removed his stoic expression, replacing it with a softer expression on his face. His change in expression relieved some of my angst, while his next question amused me. "What are you two bad puppies planning for today?

"I see Woodie has already begun on the trace. If you guys are going shopping I'd suggest you go far, far, away.

"You can leave Seaweed here with me. She seems to like sleeping on the bed, getting a treat, and a very short walk from time to time. She'll be okay."

"Eric, you're such a kind person. I want to thank you for caring for Seaweed. I really appreciate it."

Eric continued, "I'm adamant about you keeping Shadow with you. She won't let anyone mess with the car and will alert you to trouble.

"By the way, Eileen, I'm sorry about dinner last night. I didn't want you to be uncomfortable but I think I created a firestorm.

"I also thought Nina was out of place. She has always needed to monopolize any and every situation. It might have been okay and she would've gotten a free pass. However, when you left and she referred to you as the *chippie* who caused the trouble for everyone, my dad went ballistic. She has no doubt where she stands now. To tell you the truth, I don't think I've ever seen him that mad."

Both Eric and his dad were smiling, or should I just say, they had what we Mainers call *wicked grins* on both of their faces.

I turned in my chair so I could look at Ben. "I need to get myself some transportation. In lieu of this information, I don't want to buy anything that would stand out around here. I'm also concerned about registering it here in town. Although everyone knows I'm the nutty old woman out on the point who shot some poor man. If only they really knew about all the mayhem and crazy activities that really happened."

Ben was quick to reply. "Eileen, I have an ancient Jeep Grand Wagoneer, almost identical to the one you had, stored in my garage. If you would like to drive it, I'll register it in my name. It's already insured. You could drive it until this mess gets squared around."

I shook my head. "No, Ben I'm not going to sacrifice another good Jeep to them. Thanks for the offer. There must be an old beat-up pickup truck around. One they can't harm if they want to push me off the road, blow it up with a bomb, or shoot holes in it."

I thought I was being funny. From the expressions on both men's faces, they didn't share my sense of humor.

Eric spoke first. "All of those things could very well happen. This isn't a laughing matter, Eileen; unless you have a death wish."

We ended the meeting with a promised vow of silence about Eric's involvement in the matter.

Nineteen

We decided Ben and I would leave Seaweed in Eric's care. We loaded Shadow into the car, stopping to check on Woodie's progress with the project before fleeing to go shopping.

When we stopped to check on Woodie, we found him standing in the bushes shaking his head and muttering to himself like a squirrel on crack.

As we approached he nodded, "Good you guys stopped because I was gettin'ready to go looking for ya.

"Ben, when I made a pass with the dozer, I caught something with the edge of the blade. I saw it out of the corner of my eye so I got down to examine it closer. Take a look and tell me what to do."

Ben and I stepped around the blade of the big Cat to see what it was. Woodie had uncovered more crates. The same as the ones found in the cove. All wrapped in the same black, thick tarps. He had torn some of the fabric away with the force of the blade.

Ben pulled out his phone and spoke to Eric. "We've found more munitions here. Woodie unearthed them with the dozer. What should we do? Okay, I'll tell him. Thanks. We will."

Woodie was taking this all in while leaning casually against the track of the dozer. "Guess I didn't see anything, right Ben?"

Ben nodded "Eric will be down in a few minutes to remove this mess. Woodie, be careful while you're working here; stay alert, please."

Woodie pulled the biggest, meanest looking handgun with a long barrel out of his coveralls. If my memory served me correctly, it was a .44 magnum revolver. My first thought was, *okay, he really is the man for this job.* He climbed up onto the machine and produced a sawed-off double-barreled shotgun that looked well used.

How weird is this? I wondered, *It's like living in the Twilight Zone, Normal one minute, and bizarre the next.*

I had no idea how crazy this was going to get. Perhaps if I had even the slightest inkling, I would've left the cove and moved to Singapore or Prince Edward Island, Canada or some other faraway place.

If the man who'd escaped when I killed the invader thought I could recognize him, I was in for trouble. There would be no closure for him until I was dead. This was a fact I clearly understood.

I didn't know anyone here with the exception of Eric, Ben, and now, Woodie. If you asked me to describe the person at the post office, town hall, store etc. I truly couldn't. Because I'd wanted to be left alone, I only went there when I had to and never spoke to any of them. If anyone knew the truth, I still didn't want to.

Twenty

We left for our shopping trip.

Did I mention I hate to shop for anything except food and building supplies? I needed to make a good faith effort because I had nothing to wear.

I knew, with a trip to Wal-Mart for Rider jeans, turtlenecks, underwear, and a couple of hoodies, socks, and shoes, I would be in business again. I was so easy to please. These new clothes would last for the rest of my life. I wanted to re-state that... the rest of my natural life, not one shortened by mayhem.

When we got to the city, Ben asked where I'd like to start. "Wal-Mart; you can wait here. I'll only be a few minutes."

I'd guessed it was a *no* because Ben was busy getting unbuckled, lowering the windows, opening the moon roof for air, so Shadow would be comfortable, then getting out.

We strolled into the store. As I was getting a cart, a man called out to Ben. We were away from our town, but because this was the second largest metropolis, folks from down on the coast came here for regular outings.

Thankfully, nobody knew who I was. I wanted to keep it that way.

As Ben stopped to acknowledge the fellow, I strolled off and began filling the basket. By the time Ben caught up, I was done with the clothing routine, most of the personal hygiene items, and dog food. I headed for the food section. I love all-in-one shopping. I wanted to be out of this place in a matter of minutes.

We went out through the door and began filling the car. Ben was grinning like a nut. "Fastest shopping trip I've ever been on…where to now?"

Next stop was a computer store I knew about. They sold new and used. I needed a used one with basic programs already on it, internet ready, wireless with a good-sized screen and a numeric pad. The store had a great almost new one with some programs installed. In fifteen minutes, they'd loaded what I needed, added a portable printer, extra ink, a carrying case, and wished me well while holding the door for my exit. That was my idea of great service.

With a flourish from Ben, everything was stowed in the back of the automobile. He'd gotten the hang of this. He drove, opened the door to let me into the store, stood by, carried packages, and then opened the door for me to leave. He packed the back of the car, then opened my car door, hopped in and we were off again. I could learn to like this service!

I'd missed my internet because it was how I kept in touch with the kids and grandkids. It'd only been a few days since I'd been on line. They wouldn't think it was odd because sometimes when I was busy with the cottage I might go several days before I'd catch up with them.

My cell rang. I glanced at the caller ID…it was my son. I needed to take the call. Ben was stepping out of the car when I shook my head for him to stay. We chatted for a few minutes as we always did and laughed at each other, then I rang off.

Ben was polite, but I could see he wanted to ask. I thought I'd at least make an effort to explain. "My son…he doesn't need to know what's been going on. None of them will ever know. The last thing I want is to harm or involve any more folks than I already have.

Someday, maybe I'll tell them. For now, they don't need to know anything. As far as they know, I'm busy rebuilding the old cottage.

"Ben, do you know if something happened to me, would the funds go to my estate for the kids and grandkids?"

He looked shocked I would ask such a question. I needed to know. "Maybe Eric could find out or perhaps I should transfer the funds to my regular account so I'd know where they are."

I wasn't so stupid I didn't know if I transferred the funds and the Feds wanted them back, for whatever reason, they could just take them from any account. The Feds giveth and the Feds taketh away. Such is life.

I was hungry… time to have a late lunch. I let Ben pick the spot. He found us a nice, quiet, place with great food. I was sure it wouldn't be a gathering place for the coastal folks. We ate in peace.

Ben asked, "Where would you like to go next to shop?"

My reply was simple, "Other than transportation, I'm done and tired. Shopping exhausts me. I think it's because I don't like to do it, so I make it a chore."

 Ben grinned. "On the matter of transportation, I meant what I said about the Jeep. I would treat you right on the price."

I knew what he was offering. "The answer is still no. I would like, after this mess is over, to make you an offer on it if you really want to sell it. Right now, I think a beat up old truck is the trick. I just need to make sure it is mechanically sound, heavy, four-wheel drive on demand and faster than the wind. A roll bar would be a bonus, although it might give me away. Do you have any ideas?"

Ben nodded and grinned. At least I amused him. He offered a suggestion. "I bet I know who would know where we could find something perfect. Dan's into that kind of a rig and so are his friends. Let's ask him." It seemed like good thinking.

Our day over, we headed back to the shore. It would take me at least half of the night to lug everything upstairs, cut off tags, put food away, and set up the computer. I'd gotten a new hot spot so I could log on quickly without running on Ben's service.

I'd just gotten the apartment re-organized from the shopping blitz when Ben appeared at the door.

It seems he'd spoken to Dan regarding a truck. "Dan told me he was surprised I'd be interested in that style of truck. However, the man to see is Animal. I was informed Animal lives out on the Way Back Road. I had to confirm this with Dan because I know where the Back Road is, but I'd never heard of the Way Back Road. It's a dirt trace running off the Back Road. Go figure.

"I do think I impressed the young man because he called me *Sir* twice during the conversation. He also informed me if we wanted to speak with Animal, now was the best time to do so. It seems he's not a morning person, has no phone and several real mean dogs.

"I think we should leave Shadow home for this ride. Dan also told me not to take my truck or the Expedition. He said I should take the yard truck, or Animal would think we were the Feds and he would shoot us. Are you still game to go?"

Laughing, I replied, "Let me grab my jacket. I've just walked the dogs so they'll be fine for a while. Are you worried about going over there?"

"Lady, if you're game, so am I." If I didn't know better, I would say Ben likes this *walking on the wild side*.

When we went by the driveway to the cove, Woodie was still working. I wanted to see how he was doing but this was more urgent.

We did indeed find the establishment of Animal. I had rather imagined what it would look like, so I wasn't surprised. We drove down a terrible dirt drive, even worse than my road, if that was possible and then around a sharp corner into a large yard. There, each dog, it seemed, had its own junk car for a kennel. He had a lot of dogs and an equal number of cars. The noise was deafening.

There was every breed of dog chained out. I did quickly notice they were all healthy looking, fat, with nice coats and terribly mouthy.

We sat in the truck and waited, as per Dan's instructions.

After about five minutes, a man appeared, as if from nowhere, and was standing in front of the truck. He was a big person, not tall, his arms covered with tattoos, as bald as an egg wearing a do-rag, Ray-Bans, and sporting a large bushy beard. I had no clue about his age, probably late fifties, or early sixties.

Ben rolled down the window as he approached. "We're looking for a truck and Dan told us you were the man to see."

Animal grinned, reached in his shirt pocket, pulled out something, and stuck it into his mouth; the barking stopped. A dog whistle… all of the dogs sat in silence …unbelievable. "Come on out, they're fine."

As soon as he spoke, I knew he wasn't a native. I would guess Maryland or Virginia. I wondered why he was here in the back woods of Maine.

That seemed to be my *forte'* in life, to wonder why. I've never cared *what* folks did, but the *why* always intrigued me.

It also has gotten me into a lot of trouble at times.

We followed him to an extremely large metal building in the back. He led the way through a small door on the side. What a beautiful sight, at least to me… there was a full-scale machine shop set up with cars, trucks, and street rods everywhere. I could see he had a professional paint booth in the back.

Animal's first question was easy. "What did you have in mind? You don't look like my kind of client, if you don't mind my saying so."

He was speaking directly to poor Ben. I'll give Ben credit…he looked Animal right in the eye and laughed. "You are correct, sir. I'm not your client, although I sure like your shop and admire your work. This lady, Eileen, is the person you need to be talking to."

Animal looked me over. "Excuse me, sorry for the assumption. What can I help you with?"

I explained what I wanted and how I wanted it set up. I asked if perhaps he had a finished product ready to roll.

A slow, malicious smile played across his face while he beckoned us to follow him.

We walked through his shop where I enjoyed looking at the goodies displayed, one and all. He walked us out through the back door over to a smaller metal building with a sliding door. He unlocked the door, slid it open, turning on the overhead lights. He revealed the most evil looking truck I'd ever seen.

The truck had been an old Chevy in the fifties. It sat low on the frame. He'd painted it a flat dark grey with no chrome or bling on it. He stepped around the truck, opened the door, and sat in the driver's seat. When he turned the key, it was like all hell and the demons were set loose. He pulled it forward out of the shed, letting it idle while he got out.

When he opened the hood, I was thrilled! I've always loved street rods. The good rods are a combination of imagination and design taken from all makes and models. The builders then add new mechanicals, making them safer and easier to drive. The process usually includes the addition of a high-powered motor. This truck went *way* beyond that.

My son builds street rods so I knew what was going on. This man was an artist and clearly pleased I appreciated his talent.

When he spoke, his pride was in his voice. "This is a pet of mine. I call him *Down and Dirty*. He's fast; he's mean, well balanced, and stable on any kind of terrain and handles like your mother's sedan."

Animal knew I really liked it. My big concern was how low it set. If I got off-road, I'd clean everything from the underside in a heartbeat. Animal sensed my concern. He reached inside, pushed a button and instantly the truck lifted at least a foot. Now I was *impressed*. I'd never encountered a lift-kit this smooth or fast. "Get in, *young lady*. We'll take him for a ride."

Ben looked distressed.

I jumped into the passenger seat. Nice racing buckets with a three-point harness, which might come in handy if I needed it.

Animal lowered the lift to about half as we tooled around the large shop, going out a different way than we had entered the property. The truck was very smooth and quiet while puttering along the road. He swung the truck sharply to the right. Now we were onto what looked like a path in the field. Two hundred feet later, we were on a dirt course as nice as any I'd ever seen. We rolled around the track at a moderate speed. When coming out of the turn, he punched it, making a quick figure eight in the middle. The truck didn't lift, slide, buck, or spin a wheel. I was even more impressed.

He stopped the truck and told me to drive. I walked around to the driver's side. I'm short; I wouldn't be able to see out of the windshield.

Animal smiled. "It has six-way electric seats so adjust them to where you're comfortable. There is also an excellent rear view camera if you drop the sun visor. One you can actually see with, all the time."

I checked it out. He was right. On my motor homes, they had been worthless. I hadn't even bothered to use them.

The mirrors seemed to be fine. This surprised me because I'd raised the seat higher and forward. Again, the slow smile. "The mirrors self-adjust to the movement of the seat.

"Now, push the red button on the dash. Feel the truck rise up. Check your mirrors again. Are they still okay? They're all automatic. It's kind of a specialty of mine. I like things just so."

Animal inquired, "Do you like the seats? The interior's all hand-done. That is another one of my hobbies.

"I want you to drive this around the track going at a speed you feel comfortable with." I complied, finding the truck easy to handle.

"Okay, put on your belt and bring the speed up. I want you to drive it like you just stole it with the cops in hot pursuit."

I felt the engine just wanting to fly. I loved a throaty engine. The truck was responsive and quick. I dashed around the track as if I were on fire, made a figure eight while bracing for the resulting skid. It never came. I don't know what he was running for suspension but it was impressive. I was flying down the track when I hit the brakes. It stopped on the proverbial dime and gave me nine cents in change. There wasn't any wobble, and no slew either… nothing. *Damn, this is great!* I nodded my approval, grinning like a silly fool.

I had to inquire, "What is the engine, or dare I ask? What are you running for suspension? Is it turbo? Does it need special fuel? Perhaps rocket fuel?"

He was laughing so hard tears were on his cheeks when he finally got breath enough to answer. "Engine is one of mine… it began its life as a Hemi…it does have a blower, and the suspension is a combination of things I found worked really well together. It's kind of a Heinz 57 special. Do you like it?"

My turn. "I do like it. I like the performance of the engine for speed and the agility of the truck. It has awesome handling properties. This is what I'm looking for except for the appearance. What I need is all of this in a beat up body looking as if he's on his last leg. I also need excellent headlights with the ability to flick them off, including the brake lights."

Animal looked hurt as if I'd insulted his first-born. He turned and looked me full in the face. "What do you want something like this for? It isn't a trophy car for shows. You also don't fit the profile for that. How long will you need the truck? After you've accomplished what you need it for, what would you do with it?"

While I was hesitating, he asked directly, "Why are you carrying a gun? Is this something to do with the mess over in the cove? What in the hell is going on? What happened over there is giving real criminals like me a bad name. You can't tell me, can you? You're the woman who was the victim in this mess, aren't you? It's not done yet, is it?"

I kept my mouth shut. I'd promised and I didn't want to endanger anyone else. If it meant I'd need to look elsewhere for a truck, it was what I would do.

Animal just watched me in silence. "Drive it back to the shop, please."

I guess I had my answer. I would begin my search tomorrow. Animal surprised me when he asked, "Can you give me two days? I will put you together something that will make a *sleeper* look comatose.

"I'll make a deal with you and only you. You take the truck I put together for you and drive it as long as you need to. When you're done with it, you bring it back to me. I don't care if you smack it up, roll it over, set it afire or whatever. It comes back to me. I'll charge you for whatever it costs me to repair or replace it. Is it a deal?

"When this mess is over, I want you to tell me my truck and I made a difference in the outcome. That's my deal. You can pick the truck up in two days. I will make sure it has a sticker and is registered."

We drove back to where Ben was standing. He looked like he was about to give birth to live kittens. When I got out of the driver's side, he looked stunned. I walked over to Animal. We shook hands. We both said at once, "Two days."

Twenty-one

Ben drove very carefully out onto the Back Road without saying a word. I could tell he was thinking over the events of the visit to Animal's shop. He was also trying to formulate a conversation which wouldn't be invasive or upsetting to me. In the end, I think he lost his own mental argument with himself, ending with an internal chuckle.

I knew the procedure well. This was a common practice for folks who lived alone; they developed their own counseling process.

We chatted our way back to the cove, stopping to check out the progress on the drive. We could actually drive into the property without a mud bath. That was progress!

Where the skeleton of the cottage had stood stubbornly on the rocks, there was nothing but empty space. Woodie had left the floor intact in order to protect the systems, such as they were, below it while he cleared the debris from the rocks. He was a good man who knew his trade!

We walked up onto the rocks to check it closer. Ben stood surveying the water.

"Eileen, will you rebuild on the same site? The view is incredible…it changes from minute to minute.

Ben continued, "I know a retired engineer who lives down the coast from here. He stores his boat at the yard. I've seen some of his work. I'm unsure if he's still designing and overseeing construction.

Would you like me to ask him if he'd like to think about another project?"

I knew I needed a person with substantial knowledge in engineering and construction for the project I had in mind. This could be a great starting point. I was anxious to get started. My reply was instantaneous. "That would be a big boost to the project. I would like to meet with him, if he's willing. Thanks again for your help."

When I got back to the apartment, I began the task of setting up the computer and getting dinner. The dogs needed a short walk before they ate.

The weather was holding. It was crisp, but pleasant for a stroll with the dogs. They were having their usual play playtime. Seaweed seemed her old self again.

My dinner was over and the dishes washed.

Then was the time for some serious research for the house. I enjoyed delving into research. It was educational while filled with possibilities I never knew existed. I'd known I couldn't rely on my own limited knowledge.

Times and methods change rapidly in the construction world. Some things apply and some don't. I had one chance to get this right. I wanted to be knowledgeable, when and if I talked to the engineer.

I was busy reading the report, comfortably curled up in my chair, when Shadow began her low growl. It had gotten dark quickly as the evening wore on. The sky had been overcast and gloomy at the end of the day, so there were no stars.

Shadow was at the window looking out toward the ocean, still growling. Seaweed began to stir. This was too reminiscent of the night the cottage burned.

I picked up the phone and punched Ben's number. He answered on the first ring. "What's the matter?"

"Shadow is alerting to something but it's too dark to see outside. She's serious." Ben's answer was fast, "Open the door to the stairs, and hit the red switch. *Quickly!* It'll light up the entire yard with floods. We're on our way. Stay put unless you hear from us."

I'd opened the door reaching for the switch when Shadow threw herself past me on the stairs and nearly knocked me down. I hit the switch just as she jumped at something in the recesses of the stairs. There was a scuffle; she yelped and was silent. I drew my revolver and hit the light switch to light the shop floor.

I heard a window breaking, then nothing. I ran to Shadow. She was hurt. She was almost conscious when I reached her side. She had a huge lump forming on her head. I was so damn mad I was crying and rocking her body like a baby when Ben burst through the door.

"Where are you? What happened?" He spotted Shadow in my arms. I had blood on my shirt. "Oh no, tell me she'll be okay. Please. What can I do? Can I carry her upstairs where we can treat her? Do I need to get the car so we can take her to the vet? Please don't cry…it scares the devil out of me."

I could see I had to get control of myself or we would all be in a pickle. Eric rushed into the space. I didn't even hear him open the door. He was better at assessing the scene than either Ben or me. He checked Shadow's heartbeat, looked into her eyes, then scooped her up in his arms like a toy and carried her upstairs.

Eric was the first to render an opinion. "Thank God for that dog. She's one of the best I've ever worked with. Even the canines we had in combat were not as sensitive to situations as she is.

"They're getting really bold trying to break in here. I told you this was going to get messy."

His attention shifted back to Shadow, who was trying to get up. "She'll be all right. Just let her rest. I'm going to check out some things and board up the window.

"Dad, I'll check in with you. Stay here with Eileen." With that, he was gone.

I noticed he was dressed all in black with what appeared to be a ski mask around his throat. He was also armed.

I stroked Shadow and put a cold pack on the lump on her head…she wanted to get up even though she was hurting. Seaweed sat by her shoulder and from time to time licked the back of her head.

Ben sat in the chair he'd pulled over to be part of the group.

I knew what I had to say. "Ben, I have to get away from you folks and fast. If I don't, this nut-job is going to hurt you or Eric in the process of trying to get me. They could've torched this building or worse, blown it up."

Sadness filled Ben's eyes. "You aren't leaving…trust me; we have weathered worse than this. We'll be okay."

I didn't believe him.

Twenty-two

In the morning, after some restless sleep, Ben and I again set off for Animal's place. The same barking greeted us. The racket didn't continue as long or as fierce as the last time. Animal walked around the corner, gave the signal, and silence fell. I grinned; I liked a good dog handler. He walked by the first dog, an extremely large pit bull-mastiff crossbreed who looked as if he could eat an elephant in one bite. Animal reached out his hand and the dog rolled over on his back for a belly rub. Yeah, they are both a couple of tough ones... *not.*

Animal nodded to both of us, then spoke to me, "Are you ready to meet your new best friend? Come on in and meet Shag. The name is short for Shag-nasty. He lives up to his name."

Inside I stood looking at an old beaten-up Ford truck, which looked as if it had been ridden hard and put away wet too many times. Ben was clearly shocked. I was not. As I looked at the tires and wheels, I knew this wasn't a *sleeper.* The truck truly was as close to a *coma* as you could possibly get while still being upright. I was thrilled it was exactly what I wanted. Animal was waiting for a reaction. "Are you ready to try him out?"

I nodded and hopped into the passenger seat. We returned to the track where we had given the other truck a test drive.

The vehicle was very quiet. It was truly an 'SBD'… *Silent But Deadly*. When we arrived at the track, we switched seats. I adjusted the seat for height. The seat was somewhat molded. It seemed to hug my body, thus eliminating the chance of being thrown sideways on rough ground. This was a good feature. During a rapid chase over rough terrain, the last thing I wanted was to be unseated.

I checked out the dash. Most of it was standard for this type of a set-up. There were lots of gauges and no idiot lights.

I checked the sun visor. There was the same rear view camera and it was working. This one was either larger or finer tuned, because I could read the lettering on a sign across the track. I hitched the seat belt on, checked with Animal, and we were off down the track.

Responsive would be like saying a hurricane was a *breeze.*

I hit the first turn to make the figure eight; driving as if I were on the interstate while going into a slight turn…no lifting, no settling, nothing. I gave the truck more throttle and banked for the next turn, taking it very tight… still nothing. *This was a MACHINE!*

Animal looked quite pleased with himself. He had good reason; he was a *genius* in this field. He could tell I appreciated every bit of his talent. He instructed me, "Try out the lift kit. It's not as exaggerated as the other one. It will give you the clearance you need if you're in a field or cutting brush.

"I can guarantee nothing around this part of the state will catch you. They couldn't hold the road at half the speed you can produce.

"Check the oil gauge …*often*. It's the key to these motors. Also, use a good grade of gas. It'll pay off in the performance."

Animal continued speaking softly. "How're things going? You seem really wound-for-sound today. Is there more unpleasantness going down?"

I wasn't sure how to answer. I thought I'd masked my anxiety pretty well. "I'm going to have to move away from the boat yard. I'll give you my cell number so you can reach me."

I noticed one of the tattoos on his arm. *I knew the design.* I'd seen it many, many times before.

"Where'd you get that tattoo? I've seen it before."

Animal looked shocked. "I don't usually discuss my tats with anyone. It's a special design. Only two of us have it. A friend of mine did it for me many, many years ago. His name was Tex, great man. People used to say we looked like twins. How do you know about the tat?"

I considered for a second before replying, "I'm Tex's mom."

His shock was real. "Are you kidding me? How is he? He's still alive isn't he? You mentioned your son did some of this same stuff. I'm so happy I could scream. Can you tell him you met me and I want to see his damned bald head soon?"

I shook my head, "No, I can't tell him until this mess is over. I don't want anyone else involved. They tried to get me night before last. If my Rottie hadn't alerted me, I wouldn't be here now. In the fracas, she got hurt. She'll be okay, thankfully. When this is over, if I'm still alive, I'll bring him to you; I promise."

Animal was quiet for a nano second. "Come here and stay. I can keep you safe. You can be certain of that."

Again, I shook my head. "No. I'm going to meet them soon. I'll walk away, or not. I'm not spending the rest of my life hiding from some stupid jerk or jerks. I'll keep your offer in mind.

"I'll be certain to let you know how to contact Tex. The deal has to be, and you have to swear, you'll not contact him until I tell you, or I'm not here. I never want him compromised again. I love the crazy kid.

"We need to get back or Ben will think we've eloped. He knows nothing of my family history either."

Animal was shaking his head. "Tex's mom, damn, we used to talk about you all the time. I never thought I'd meet you. Thank you for sharing the information. When I see him I'm going to hug him to death."

When we returned to the yard, we found Ben was pacing. He was clearly not pleased. I wondered if something else had happened while we were gone.

As we got out of the truck, Ben mentioned, "I noticed it smoked when you were driving out. Does it burn oil?"

Animal chuckled and continued with the malicious grin on his face. "No sir, I built it to give this appearance. If you met the truck on the road, what you would think, just another old rust bucket with a sloppy engine. Right? Wrong. This will clean your clock while you're thinking about pushing on the pedal. Don't worry sir, I wouldn't give her anything that's unsafe. This puppy has traction control, which is state-of-the-art, and a braking system you couldn't find in anything on the road today.

"Shag has a valid sticker and I left my registration on it. The papers are in the glove box because you're *just trying it out*. Now, get out of here and drive as if you stole it.

"By the way, this is a clean piece; it hasn't been seen around here, so nobody will associate it with me.

"If you have any problems and I do mean *ANY* issues, call me. Here's my number. I always have my phone with me, okay?

"Now git, so I can get some work done. I want to thank you, sir, for bringing her to me."

Animal continued, "Dan's a real good boy and he knows how to be private, if you know what I mean."

The truck went over the rough road like a Cadillac on asphalt. I was feeling confident. I just prayed I wouldn't have to wreck this jewel in order to settle a score. This was a game where I didn't even know who or how many players were in it.

Twenty-three

For the next two days, I drove the back roads. Some I knew, some not so much. I wanted to be as familiar with Shag as I could possibly be. I was happy nobody had observed me. I looked like straitjacket material. I drove him fast, slow, did donuts in the middle of the road, and tried the lift kit while taking him off-road into the blueberry fields. At one point, I even took the truck through a brook. I was as familiar with the equipment as I was ever going to get.

I was ready to start my plan. If you want to beard a lion, you have to go to his den.

I had a visit from Eric late the same night. I was surprised, because usually Ben and Eric were almost always together. When I opened the door for him, he looked a little sheepish putting his finger to his lips in a shhh-signal. I kept quiet and stepped aside. Eric entered, closing the door quietly behind him. In hushed tones he asked, "Are you going hunting for whoever is after you?"

I nodded and said, "Yes."

Eric reached behind him and produced a lethal looking black .45 automatic in a black holster. The holster had several quick release, loaded cartridge clips, all with what appeared to be hollow points.

He spoke so softly I had to lean toward him to hear. "Before you begin the hunt, go out to the old gravel pit on the Way Back Road, and practice with this. Your snub nose is too light for this type of hunting.

"Are you familiar with this model? I truthfully replied, "Yes, very."

Eric passed me the weapon with a big grin. "Wear it, use it, stay safe, and keep my number on speed dial, promise?"

All I could do was smile and nod. I really liked Eric.

I was also so sorry for the problems I'd dumped on his doorstep. I hoped I could end the situation without anyone else getting hurt.

Ben called me early the next morning to tell me Woodie had a problem. He needed us to come at once. I dashed down the stairs with Shadow on my heels just as Ben arrived.

We drove to the job site to find Woodie standing in the middle of the trace shaking his big shaggy head.

"Thanks for coming so quickly. We got trouble...when I began digging to make an upper catch basin to drain the area, I found something you need to look at. This is different than what I found the other day. If I'd gone any further, both the machine and I could've been in paradise. Be careful, but come and see.

"Thank God I was in Viet Nam or I would've been clueless."

We started to follow Woodie when he stopped short saying, "Put the dog back in the truck. It's too dangerous for her to be loose."

I complied. Shadow wasn't happy, but she stayed watching carefully from the car window.

Just ahead of the dozer sat an old excavator. Both were quiet. Woodie stepped around the track of the machine and pointed. There was a line of what looked like dark colored twine stretched taut between, then around, the trees about six inches from the ground. The bucket of the excavator was almost touching it. If Woodie hadn't pointed it out, I wouldn't have seen it.

Ben shook his head and patted Woodie on the shoulder. It was obvious they knew something I didn't.

Woodie seemed reluctant, but determined, to explain this to us. "I thought when I first saw it I was having a flashback. I hate to say this, but from time to time, it still happens.

"It was early when I started and there'd been heavy dew. The glint of the sun on a bead of moisture drew my attention. I stopped, thinking I hadn't really seen it. Not here in a Maine swamp.

"I shut the machine down and just sat there to see if the moment would pass. I haven't been bothered much in the last few years.

"Truthfully, Ben, it rattled me. I thought perhaps the PTSD was going to re-cycle again. I honestly don't think I could do it again.

"After a few minutes, I got down from the cab and took a closer look. When I realized I was okay, I called you.

"Ben, this is bad business here. What do you think?"

We all walked back out to the trace while Ben called Eric. When Eric arrived, he inspected the site then called a number on his cell. He walked away so we couldn't hear the conversation.

When he returned, he told Woodie not to do anything until folks arrived to take care of the issue. He thanked him for his keen eyes and knowledge.

Then Eric shooed Ben and me away.

What, I wondered, would they find now?

I was anxious to get on with my hunt. I realized I had to wait until we knew what they'd find at the dig site.

I heard a small helicopter arrive and set down in the field across from the trace. Ben and I stood in the yard at the shop and watched. As much as we wanted to go down and be on site, Eric had been adamant for us to stay far away. We decided we would respect his request.

We retired to the shop and worked on the drawings for *Survivor*.

It didn't take long before the entire troop minus Woodie arrived in the shop, where without a word spoken we were ushered into Eric's office.

When the crew invaded the dig site, what they found was far from what was expected. The area wasn't booby-trapped, as we'd feared. Someone had used the twine to lead to the spot of another buried stash.

They'd anticipated more munitions. What they uncovered was a large stash of cash in several containers, duly wrapped and carefully waterproofed.

Along with the cash, they had unearthed a batch of drugs, bricks of heroin in containers. Not far from the drugs were more remains that were human.

After some conversation, then more phone calls with more discussions, they concluded where most of the cash had originated by tracing the serial numbers. Some of the cash was from a never-published robbery of a transport from a mint. On some of the stash they had to complete additional queries. The drugs they would trace. A team to sanitize the area was on the way.

They were mostly concerned about Woodie, Ben and me being able to keep this quiet. Eric assured them it was under control.

They returned to the site to manage the clean-up leaving the three of us to stare at each other.

Finally Eric spoke, "This is way too big. I wonder where else in this state they have the same mess going on. I'd guess from the number of remains we've found so far, if they use someone for a job, when they finish with them, they kill them. I wonder how many have just disappeared. We have many ex-military personnel who, when they return home from duty are unable to re-integrate into society. Their personal damage is too excessive for them to carry by themselves. It leaves them with no place to go. I'm wondering if they're not using those people to help with the operation. Either when, or until, they become too hard to control, or they're afraid they'll turn the ring leaders in; they kill them.

"No one will look for them. They won't be missed because they've become like ghosts who wander around lost to the world they've left."

Ben and I just looked at each other as the horror of the statement sunk in.

It was time for me to get on with my hunt. I needed to see if I could put an end to some of this madness that had descended on all of us. I excused myself, leaving the men to talk.

I was sad beyond words. I liked these folks, although I no longer felt I *personally* had brought this trouble to them. If I hadn't come, perhaps the stuff would've stayed hidden. The crooks would have just quit without problems for anyone.

I knew from years of experience, even when you left poop undisturbed, it still stunk; then when you stirred it, the stench became unbearable. This had become a situation requiring an immediate solution.

Twenty-four

Shadow seemed to be herself and fully recovered. I put her into the new seat harness I'd made for her, using some suggestions from Animal. That way she would be secure and not bounced around if we got into a skirmish.

I checked my revolver, placing it in the holster attached to the side of the driver's seat for a quick grab if needed. I did laugh to myself as I stowed it. I'd always called it my *hugger* gun. You needed to be that close to hit anything with any accuracy. It was a snub-nosed Colt Detective Special, easy to conceal, but no distance. Now with the addition of Eric's .45, I was less concerned about the range. The noise would be a problem if I needed to discharge it inside the truck. As I was laying it aside, I noticed there was a silencer on the holster. I wasn't familiar with it, but I was certain I'd figure the device out.

Off to the Way Back Road to follow Eric's suggestion about practicing first. What was the old saying? *Practice makes perfect*? I would soon know if it was fact or fiction.

Ben came out just as I was ready to leave. "Hey, where are you two going? Can I come along?"

With a headshake I called, "Not today, going on a mission. Hope to see you later, though." With that, I left quietly, like the little old woman I was supposed to be.

I said a quiet prayer. I prayed I *would* be back and I really still possessed the courage I thought I did. One thing I was sure of...*I was not living like this anymore.*

I've lived in situations so frightening I didn't dare to go to sleep for fear of what would happen next; I wasn't going to be pushed around again, by anyone. I was going to end this. I would do it in my time, on my terms, and without anyone else involved.

The trip to the pit was not only helpful, it increased my confidence by about two hundred percent. I'd always been a good shot with both handguns and rifles. I hadn't been target shooting for years; however, the skill remained.

The .45 was comfortable, although heavy, after the small .38.

I had large, working hands, from all of my years of working on houses and construction. I'd also retained a lot of strength, even for my age.

I was as prepared as I ever would be.

I had my cell in my hoodie pocket just in case I needed backup. My first stop would be the post office...a.k.a. *gossip city*. I parked, walked to the counter, and asked the mail person to hold my mail for a while. After all the rules were thoroughly explained about how long it could be held and so on, she wanted to know if I was still staying out at Ben's place. I shook my head and simply stated, "No!" Then I bolted for the door. It would be all over town in a heartbeat, I was sure.

I cruised slowly through town, stopping at the general store... just to see how good the gossip line was working. I walked in and purchased a pack of gum along with a special dog biscuit for Shadow.

While I was paying, I overheard a couple of men in the background talking about the truck. One was remarking, "The woman who was staying out at Ben's place was driving it."

The other person was quick to correct him, "She ain't there any more…left today."

Yes, the gossip line was on track.

I gave Shadow her treat and drove off, heading out of town toward the road they call the Whale Back because of the humps in it. At forty-five miles an hour in a car, it'll stick your stomach to the roof of your mouth. I'd been driving it in this truck at eighty with perfect control. If necessary, I knew this truck could produce more speed while retaining its handling quality.

There wasn't any traffic on the road. This wasn't unusual for the time of day. Most folks either fished or worked in the woods, not wasting time out riding the roads mid-day.

I drove along at forty-five. On the top of the second hump, I spotted a big black truck behind me. There was enough chrome on it to stand out anywhere.

Whoever it was had to be flying, because when I made the top of the next hump he was right behind me. Game on!

At first, I thought he was going to ram me. Instead, he began passing on the next hump. When he was beside me, he shot me a wicked grin while giving me the finger.

I didn't change my speed. I paid attention as he pulled in front of me and hit his brakes...hard. I swerved out around him. While I was passing, he gunned it. I let him go.

So far, I hadn't played my hand at all.

I called Ben's number. When he answered, I said, "Write down this registration number…Ford, either a 250 or a 350 black covered in chrome, Maine plate 458-293."

Ben yelled, "Where in hell are you?"

"Whaleback… gotta go."

The truck was out of sight. *That meant trouble.*

I spotted something shining in the woods up ahead. *Chrome, do you suppose?*

I drove on, not speeding up or slowing down. I knew this road only went about another two miles so it would happen soon. I was ready. *Bring it on, jerk!*

He did. When I drove past the skidder road, he blasted out of there with mud flying and tires squealing when he hit the tar. His truck fishtailed all over the road, rocking with the force of the corrections he was making.

Maybe I should just let him kill himself. Then he came. He was right beside me. He was going to ram my front end. Damn, I was on the top of one of the humps with no guardrails and a steep drop. I saw him swing the wheel. I braked. He misjudged on the correction, almost going onto the soft dirt shoulder.

He recovered but he was mad. He was also erratic. This would be my redeeming feature. I paid attention. He slapped his brakes, trying to get me to either hit him or go around.

He was not in control of this game. He hadn't figured that out yet.

I hit the brakes then swung the wheel, punching Shag, and did a one-eighty in the middle of the road. He must have figured out how to turn around because then he was behind me again.

Lord love us, the fool was going to try to race me. I braked; he shot by. I spun a one-eighty because I wanted him on my other side when this ended.

He had again figured out how to turn around and was back with a vengeance.

I breathed a quick prayer…*God please help, take the wheel*! This would be it. He was abreast of me. We were driving seventy and the idiot was still giving me the finger. I was wrong! He was pointing a gun at me.

I braked; he pulled ahead. We were starting up the biggest hump.

Shag, I hate to do this to you, but no choice. I caught his front wheel, hit the lifter, and turned my wheels. Too many bad noises with the contact, then his truck just flew out into space, off the road, down the banking, nose over tail repeatedly.

I pulled over and backed up. I could see the wreck but didn't see any movement. I called Ben to send police and a meat wagon.

I should go check on him. I didn't and I wouldn't unless he started climbing the banking. *If he does, I'm going to shoot him somewhere where it will hurt, a lot.*

Shag had not sustained any damage. I released the lift kit so he just looked like an old tired truck sitting there. I heard sirens so I stood there watching his truck until they arrived with Ben bringing up the rear. He had Eric with him.

Eric was the first to speak. "You're going to get yourself killed. Do you know that?"

I nodded "Yes I do, but it's going to be a fair fight. I don't know who he is, but he tried to put me off the road a half dozen times. He was getting ready to shoot me from the window. I disarmed him.

"It was a nice truck…too bad he didn't know how to drive. Do you know him?"

Eric responded, "He hangs out at the garage in town. Dad pulled his plate but I didn't recognize his name."

Eric's phone rang. "Yes sir, that is correct I'm here now, and I don't know yet. Did you make the name? Oh, okay. Let me get the officer."

Eric went down over the banking with the speed and agility I envied, considering his size and age. He was talking to the officer and handing over his phone.

I could hear an ambulance wailing.

I wondered if I should move the truck. Eric was coming back up and heading straight for us, so I stayed put.

People were arriving from town. What did they do? Had they closed up shop for the day to come see the show?

I took Shadow out of the truck on her lead and stood with Ben.

As Eric neared the top of the grade, what looked like an old wrecker arrived. They'd never get the truck out of there with that piece of equipment. It wasn't my problem, nor did I care.

I had to know, "Eric, is he alive?"

With a nod, "Just barely and the officer has the gun with a silencer on it. He also has orders to take him to the hospital under guard and not leave him until the Fed-boys show up. You got a hot one there, kiddo."

When the wrecker parked, the driver, Bart, walked over to the edge of the road to look down into the ravine.

Suddenly, Shadow made a lunge, nearly pulling me over and knocking me into Ben and Eric. She was growling with her teeth bared. I was having a tussle holding her. She wasn't listening to me at all.

Eric took her lead. "Stand back, Eileen, I've handled k-9s and I'm well trained. Something's not right here. Dad, are you carrying? Hell, how dumb was that question?"

I opened the door and passed him my .38 as Shadow continued to lunge. Eric walked forward with her. She was almost dragging the big fellow. What was he going to do? I knew he wouldn't hurt the dog. He held the gun low by his leg. Whatever he was going to do, he was deadly serious. Shadow pulled him right to Bart, the wrecker driver, and then alerted… she knew something, but what? When the driver spotted the dog, he panicked, but he was too slow. Shadow had him by the forearm and wasn't going to let go.

The driver kept backing to his truck, pulling Shadow along with him. He reached inside the window for his gun just as Eric quietly brought the revolver up and placed it on his neck. Strange thing... with all the people milling around, they'd missed the whole show. It seemed only Ben and I had seen any of the performance.

I slowly became aware that Ben had a death-grip on my shoulder. I turned my head and he relaxed his grip, then patted me as if I were a child or a pet.

He was as white as a sheet. Was he having a heart attack? I needed to know. "Are you all right or do you need to sit in the truck? Do you need a doctor?"

All I received was a lopsided grin. "I'm okay. I think I'm just getting too old for all this excitement."

Amen, so am I.

A trooper approached the wrecker, took in the situation, and without any fanfare he cuffed Bart, the wrecker driver.

At some point, Shadow must have released his arm. She was sitting next to Eric as if he were her best friend in this world, being as good as ever.

Oh great, I heard a chopper flying in. Here came the Feds and the merry men again. I'm going to write a book about this, if it ever gets over.

I think the Feds are tired of this group. They landed and hastily walked toward Eric and the trooper, grabbed the wrecker driver, and threw him into the chopper.

I recognized this one… it was Hank, coming my way. I braced myself; I hoped there wouldn't be more stupid questions.

The road was totally blocked. What a state of affairs!

They still hadn't retrieved the driver from the wrecked Ford truck. Thankfully, Hank passed by with only a passing nod and, "Hello." He went down over the bank to where the wreckage was scattered on the ground.

I spotted a car parked way down on the end of the gathered cars lining the road. Some had arrived by driving in from the other direction. The person was just sitting there, but something about his posture reminded me of my son. I knew it wasn't…I *did* know who was in the car. I told Ben I'd be right back. I didn't want to draw attention to the car, so I pretended to be looking for something along the side of the road.

When I was even with the car, I averted my attention, never looking directly at the car or driver. I continued to search the shoulder while speaking softly, "Shag is fine, and he did a great job. There are Feds all over the place up there. Good place to avoid. There's a nice, well-wrecked, Ford truck smushed in the ravine. At this point, I think you could also buy the wrecker very cheaply. Stay cool, I'll talk with you later and thanks."

I searched beyond the car for a ways then shrugged and walked back to my truck.

The trooper asked me what had happened and I told him. He made a couple of notes on a pad, closed it, then muttered, "Damn fools from away never obey the speed signs on this road. This happens all the time. They should learn to read and to drive. I'm sorry to have held you up. You had no part in this mess."

Hank made it up the banking, puffing and red-faced. "That one will live. He'll be sore for a while and sorer still when he figures out I just served him with a Federal arrest warrant. He's going to prison for the rest of one sentence before he can begin the next one. I think this is over.

"I'm definitely going to retire, and not to the State of Maine. I wish you well, lady, have a good life." With that, he boarded the chopper and they left.

I wanted to go home and sit on my rocks. First, I needed to get my dog back… no sooner said than done. She returned with her leash in her mouth, wagging her tail-less butt at Ben. She gave us her big, happy Rottie-smile. She was *some proud* of herself, as they say Down East. She had the right to be; she was a good girl.

Ben seemed more relaxed than I'd ever seen him. "What do you say about us going home and building some boats?"

My reply was simple. "Sounds good to me… along with building a house, garage, doing some landscaping and planning a peaceful life in the cove."

We tired of watching them try to retrieve the truck from the gully. I thought *what a circus! Good luck with that!*

Twenty-five

The next few days were peaceful and relaxing, allowing me to meet with Jay and finalize house plans. He was amazing. He listened to what I'd said, understanding the use of the materials I specified. His engineering knowledge was a bonus. He had a crew in place to begin the erection as soon as the foundation work was completed. Attaching the foundation to the ledge proved to be challenging.

I returned the truck to Animal with *great* reluctance. I'd liked the power and the handling of the machine with full knowledge it would get me into massive trouble. I'd always loved a gutsy ride.

I reassured Animal that I would bring Tex to visit him.

I took one last look around his shop, drinking in the art of his craft. I'd wanted a street rod for most of my life, knowing it was way out of my price range. Still it'd been, and still was, fun to dream.

Animal wouldn't accept any payment for the use of Shag. He'd saved my life by modifying and loaning me the truck.

When we returned from the delivery to Animal, Ben drove us over the same road we'd taken when he explained his problems with Nina. We drove to the garage set apart from the house. He beckoned me to get out of the car while he unlocked the side door. Ben stepped inside and hit the button, opening the door and pulling off the cover of the auto stored there. There sat a beautiful, vintage, silver Jeep Grand Wagoneer.

Ben's face said it all. "What do you think, Eileen? Just like new. Twenty-two thousand miles, one owner, maintained perfectly, and ready to go. He opened the driver's door with a flourish. "Sit, madam! Tell me what you think."

I sat. I also smelled and touched. Because I'm a very tactile person, smell and feel are very important to me. The car smelled of clean, soft leather. I had also detected the faint hint of the aftershave Ben always wore, mingled with his subtle personal scent.

As with my old Jeep, the seat fit me perfectly. I bet he'd been over there prior to today and dusted the dash. I smiled.

Only one question popped into my head. "You're not serious about selling this, are you?"

Ben patted the roof with what seemed almost a caress.

"Only to the right person. I've loved this since I first saw it years ago. I didn't drive it much because my wife hated it. She said it was ugly and rode like a truck. She would never drive it. I stored it, but seldom used it. I knew someday I'd know my reason for storing it."

With a wicked grin, he made a grand sweep with his arm and declared, "This can be yours today, if the price is right."

I was afraid to ask, but I did. "What is the right price, sir?"

Ben asked so little I felt I'd stolen it. We both knew it while enjoying the barter and the banter.

We drove both vehicles back to the shop.

Eric was standing outside the shop laughing at us as we approached. "My goodness, I *am* raising children again. Dad, we're in for a blow. They're predicting it to be strong. Don't you think we should lift *Survivor* and cradle her? I can fit her into the number four building so you two can still have access to her."

Ben looked at me for affirmation. I nodded my approval. We went to watch.

Later we drove into town and registered the Jeep to me. It would be *so* good to have my own wheels again. Eric gave me garage space until my house and garage were completed. It was wonderful to have people who cared.

The evening was cold and blustery with the wind really picking up velocity around four in the morning. The apartment stood firm, even if the noise was unbelievable. I was happy we'd lifted the boat.

In the morning, everyone was out checking the stored boats and buildings before they met in the shop downstairs. Eric called up to me to come down so we could chat...*this was strange, chat about what?*

He and his dad were at the drafting table when I arrived. Eric pointed to the hidden door with a finger to his lips. We all moved into the office, locking the door. *Oh, oh, something is up.*

Les had contacted Eric during the night. The Feds had completed the initial interrogation of both Bart, the wrecker owner, and the wrecked truck driver. Les told Eric the driver of the truck and Bart were both so strung out on heroin during the incident on the road with me they were incapable of conversation. It explained Bart's behavior with Shadow when she bit him, along with the confession that he was the one who had broken into the shop and struck her that night. His intention was to silence me so I would not identify him as the person from the first incident on my beach.

By the time they'd gotten them to headquarters and through being booked, they both would've sold their own mothers for a fix. Les told Eric there wasn't any doubt everything the truck driver and Bart knew, thought they knew, hoped they had known, or ever would know, was spilled.

Both Ben and Eric agreed Bart was a victim of his own greed and addiction. He'd been an okay kid growing up, with only minor problems. He had done a very short stint in the service then returned home. He'd never settled back in. Les told Eric that Bart had a terrible heroin habit, which would take a long time, if ever, to break.

The Feds knew the truck driver. They'd been hunting him for some time; he and Bart had served together in the army at a couple of posts. One of them was in charge of moving munitions from base to base while readying them for shipping to troops overseas. Someone in the military figured out more and more of the supplies were coming up short. They were ready to seize both men when they went AWOL.

The amount of small arms missing was staggering. It was only confirmed when the authorities did an inventory.

However, they'd both worked on different bases, and been transferred several times; it compromised getting the inventories coordinated.

The Feds still hadn't found the other man involved. They described him as very dangerous and a real psycho. He liked knives, hand-to-hand combat, and explosives. They wanted us to know because the Feds believed, based upon the confessions, there was still a lot of inventory out in the water and this nut-job wanted it.

They warned us to be extra diligent.

Eric said, "When the seas calm down tomorrow, I'm going out to some of the locations. I'm hoping I can spot something. I just wanted you both to know. Continue being careful and observant. Just as a precaution, I want you both to carry your guns and keep my number on speed dial on your phones."

I was as tired of all this as I knew they were. Eric had said he wouldn't bring his family home until this was over and finished. He missed the children terribly.

I understood how he felt. As nice as they were, and as great as the apartment was, it wasn't my home.

When we left the meeting, I took my dogs and drove to the cove. I knew I'd find peace there. They were excited to be back, although they seemed confused. The cottage and shed were all gone.

Jay's men had poured the concrete on the rocks for the base of the new house. I climbed up on it and stood. Soon, and very soon by God's grace, I would be home.

I walked out on my point. The ocean was still wild with the waves crashing in. It was a neap tide due to the phase of the moon along with the storm. I could see things I hadn't seen before because the water was so low.

Then I spotted something odd. I didn't know what I was looking at until I got closer. I recoiled!

Pulling out my phone, I punched Eric's number with a shaking finger. It took three tries before I was finally successful.

When he answered, I could tell he was with someone. "Eric, it's Eileen, come quick and don't bring your dad…this will be too upsetting for him."

Trying to sound normal, Eric replied, "Okay, be there in a few, thanks."

I walked to the concrete platform and sat waiting with the dogs. I couldn't look again.

How Eric got there so rapidly I don't know. He slid into the spot by the Jeep and ran down the path to where I was. "It's over there in the rocks."

Eric walked over and climbed down into the rocks. I heard him retch once. He moved down lower onto the shelf of rock then walked back toward me. He had his phone to his ear listening. "Yes sir, it is him. I checked the tattoo on the ankle.

"Sir, there were also remnants of what looked to be a Zodiac. From what I could see, he was either getting ready to use or set up a rocket launcher. He made an error or misjudged the discharge. It blew a hole in the boat filled with crates.

"I don't know how long ago this happened, but it's recent. The storm last night drove the mess into the rocks and pounded it pretty badly. I could see the crates on the bottom. It's too rough to retrieve them now. I'll get them, perhaps tomorrow.

"Yes sir, I'll take care of both of those things.

"No, Eileen found him. I'll do that, sir."

Eric stopped in front of me as if he were talking to a small child. "I'm sorry you had to find that mess, but there is good news in this situation. You've just found the missing link. He was the man I was warning you to be on the lookout for. I'll have this removed shortly and it's over and done with. I didn't tell dad where I was going."

Eric lifted his head to listen. "Too late, I can hear him coming right now. We have to let him know. He'll be okay.

"Eileen, I must tell you he's better right now than he's been in years. He's back on track and happier than I have ever, and I do mean *ever*, remembered him. Thank *you* for that."

Ben parked in the expanded parking lot. The dogs ran to meet him with yips and wagging tails. He arrived on the rock with his furry friends. "Okay, did I get uninvited to this meeting for a reason? I knew you were up to something when you left in a cloud of dust. What's up?"

Eric filled him in, then left us with orders not to touch anything. *As if we wanted to.*

He returned with a camera and equipment. Setting about the task of getting the remains off my shore, he secured the Zodiac. I offered to assist him to carry the bundle to his truck. He declined both my offer and his dad's.

Ben cocked his head in my direction and smiled. "I just spoke with Jay; he told me the trucks and crew will be here in two days to erect the walls and roof. With weather cooperating, he'll have it sheathed and shingled in ten days with the doors and windows in place. The doors and windows are coming from somewhere in Indiana. The crew delivering them will install them. Why don't we go shopping in the city for some furnishings and a good dinner. Would you like that?"

I thought for a moment, "Okay Ben, your lovely chariot or mine?"

It was good to joke and laugh again.

Twenty-six

The building of the home progressed rapidly. Now, my hope was to be moved in and living in the house before the winter really arrived.

I wanted to spend Christmas sitting in front of my fireplace watching the ocean. This idea had been the inspiration for the installation of the beautiful glass doors. They'd look out onto the surrounding porch, which wrapped around three sides of the cottage.

The kitchen was almost completed. I wanted to unpack the things I'd purchased. I had enjoyed each of the trips Ben and I made to the city. We always started with the guise of getting a specific item. We returned like pack rats with whichever vehicle we'd taken full to the brim.

If we were not at the house, we were in the shop working on the hull of *Survivor* or the first reproduction. We couldn't wait until we could test-sail our new one to compare its handling abilities to the original. Ben and I became great friends and partners in the *Survivor* series of specialized small sailing boats. We kept ourselves busy building the new boat for our proto-type and planning marketing strategies. Funny, we were both old and retired, yet we had begun a new business venture. We were enjoying our creativity and productivity to the limit.

Spring would be wonderful. I was planning the landscaping, along with new garden plots for the house. I prayed God would bless us with an early spring. It had been a mild winter so far on the coast this year.

I moved into the new house one week before Christmas. I was moving in one door while the workers were moving out of the other. Trucks arrived with furniture and boxes as others were hauling away materials and trash bins.

The confusion was wonderful; I was in high gear, and I couldn't wait to put up the Christmas tree. The tree was artificial, but all the outdoor wreaths were made of wonderfully fresh Down East balsam. The smell was breathtaking. The wreaths were a gift from Ben and Eric.

Ben arrived in the middle of the melee. Thank God, Woodie had made a very large parking area; it was full to capacity. Looking around at furniture being set up, he just stood shaking his head. "Great skills, Eileen, you're a cross between a supervisor, traffic cop, and a choir director. You're doing a good job.

"I came to inquire if you'd please go with me to the Christmas Eve service at church. I really want to go, even though it's been years since the last time I went. I don't want to go alone. It would really please me if you would go with me. Think about it and give me a call. I know you're pretty busy right now."

Then he left, still looking around and shaking his head.

Smiling I nodded and thought to myself about how strange the request was. I'd also wanted to start going back to church. I wondered how he knew. I'd always gone to church, no matter where I was, until I moved to this town.

The other day, when I first began contemplating going into town to attend church, I wondered how, or if, the town folks would be receptive to my attendance. I asked myself, *after the last few months what could folks say that wasn't true?* Who cared? I didn't anymore. I was going to enjoy what I had left of the life God has given me.

I called Ben to tell him I'd love to go.

Perhaps we'd both come to the same place at the same time. It had been a terrible few months. Both Ben and I had a lot to be grateful for…God had blessed us.

I knew people, wherever I was, had always considered me odd, because I was a consummate loner. After all these years and life issues, I'd grown a thick skin so it bothered me less.

Finally, the last of the trucks left with tons of cardboard and shrink-wrap loaded into them.

Then it was time to put dishes away, make beds, move things to my liking and then relax for a few minutes.

Looking around at my new home was a heartfelt pleasure.

The one thing I missed was my artwork. Over the years, I'd painted some, but now it had all been lost in the fire. Perhaps this winter I would set up a space in the spare room and begin again. I'd like that. I wondered silently if maybe I'd lost my touch with the paints and brushes. We would see.

It was a time for new beginnings. I took a few hours to steal away to refresh my appearance with a new haircut. I hadn't cut my hair for years, wearing it in a long almost white braid to keep it in place because of the natural curl. I had heard of a salon in a neighboring town that was collecting hair to make wigs for cancer patients. I thought it would be a good gift to someone in need. I called, made an appointment and returned with a manageable short curly cut.

I had laughed at Ben…he looked shocked by the change of hairstyles. After his initial surprise he managed, "I love it, now you look cute. The look suits you perfectly. Great hair-do for sailing and fishing in the wind."

Christmas Eve arrived with Ben coming to pick me up for the drive to the church. I think we were both apprehensive about going, although neither of us would voice it.

We arrived at the door of the church in softly falling snow. The church was a lovely old building in the center of the village, its stained glass windows glowing with light from the interior. It looked like a Norman Rockwell painting. We both took a deep breath, then Ben opened the door, and we marched in.

An elderly man with lovely white hair and twinkling blue eyes behind his rimless glasses warmly greeted us. "Ben, how wonderful to see you again."

Turning in my direction, he extended his hand, "Welcome to God's house. It's a pleasure to meet you."

We found seats where we could sit together. I wondered where so many folks had come from. The church was full to overflowing.

The sanctuary's decoration of real balsam boughs and wreaths gave off the most wonderful scent, which mingled with the smell of burning candle wax. The choir was already in place with the pianist softly playing Christmas hymns.

I took a long breath and realized how much I'd missed this. Glancing out of the corner of my eye, I could see Ben was experiencing the same feelings. Perhaps, without knowing, we'd managed to do something nice for each other.

We had become good friends since the time, which now seemed so long ago, when I'd threatened to shoot him. Now, I would want to protect him. How funny was this? *Must be the season's getting to me.*

Just as the service was ready to start, I felt a tap on my shoulder. When I turned to see who was touching me, I grinned like a kid. Sitting directly behind me was Animal with a big smile on his face. Ben turned and nodded, smiling a welcome.

The church service was one of the nicest I ever remembered. We left the church feeling safe and comfortable. I'd invited Ben and his family for Christmas dinner the next day. I extended the invitation to Animal. He was pleased and promised to behave. Ben and I laughed together as we got into his car for the drive home.

When we pulled down the drive, no longer referred to as *the trace*, and rounded the last slight bend, we saw the cottage. It was standing proudly, all alight, on the rocks looking out at the ocean in the starlight. The dusting of snow made the ground glow as though someone had scattered diamonds all around.

As I was getting out of his vehicle, Ben passed me a wrapped box, surprising me. I thanked him, said goodnight and walked up the path with the pleasant smell of the ocean and the balsam from the wreaths. I thought *this is what Paradise must be like*. It had been a wonderful Christmas Eve. As I stepped inside my home, I hung my coat; then I unwrapped the present. Ben had gifted me with a beautiful, leather-bound Bible inscribed with my name in gold leaf. This would replace the paper-back one I had purchased after the fire.

Twenty-seven

During the period after the last skirmish, I'd managed to get away for a couple of days. I'd gone back to the southern part of the state for a quick visit with the kids. Then I kidnapped my son without telling him where I was taking him. We returned to visit with Animal. I'd promised and I keep my promises.

To say they enjoyed their reunion would be the understatement of the century. They laughed and hooted as only boys like them could. They inspected cars and trucks in various states of design. They fired up engines, driving out on the track in the partially snow-covered field. They reminded me of two bad boys let out, without supervision, to play. I really believed they had been two lost souls who somehow years ago found each other when they were incarcerated in the same prison. They'd formed a bond that would never end. Both were kind men who'd made mistakes during their youth and had become productive members of society.

My only deal with Animal was he shouldn't tell my son anything about the mess, or what had happened. I don't ever want my life problems to impact my children negatively. It had ended okay… I was still here, and my theory is, *no harm no foul*, so leave it alone.

I'm not certain Animal respected all of my desires for being quiet. When we were leaving I heard my son say, in that intense voice he gets when he's serious, "Now you take care of my mom, you hear?" Animal's reply was a nod, "Damn straight, Tex, she's important to me also. Remember to keep your lip buttoned. Okay?" Big hugs and we were off.

My son was quiet for a long time with a sly smile on his face. He had thoroughly enjoyed the visit. I'd never inquire what memories he was reliving. It was none of my business. I was happy I'd kept my promise.

It's sometimes good to re-connect with your past even if it is under dire circumstances. I've always believed the past gives you the benchmark you use for going forward.

Twenty-eight

The winter sped by. We filled it by working on the boats for the *Survivor* line Ben wanted to launch in the spring.

I'd spent a considerable amount of time on the artwork for my home. I worried that, perhaps during the long absence from painting, I had lost my skills. However, I seemed to have developed a new dimension to my painting. At first this seemed odd to me, because for once in my life, I not only had time to do things I enjoyed, I wasn't worried about funds. I had always found art supplies to be expensive.

One afternoon while Ben and I were working in the shop, Eric came by. He referred to us as the children, always with good humor. He also called the shop our playroom.

I hadn't seen Eric for several days. He'd been very busy in his own set of buildings down in the yard where he worked on the motorized boats. He also had a special shop where he and Dan, with a couple of other men, built race motors for boats.

Today he had something on his mind. Although he was smiling, I could tell he was here on business of some sort. I offered to move to the back of the shop so he could speak privately with Ben.

Then he spoke up, saying, "This involves both of you, really all three of us. Eileen, this is about last fall when you were involved in the wreck out on the Whaleback. The man in the truck was a known criminal with a Federal reward on his head. Les called me a couple of days ago to let me know he was sending this out. He wanted me to make sure you got it." He handed me an envelope with a Federal check in it for fifty-thousand dollars.

"Eric, I didn't *capture* anyone; this isn't mine. This needs to be returned to someone."

Eric laughed and shook his head. "I call it a capture when this guy had been on the run for over two years and neither the Feds nor anyone else could find him, let alone arrest him. Nope, it's yours to do with as you please. Dad, you're my witness. I delivered the goods."

He was still chuckling as he walked out the door with, "Now you kids behave" tossed over his shoulder.

"Ben, I don't want this and I don't need it, thankfully. They were talking last week at church about how to raise money for improvements to the building. I already planned to donate a gift to the fund. What do you think Pastor would say if we were to give him this check as well? The only condition would be he couldn't tell who gave it to him or where it came from."

"Let's go find out."

We were a strange sight, because wherever we went the two dogs tagged along. Shadow hopped in and Seaweed waited for one of us to lift her to the seat.

I don't think the pastor cared if we were strange or not. Tears filled his eyes when we handed him the check. I felt my request of anonymity was safe.

Twenty-nine

Spring had finally arrived at last!

Jay called one morning and informed me he had the landscaping all set. I was to leave it to him. He had a tremendous interest in plantings tolerant enough to withstand Maine winters on the coast with the salt air and harsh winds.

I informed him that'd be fine with me as long as he left me a place for some raised beds to garden. It had always been one of my great pleasures during warm weather, along with fishing, clamming, sailing, and everything else.

Ben and I were *very* excited…we were launching *Survivor* after her long winter rehab, as well as the first of her prototypes. We'd enlisted some assistance from Eric, Dan and another yardman.

Eric had informed us we were too old to be horsing boats around and there were others with equipment which could do it easier and safer. We laughed, not caring that one moment he referred to us as children and in the next breath, we were too old, as long as we could get out on the water.

Later during the day, Eric, unknown to us, filmed the two of us sailing up and down the shoreline in front of the boat yard. Ben was teaching me how to sail by coaching from his craft.

Shadow sat on her seat in the prow as if she owned it, while Seaweed lay quietly at my feet, content to be together.

Survivor didn't leak a drop. The winter's work had been well worth all the effort.

Eric put the video on the internet as a surprise without telling Ben. The next day Ben was taking orders for his new line. He looked like a kid with a new toy. He wanted to draw up a partnership agreement, set up books, order supplies etc. He was a new and energized man.

When I returned home from the shop later in the day, I had two surprises waiting for me. Jay's men were just finishing the plantings.

I'd always loved to garden and landscape, but never had the resources, financially or work force, to come anywhere close to this level. It was *breathtaking*. He'd used mature plants along with some smaller ones to achieve the desired effect. The garden area looked like it'd been there for years.

He'd laid a stone pathway which wandered through a wrought iron gate with a weathered finish to an area of raised beds. He called this 'the garden area.'

I took this to mean I could plant and play in *there*, but not to touch the other.

Jay looked like a proud father of brilliant twins.

He'd requested permission to photograph everything when he was done to promote the new plant section of his brochure.

Jay had just driven away with his men when I heard a vehicle drive by on the road heading down toward the boat yard. I made a mental note, because it was a high powered, throaty sounding engine.

I continued inspecting the yard. Because of the earthwork Woodie had completed, with Jay directing, I had a lot more usable ground space.

This was Heaven.

I needed to purchase some outdoor furniture for the garden area. I would spend a lot of time out there. Thanks to the constant breezes, we had very few bugs during the summer.

I heard the engine again. I was tempted to go out to the end of the drive and sneak a peek. *Nosy old bat*, I chastised myself. It's *none* of your business.

I busied myself planning the placement of the furniture along with a fire pit.

I heard the engine sounds slowing down. Whatever it was, it was coming closer.

What a sight drove into the parking area! Ben and Animal in the greatest street rod I'd ever laid eyes on! I think it'd been a Model A at one time. Now, along with a bright metallic candy-apple red paint job, it sported leather bucket seats. *Wow!*

I ran down the path to get a better look. Animal was grinning like a fool and Ben was not far behind in the grin department.

Animal gave me a hug. "Well, what do you think? Is it the right color? Does it sound good? Does it have the perfect wheels? Do you like the interior? It has a soft top and a hard top. Do you not like it?"

I hadn't had time to utter a sound.

"Animal, that's the greatest rod I've ever seen. I heard it go down to the yard and even though I hate nosy people, I wanted to run out to the road so I could see who and what it was. You have outdone yourself with this one. Has Tex seen this?"

I wondered, after I asked; why I had. It was so similar to ones I'd seen him draw years ago. Perhaps he'd shared some of his drawings and ideas with Animal.

Animal nodded and drew a piece of well-worn paper out of his pocket and passed it to me. It was the drawing I remembered so well from all those years ago. To look at the drawing, then to see the finished product sitting here, brought tears to my eyes.

"Can I take a photo of you with the car and the sketch to send to him? He did that drawing a long time ago under terrible circumstances. I know he would appreciate all of your labor."

Head shake, "No" from Animal. I was surprised…I thought he would have liked sharing it. The surprise must have shown on my face.

I got a big grin in return, "We both worked on this, so he already knows all about it. You need to see the door. I walked around to the driver's door where a small brass plaque was mounted.

It was brief, *To the Best Mom, from Tex and Animal*. Animal spoke quietly, "Thanks, this is our gift to you. Years ago every letter, magazine, photo you ever sent, I shared. Without you, neither of us would have remained sane or be who we are now."

With that, he passed me the keys and a certificate of ownership.

Ben ducked his head and walked to the garden area calling back, "Eileen, take Animal and your new toy for a trial drive. I'm just going to sit here and admire Jay's handiwork. Don't hurry."

Animal and I drove off. I didn't rev the engine or slew it. I stayed true to my rule given when my son was growing up building motors and cars. He couldn't make black tire marks in the road in front of my house. Good rule. I wouldn't want to act like a *gearhead* on this road.

We went out to the whaleback and played. The rod was spectacular from start to stop. I loved it but these two fellows couldn't afford to be giving away their products without payment. I also didn't want to hurt either of their feelings. I needed a plan.

I drove Animal home, thanking him again.

I had been gone for over an hour. I wondered what Ben had done to entertain himself while I was gone. Perhaps he'd called the shop to get a ride home. I felt guilty as I drove into the parking area. It had been rude of me to leave him alone like that.

When I walked up the path, I saw a note on the gate. Hummm…he had gotten a ride home. I took the note, opening it carefully against the breeze which had sprung up. Two words "Happy Birthday."

I stood there quietly for a moment. It was my birthday, and I'd forgotten. How funny was that?

I caught a flash of white coming in my direction, which meant Seaweed was out. I scooped her up and walked into the garden area. There I stopped dead in my tracks.

Where I had stood before, making a mental list of lawn furniture to purchase, were chairs, benches, tables, a fire pit, and more. I must be hallucinating.

Ben walked around the porch and called down, "How'd I do? What did I forget? Do you like it, partner? Happy Birthday! Dinner party at Eric's house tonight begins at six."

Life would never get any better than right that second, *ever*.

Thirty

The winds of evil were blowing again like a deadly gale of monstrous proportions... how quickly things change.

How can a phone call wreck your life? One minute the sun is out, life on the rock-bound coast of Maine is great, there isn't any danger, and the next... your property is under surveillance, and invaded by strangers with bad intent carrying weapons.

Would I be able to live through this situation? I survived the last one, but this one was different.

Last time I didn't know what they thought I knew; this time I do and I'm not going to tell. I no longer know who the enemy is or who to trust. I'm not at all sure if I ever really did know.

I'd received a phone call from my sister, Kate, in Virginia who's involved with a shelter for battered women. She asked me if I would be willing to shelter a severe case. She'd never asked before. I could tell from her short, stilted conversation, this was extreme.

Because I have always been a very private, independent person, my sister only knew I'd moved to this remote location over a year ago, the home was on the ocean, and I liked it. This, in my opinion, was *all* she needed to know.

I had zero intention of sharing with her, or anyone else, including my children, what had happened to me during that time span.

How did you tell someone, "Oh by the way, I've been shot at, killed a man, had my house invaded with the law, the Feds, DEA and most everyone else with a badge. There have been agencies with titles only pronounced in acronyms.

"Then the house got blown up, and, oh yes, they blew up the Jeep too. But, not to worry, the dogs and I are okay.

Sounded flippant even to me and I might also add, even in recounting it here, it still scares the living hell out of me.

Because it appeared to be an extreme situation, I agreed to shelter the woman until she recovered. I was completely unprepared for the extent of damages done to her.

I knew about spousal abuse. I'd been there. Thankfully, I survived to walk away and smart enough to keep walking. It's the most demeaning thing that can happen to anyone, female or male and next to child abuse, it is high on my *hate list*.

I believed in paying it back as well as forward, so I agreed to help. After the fracas of the last year, my life seemed great, so I could share for a couple of weeks.

Dena arrived late at night in a large black truck. It blended so well into the local traffic, what little there was, it was seemingly not noticeable. That's the advantage of living in a small, Down East, mostly unnoticed and forgotten, town in coastal Maine.

When they drove into my long, winding driveway, my gate alarm and monitor let me know they'd arrived. The driver was trying to assist her. I witnessed it wasn't working. I stepped to the side of the truck and introduced myself. "Hello, I'm going to be your hostess. Could I assist you in some way?"

The poor driver just shook his head and scooped her into a bundle. I led the way to the entry door, holding it open so they could enter. I motioned him to a large recliner in the open living room. He gently placed her onto the chair while carefully re-wrapping the blanket around her. I tilted the chair back to give her more comfort. She uttered a stifled moan.

The driver passed me a packet of papers, leaned over and said a quiet goodbye and good luck to her, then left.

I stayed close to home after Dena's arrival because she was so battered. I didn't know medically or mentally how stable she was. Her first day with me, she stayed in the chair without stirring. I did get her to drink small sips of a power shake I prepared and some water. This woman was critically ill. I tried talking to her about having the doctor come to check her, knowing he would make a house call for me.

She was adamant, or as adamant as a mostly dead person could be. She became so agitated I didn't bring it up again. However, I resolved if the next day didn't bring marked improvement, I would call the doctor. If necessary, I'd transport her to an emergency room.

Later in the day, she roused herself enough to inquire about security. I assured her I had state-of-the-art security along with the backup of my neighbors just up the road. I explained they were a phone call away.

I wouldn't explain Kate's background or our relationship…all I knew was when they moved battered women from one safe place to another, none of the stops was discussed with anyone. I respected that. I had been certain this would be a short-term placement. Now, I wasn't sure it would be.

Over the years, folks had been kind and helpful to me. I felt this was payback.

I wanted Dena to know if someone came to the house, she'd be safe. I also knew by keeping a normal schedule it wouldn't raise any flags. The fact I hadn't been to the shop for a couple of days would soon bring either phone calls or a drop-in from either Ben or Eric.

Thirty-one

Eric arrived in the early morning with a guest…the most magnificent Rottweiler I'd ever laid eyes on. He was big, even for a Rottie, with a head like a bear. He was walking off leash in perfect step with Eric. I noticed there was a small hitch in his step. On closer inspection, I saw part of his ear was missing. As always with a Rottie, he had a big grin on his face.

Eric walked up to me as I was standing in the garden with Shadow. I'd been admiring the plants, which seemed to be thriving in spite of the rugged coastal weather in this area of Maine.

He stopped just a few feet away. The dog sat, seemingly without any command from Eric. "Eileen, I want you to meet your new best friend. This is Bruno. Bruno, say hello, please."

The large dog stood, walked forward, sat in front of me and extended his paw as if introducing himself.

With the human introductions completed, Bruno turned his attention to Shadow, who was sitting by my side, quietly assessing the situation. Shadow is small for a Rottie. Bruno was more than twice her size. I would guess he weighed well over a hundred pounds. He was a *big dog*.

Bruno made eye contact with Shadow and in the language only dogs knew and appreciated, they decided they liked each other. Both stood at the same time, stepping forward to touch noses then completed the sniff-test and then moved to the washing of faces. Without a sound from either of them, they laid down side by side at my feet.

Speaking softly Eric said, "He's a great guy…saved my life during a scuffle. He was shot and pretty badly injured. When he recovered, I was able to keep him. He's only been out of rehab for about a week. In time, I think he'll recover all of his range of motion in his rear quarter. The ear won't grow back, but being a guy, he wouldn't hear of plastic surgery."

I had to laugh. Eric possessed the same dry humor as his dad. I so enjoy them. I literally owe them my life.

Out of the corner of my eye, I saw a slight flurry of fur coming up from the porch area. It was poor old Seaweed.

She was so old she preferred the porch, with a spot of sunshine and not too much activity. When she saw Bruno, she stopped dead in her tracks. I needed to encourage her. "Come, it'll be okay, girl, meet our guest. This is Bruno." She came forward slowly, never taking her eyes off the other dog. Bruno didn't move. Seaweed ventured forward while she sniffed the air.

Shadow gave her a low woof, encouraging her as she completed the last few paces. She smelled Bruno's head, turned her head slightly, and licked his cheek. With all of the regal airs of a queen, she placed herself between the two dogs and lay down.

I surmised the meet-and-greet went well.

My home had always maintained an open door policy for Ben and Eric. After what we'd endured, we were as close to family as one could get.

I heard the small bell I'd given Dena to summon me so I turned and started for the porch at a run. I never gave Eric a thought. I was only concerned about Dena. In all of the time since her arrival, this was the first time she'd rung the bell. I was somewhat alarmed as to what the problem might be.

I hit the porch almost at a run with the entourage of Eric and dogs in tow. I opened the front door and hurled through to find Dena on the floor on her face. She must have been trying to get out of the chair. She'd either fallen or tripped on the blanket she always kept wrapped around her. Somehow, she'd managed to hang onto the bell. When it hit the floor, it rolled and rang.

She was moaning. I got down on my knees to see how I could help her. Eric took in the scene in one heartbeat then looked at me out of the corner of his eye with a quizzical look. I carefully put my hand on her shoulder, leaned close to her ear and whispered, "Dena, can you hear me? If so, nod your head." A slight nod…this was good. "Someone is here with me and we're going to sit you back in the chair. It'll be all right; just relax." I tried to wrap the blanket around her to cushion the contact of the lift.

Eric assisted in the wrapping with skilled hands, then in one swoop picked her up and gently placed her in the recliner I'd put back into a more prone position.

I knew the extent of some of her injuries, but not all. I knew it was extremely painful even for a carefully executed movement. Her pain became evident by the moan she emitted, even though she suppressed it. Once we had her laid back, I moved the blanket away from her face so she could breathe.

I certainly was not, nor could I have been, prepared for anything which happened next. She opened her still swollen and blackened eyes slightly and saw Eric at the same time I stepped away from the arm of the chair and he saw her.

I read people really well. I was thunder-struck. I don't know how... but they knew each other. I mean they *KNEW* each other.

Dena gasped and fainted dead away.

Eric bolted out of the door.

As I was trying to help her recover, I heard Eric driving out of the parking area squealing his tires. He *never* acted like this. He had always been my rock. What was going on?

When Dena finally came around, she wouldn't say a word.

It was as if it never happened. Something was strange. I needed to get this straightened out immediately.

Ben called me a few minutes later, frantic. I have never heard Ben frantic. What was happening to my friends?

"Eileen, you have to come quickly. Something's wrong with Eric. I think he's having some sort of psychotic break or something. I can't reach him at all. Please come, I beg you."

What in the devil was happening? I couldn't leave her alone, but I knew I had to go to Ben and Eric.

I called Animal, my other good and trusted friend. "Animal, I have a problem. How fast can you get here? I have a woman staying with me and I need you to make certain no one shows up. My dogs and another big Rottie will be in the house with her. I need to go to Ben's place at once. There's a serious problem. Can you do that?"

I knew what he would say and I would trust him with my life; I already had.

As soon as Animal arrived I flew to Ben's shop, noticing both of the cars were at Eric's place. I slid to a stop and dashed into the house. I cannot describe the scene when I entered. Ben was trying to stay calm and Eric was hell bent on destroying the place.

I spoke very quietly and calmly. "Eric, talk to me and tell me what hurt you so badly. Why are you so devastated? Please, come here and talk to me."

He went from being a wild beast to a child in front of my eyes. I took his hand and walked him into the destroyed living room. I sat him on the sofa.

Eric is a big man, like his dad. He's tall and well developed muscularly. Sitting beside him, I felt like a tiny person.

Eric sat with his head down and his hands hanging loosely between his knees. I put my arm behind his back and just stroked his shoulders gently, as you would a child. He began to sob as if his heart and soul were in the process of being ripped from his very being by the devil himself. I said nothing, just continued to stroke him.

Finally, he spoke from somewhere deep inside himself. "They told me she was dead. They *lied* to me."

He'd said all he was going to, or could say.

I was sure, so I asked quietly, "How well do you know Dena?"

He turned his head to me with tears still on his cheeks. His eyes carried a haunted look; perhaps they'd seen straight into the bowels of hell.

When he spoke, his voice was ragged with emotion. "Her name is Victoria. We always joked her name suited her because I always called her 'Tricky Vicky.' She was my partner in Special Ops for a while. They were concerned we were getting too involved with each other. There'd been talk of splitting us up. We decided we would retire from the service and live our lives together.

"On the last mission, we got into some really tough shit. I was shot and roughed up pretty badly. They were going to take after her when Bruno got into the fight. I thought she got away, but they told me she died, died a hero, but was dead. I never heard from her again. Why is she with you? What happened to her?"

I tried to keep my voice even while I stood and took him by the hand. "Eric, you need to come with me right now. We both need answers. I didn't want to leave her alone. Animal is watching the house for me."

Poor Ben…he'd been standing there like a statue, listening to Eric's statement. I was certain he knew nothing about any of this. I didn't know whether to ask him to come with us or to allow Eric some private time with Dena/Vicky.

In the end, Ben just nodded. His nod implied *I trust you to do what is right. I'll wait here. Call me if you need me.*

When I arrived back at my place, I could see Animal was guarding the property. One of his favorite big, make that *massive*, pit bulls was sitting at the end of my drive just daring anyone to pass.

In spite of all the problems, I had to smile. Rolling down the window, I spoke to Zeus. "Hello, it's okay, boy." He moved to the side of the drive, returning to his guard position as soon as I passed. At the house, Animal opened the door as soon as I entered the parking area, but didn't come out. Damn, I'd never seen him with a weapon. Usually just the sight of him would demand compliance, but today he had a stainless .45 caliber automatic pistol in his hand.

Eric looked like a man in a walking coma. His eyes were open and I knew he could hear me, but I also understood he was in shock. Nothing was registering with him. I wondered if this would be too much for him. This was way out of my skill set.

I'd brought him there, so I would just go with my gut and let it play out. Good, bad or indifferent...we were going to discover some truth for both of them.

I parked, walked around the car, and opened the door for Eric. He made no move to get out or even look at me. I held out my hand to him. "Eric, come. I'm with you. It'll be okay. Remember, you're not the only person who's in shock and most likely scared to death. You need to be strong to help her."

Lord, I prayed it was the right thing to say. It must have been, because I could see an immediate change come over Eric. He straightened his spine, set his shoulders back, and stepped out of the car. He nodded to me, so like his dad; I knew he could do this.

I didn't know Dena at all. She was the unknown factor in this situation. I was certain in a short time I would know a lot more than I should.

Bruno, Shadow, and Seaweed were all guarding Dena. What a strange sight. Dogs know so much more than humans do. They can sense a situation even before it happens.

Dena remained in the chair where I'd left her, wrapped in the blanket. Her eyes were as open as she could get them, considering the bruising and swelling. She didn't appear anxious at all. Knowing her background and training, I was not surprised, even under these extreme conditions.

Animal assured me she'd been fine while I was gone, even though she hadn't uttered a word.

He glanced at Eric, nodded, and then told me to call anytime if I needed him, for anything. I knew he meant it, in every sense of the word.

I moved a chair over to where Dena was so Eric could sit and talk privately with her. He shook his head, "No."

I was confused. Didn't he want to talk with her? I indicated I would be in the kitchen if they needed me. Again, I got the headshake, "No."

"Eric, please tell me what I can do to assist you and Dena."

His answer floored me. "Please sit here with us for a little while. We both need a good, honest, caring person to help us through this. You've always been a rock to me with the most common sense of anyone I know next to my dad. Please, sit."

I sat. I could only guess at the turmoil going on in their minds. I'd encountered some really odd things in my many years. However, I'd never had a person or persons return from the dead, especially someone I loved and cared about.

Neither of them spoke. It appeared it was almost too painful for them to look at each other. I wondered would the hurt they both had endured over the original loss be so traumatic they'd feel it was too risky to go there again. Time would tell. We would just sit and wait.

Finally, Eric lifted his head. After what seemed to me a tough mental argument with himself, he spoke quietly. "Vicky, what happened to you? Who did this to you? How did you get here? Are you still with the unit?"

There was no reply. Nothing changed in her expression or position, with the exception of her eyes. I saw an instant flash of fear, and then what I thought was frustration. I didn't know anything about her so it was all guesswork. Her eyes closed. I thought she'd drifted off again. Eric stayed silent and just sat, watched and waited. He gave me the impression he would remain this way for a thousand years, if necessary.

It took less time than I thought. Vicky seemed to be trying to sit up straighter or just get into a more comfortable position. Then she opened her bloodied eyes and spoke.

Her voice was husky and low, whether from the trauma she had withstood or naturally, I had no way of knowing. "I need to get away from here fast... you'll all be in imminent danger when they find me. I thought I was okay before in a government safe-house; I was ratted out. For the moment, they think I'm dead. It won't take them long to find out I'm not. They'll come and kill all of us.

"I left the unit when they told me you were dead. I couldn't do it anymore. I took leave, did R & R. My heart was dead, so I quit. After the last mission we were on, when they finished with you, they attacked me and nearly killed me.

"If Les hadn't shot one of them, I wouldn't have gotten away. In the process of trying to save us, he was injured. I never saw him again so I don't know what happened. I knew you were dead; they told me Bruno was dead because he'd been hit trying to protect us. I was too hurt physically and mentally to go any further."

I don't know how, but Vicky continued to speak. "I hid in the cabin and healed most of the physical stuff, but I was done. When I tried to go back to being a civilian, they caught up with me. The chief put me in three safe-houses and each time they found me. There's a mole deep in the department; I know this.

"This last time I escaped on my own. I landed in a battered women's shelter; they thought my partner did this to me. I never told them differently. Because of the injuries and the fact I wouldn't get medical attention, the person who picked me up off the street became my guardian angel.

"She's one tough gal. I could only tell her this wasn't the first time and they would find me and kill me. She arranged to get me here. What happened to you?"

Tears were streaming down Eric's face and my heart broke for both of them. When Eric composed himself, he spoke in a very quiet, calming voice.

"When I finally got well enough, I came home and stayed till I could physically handle the job again. I was so devastated mentally about losing you I was trying to drink myself into a fog all the time. They sent me off to a 'soft' assignment, hoping I'd pull myself together.

"I met a woman who had a couple of children. The kids and I hit it off great; it helped some. Thinking it was the right thing to do, I asked her to marry me and came home to live. It was a great place for the kids. She came, but the truth is she spent more time gone than here, leaving the kids for weeks on end before she'd return. I didn't care. I liked the kids, but her, not so much.

"Occasionally I'd get a call for service from command and would be away for a short while. Never long.

"Last year we had a free-for-all here which involved Eileen. Before we knew it, we were in the middle of an all-out firefight.

"Belle and the kids were away. For their safety I wanted them gone until the problem here was over. While she was gone, she divorced me and disappeared. I was relieved it was over, but I missed the kids."

Eric regrouped and continued. "I went once and checked the cabin. I had such a strong feeling you'd been there I hated to leave. I told myself mentally I wanted you to be alive and there. I was playing head games with myself, so I left."

They sat staring quietly at each other as if to take their eyes away, even for a second, would cause each one of them to disappear again. I moved slowly and quietly and left the room.

I retreated to my office, and called Ben. "What's going on? Should I come? Do you need help?"

How like Ben. I was quick to assure him everything was under control and Eric was doing fine.

I didn't want to concern Ben nor did I feel it was my place to explain the unfolding situation. I was certain Eric would include his dad shortly, once he got his mind wrapped around what happened.

I prayed the shock wouldn't be too much for either Eric or Vicky. I told Ben I would call him in a little while and rang off.

Thirty-two

When I returned to the living room, it was empty. Dear Lord, where are they? I prayed they were safe.

Seaweed was asleep on the couch and both Shadow and Bruno were among the missing.

I ran to the door and out onto the patio… nobody... the garden area... nobody either. With my stomach churning, I ran to the porch, which circled the three sides of the house, allowing a great view of the cove, rocks, and the water.

I saw a flicker of movement down in the rocks. I bounded off the porch and over the wild grass to the beginning of the boulders. I'd reached the crest of the ledge when I looked down just as Eric, with Vicky in his arms, scooted toward the cave.

Those same rocks had saved my life and the dogs' during last year's episode.

I'm not a paranoid person. However, after the riot here last time and considering what I'd just heard from Vicky, there might be others looking on as well. I wasn't certain we weren't being watched.

I knew where they were…the dogs were with them, and I left them alone.

I was returning to the front porch when I heard the drive alarm sound. It was a very subtle, natural sound. Unless you were familiar with the sound, you'd never hear it.

I was concerned because Shadow wasn't there with me. She'd saved me so many times I felt naked. That thought came and went in a half second, and then I felt her soft nose in my hand… she was there I relaxed in my relief; she understood.

The car that drove into the yard was an ordinary sedan, but not anyone I knew. I walked slowly forward as the driver opened his door and stepped out. I didn't recognize this person at all.

Shadow blocked as he walked around the front of the car. She made no effort to move, staying firmly at my side.

The man lurched toward me with an uneven gait, appearing to be in pain with every step. He was within six feet of me. Shadow hadn't moved. He hadn't uttered a word.

I wished I had my weapon, but it was too late.

He took one more halting step and seemed as though he were trying to catch his breath as he leaned over.

He spoke very distinctly and softly. "The Fuller Brush man sent this…he said to use it now. He'll be in touch soon."

He handed me a bag with carrot greens sticking out of the top and turned to leave.

I was certain this man was Animal in the oddest get-up I'd ever seen.

Before I could say a word, he was in the car and driving slowly away. I couldn't make out the plate on the auto.

Why? *Here we go again* was my only thought.

The reference to the Fuller Brush man was from last year's run-in with the Feds, all kinds and ranks of them. When it was finally over, the person in charge was Les.

When he'd left, he told me if he needed to return for any reason, he would be the Fuller Brush salesperson.

We had laughed then. I wasn't laughing now.

I took the bag of carrots into the house to the corner of the kitchen where I knew nobody from outside could see in.

I reached into the bag. There were in fact, carrots. At the bottom was a small, oblong, battery device like the one you'd use to scan an animal for an information chip. The type that would be surgically implanted for identification and medical information purposes.

The next problem would be how to get this device and the information to Eric. I needed to do this without our current surveillance situation seeing me.

I already knew we were being monitored; why else would Animal arrive in character?

I called Shadow to my side. I had an idea. I prayed it would work. I took one of her old large balls we play with outside, cut a slit, and inserted the scanner along with a note. I asked Eric about food, meds and if he needed assistance. I also added the information from the Fuller Brush man. I briefed him regarding Animal's assistance in a get-up no one would expect him to use.

The next step was to see if my plan would work.

I took the taped ball and Shadow through the garden area. We stood on top of the large granite ledge, which stood barren and exposed to the coastal winds and weather.

I tossed the ball into the air as if to play. Shadow watched intently, never taking her eyes off the prized ball. I tossed the ball to her and true to form, she caught it in midair.

I patted her head and spoke very softly to her. "Give. I want you to fetch, then take the ball to Eric."

I had her attention, but was unsure if it was too lengthy or complicated a message for her to understand.

Taking a leap of faith, I tossed the ball toward the rocks outside of the garden. I aimed it toward the entrance of the cave.

Shadow bounded off after the ball, almost catching it on the first feeble bounce. She then chased it as it rolled and bounced over the boulders. She disappeared from my sight. I walked out onto the rocks looking for her. I was hoping she had grabbed the ball and gone into the cave.

She reappeared with the ball in her mouth and a happy expression in her big brown eyes. I was sure it'd been a failed attempt. I took the ball, patted her head, and repeated my command that she fetch and take the ball to Eric.

She looked puzzled but ready to play, so I tossed it as hard as I could in the direction of the cave. I was certain she knew where Eric was. I was sure he'd gone into the cave.

I began to worry...perhaps he had forgotten about the cave with the passing of time.

Perhaps he'd called Ben and moved Vicky by boat. I didn't know. I also wasn't willing to give away the location of the cave in case I needed it later, as I had before, for hiding.

This time I could see Shadow looking like she was hunting for the ball, then bounce back out of my line of sight only to pop up again on a distant rock and drop back out of sight again. Then I couldn't see her. She was gone for a long time. At least it seemed like a long time to me. When she bounced up over the rocks at the end of the garden, she had a look of, *I found him*, written all over her face.

I recovered the ball from her, ruffled her ears, and then we walked slowly back into the house.

I discovered Eric had opened the ball; it was also lighter, indicating the device was gone.

I opened the slit and removed the note I had sent. Eric had written on the back. "Shit! All OK! Keep me posted, working on a plan."

It was time for me to call Ben. No! I needed to go to the shop.

I didn't know how long they'd been watching my house. Had they seen Eric come and go, and then come back with me? Had they seen him leave with Vicky? Had they seen Animal here before to watch Vicky? Had they seen the carrot delivery? My mind was rife with questions I had no answers to.

I knew I needed to be careful. I didn't want to give them any additional information. It meant no cell calls or e-mails. I was sure they were monitoring the whole situation.

Not for the first time I wondered how I got myself into these messes. All I wanted was to have a quiet life here on the coast, painting, sailing and working with Ben on the boat designs and sales.

That was it!

I called Ben on his cell. When he answered, I began the conversation with a terse tone, without giving him a moment to speak, "We have a problem with the advertising design on the new prototype. It won't work and we need to discuss it at once or we'll be in a crisis if this hits the market, on air, or e-mail. Sorry to dump this on you, but we need to iron this out right now before you post anything, anywhere. Do you understand?"

Blessed be! Ben got it. That was evident in his quick response, "Gee, I'm sorry, I was sure the bugs were worked out on our campaign. I must have missed an important part of it somewhere. I'll bring the copy and come right over as soon as I shut everything down here."

Thirty-three

I loved these two people. They'd put their lives on the line more than once for me during the scuffle here last year. I never thought we would be back at it again.

Had I brought them more trouble? I hoped and prayed not.

Ben arrived almost before I got the phone turned off. He strode to the door, entering without knocking as was our usual pattern.

I motioned with a finger to my lips for silence. Although he looked stunned, he said nothing.

His face saddened and showed his anxiety. I could understand that.

"Good morning, Ben, we have to revise this copy for the advertising. I've jotted down some ideas. If you'll take a look at them and add your comments, I think we can fix this before any damage gets done." With that said, I headed for the office while I passed Ben a note I'd written. It described some of what was happening, where Eric was and why he left without talking to Ben.

After a moment with some shuffling of the papers in his hand, Ben spoke haltingly, "Well I can see your concern about the wording in the copy. It could leave the wrong impression and we don't want any issues. I like some of your new wording. However, I'm not sure it gives enough information so they'll understand the complexities of the craft. Can you come to the shop where we can flesh it out a little more? Are you tied up here?"

I knew what he was asking, because at the shop we could use Eric's safe room. There we could talk without any electronic eavesdropping, no matter how sophisticated.

I wondered how I was going to pull it off without giving whoever was doing the snooping a clue that Vicky was not in the house. "Let me call and see if I can get someone to come and sit with my guest while I'm gone. She may need something while I'm away and certainly Shadow can't supply that."

I didn't want to call Animal again for fear he'd get too involved in a harmful situation.

When the gate alarm sounded, it saved me; someone was coming down the drive as we spoke. I wasn't expecting anyone and I seldom had any drop-ins.

As the vehicle got closer, I recognized the sound of the engine. The driver was Dan, one of the workers from the yard. He was driving his monster truck, which was his pride and joy.

How he ever kept the thing on the road was a mystery to me.

He parked and bounded up the walk to the door. "Hi Dan, good to see you, come on in."

He was about to speak when Ben shook his head to silence him. I continued to address him. "Dan, I have a guest who's resting in her room, and I need to run to the shop to see to some paperwork. Could you just sit here for a few minutes until I get back? I doubt she'll need anything. I don't want to leave her alone in case she does want something.

"Have a seat and raid the refrigerator if you want to. I won't be long. I'll leave Shadow with you. I have my phone in case you need me."

Ben had been writing on a tablet all the time I'd been speaking. He passed the pad to Dan with a sign for silence.

Dan looked up at Ben, nodded, and wrote on the pad, "Damn, not again?"

The look on Ben's face said it all.

We walked to the parking area and I indicated I would take my car so I could return without interfering with Ben.

As we drove off, I prayed whoever was watching the house would not mess with Dan.

I needed to hurry. When we got to the shop, we went directly to the safe room so we could talk.

I gave Ben a rundown of what I knew, where Eric and Vicky were, and how I'd communicated with them.

I also informed him about the carrot delivery with the scanner in the bag.

As I watched, Ben aged before my eyes. I felt such deep sorrow for him. I almost felt compelled to put my arms around him, as a shelter from the hurt and angst that I knew was coming.

When we were beginning to enjoy some quiet and productive time with everyone feeling safe, I had brought trouble again. As before, I had no clue as to why, or what I'd brought.

Could it be worse than the last time? Lord, please, no. We had all nearly died in the melee.

I spoke simply and carefully. "We need to get them out of the cave to a safe location. I don't know what's safe anymore. What do you think, Ben? Who can we trust?"

We stood looking at each other like two lost souls. We also knew whatever it would take, we *would* do it.

"Ben, I'm going to see if I can get another message to Eric with the ball. If I get a reply, I'll contact you by phone without telling you anything. Will that work for you?"

Ben's nod of approval was hesitant, indicating he would prefer to be on the front line. I just didn't know how else to make this work without giving Eric and Vicky away.

We walked into the shop and chatted about the layouts from the photo shoots and the trial runs. Then I left for home.

Arriving back at the house, Dan informed me there had been telephone calls. He told me someone had left messages on my machine. He'd not listened nor answered the phone.

I thanked him and asked after my guest. He quickly stated he hadn't heard her stir, although he worried the ringing of the phone might have awakened her. I assured him I would check and thanked him again for his assistance.

After Dan left, I checked the answering machine and set the lock on the gate. I didn't recognize either of the numbers displayed on the caller ID. One message stated they were selling some product. I deleted it.

The second call was Animal telling me he needed to come and service my street rod. He'd call me later. I knew there was a hidden message, but I didn't know what. With all the care the street rod received, we serviced and coddled it as if it were a baby.

I called Animal back. I knew he'd been waiting for my call.

"Hi there, I got your message; sorry I was at the shop talking with Ben about our campaign. What's up?"

His answer floored me. "I have a recall on a part in the engine. It's a real problem. This thing could blow at any time. This *is* serious and needs instant attention. I'll come over and see if I can replace it there. I may need to move it back here to the garage. Will you be home? I may need Ben to help me move it because we can't start it without damaging the engine. I'll be there shortly. Okay?" With that, he rang off.

He knew something I didn't. Whatever it was, he felt it was very important.

I scribbled a note to Eric, stuck it into the dog-delivery-ball, and took Shadow and Seaweed out to *play*. I knew the first time had been pure luck and just prayed I could do it again.

First toss, Shadow bounded after it down through the rocks and returned at once with the ball in her mouth. I tossed it again and

Seaweed tried to give chase but had to quit. She was just getting too old for a workout.

Shadow returned with the ball. I gave her a 'good girl' and a pat. This time I told her to take it to Eric, then threw it hard in the direction of the cave.

She was gone longer, but when I took the ball, the tape was still secure and in the same place as I'd marked it. I began to worry it might not work this time. I tried again and off she went in hot pursuit. When I was beginning to wonder if she'd lost it in the rocks, I heard a mighty roar and growling…this was not good. It was Shadow alerting me someone was nearby who shouldn't be.

When this first began, with Eric and Vicky disappearing, I started carrying my .38 Detective Special. I reached for it and started over the rocks toward the noise.

Sitting on a rock just at the edge of the scrub woods was a man with a pair of field glasses around his neck.

The property is not only fenced and alarmed, it's clearly marked and posted against hunting animals and people, for a damn good reason. If people are within my area, they have more to fear from me than they do anything on the other side of the fence. I shoot first and ask questions after. If they're still able to answer, that's good; if not, too bad for them.

I walked up the rocks toward this person just as Shadow got within striking distance of him. I noticed she didn't have the ball in her mouth. Where was it?

The man stood with the field glasses in one hand and his other hand in the pocket of his shorts.

"Get both hands where I can see them, *NOW*! Who are you and why are you trespassing?" I already had the .38 out, cocked, and pointed.

He threw both hands into the air with a look of mock horror on his face. He was about his mid-thirties, too athletic and honed to be trying to play this part.

Shadow wasn't buying him either…she was blocked with the hair on her neck and back standing straight up. She'd saved me so many times I never doubted her instincts.

I pulled out my cell and called the local sheriff. The man began to shift his weight slightly. His reward was a toothy snarl from Shadow, along with the changing of my aim with the revolver. He froze.

I relayed the information to the sheriff, who assured me he was on his way and for me to stay put, and to only shoot him a little, and only if necessary.

The last statement was a direct reference to the fact the last time when a person was trespassing, I shot him dead after he shot at me.

I must admit it did create a firestorm down here on the coast when it all unfolded. I'd certainly succeeded in making a lasting legacy for myself. When I called the law these days, they responded in a *real* no-nonsense way.

I could hear the siren wailing as the police car approached. A good sound for me; however, it seemed not so good for this man. He was trying to decide what to do. He had two choices: me with a gun and the dog, or the police. Too late, he made the choice to run. As he spun around, Shadow grabbed his leg, sending him sprawling to the ground. All he could do was bellow in pain.

Larry, the Local Law, as I liked to call him, was making fast tracks over the rocks, gun in hand. I gave Shadow the command to release and she sat shaking her head as if he hadn't tasted very good. Other than a couple of minute puncture wounds on his leg, he seemed fine.

I didn't give a damn.

The officer wasted no time in cuffing him and dragging him off to the squad car. I told the deputy I had no idea who or what he was but needed some serious research on both state and Fed databases. The officer looked like he had the catch of a lifetime when he left the yard with the man secured in his back seat.

Larry had a great big German Shepherd who rode with him in the front seat. Her name was Greta the Great. Don't ask; I don't know. She never appeared to be very friendly.

I called Shadow and commanded her to find the ball. She retraced her path from before and worked back and forth until she found it. Tape still in place. I tossed it again toward the cave and told her to take it to Eric.

Not expecting much success, I waited.

When she returned with the ball in her mouth, I could see the tape had moved. We returned to the house while playing by tossing the ball in the air. Once inside I tore off the tape. Eric had inserted a note of his own.

Thirty-four

He had used the scanner and found a chip in Vicky. Somebody had inserted it into the head wound some time ago. Eric had removed it. He didn't say how and I really didn't want to know.

He needed his dad to bring the electric Zodiac to the base of the rocks tonight at dark. He had a plan and knew where they could go to be safe. He also needed him to bring scuba gear for two and full tanks. He also had a plan about what to do with the chip.

He needed us to throw in some of the survival food and gear from the safe room.

As always, a hastily scratched, "Thanks."

Eric then had a quick question, regarding who Larry had taken into custody and why.

That info I couldn't give him because I didn't know yet. I hoped Larry wouldn't just release the man without letting me know. Because of his involvement in some of the problems last year, I doubted he would just set him free without notifying me.

The driveway alarm went off again. For a quiet back road area, I had more traffic than a main highway, or so it seemed. This time I knew by the engine sounds it was Animal.

I walked out to meet him with Shadow on my heels. He wasn't alone. I was surprised and alarmed. He is the quintessential loaner...was he forced to come here? I was relieved I was armed. I really was getting too old for this lifestyle; however, I was here and this was it, at least for the moment.

Animal got out of his truck and the other person opened his door and was standing by the side of the truck waiting. Animal reached into the bed of the truck and pulled out a large toolbox, setting it on the ground. I walked forward and Shadow didn't alert, so I spoke with Animal quietly. "What's wrong with the rod and what makes it so dangerous?" Animal was fishing in the toolbox for something. Without glancing at me, he passed me a folded sheet of paper with a considerable amount of print on it.

At the top in bold black letters were the words, "RECALL NOTICE." I opened the sheet and began to scan the print... my hair stood on end, my gut clenched and I thought I would heave right there and then in front of these two.

In essence, the paper outlined some of what I already knew about the chip, as well as Vicky and Eric's stories, and what was happening to catch them and silence both of them.

It seemed someone in the organization thought one or both knew something which could jeopardize either them, or the organization's, standings.

There was, according to this copy, only one alternative. They both needed to be silenced…immediately.

Nothing was to be off the table in order for it to happen and the fact they could get them both at once was a bonus.

I was shaking all over. I tried to pass the sheet back to Animal but he replied with, "That's your copy of the recall notice. I'm sorry this happened. I've never had a problem with this product before. Oh, excuse my poor manners; he's the factory rep who's here to check it out."

When I turned to meet the rep, I knew the man. He looked very different from the last time I'd talked with him. Even with glasses having a slight tint, different hair, and his body looking bulkier than before, I knew it was Les, aka the Fuller Brush Man. I didn't know if I should be excited or terrified. I opted for terror. Unless the world were ending immediately, this person wouldn't show up.

Animal said in a gruff voice, "Well, let's not stand around here all damn day. I've got work to do." He picked up his box and headed for the garage bay where the rod sat in its spot.

They tinkered around under the hood for a bit then came back to me with sad faces. "I don't have to take the car with me today, but you can't use it until I get the replacement part. It could be a week or more before it shows up."

I thought I should at least let them know Larry had taken a man off the property a few minutes prior to their arrival. "Animal, did you guys meet Larry on the road when you came out? He removed a person from my property immediately before you arrived. Life in the Cove hasn't been as tranquil as it should be."

I could tell from the looks they exchanged they hadn't met Larry and were more than a little concerned about my comment.

Damn, it would be nice if we could have a conversation and clear this mess up for the last time.

"How's your guest doing with all this excitement"? Animal inquired while the 'rep' was busy writing his report.

"I think she's doing okay and will improve greatly once I can get her outside and breathing this fresh salt air. That can cure most anything, as you well know."

The 'rep' handed Animal the sheet he'd been writing on while we were talking. After a quick scan, Animal handed it to me. It simply read, "Working on a plan...can you keep them safe for a bit...if not, shake your head, say no and give it back to him."

I didn't want to give Eric away and I didn't trust anyone, even Les. Without more knowledge, I was wondering what to do.

Of the whole group, Eric was the one I trusted the most. I said, "I guess I'll have to live with the recall notice and trust you can get it fixed shortly. Thanks for trying. I won't touch the hot-rod until you return with the parts. I appreciate your help and the warning, because I would've been using it.

"As you well know, I love to drive it sometimes…even speeding. I'll try to act my age for a few days. Good luck with getting it fixed."

They returned to the truck and drove away. I wasn't relieved Les had been here; this was bad, *even worse than I thought.*

I didn't think I should try to get another message to Eric. I was sure he knew how serious this was. I needed to get to Ben with the latest instructions from Eric.

I left Shadow in the house with Seaweed, reluctantly set all of the alarms, and tore to Ben's workshop.

I passed him the sheet I'd received and the handwritten note from Eric outlining what he wanted.

To keep our cover, I promised him I would have his copy changes in the morning. I also told him about Animal, the factory rep, and the hot-rod, then returned home.

When I got home, as always, I closed the security gate at the entrance of the driveway. The only way to open it was by me releasing it from the house with my remote or with the special code the emergency folks, Ben, Eric, Animal and I had. All seemed to be peaceful when I arrived.

As the afternoon wore on, the usual fog bank began to roll in across the water. I loved living on the ocean; however, this time of the year, each afternoon it seemed we got a heavy, damp fog. It was great for the gardens and for cooling things off, but it cut the visibility to almost zero, so you have to plan when you are sailing around it.

As darkness approached, the fog thickened. So did my anxiety. I wasn't sure when Ben would be here, or if Eric could get down to the boat with Vicky without scrutiny.

I'd taken Shadow out several times during the late afternoon. She hadn't alerted. Based on her demeanor, I didn't think anyone was prowling about in the tree line.

I also knew that, with night vision/thermal imaging gear, I was certain they could spot someone no matter how well hidden the person was.

I was more concerned about the safety of everyone I knew. I didn't need or want to have a repeat of the upset of last year. I'd lost my home along with everything in and around it with the exception of my sailboat, *Survivor*, and my dogs. Old memories die hard…they just don't stop.

Strange word, I mused, *upset*. More like World War III and then some.

On my last walk with Shadow and Seaweed, when I turned from the garden on the ledge, Shadow bumped my hand with her muzzle; taking my fingers into her mouth. This was something she'd done since a pup when she wanted me to follow her.

Strangely, she didn't release my fingers, and just kept walking toward the cove. I plodded along with her as Seaweed followed at a slower pace. We walked down to my sitting rock at the edge of the cove.

This was my place where I often sat and either drank my early morning coffee or in the evening sipped a glass of wine while reflecting on my day. It was a large rounded boulder with a space carved out by waves and weather over the years, leaving a pleasant seat.

Even in the fog and the darkness, it was comforting to sit there and listen to the water softly brush against the shore. There wasn't any wind and, other than the soft lap of water, there were no other noises.

We sat like three statues for a short time. Shadow leaned her shoulder into mine looking toward the water offshore. I moved my head just enough to follow her sight line. I'd been there long enough so my eyes had acclimated to the light and shadow. I knew this rock formation as well as I knew my own face.

Something was different. Nothing was moving but there was something there which didn't belong. Shadow hadn't alerted so I wasn't frightened, yet.

I reached for the small .38 in its holster and just cupped my hand on the butt. There we sat in absolute silence without moving so much as a twitch; but ready.

The formation changed again and I knew someone was moving slowly and silently among the rocks toward us. I unholstered the gun just in case. As I did, Shadow nudged me again with her shoulder, but made no sound at all.

This was getting freaky... I waited, not moving and hardly breathing. I knew if Shadow alerted or moved quickly, all hell would break loose. I wanted to be ready.

The touch on my shoulder almost panicked me into a scream. Instead I froze.

I was fully ready, alert and strangely calm. A voice whispered in my ear so close I could feel the breath on my skin. "Don't move, just listen, and then walk back to the house. Leave Seaweed, but take Shadow with you and go meet Dad at the shop. Change into wet suits under your clothes. Then the two of you go to the dock and get into the Zodiac.

"Talk about a nighttime experiment in the fog with new GPS gear you two have been working on. Keep Shadow with you. When you folks get back here, we're going to change places with you. As you get out on one side, we'll load on the other. Stay in the water for a bit then come up over the rocks to the back of the house. Don't expect Vic or me to say anything to either of you. I know Les was here today; I'm not ready to talk with, or trust anyone. I'll get in touch with you when I feel we're safe. Take care of Dad... now go and stay safe."

I waited for the count of ten then spoke quietly to the dogs to come with me and we strolled back to the house as if we'd been out for our usual evening breath of air and potty breaks.

I had arranged with Dan to come and housesit with my guest. I gave his cell a call, then closed the door to the guest room. He arrived as I was getting ready to leave. I gave him the usual instructions to raid the refrigerator, watch television and to let the answering machine take any calls. I assured him my guest would be fine until I returned.

I left all of the house alarms on, changed into black running gear and sneakers, took Shadow, and hurried down to the workshop where I found Ben pacing the floor.

I truly am getting too old for this life-style and I'm certain Ben is, too.

I greeted Ben and began to chat with him about the GPS test while I was handing him the note relating what Eric had told me. He nodded, kept the conversation going as he burned the note with a lighter.

We changed into the wet suits, put our clothes back on, then he set the alarms and led the way out the back door.

We headed off to the small dock where the Zodiac sat in full fuzzy view from the fog and the dock light. We laughed and chatted loading the dog and untying the craft.

We moved out of sight from the dock light, using the usual gas motor on the rig. Ben kept us close to the high and rocky coastline, hoping to avoid detection from anyone on shore. I began to pull off my running gear, exposing my wet suit, adding the hood. Ben was doing the same thing without moving about much in case anyone with night vision could see us. I stuffed our clothing into the waterproof pack we'd brought. We put on the single tanks and secured our masks on our heads. Neither of us had bothered with flippers.

Ben switched the gas engine off, running only with the electric one. It was so quiet the only sound was the hissing of the water along the sides of the craft.

It was eerie being out there with no sound or sightings of anything. With so much fog, even Ben looked blurry.

Shadow sat calmly on the small deck as if she did this every night. I always marvel at her sense of trust in us.

Ben cut the power and began drifting. I didn't honestly have a clue where we were, but I trusted his skills. I followed Shadow's lead and sat quietly, waiting.

We brushed against something in the water, and then felt another object. I felt a tug on the boat as someone took hold of the line draped around the craft.

A voice so quiet I barely knew it was there said, "You guys and Shadow just roll off the port side and swim to the cove... love you both. I'll be in touch. Stay safe; this is going to get very nasty, very quick. Don't worry about us…we'll be okay; love you both. I'm sorry for the trouble. Go and be real quiet."

I went first. I just rolled over and slid into the water without a splash or a sound. Shadow seemed to understand the game. She put her front haunches on the gunwale, slid in behind me, and began swimming in a circle. Ben was in the water, too. All three of us left without any sound other than the soft lapping of waves on the rocks.

I looked again at the craft, which now held two people and a big dog. It was moving away from the rocks, a seamless transition. I hoped whoever was watching would see and believe the same thing.

Ben touched me on the shoulder and pointed, beginning to swim away. I followed with Shadow staying with us. As we began to move away farther from the rocks, Ben motioned for me to put on the facemask and the regulator. He signaled for us to dive under.

I *hate* night diving. I'm so claustrophobic it's a real trial. I'd only do this for Eric.

I worried about what Shadow would do. No need to worry; she was right by my side with only her nose out of the water. How could she understand?

I think of the strangest things under pressure.

I followed the swirl of water created by Ben's swimming. Made sense to me…I didn't know where we were or where we were going. I just prayed nothing would touch me…I hate that even in the daylight when swimming. I tell everyone if even a piece of kelp touches me, I look like an Evinrude at full throttle.

Ben slowed. I came abreast of him. He indicated we should swim toward shore. A few moments later, I felt something under my feet, then nothing, then my hand touched what I thought was a piece of ledge. Ben signaled up and I went. The climb wasn't more than a few feet and I was, thankfully, out of the water.

He led the way to another of the inflatable boats moored there. Getting in was not easy. I let him try first; he climbed in and then gave me a hand. I was lying on the deck, when Shadow, with Ben's assistance, landed on me. We were all safely out of the water. What a relief!

Ben signaled me to remove the air tanks. He promptly lowered them over the side attached to the line that'd held the inflatable; he allowed the gear to sink out of sight.

We pulled our running suits on over the wet suits. Thankfully, they were large enough to get into without too much effort.

He passed me a paddle. We paddled out away from the rocks, continuing for some distance.

Ben spoke as he started the outboard engine on the boat, "Well, I think that's enough experimenting for now. I'm satisfied the GPS system will work well enough for our purposes with the sailboats. "Let's go to the shop and get some coffee."

Thirty-five

We motored back to the dock, tied up and strolled to the back door of the shop. It'd been so damp with the fog, if we'd met someone, our being wet would seem reasonable.

I had to admit, though, I was frigid... scared for Eric and Vicky, the whole experience left me longing for a hot shower and fire in the fireplace at home.

We enjoyed a cup of hot coffee laced with a small shot of brandy, sugar, and light cream. Wow, that was a treat! I was ready to go swimming again right then.

However, if you'd given me five more minutes, my brain would've come back to earth. Then, I'd go with my first plan for a hot shower and the fireplace.

When I arrived back at the house, all seemed secure with Seaweed greeting us at the door.

I made a show of going into the guest room to check on my houseguest and inquiring if she needed anything. Then I thanked Dan for his assistance.

Dan assured me it had been a pleasure to just sit and watch television, eating good food. I was to feel free to call him anytime I needed the refrigerator cleaned out. With a wave and a big grin, he fired up his monster truck and went home.

I went into my office to check messages as usual; old habits never stop.

When I turned on the desk lamp, something was out of place. I am almost anal about things. Anything moved or something placed in my space gets my attention immediately. There was a corner of an envelope sticking out from under the big desk calendar.

I'd learned years ago not to put anything under the blotter on your desk as it would, or could, disappear for an entire year.

Very carefully, I slid it out, lifting it gently to the light. I could see what looked like a note inside and something tiny. I opened the envelope and extracted the paper. The message printed on the sheet said, "Trust you to creatively make this/her disappear." I looked into the envelope and what looked like a tiny, flat, white battery was in there. I knew this was the tracker.

I brushed out Shadow and contemplated my next move. I knew Eric had put this here, without setting off the alarms, before he left in the Zodiac.

The ball was in my court. After some prayerful thought, I called Animal. He answered with a cheerful, "Howdy, don't tell me you can't wait for the part to arrive, and you now want to trade the hot-rod?"

My answer was just as upbeat, though carefully worded; we both knew someone was monitoring our conversation. "Not yet, but after looking at the paperwork I'm not satisfied with what it states in there. I need some serious clarification for my peace of mind. Do you think you could do that?"

The reply was instantaneous, "I knew after you thought about it you'd question it. It *is* a bit complicated. I could draw it out for you. I'll come over in a few minutes and do a better job of explaining it. Are you up to doing it now?"

My reply was without hesitation. "Sure, I hate things to drag on unresolved, as you well know. Come on over; I'll make us some coffee. Thanks."

When Animal arrived, I greeted him and passed him the scrap of paper Eric had left in the envelope.

We continued to banter back and forth while I got us coffee and went into my office where he said he needed some paper to draw me a diagram.

I'd written out what I thought was needed. I wanted a large black SUV with heavily tinted windows to come and take my houseguest away. She wasn't going to be staying here any longer due to her injuries.

I'd also outlined to him how I thought we could package the chip and send it by bus to some distant place.

I didn't know if it would work. It was worth a shot and would certainly be distracting. Could he arrange it for me ASAP?

He nodded, put up one finger and mouthed, "Hour."

We continued to talk about the hot-rod in very technical terms to a point where I didn't understand any of it.

I just laughed and said, "Well, if you say so, I trust you to do what's right." Walking him to the door, I thanked him for his time and coming so promptly to relieve an old woman's mind.

As he was ready to open the door, he made a gesture of wrapping something big up and carrying it like it was heavy while he mouthed again, "One hour."

I had no idea what he was planning. He'd never failed me yet.

The fact he was wearing a bulletproof vest and carrying a weapon was scary, but I didn't mention it. He opened the door, stepped out and walked away to his truck.

Going into the guest room, I left the shades drawn as they'd been all day.

I turned on the light, found a blanket similar to the one Vicky arrived with, and then I gathered the large pillow roll used for decoration on the bed and proceeded to wrap it up. I tied it so it resembled a body.

Going into the office, I got the small chip. After I'd placed it into a paper clip box with cotton, I inserted it into a padded mailer.

Lord, please let this work, even if only for a short time.

The gate alarm sounded, setting off the dogs. I checked the camera and pushed the talk button. "Yes, state your business please."

A man's deep voice answered, "I'm here to pick up a passenger needing immediate medical transport. I also have my assistant with me."

A very large head appeared on the small screen. One I knew well. I opened the gate. He pulled into the parking area, maneuvering the vehicle into position. He parked it where no one by the tree line could see into the interior.

When he stepped out, here again was someone I'd never seen before. He was taller, heavier, bald, wearing a black uniform with a chauffeur's hat.

This man must have a wardrobe half the size of Hollywood. He walked to the door, gave me a formal greeting as if it were the first time we'd ever seen each other.

He followed me to the guest room, lifted the *body* gently, took the *paperwork* and carried it out to the waiting auto.

He made a big show of tucking and positioning while speaking quietly to the parcel, as he placed it onto the seat. Affixing the seat belt, he inquired if it was too tight. I stood holding the door.

When he stepped back, I stuck my head into the interior and said I hoped *she* would be okay. I assured her she could contact me if necessary.

I stepped back, closed the door, and walked up the pathway to the house. As he drove off into the night, I prayed this would work.

Thirty-six

After a long and restless night, I awoke again to another dreary, foggy day. It seems as though God has forgotten us here on the coast. We've had no sun for days. It feels like weeks.

Seaweed hadn't seemed to be herself and Shadow was staying close by her side. I understood she was old. I wasn't willing to relinquish her yet. I'd called the vet. I would take her in to make sure she wasn't uncomfortable. Most likely it was just age related, something we sadly couldn't reverse.

I had planned to go down to the shop to see if Ben would like to go with us. He'd been at loose ends since Eric left.

It would also give me a chance to tell him about sending my *parcel* on its way.

I missed Eric. I'd just like a sign he and Vicky were okay. I hated waiting but I guessed no news was good news.

I got my Jeep out of the garage and loaded the dogs. Lately Seaweed has been riding on the back seat and Shadow rides shotgun on the passenger seat. When I lifted Seaweed onto the seat, she made the effort to hop onto the console then into the passenger seat where she laid down. I was elated; maybe she's recovering from her low period.

Shadow seemed fine with the swap of positions and sat in the middle of the back seat looking through the windshield out over the console. The alarms were all set as we left the yard with the security gate closing at the end of the driveway.

I thanked God for all the security measures built in from the last disaster. I felt good about them but I was still conflicted. I was taking this stroll down memory lane as I often do when counting my blessings.

I'd moved here for peace and quiet; however, in less than a year and a half, I had shots fired at me, killed a man and my house and Jeep were blown to bits. I wanted to add that this didn't enhance my comfort level.

I caught a flicker of movement from the corner of my right eye. With no good reason, I ducked. The blast took out the passenger window and the driver's side window. It happened so quickly I neither braked nor turned the wheel. It had been *pure reflex.* I stayed low and gunned the Jeep around the slight bend in the road; not slowing down until I slid into the yard at the shop.

Ben must have heard my arrival. I never speed into the boat yard. Before the car stopped, he was out of the shop and coming my way with a look of horror at the sight of the car. His first bellow was, "What in the hell happened to you? Are you all right? Are the dogs okay?"

I really didn't know if we were okay…I knew there was broken glass all over me; the dogs remained silent. I was shaking like a leaf in a gale.

Ben opened the car door, while dialing his phone.

He offered a hand to assist me from the auto. I took it, trying to stand. I was willing, but I had legs like wet noodles. I had to pull myself together.

Think of the dogs, my mind kept telling me. Finally, I got the message and stood. I walked around the car to lift Seaweed off the seat brushing off more glass.

I walked to the back door, letting Shadow out while putting Seaweed on the ground. She began shaking herself as if to dispel rain.

It was working; glass was flying off and out of her fur. Thank God for safety glass. It was just pellets and not shards.

Shadow followed suit with the shaking, even though it appeared she had less glass on her.

I could feel the glass in my hair and down my neck around the turtleneck on my sweater. I could also feel something wet running down my head by my right ear.

Ben looked horrified as he still managed to talk to the sheriff or the State Police.

Whoever shot at me was using a silencer and a high-powered gun, a rifle, I suspected. They must have been close to the road. What I'd glimpsed was the movement of a bush or a branch when they aimed.

Thank God, yet again, for good eyesight and quick reflexes.

I was trying to look into the side mirror to see where the blood was coming from. I wondered for the umpteenth time what I knew, or what someone thought I knew, which was so important they wanted to shoot me…again.

As usual, there were the sound of sirens and cars driven too fast on the dirt road. We should install a racetrack course out there. I knew that soon I'd need to leave this town so it could resume the slow and sleepy pace it once enjoyed.

Poor Larry the Law slid to a stop and looked anxious. "Are you hurt? Are the dogs okay? Who did this? Why'd they do this? I thought we were done with this shit."

I laughed in spite of my anger and frustration and gave him answers as he'd given the questions. "Not hurt, dogs okay just covered with glass, don't know who did it, and don't know why they did it. I agree with you…I thought we were done with this shit also."

The next to arrive was the state trooper stationed in our area. This was the same show, only with a different car and characters, but same questions. I wondered if they'd compared scenes and notes before they got there. After a look in the woods, along the road, and asking the same questions, they'd conferred. Then they returned with one last question, which proved they hadn't been listening to anything I'd said.

Larry asked, "From the sound of the shot, do you think it was a hunting rifle?"

I shook my head and replied, "I told you, it had a silencer on it. I heard nothing until the glass started flying."

Larry seemed to be distracted and somewhat anxious. I walked over to him and inquired if he was all right. His answer surprised me. "I'm okay, but I'm thinking this job may not be for me. The thought of doing anything else has really bothered me. This was a nice quiet job with the run-of-the-mill problems. Conflicts were almost all local. Occasionally there were a few out-of-state folks, but nobody too dangerous. Now it's so unpredictable I wear a bullet-proof vest all the time and wonder if I'll get home to my wife and kids."

I was shocked, but I understood. The mayhem had begun when I bought the cottage…if I'd never moved there, nothing would have happened. I couldn't stop wondering what would have happened when someone discovered the cache of arms and drugs flowing through my cove.

I responded, "Well perhaps this will stop soon. Either they'll succeed in killing me or figure out I'm not worth the effort."

Larry looked at me for a long time, then spoke very quietly so I could barely hear him, "It isn't just you… late last night someone shot up a big black SUV as it was off-loading a passenger onto a chopper in a field outside of town. I guess they managed to get aboard and into the air far enough so they got away. Then someone set the vehicle on fire and burned it to the frame. By the time we got there, it was all over and whoever did it was long gone. The State Police are taking care of the investigation. Thankfully, I'm just local. Do you need a ride home?"

I shook my head, "No, but thank you for the offer."

I was so worried about Animal I almost panicked. I had no idea if he'd gotten hurt. I couldn't ask Larry without telling him about the mission I'd sent Animal on.

There must've been more police scanners in Down East Maine than anywhere on earth. Cars and trucks were coming down the road as if we were holding a county fair at the boat yard. They pulled up and parked willy-nilly all over the grass. The town folks were getting out and walking around the Jeep, talking with Ben and Larry like it was old home day or something.

I took the dogs and went into the shop where I could check them over carefully while I cleaned my head. What a damn mess!

I was busy in the bathroom when I heard the door open and close. No dog sounds. It had to be okay.

I was almost done when a soft knock came on the door. I opened it slowly and could've fainted for joy. There stood Animal, as himself, with his hair in a wild ponytail, bearded, tattooed, and scruffy. I just hugged him and whispered in his ear, "Thank God you're okay."

His reply was a booming, "What did you do to the Jeep?"

I chuckled. "Had a scratch on one of the windows so I thought I'd order a new set, silly."

He passed me a note that said, "Package on way to Haiti." I happily smiled my thanks and flushed the note.

Animal helped me re-check the dogs for glass, then we stepped out into the crowd.

He assured me he could have the Jeep repaired, cleaned and returned by next day, late afternoon.

If I needed wheels in the meantime, he'd leave his truck as a loaner.

I told him I guessed I didn't need to go anywhere until he brought the Jeep back. I'd drive his truck back to my house, then he would have it when he returned with the Jeep.

Good to his word, the Jeep was returned late the next afternoon just before dark.

Thirty-seven

The next morning broke slowly with a cool, heavy, misty rain and fog, which chilled the bones along with offering no visibility. It seemed as though the house, sitting on the large ledge, floated in midair. Even the cove, a few hundred feet away, was shrouded in the mist, making it invisible. This whole scene was eerie, even to me; who loved the changing weather on the coast.

Both of the dogs were edgy. This was very unlike them. I thought even though it was chilly and wet, I'd take them for a short romp down to the cove.

I threw on my old orange slicker with the hood, a pair of clamming boots, stuck the phone in my pocket and, as an afterthought I stuck the revolver in my other pocket.

Strange, I thought to myself, I have a state-of-the-art security system and haven't had an issue for a couple of days. Why would I add the gun to a routine walk?

I'd learned over the years to trust my inner thoughts and not question the wisdom of being careful. It had saved my life several times.

We trooped out through the side door and down the path closest to the cove with Seaweed and Shadow leading the way.

I wondered, do they really have better sight than humans, or are they just braver? Maybe they just don't care as much as we do.

We were almost to the cove. I could tell by the footing and the soft swoosh of the waves on the beach.

Shadow returned abruptly with Seaweed on her heels and then she sat directly in front of and facing me. I stopped, listened intently, but didn't hear anything unusual. Still she sat, demanding my attention.

I knelt and looked her directly in the eyes. She was looking at me with an intensity I hadn't seen before, not making a sound. Something was wrong!

I stood with the intention of going forward toward the cove when she moved in front of me and sat again.

"What do you want, girl? Can you show me what's wrong?" Shadow stood, and then walked over to Seaweed. She stopped to give her a soft nuzzle, along with a little grunt, so silent I almost didn't hear it. I don't begin to understand dog-talk but Seaweed sat and remained when Shadow returned to me.

She took my hand in her mouth, making it clear I needed to come with her. She took me to the far side of the cove, out onto the large rocks jutting out into the ocean. My heart was pounding like a blacksmith's hammer.

What had she found?

She'd not been far ahead of me on the initial start of the walk so I didn't think she could've gotten this far around the cove. We'd climbed up onto the upper ledge before she edged her way down closer to the water's edge. It was slippery and I thanked God I'd put on my boots so I could hold my balance. We rounded the edge of a large boulder; she stopped, looked back at me, and then pulled me two steps toward the shoreline.

There, huddled in the rocks, were Eric, Vicky, and Bruno. None of us uttered a sound. We looked like we were looking out at the ocean as casual as could be.

I could see, out of the corner of my eye, Vicky looked nearly dead. I was alarmed. Eric offered a piece of paper. We all knew there was surveillance. They could see us with thermal imaging, even in the dense fog. I prayed Eric and Vicky were around the bend in the rocks far enough so they wouldn't be detected.

I picked up some small samples of seaweed, a rock, and then the paper from his hand. It simply read, "Need help! Vic real bad, call Animal ASAP!"

I nodded slightly, then turned to go without a backward glance.

Even though they had a survival blanket wrapped around all three of them, I was certain Bruno was the heat source. Eric hadn't looked much better than Vicky.

Shadow led the way back across the rock maze to the shore where poor old Seaweed was sitting where we'd left her, wet and shivering, but nonetheless, ever obedient to her friend.

I had to get her toweled dried and warmed up. She was too old for this.

I needed to call Animal. Should I go to him? This was never an easy call. However, I knew time was of the essence. I knew from her appearance that Vicky was slipping away, she wouldn't survive much longer without medical care.

I'd made it to the porch when the alarm sounded on the driveway gate. Damn, who could it be just when I didn't need an interruption?

I pressed the button on the call box, only getting a cheery greeting, "Your favorite person is here to repair the rod." I pushed the gate lock button and nearly fell down with relief.

Using the call box was for show because Animal had the code. Blessed be, it was Animal in all his glory with a large van I hadn't seen before.

I was no longer surprised. I have no idea where he gets these vehicles or where they go. I probably don't want to know.

I scooted Seaweed into the house, grabbed my goose-down vest off the hook and wrapped her in it. It would keep her warm until I could get back to her. She snuggled and looked grateful. I felt less guilty for having to leave her there alone on the entry rug.

Shadow walked ahead of me to the truck parked in front of the garage where the hot-rod lived.

Animal wasn't alone. I had to be where I could talk to him about Eric and Vicky. I couldn't see who was with him. The person hadn't exited the truck yet.

Then Animal's super huge pit bull, Zeus, opened the passenger side door, and let himself out. Man, that's one big dog. He must be part mastiff. Zeus is smart, athletic, and kind.

That statement needs clarification…my mind told me he was kind to those he knew and liked and could be vicious to someone he didn't trust or seemed threatening to one of his people.

I gave him a pat and an ear scratch, then he and Shadow talked or whatever they do.

As Animal was putting up the garage door, he whispered to me, "What?"

Because I hadn't known who was with him, I had been afraid to tell him about the situation. I glanced at the truck. Animal nodded and gave me a thumbs-up sign. I reached in and hugged Animal. The shock on his face said it all. Using the hug to hold him close enough to hear me, I whispered, telling him the situation; pleading with him to help without giving them away. He just stood there holding me, like this happened all the time. He told me he already knew. It was the reason they were here.

I had to know. "Who are *they*?"

I should've guessed. It was Les masquerading again as the technician.

I was concerned and when I stepped away from Animal, he read my dismay. "It'll be okay. We can get this fixed shortly.

"Do you mind keeping Zeus for a couple of days for me? He prefers to be outside and not in the house. He's been here with me and he knows the boundaries. He won't leave the property."

I knew, as usual, I didn't have the full story on this nor would I ever really know.

I simply expressed a heartfelt, "Of course! He's always welcome to stay. I'll call the grain store and have them bring me a truckload of food. You know I love horses. Can I ride him?" We laughed together.

His next question floored me. "Is the tide coming or going?" I realized while we were standing talking the mist had increased. Visibility wasn't more than twenty to twenty-five feet, so he certainly couldn't see the shoreline.

"It's a going tide for another two or three hours, I would guess. Why?"

Animal looked at the ground then back at me before speaking. "I have friends who lost their favorite big dog and they don't want to bury it on their place. I was wondering if you'd mind if I buried him at sea off your far shore. He's in a container that'll float off on the tide then will biodegrade with time. His name was Boatswain. He sailed with his master all his life."

My mind flat-lined…what do you say to a request like that? "No, I don't mind at all. When would you like to do it?"

Animal winked at me. "Now. It's part of the reason I came today."

He went to the back doors of the van and opened them. The inside of this van looked like an ambulance. I was stunned. There was another person in there besides Les. That was an even bigger shock. I knew what they were going to try to pull off. How would they get Vicky, Eric, and Bruno in there without detection?

I was going to be just a spectator, I was certain. However, I was a *very* grateful spectator.

Animal began unloading the *container* with the assistance of Les, who began whining, "I don't get paid to do burials of animals. Why can't you do this some other time? I can fix the hot-rod while you do this."

I could hear him muttering as they disappeared into the mist. I didn't know what to do. I closed the back doors to the van and walked after them. I wasn't going out on the rocks again; I'd wait on the beach.

As I stood in the cove, I wondered for the umpteenth time how I *ever* got myself into this mess. Not once but twice, it seems, or did this all count as one mess, just elongated, with no end in sight.

Soon Shadow came bounding up to me with Zeus at her side, both looking like they knew something I didn't and they were not going to let me in on it.

I heard the crunching of feet on the sand before I saw Animal, still carrying the container, while he was dressing Les down.

"I don't give a damn what you think…it *was* a good idea. I told you I needed your help to put it overboard, but no, you're too friggin' chicken to get out on the rocks because it's slippery with seaweed. What in the hell did you think, dumb ass? This is the ocean; we grow seaweed on the rocks.

"Now we missed the tide and I'll have to do it tomorrow without you. I sure as hell hope you're a better mechanic than an assistant or the rod will never run again.

"Can you at least help me put the container back into the van or will it affect your working contract as well?"

Wow! Animal was on a rant for sure. I'll give him a wide berth.

I walked behind them to the van and stood as they opened the doors and slid the container into the back. Les seemed to be pissed off and said nothing. He just got in first and pulled it inside. Animal was really acting nuts. He slammed the back doors shut, spun on his heel and walked into the garage where he punched the button to close the door, ducking out before it came down.

As the door was rumbling shut, he whispered, "I got 'em... be back... I left you a present. Have fun. Don't kill me."

Then in an angry voice he said, "I'll come back and finish the rod but I can't stand this idiot any longer. I'm dumping him out the first chance I get. If you see him hitchhiking, don't bother picking him up. He ain't worth it.

"Take care of Zeus.

"See ya." He jumped into the van, turned around, and left the yard.

What in the devil was he trying to tell me? I'd figure it out later. At that moment, I needed a cup of hot, strong coffee while I got dry and warm.

Seaweed had moved off the entryway rug, though still mostly wrapped in the vest. She was lying on the rug by the glass patio doors sound asleep.

Shadow had opted to stay outside with her new best friend. They were sitting on the porch shoulder-to-shoulder, with Zeus dwarfing her.

I pulled off the boots, hung my slicker on the coat rack, and headed for the kitchen and hot coffee. In the back of my mind, I wondered if I'd forgotten to turn the coffee maker off. I could smell coffee. Mystery solved…the pot was nearly half-full; I hadn't left it like that.

Alarm bells went off in my brain.

I stepped back to the coat rack, drawing my revolver from the pocket…better safe than sorry, or dead…neither a good choice for me. I proceeded very carefully into the kitchen, gun in hand, and ready. I knew I looked funny. I could laugh at myself later.

The counter looked just as I'd left it with my cup sitting near the sink.

I knew the coffee pot was all wrong. I make one pot in the morning. It holds just two of my big mugs. I drank all of it before we went out. Now the pot was on and half full.

Before I could finish my thought, Zeus began barking. I was torn between seeing what was going on out there or finishing this quest.

Decision made. I stepped into the kitchen with the gun at the ready and made a quick sweep.

Problem solved. There in the corner, comfortable as ever, sat Les drinking coffee. He raised one hand as if he were going to surrender and drank with the other.

"Don't shoot," came out in a whisper. I noticed he was wearing a holster, holding what I assumed to be a .45 auto pistol. I'd always suspected he carried, but this was the first time I'd seen it displayed.

Zeus was really making noise.

I grabbed my slicker, pulled on the boots, and, still with gun in hand stepped quickly outside.

Shadow was all blocked up and growling. "Go get them," I told the dogs. They were off to the tree line at full speed, with me right behind them.

My land was fenced, alarmed, and posted. Anyone would know it was private property. They knew they were trespassing.

I didn't think Shadow would attack a stranger unless they were a threat to me. However, I hadn't any idea what Zeus would do. I'd know in a minute, because they were much faster than I was. They were nearer to whatever was upsetting them.

I arrived in time to see Shadow confronting a man with a pistol with a silencer in his hand.

I could see Zeus had gone outside of the intruder's field of vision and had just sprung onto his back as the man raised his hand to fire at Shadow.

There was a shot. When the gun discharged, Zeus had him on the ground with his massive jaws around the back of the trespasser's neck. The gun had gone airborne, landing into the rocks during the attack.

Shadow was watching intently. Zeus sat on the man's back, not letting go of the intruder's neck.

I pulled out my cell phone, thinking, it was a good thing I hadn't emptied my pockets when I'd hung the slicker.

I called 911 and got Larry the sheriff, aka Larry Law, "Yes, Eileen? Don't tell me you have another passenger for me."

That was a simple question, so I gave a simple answer. "Yep, up by the fence, behind the garage. You'd better hurry; Zeus has him by the neck and I've no idea what command would make him stop."

Whoever this was, he was smart enough not to move. Zeus was not going to let go. I didn't even want to get close enough to see if the dog had drawn blood.

More importantly, I didn't care.

We were an interesting group. There was a man on the ground with a massive pit bull/mastiff seated on his back. The huge critter had his jaws around the back of the man's neck.

At the same time, a Rottie sat, firmly ensconced in front of the man with her teeth bared. She was controlling the situation by her growling.

An old woman in an orange rain slicker, wearing clamming boots, was holding a .38 Detective Special in her hand, aimed at the man. The person remained nameless and quiet.

When Larry made his way up to the tree line the situation seemed to amuse him.

He took in the scene, looked at me, and asked, "You really don't know what command will get him to release, do you?"

My reply was easy. "Nope. I don't even care. Just get him off my property. I'll file charges. I want a restraining order on who/or whatever he is, or thinks he is. Can you handle this by yourself?"

Larry smiled his little boy grin, and told me what I already knew. I heard sirens coming. I'm the only troublemaker on this road. I knew where they were going to stop.

"Nope, when you call, I always phone all the Staties and Feds in the area and round up the National Guard."

He exaggerated.

I'm again thanking the vision of the security system installers. They'd provided all law enforcement and emergency responders with the special code so they could get through the gate.

There were two of them and when they assessed the immediate situation, they smiled and nodded. The troopers then pondered how to get Zeus to leave his post so they could arrest the clown.

Well, it was worth a try; I guessed. "Zeus, it's okay…leave." His eyes focused on me. I tried again. "Leave." That time he relaxed his mouth but stayed seated on the man's back. I commanded, "Zeus come!" He looked at me, like *really*, but he came along with Shadow, and sat beside me.

"His gun fell over there somewhere."

Mission accomplished. The dogs were safe, and the police had the invader, his gun, and the discharged shell casing. My next step was to see what happened in my kitchen.

Does it *never* end? Was this my new mantra? At least it changed from last year when it was *why me, what did I do?*

As a side note, I never did figure out what it was I'd done, other than buy an old abandoned cottage.

The dogs and I returned to the house with them taking up their guard-post on the porch. Those two were *serious* guard dogs.

Thirty-eight

I removed the boots and slicker again, retrieved two giant dog bones from the container by the door. I paid my guards for a good job well done.

Back to the kitchen and perhaps, as a reward to me, a cup of coffee.

Les was where I'd left him, seated in the chair with coffee mug in hand. There was a new pot of coffee so I knew he'd had a refill.

Les held up his hand and made a gesture to wait for a minute.

He stated quietly, "We can talk now; I've set up a jamming device so they can't understand what we're saying."

I was ready. "Okay, what in hell is going on? Why are you here? Who left in the van? No, don't even answer. I already know. How come I got stuck with you?"

With quiet assurance, Les explained it to me. "Eric contacted me about Vicky's condition and the need for immediate medical attention without any fanfare. He knew the house was under surveillance. We, Animal and I, devised a plan to make it happen. God provided the weather for cover. Considering what just happened, I may be here for a few days."

This was so reminiscent of the previous mess where I had an in-house agent who stayed for a length of time. I would like to add, it was to no avail. They blew up my house directly after he left. I'm not sure I wish to participate in the game again. I sipped my coffee while considering my options. Les tried to be inconspicuous in his inspection of my mental deliberations.

He failed.

I decided to be blunt and honest. "I don't trust you, Les. I did when you were here before; now I don't trust any of you Feds.

"And while we're on the trust issue, are you going to tell me who Animal is? I know him from a very different situation and have it on good authority I *can* trust him. You, however, don't get a free pass along with him."

Les didn't seem to be upset with my assessment of his trustworthiness. In the true Les-style I remembered so well from the last time, he took his time, seemingly to ponder his approach.

I was certain he knew Vicky had told me there was a mole deep in the department creating havoc. She'd also told me Les was involved in saving her and Eric's lives, even if someone neglected to tell either of them the other person wasn't dead. I'm almost sure he was going to gloss the situation, blowing me off. I wouldn't buy it. Talk was cheap. I wanted facts.

Les opted for the old line, "Could I get you to give me a refill on the coffee? I'd do it myself, but this area is the only place where they can't see me.

"Crawling over to the counter again wouldn't be a pretty sight for you to witness. In fact, I might have to shoot you not to relay it to others. I am only kidding, of course, but only about the shooting."

I chuckled and turned my back to the windows. I carried the pot over to him.

I'd thought, when rebuilding the house, the windows seemed like such a great idea. I loved lots of light, and the ability to enjoy the panorama had been a great idea. I could look at the water, my cove, the gardens, and the garage area constantly.

He continued, "I don't know how much I can tell you without getting you into more jeopardy. As usual, you know enough to be dangerous, and *in* danger. The proof of the fact was having two invaders removed from your property. Soon they aren't going to be watching you. They'll try to get rid of you, like shooting at the Jeep. I think they wanted to scare you. The only reason they haven't killed you so far is they think you can lead them to Eric and/or Vicky.

"I don't think other than watching Ben's place they'll do anything to him. I have a back-up plan in place there. I'm technically retired from the department. However, I still have some very useful people in place.

"How *did* Vicky get sent to you in the first place? Somehow I don't know or understand that part of the puzzle."

I didn't see any reason not to tell him because he could trace it if he really wanted to. "My sister, who lives in Virginia, works with a system for domestic abuse cases. The agency works with women, men, and children, if they're involved, along with their pets. The organization provides them passage to safe houses while assisting them to obtain legal help to stay safe.

"Vicky made it to one of those shelters after she was picked up on the street in horrific condition by my sister, Kate. She was refusing any medical attention. Each time your men found her, they brutalized her again.

"They thought she was dead when they finished this last beating. The men left her unattended for a short period. She managed to get away.

"She knew from what she'd overheard them saying, when they thought they'd killed her, that if they caught her again, she would be dead.

"Her condition was so severe the shelter didn't know what to do with her. The rescuers needed to hide her outside of the usual contacts their system had.

"My sister knew I'd keep her safe, if she could survive the trip.

"Vicky is one strong, stubborn lady. I had no idea who, or what she was until Eric came to introduce me to Bruno.

"After the dog recovered from his injuries, the department no longer wanted him. Eric had been keeping track of his progress so when Bruno was well enough he went to get him.

"When Eric came in, I was in the process of introducing him to my house guest when he went nuts and ran out of the house. When he saw Vicky and she saw him, I knew they had a substantial connection to each other.

"I called Animal to come stay with her while I went to see what was wrong with Eric. Ben called to tell me Eric had gone berserk and was wrecking his house. I brought Eric back here and they talked.

"I don't need to know why, or what, I just need to know they're safe.

"At some point I have to go tell Ben what's happened. He has a right to know. Eric is his only son, whom he loves dearly."

Les appeared sad and discouraged. This was unusual for him. In my past dealings with him, Les had always looked in control, no matter what.

He looked defeated, but by what, or whom? This thought didn't quiet my anxiety at all.

When he finally spoke, I heard the sadness in his tone. "When we were finishing up the mission, Eric and Vicky were partners. They were working well together but they'd also become lovers. They were so tightly bonded it was dangerous for both of them. They'd told command they were going to retire from the service. They wanted to get married, and live like normal people. I don't think when you're in so deep, it can happen. I thought if anyone could make it work, Vicky and Eric could.

"I probably shouldn't tell you this, but I firmly believed they were both set up. They knew too much about too much, and were ready to blow it wide open. It would have exposed some key people in the service who'd gone rogue for profit. I smelled a rat. Then I got wind of where it was going down. By the time I got there, both Vicky and Eric, along with Bruno, had been beaten and shot.

"I was barely able to control it long enough to get them out to medical treatment. They sent them to separate facilities and I got a notice Vicky had died.

"Eric was in real tough shape but pulled through and you know the rest of his story.

"I never found out Vicky was alive until she showed up here with you, and Animal contacted me.

"Some of this resurfaced again for Eric with the dust-up here at your place last year. We ended one arm of the problem, but it was far too lucrative for the head to let it go.

"Now the only thing I'm going to tell you about Animal is this…he's good people. You can trust him for anything. Anything else you need to know has to come from him.

"Eric and Vicky are going to a medical clinic. It's private and not known to the department. I'm just praying Vicky will survive the trip."

My heart broke for both of them, although I was unsure of the extent of Vicky's injuries, I knew it was bad and getting worse.

I needed to know so I asked, "Will you have contact with them so we know if they make it to the facility and about her condition? Will this be another waiting game with no end in sight?"

Les shook his head as if to clear his thoughts and I wondered how long it had been since he'd slept, or where he'd been staying. He had no carry bag or even a jacket with him.

I needed to inquire. "Do you need to rest? You seem to be out of sorts. Do you need something I can get for you?"

After careful thought, and a sip of now-cold coffee, Les stood and stretched, taking in the view from the window next to him. The fog was lifting and the visibility was improving. We could see beyond the rocks at the end of the point.

He asked, "How safe is this house? I know you have security all around the wooded side with the gate in place. You've had two intruders in the last few days that breached the fence without sounding an alarm. The dogs are the best protection you have. If someone got to the house, do you have a way out without being seen?"

I saw no harm in showing Les the trap door, which led to the cement room below the house. When the house was re-built, I kept the space, with modifications. It'd saved the dogs and me before. I told Les where it was located in case he needed to hide there.

I had also reconfigured the locking system on the door leading out, so I could lock and unlock it with a code from either side. I gave Les the code.

I prayed I hadn't made another error.

His next request surprised me. "Eileen, I need to get to Ben's shop so I can use the equipment in the safe room. I have no clothes, not even a jacket or any personal care items.

"I do have my phone. However, due to the circumstances, I wouldn't use it. Everything is too easy to track. The only people who know where I am are Eric and Animal. I'll tell you this much... when and if they get Vicky stabilized, Eric and I are going to stop this thing.

"We may not make it out the other side, but we will stop it. How can you get me to Ben's without anyone seeing me? You're right; I need to get at least an hour of sleep if you don't mind."

My reply was simple. "Can you get into the guest room without being seen in the windows? I still have the drapes pulled in there. As for getting you to Ben's, I'll need some time to think of a solution.

"I think it will be calm here with both of the dogs on guard duty. However, I don't expect this calm to last for long. I still remember how fast it fell apart last year.

"Can you swim? Do you know how to use scuba equipment? How long can you stay in the water? Think about it and take a nap, if you can.

"I'll take Shadow and go to the shop. Zeus will watch over you. I could get you a jacket from the shop. There are always jackets hanging there in case anyone needs one. I'll also tell Ben what's happened."

Les dropped to the floor and began the crawl to the guest room while muttering, "Of course I can swim, scuba, stay in the water…all of the above. I really am too damn old for this; it's a young man's game. How'll I know it's you coming back and not someone else?"

"I'm taking Shadow with me. When I return, she'll bark to Zeus. In the meantime, your guard dog won't let anyone except Animal near here. If you hear a ruckus from him, shoot to kill, I guess.

"Welcome to my world. I won't be long."

My trip to the shop was unsettling because I had to tell Ben about Eric. I had told him Eric and Vicky were gone and I didn't know where or when we'd see him.

I was still leery about going, considering the shooting incident the other day. I had to go. I needed to talk to Ben. I gathered my courage as best I could, loaded Shadow, commanded Zeus to stay and guard then headed down the road.

On the seat lay a paper left by Animal for the windows. Odd, I had forgotten to ask him what I owed him. Perhaps this was a reminder. After a closer examination of the paper, I understood. The sticker came from the replacement glass. I realized why he'd left it there on the seat. The new glass was bulletproof and he had changed all four windows.

I made a mental note to thank him.

I made certain the gate closed behind me with the locked light on before pulling away.

Ben was so glad to see me when I walked into the drafting area of the shop he gave me a hug. We greeted each other and chatted idly about the plans he was working on. I indicated to Ben we needed to get into the safe room so we could discuss the current events.

As the door closed and locked, I began updating Ben on the most recent activities. I watched as his eyes mirrored the sadness. We both knew none of this would or could have a good outcome.

Honestly, how could it?

We quickly discussed how to get Les transported to the shop without detection. I thought if I could get him around the point and out of sight, perhaps we could pick him up with the Zodiac.

We had no idea of the amount of surveillance there was for either my place or Ben's. Even if I could get him into my car, we would be sitting ducks on the road. The water seemed to be the only escape route. However, how could I arrange it?

We ended our conversation in the room, then returned to the shop to chat.

As I was getting ready to leave, I spotted the packing crate we used for storage of small sails. We kept it because it was long, narrow, and sturdy, not taking up too much of the floor area of the shop.

My brain went into overdrive. I motioned to Ben to come to the drafting table. Grabbing a sheet of paper, I wrote the instructions for him. He nodded, grinned, and slapped me on the back. I said my goodbyes and headed for home. I knew this would work slick as a whistle.

My greeting when I arrived home was a big slurpy kiss from the guard-dog sitting on the porch. Then he and Shadow played in the yard before returning to the porch to sit shoulder to shoulder. To see them, you would have thought they'd always lived together.

As I went into the kitchen, I saw Les back in his chair with still another cup of coffee. From the looks of him, he hadn't napped.

He looked at me and mouthed, "I need to get out of here."

I nodded, walked slowly over to the window beside his chair and whispered the plan. With any luck, I would have him out of there within the next half hour. He looked reluctant but desperate enough to try anything.

When I asked him if he could duck-walk, he looked puzzled. I guess he didn't have much of a childhood. Therefore, I demonstrated what I was asking him to do. I squatted then walked in that position around the kitchen. I even flapped my elbows for effect.

Oh, I knew my old knees would protest the move tomorrow.

The reward was a big grin and a nod. "How far can you go doing that?"I whispered.

Still grinning, Les replied in the same whispering voice, "Not more than a mile."

My phone rang with Ben on the other end of the line. "I'm sending Dan on a dump run. Do you need a pick-up?"

My reply was instant. "I have two barrels of trash and, if he has enough room, I'd like to get rid of the rest of the big cardboard moving cartons I still have. I was going to use them in an art project, but I've changed my mind. Are you sure Dan won't mind helping me smash them down? If so, I'll wait until later to send them and he can take the barrels. I'll drag everything out so he can load them. Thanks."

Les was listening to all this with a quizzical look on his face. I leaned over and whispered to him, "This is going to be your ticket to freedom …get ready.

"I have two big boxes I have to go drag out of the other room. I am going to drag one out the front door down to the garage. I'll pull out the trash barrels then come back for the last one. You're going to get under it with the bottom flaps open and duck walk to the garage.

"There's a hydraulic lift gate on the truck. I'm going to put you, along with the rest of the stuff, on it.

"There's a canvas cover over the truck body. Inside of the truck with the junk from the yard, there'll be a long wooden crate at the side of the body. Lift the lid up and get into it. Dan will take you to the dump and return you to the shop.

"Dan will park the truck because he has no idea you're on board. Later, either Ben or Dan will park the truck in the bay on the end of the shop. Ben will be looking for you to get into the shop. Good luck."

I hauled out the first big box and, with the help of the dogs and a lot of playing, we hauled it to the garage. Trash barrels pulled out and covers secured. I ran back to the house to get the household trash while moving the other box into the kitchen area. I prayed it would fit through the door. I picked up the newly bagged trash, taking it down and stuffing it into the can then re-secured the cover. I returned for my last *package*.

I hoped Les could do this. I opened the door and, not seeing Les, I assumed he was loaded to leave. I'd pulled up the end of one flap on the top to give me a handhold. I began walking off the porch and down the path while secretly thanking Jay for making the whole house and exterior wheelchair friendly. I didn't hear any noise from inside the box so I guessed Les was doing okay.

The dogs had played with the first box and they were ready to do the same with this one. Shadow wanted to pick up one of the flaps and drag it. She had no idea why I kept giving her the command to *leave*. She was so playful I was surprised she just chased Zeus around the yard barking like a nut. We made it to the garage area as I heard the truck coming.

I thumped the top of the box just to let Les know I'd be loading him shortly. Dan backed the truck up to the boxes and barrels, popped out to unhook and lower the tailgate, then he grabbed the barrels one in each hand. I pushed the box onto the gate while Dan grabbed the other one. Dan was in the process of flattening the other box while I put the gate up and shoved the carton into the body of the truck. Dan laughed. "You do love the mechanical things, don't you? It surprises me how you and Ben would rather sail than run the race boats. They're a lot more exciting, you know. Now bring the gate down so I can smash the other box."

I'd seen the box shift, so hoping Les had gotten into the hiding spot, I lowered the gate. Dan grabbed the box and jumped on it, making short work of unfolding it.

He called back to me as he entered the truck. "I'll drop off the trash barrels on the way back."

I waved my thanks as he drove out of the drive.

Thirty-nine

I puttered in the garden to take my mind off who was where or why. All three dogs enjoyed a little sunshine. They were calm and quiet. For the first time in a long time, I began to feel some peace of mind.

Dan returned after a while leaving the barrels then driving away. I watched him go, wondering if he had any clue Les was in the back. At least I hoped he still had Les in the back.

The gate alarm sounded, then I heard it open so I knew it was someone with the code. I waited to see who.

Zeus became so excited I was worried about him. He never left my side but he was on level nine for alert, so was Shadow. Seaweed didn't move.

A truck came into view. I didn't recognize it but I knew who the driver was. Animal stepped out with a big grin and walked toward us. That was all it took; the dogs were off and flying. I knew he could handle the onslaught. There was growling, hooting, patting and kisses with lots of laughter. After the greetings were over, the dogs sat with playful looks on their faces. Animal then rewarded the three dogs with treats.

Animal looked great. I was so happy to see him I gave him a hug. This was becoming a habit. Maybe getting a hug was the only reason he came. Who cares? I think he's very special.

He spoke first. "Good news… I have the new part for the rod. I'll have you out getting speeding tickets shortly. Do you still like me?

"You wouldn't have a cold soda in the fridge would you?"

I laughed aloud because he never would take anything you offered him to either eat or drink, with the exception of Christmas dinner. "Come on in and we'll look."

Once inside he whispered, "Vicky is doing great! We got her there in time. Eric will be showing up soon. He'll call Ben. Where's Les?"

I smiled and whispered back, "I threw him out with the trash. I think by now he's at the shop, maybe."

Aloud I asked, "What's your pleasure? There's lemonade, Coke, wine, beer and water. Take what you want."

Animal grabbed a cold beer and headed to the garage with me on his heels.

In minutes, the rod was rumbling happily. "Put Seaweed in the house and we'll take this thing for a spin to check it out."

I put Seaweed in the house then jumped in the rod. We headed for the shop. I loved my hot-rod.

Ben was excited to see us. It was a pleasure to see a grin on his face.

Animal left the engine running as he checked something under the hood while Ben stood close to him pointing. From the look of relief on Ben's face, I knew Animal had given him the same news.

We were just getting ready to return to the house when Ben's cell sounded. I knew from the ring-tone it was Eric.

Ben answered quickly and we could hear Eric's voice loud and clear, "Good news, Dad, the auction was great. I got us a real bargain. I should be pulling in late afternoon if everything continues to run well. See you soon, bye."

Ben looked both relieved and very confused. We would just have to wait and see, I guessed.

Ben laughed and asked Animal to come see his new drawing. We trooped into the shop, still chattering away.

Sitting at the drafting table was an old man I'd never seen. He was a bit portly, wearing wire-rimmed glasses, with an old Greek seaman's hat perched at a jaunty angle on his curly grey hair. Although he was wearing suspenders, he looked solid in his frame. When he turned, I knew Les had made it there safely. His eyes gave him away even though they were a different color. Ben couldn't wait to share the news of the phone call.

My cell rang. I didn't recognize the number at all. Ben nodded for me to answer it. Animal looked over my shoulder and nodded. "Hello."

A voice spoke softly. "You have company at your house. It's all right." What were they saying? Who was that?

"Animal, I need to go home right now." I nodded my farewell and we left.

When we arrived home, the gate remained locked, as it should have been, with the security system turned on. The dogs were on the porch, waiting, sitting in their usual places.

Had the call been a prank?

Animal drove the rod into the garage, closed the door, and then walked with me to the porch. "It's okay, honest."

I knew someone was in the house. I could smell a very faint scent, which was unfamiliar.

I wasn't carrying; I felt naked.

How had they gotten in with the dogs outside? Who was here? The door to the guest room was open slightly. I knew I shut it when I left.

I reached for the pocket of my jacket hanging on the wall-rack.

Animal shook his head while touching me on the shoulder. He stepped ahead of me into the room.

There was Vicky lying on the covers with the pillows behind her. She looked so much better than the last time I'd seen her, I was overwhelmed. Thank God she was alive, or seemingly, almost alive. "I'm so glad to see you. You certainly look much better."

As I stepped toward the bed, my eye caught a movement in the corner, I spun, and sitting in the chair was an older man I'd never seen.

He smiled, stood, and then walked forward with his hand outstretched.

"I'm Vicky's father. My name is Roger. Thank you for allowing us to stay with you. We'll not be any trouble, I can assure you."

I was speechless. There was Vicky along with her father, here? How did that happen?

I turned to Animal, who was grinning from ear to ear. "Vicky's dad is a retired trauma doctor. He's on vacation here for a short time. I think you'll all enjoy each other.

"By the way, there's a van coming with some supplies shortly. I hope you like my choices."

As soon as the words were out of his mouth, the gate's alarm sounded. Animal took charge of escorting the van in, the unloading, and the exiting.

It was kind of fun because he had enlisted Zeus and Shadow in the process by giving them small bags to carry.

I went into the kitchen to see what was there... Oh my, where would I ever put all of that food, wine, liquor, paper goods, and other sundry items, which covered the floor? I was sure I would manage; after all, the house was large with good storage. So unlike the small cottage it had replaced.

True to his word, late in the afternoon, Eric arrived at the boat yard with a very large motorized sailboat. Ben called me when he first spotted the boat out in the harbor. This wasn't a local vessel, one Ben would've known. He'd used his telescope to try to identify it and then he spotted Eric at the rail.

All Ben said was, "Can you come now?" I checked with Vicky and her dad before I left. Zeus was still in command of the porch.

Animal had left him with me for a little while longer. Why, I wasn't sure. However, I loved having the goof and he was a sharp watchdog.

Ben was standing on the wharf as if he were waiting for the Queen Mary to land carrying a precious cargo.

The old fellow from the shop was with him; standing with his hands in his pockets and a pipe in his mouth. He was still wearing the Greek sailor cap.

I snickered. The man had a grey mustache, which had miraculously grown in the last few hours. Nice touch, Les.

They must send these folks to acting school prior to working for the department.

The vessel was large for the wharf.

Eric knew what he was doing. Soon he was sliding out a gangway. I noticed he had a crew aboard. Perhaps when you buy a boat this large it came already equipped with a crew. I didn't think so.

Eric looked great. He hugged his dad, then me, while he whispered, "It's almost over, hang in there."

"What do you think, Dad? Good thing to go mackerel fishing in?" It was so good to have Eric home. Ben just shook his head and smiled his old smile.

Eric inquired of his dad, "What's the weather for the next few days? Do you think I can secure the vessel in this spot or should I set a mooring for her?"

Ben reassured him the weather would hold for a few days, according to the forecasts for the area.

What a beautiful vessel…all white and teak with enough brass to create a marching band. To be honest, I couldn't wait to see the inside.

It made quite a statement sitting on the end of the pier with the lobster boats on moorings and racing boats along the other side of the wharf.

Even Dan, who'd arrived during the docking, was impressed. "Glad to have you home, Eric. These children of yours are a handful to keep in line."

Eric laughed and slapped him on the back. Eric always treated Dan like a younger brother. They were both great people.

Les hadn't uttered a word…strange!

I began to worry. It was never good when Eric and Les were there. I was there and Vicky was at my house. If they, whoever they were, still wanted all of us gone, they had us bunched up in one pen. It would be like shooting fish in a barrel.

I remembered, years ago, there was a saying, "Bunch them up, and you can get them with one grenade." I wondered…was this going to be the case now?

Forty

I never have long to ponder something like that because everything always seems to move at warp speed.

Shadow, who'd been sitting quietly beside me, began to whine. She was clearly anxious about something.

Just as I was getting ready to leave, the old man sidled up next to me. He brushed against me, making it look like he was unsteady on his feet. He spoke so low I almost missed what he said. "Can you use a knife? Make sure Vicky gets one and keep the other with you at all times." He toddled off toward the end of the wharf.

It was apparent Shadow wanted to leave *now*. We got into the Jeep and headed for home. She didn't sit on the seat, but stood at rapt attention. Something wasn't right.

I drove faster. I had the gate opened before I was even near it. Shadow was more agitated than before. The hair on the back of my neck was prickling.

What was wrong?

I grabbed my cell and rang Ben. He answered at once. "Where did you go?"

I couldn't talk I just wanted him to know something was up. What, I didn't know.

"Ben something's going on. I haven't a clue. I'm just going through the gate. If you don't hear from me soon, send help."

I pulled into the space by the garage, finding no Zeus. I had no gun; this wasn't good.

Shadow didn't wait for me to open her door. She jumped out of the open window, tearing for the porch with me on her heels. Zeus was lying in a heap on the ground with a huge bloody lump on his head.

I pulled out my phone and dialed Animal. Just as he answered, I heard Shadow growl. All I said was, "Help, Zeus has been hurt."

Before I could utter another word, someone yanked the phone from my hand and violently flung it to the ground.

The meanest looking man I'd ever seen was getting ready to shoot Shadow. I stepped in front of him. *Yes*, I had a protective instinct. She's my child. My move so unnerved the man he hesitated. Shadow leapt like lightning striking, and had him by the neck! I was horrified; she was truly going to kill him. He'd dropped the automatic pistol in his need to dislodge the dog. I snatched it up and pointed it at his knee. I pulled the trigger. He went down.

I'd forgotten how much damage a hollow point at close range could do to human flesh and bones.

Shadow was reluctant to let go, but she backed up a step.

I picked my phone up off the ground where he'd flung it. I punched in nine-one-one. When they came on the line, I told them I needed an ambulance and police ASAP. A man was bleeding to death. At this point, he was out cold.

I told Shadow to guard. I yanked off the man's belt and fastened it around what was left of his upper leg. I heard sirens.

Before the emergency vehicles arrived, Animal flew into the yard. I don't think he even shut the engine off or put the truck into park before he jumped out. He just nodded at the mess then rushed to Zeus. He carefully examined his dog.

Shadow was torn…she wanted to obey me, but she also wanted to go to her canine friend. When the attendants arrived to treat the man, I explained what he'd done. The officers were there and I recognized the one who worked with the department last year. He took charge of the man.

Zeus opened his eyes, clearly dazed, but he made one feeble wag of his tail. I prayed he'd recover. I felt horrible because he'd been hurt at my home.

Animal looked so concerned I wondered if we should have the medics check the dog. When I leaned over to ask him, he whispered, "Are the folks inside all right?"

"Oh dear, I don't know. I haven't looked yet! I'll go check."

Animal picked Zeus up, carried him to the porch, and placed him gently upon the padded wicker settee with a soft pat to his side.

Then Animal snuck up to the front door. As he moved silently to the door, he pulled his .45 auto. With his hand on the latch, and me practically in his hip pocket, he slowly and gently moved the latch. Shadow was backing me up.

We flew through the doorway. I grabbed the .38 from my jacket pocket as I sped by. Animal, with a show of speed and agility I never would have expected, rolled across the living room floor with the weapon at the ready.

I slid along the wall; the door to Vicky's room was ajar. I really didn't want to look; I knew I had to. I quickly checked Animal's position and shoved the door with the toe of my shoe.

I could see Vicky lying on the covers. She wasn't moving. I swung around so I could see the corner where her father had been. He was there, but he also wasn't moving. Animal dashed out of the door and grabbed the medics.

I didn't see any blood on either Vicky or her father. I prayed they weren't dead.

The medic rushed in with his box while he was sputtering about the man who was bleeding out on the gurney.

Animal put it into the right perspective, and I agreed with his statement, "Tough shit for him. He caused this. Now see what you can do here."

I felt sorry for the poor EMT. He clearly didn't know which one to look at first. Animal walked over to Roger. He checked for blood, then checked his throat for a pulse. The EMT seemed to take a hint from the move and checked Vicky.

I spotted a small bottle on the floor along with a hypodermic needle under the edge of the bed. I picked it up and passed it to Animal to see if he knew what it was. Animal passed it to the paramedic.

The EMT looked at the bottle; shook his head, then called for the other EMT to come in. She looked at the bottle then the needle, checking to see how much liquid was in each.

She shook her head slightly. "In my other life I was a nurse. This is one of the common sedatives used to put patients out. I don't know how much of a dose they received. I would strongly suggest you continue to monitor them very carefully until they regain conciseness.

"I don't think we can transport three in this unit. It'll take too long for anyone to come from another town. I'll call the retired doc in the village and ask him to come if that's okay with you."

Thankfully, the doctor came directly. He'd been on another call nearby. He had rushed out to the house.

When he arrived, Animal went out to assist him and fetch his bag from the car.

If I didn't know better, I would swear Dr. Brann was the minister's twin brother. He had the same white hair and blue eyes. However, he had a very serious expression on his face as he walked with purpose through the bedroom door.

First, he checked Vicky's pulse; then moved to Roger. "They are both too heavily medicated. Not knowing their health issues, it would be dicey to give them something to counteract it. Do you know how long they've been out?"

I shook my head, "I just came home a few minutes ago. Then I had the dust-up in the yard. When the EMTs came, we entered the house. It had been maybe fifteen or twenty minutes or possibly a little more. It's hard to judge time when you're having so damn much fun.

"Sorry, I think I'm a little tapped out here, please excuse my bad manners."

The doctor explained, "Depending upon their state of health and metabolism it could be soon or hours before they come to. He looks reasonably healthy." Then he looked at Vicky, shaking his head before resuming. "They should be able to throw off the effects of the drug in a reasonable fashion."

I know he wanted to ask me what had happened to Vicky so I just shrugged my shoulders and said, "Domestic abuse. She is, or was, much better than before."

The doctor looked me in the eye and stated, "I hope the man with the shot to the leg was the abuser. You should've shot him in the crotch."

I didn't want to tell this nice country doctor, but that had been my first choice. Sadly, common sense ruled my choice.

While we were conferring as to what I should do, when/or if they awoke, Roger began to stir. The doctor moved to his side, listening to his heart with the stethoscope. Roger was trying to regain consciousness, although he was confused. However, he didn't seem to be agitated.

The doctor was speaking very calmly with a good level of success. Roger was beginning to speak as well as trying to move.

The doctor explained to him what had happened. Roger nodded, inquiring about Vicky just as she moaned.

The doctor was quick to get to her side. Using the same technique, he listened to her heart and checked her vital signs.

She was coming around also, but there the similarities ended. Vicky was agitated and ready to do battle with the doctor.

I stepped to the side of the bed and touched her arm, saying as softly as possible, "Vicky, it's Eileen, you were drugged. This is the doctor from the village. It's going to be all right. Stay calm, we have this under control."

To my amazement, she calmed down after asking about Roger. The doctor answered her question, using a quiet voice. He also told her I shot the man who did this. She had nothing to cause her to be concerned.

Oh, if only he knew, I thought.

I heard the troops coming. I'd forgotten to call Ben and tell him everything was under control. Such a statement would have been a lie, and I knew it.

Animal was splitting his time between dog care and door attendant.

He filled them in with most of the facts, saving me the energy.

Both dogs were sitting up on the settee like two old folks watching the afternoon wane. I snuck out and gave them both a dog treat... too bad they don't drink wine; I would've served them a nice large glass. They had certainly earned it.

Eric made a dash for the bedroom, almost knocking Dr. Brann down in his haste.

Ben was patting me on the back as if I needed to be burped. Les was quiet.

What a bunch!

Forty-one

My cell rang. It was my sister. There wasn't any way I could share any of this situation with her. I stepped out onto the porch and casually chatted with her.

I knew she wasn't going to ask me about my guest, as it would go against the rules. This was a good thing. If I told her the truth, she'd have a stroke.

I assured her all was well in Maine. It was *finest kind* as we say locally. I promised to talk with her soon. However, now I had guests here.

Her inquiry about if I was sure everything was okay nearly had me in hysterics. I took a deep breath, reassured her everything was fine.

I lied again and told her I was in the middle of cooking a meal for guests.

She understood and told me she was pleased I had friends. We said good-bye. She was wishing she were here so she could eat one of my meals.

I laughed then ended the call.

Probably feeding this gang would be a good idea. Thanks, Sis, for reminding me I had things to do.

First, I needed to find out how the man had gotten in here. I checked the code reader on the gate. Someone must have given out the code. However, who would do that? It had to be someone I knew. It appeared the man came in using a code, not the emergency one. *I was very frightened.* This was a serious problem because so few people knew the code. Who could it be? I didn't think Les knew. The only people who had access were Animal, both Ben and Eric, and me.

I needed to review the video from the gate. I went into my office, locked the door, and rewound the video. There was no vehicle there. How did he arrive?

Then, there he was, driving up to the gate on a motorcycle. Mystery solved. He had pushed the call button and Roger answered. Motorcycle man told Roger he had a special delivery parcel for me. Roger had opened the gate.

Right then, I realized Roger hadn't a clue what Vicky did for work. Damn, that would be shaky ground to tread.

There was a quiet knock on the office door. When I opened it, I saw Ben and Les. "Eileen, we need to talk to you. Can we come in?"

Suddenly, I was finished. Much more of this and I was afraid I would shut down and never return to the alleged land of the living. I hated violence. It was all I'd dealt with for what seemed like forever. The sad thing was, I knew there was no immediate end in sight.

I allowed them in while making an understanding with myself. All I would do was listen, until I couldn't absorb any more, then they'd have to figure out for themselves what to do.

Ben pulled a chair over so he was sitting almost directly in front of me with his knee touching mine. At another time, I would've moved away. I didn't like anyone in my personal space. Les moved the other chair over so the three of us were all close. Leaning in, he began to speak, "Eileen, this isn't good... the man you shot is one of ours."

My heart sank. Then I was pissed, *really* pissed.

"What in hell was he doing here then? Why'd he drug them? Why hurt the dog and try to shoot Shadow?

"I want some damned answers and I want them quickly! This may be a game to you yo-yos but this is *my* life and I no longer want to participate in a game of stupidity. Is that clear?"

Les rubbed his hands together, and took a deep breath. After his usual internal argument with himself, he leaned closer and began to speak. "He was one of the people who'd gone rogue. We don't know who sent him here.

"As a precaution, I've put a set-up on him at the hospital to monitor who shows up or who he contacts. I don't even know what he was looking for, other than to be certain Vicky was here.

"We were so careful when we transported her for the return trip. I have no clue how he even knew. We didn't use anyone except people we trusted. This may have gone deeper than we suspected. Could you tell from the gate record how long he'd been here?"

I re-opened the system, checking the time and date stamps.

"He must have stashed the motorcycle in the woods and walked down before Zeus cornered him. He arrived at the door and Roger allowed him entry. He went about his nasty business with the drugs. He wouldn't have been in the house more than a very few minutes before I arrived.

"I came in right behind him, as you can see from the tape. I parked and ran with Shadow to Zeus. I must have interfered with whatever he was looking for, or what he'd planned to do.

"Would Vicky have recognized him as one of you?"

Les nodded. "He was one of the men who tried to kill her, me and Eric."

I asked, "What does this mean, Les? It was bold to have shown up here. Would he have known you were here? Where's this mess going?"

Ben hadn't said a word. I knew he was busy processing everything. Ben finally spoke. "Les, I don't believe Eileen could do another round and I know I can't. I know this is important and needs to be finished. However, the collateral damage to people not involved is too high. What are the alternatives?"

Les sat with his head hanging down. He looked like a man who'd lost his battle. He was clearly out of options.

In a way, I felt sorry for him... it truly wasn't his scrap anymore. He'd left the department. It just hadn't left *him*. The truth of the fact was obvious.

Just as Les was getting ready to reply, his cell rang. It seemed to surprise him as much as it did us, in my quiet office space. He answered quickly with a finger to his lips. "Yes sir, no sir, I'm sorry sir. Before I can answer your question, I need to ask the parties involved. Hang on for a moment, please."

Les turned back to Ben and me with a look of total disbelief in his eyes. "It's the Bureau Chief. He's requesting permission to come here to meet with everyone. This is either *very good* or *very bad*. It's your call, Ben and Eileen. What do you want me to tell him?"

Ben and I exchanged glances; saying almost in unison, "He can come if he can clear this mess up. We're done being pawns in a game we have no skin in. When will he arrive?"

Les turned his attention back to the phone, nodded once, saying only, "Yes sir."

"He'll arrive within the hour. I honestly don't know what he wants at this point. He may want to shoot all of us. That's how crazy this situation has become.

"On the other hand, he may want to promote us to become full-fledged agents. I guess we'll just have to sit and wait. We should tell the others about his impending arrival."

Les looked unenthusiastic about the encounter that was about to happen.

I needed to know, "Les, do *you* trust this man?"

He stood, looking totally lost and dejected. "I did, always. I also felt he was the last honest person I knew and could depend on... now I don't trust anyone or anything. I'm out of reserves, I guess."

Les continued speaking, "If the man you shot was here on orders from the chief, we're in for a go. I'm certain his being shot spurred the call. I need to go talk to Eric and Vicky."

I stopped his exit with a quick question. "Roger doesn't have a clue what Vicky's profession was, so does he understand the danger here?"

Les turned slowly and shook his head, "No, he doesn't."

Could this get any worse? I knew the answer to my own mental inquiry...*oh hell yes, and it probably would, soon.*

I reached over and patted Ben on the knee. He looked old and sad.

I was sure I didn't present any better.

I tried to lighten Ben's spirits. "Well kiddo, it was a good run while it lasted, huh?"

Ben didn't utter a sound. He looked like he was going to cry. How sad was that?

As Les exited the office, Animal entered and closed the door. He remained standing and seemed very uncomfortable.

I hoped Zeus hadn't relapsed or something worse. When Animal spoke, he seemed strangely unsure of himself.

My rocks were all turning to gravel before my very eyes.

Forty-two

Animal spoke slowly. "I need to leave for a while. Can I leave Zeus here? He's not up to speed, but with Shadow, I think you'll be okay. I've asked Dan to bring Bruno over as well. They all know each other so they'll be fine together.

"Please be careful and make sure you're *all* carrying, without being obvious.

"I think we're in for one hell of a scrap. I may be wrong. I pray by all that's holy I'm mistaken."

"I'm with Les… I don't trust anyone anymore." After all these years, that was hard to admit.

"I'll return soon. Stay safe and don't let anyone in except Dan with Bruno. As soon as the dog is out of the truck, send him back to the yard at once."

He bolted out, leaving Ben and me to sit and stare at each other. Ben reached his hand over and clasped mine. We just sat there in stunned silence, with our own thoughts. We were taking comfort from each other.

Eric was the next to arrive in the office. To say he looked like hell would have been the understatement of the year. His face showed the ravages of his very soul.

I stood and wrapped my arms around his neck and just held him close. "Eric what can I do to help?"

Under most circumstances, it would've been a normal and reasonable question. However, these were not normal or reasonable times. My heart was breaking for a man who was so dear to me.

God, I prayed, keep us all safe.

What was so horrific they couldn't share it with Ben and me?

When Eric stepped back and found his voice, he prompted us as Animal had. "Arm yourselves, but be discreet.

"I'm not sure what I should do with Roger. All these years he thought Vicky worked for the IRS investigating tax fraud. He knew who I was, but not what I did. Neither Vicky nor I think we should tell him. Les is also advising against it. What do you two think? Where can we put him so he'll be out of danger?"

We knew he couldn't stay here or at the boat yard. Where could we put him out of harm's way? I didn't want to involve anyone else in this mess. Animal had left for God only knew where. "How long will this mess take, Eric? I'm out of hiding places. Would he go willingly? How about we get Dan to take him for a scenic boat ride?" Boy, that sounded stupid even to me, but it would get them out of danger for a while.

Eric's eyes lit up and the crinkle around his eyes made a brief appearance. As he burst from my office, he tossed over his shoulder, "Good thinking! It will get both Dan and Roger out of this mess. Dan is almost here with Bruno. This may be the sales job of the century, but it's worth a shot."

Ben shook his head. "How do you think of this stuff?" I shrugged my shoulders and smiled as the gate alarm announced Dan and Bruno's arrival.

Eric must have been a good sales rep because Roger was talking and animated as Eric explained to him how Dan was going to test one of their special low profile racers. He also added how Dan would love to show off to anyone who had the daring-do to ride along with him. Eric ushered Roger out of the door just as Bruno arrived amid the barks of the other three dogs.

First, Bruno ran to check with Eric, then on to the canine fan club lined up on the porch.

Strange, I thought, Bruno and Zeus did know each other. I wondered how. As far as I knew, they'd never been together. I stored the thought for later reflection, if there was a *later*.

I walked into Vicky's room. Even though she was still on the bed, she looked stronger and more resolved than before. I hoped the meeting wouldn't be too much for her fragile health and mental state.

I stuck my hand into the pocket of my jeans and touched the two knifes Les had given me earlier. I palmed one, and passed it to Vicky. To an outsider, they would have only noticed a hand pat as I asked, "Are you feeling better now?"

She nodded and seemed to rally. Only her eyes gave her away, reflecting the fear she carried. I leaned closer as if to fluff her pillows and whispered, "Do you have a weapon where you can reach it?"

Her nod said it all. Still she whispered in her hoarse voice, "Thank you for everything no matter what happens."

I patted her hand and walked out onto the porch to look out over my cove. What would happen? Only God knew.

I prayed silently. *Dear God, I know You have a plan, but could You please share some of it with us before we die of fright? Thanks for all You have given me. I have always been grateful for all the good times, people and pets You allowed me. Please keep all of these folks safe.* They were good hearted, kind, and caring people. As if in answer to my prayer, Ben came and stood beside me looking out to the water. His big presence comforted me. We were still standing there when the gate alarmed and Animal arrived.

Animal wasn't alone. There were four men with him…three wore combat gear and carried assault rifles. The other wore business attire. Nobody I recognized.

Eric didn't look pleased. Neither did Les.

My radar went off big time.

Ben watched Eric. We couldn't see Vicky. Her door had swung closed, leaving it only slightly ajar.

All the dogs were at attention; lined up on the porch, even poor old Seaweed. They were deathly silent, not making a sound. I found that odd and discomforting.

The squad headed toward the front door. Then the three military men split off from the group. One headed to the tree line above the cove. He instantly blended into the bushes out of sight. The second one climbed the ledges and disappeared into the tree line behind the garage. The third vanished into the rocks on the point below the house. Good choreography well planned. The men moved into place silently with no voice commands uttered. Animal advanced to the door with the remaining man.

All I thought of was the jacket I was wearing. It concealed not only my .38 revolver but also the .45 caliber automatic. Eric had given me the .45 just before the car chase, which seemed like ancient history.

I prayed my knees wouldn't shake so hard my spare ammo would rattle in my pockets.

Ben stood, stoic as usual, with no visible emotion showing on his face. My plan was to mimic him.

Animal walked into the living room, as if he visited every day, and introduced strangers to me.

His inquiry was all business. "Will Vicky be able to join us in the living room?"

I wondered if she could, and if so, how would she be able to conceal a weapon? "I'll inquire and see if we can make her comfortable out here. It may take a few moments."

I entered her room to find her sitting on the edge of the bed. She had apparently heard the request. She was still dressed only in her gown and robe. I helped put on her slippers.

She whispered she needed her small pillow. I reached over to get the pillow and she shook her head. I touched the other one laying there, getting a nod.

I asked gently, "Can you stand and walk, or do you need to be carried?"

What guts this woman had. She stood with great effort, put her hand on my shoulder, and we made our way slowly to the recliner. She sat while I adjusted the control, then passed it to her so she could use it.

She took the pillow and swaddled it against her stomach, clutching it to her as if in dire pain. "Are you able to sit? Will that be too taxing for you?" She closed her eyes and nodded.

We were quite a bunch. Animal stood by the door with a look which indicated he could be gone in an eye-blink. Eric stood near the entrance to the kitchen, with his back against the wall. Ben was near the fireplace gazing out through the window, with seemingly subtle glances. They were watching the areas where the men had deployed. Les stood where he had a direct sight line to the new man. *His watchfulness was not friendly.*

The only thing missing from the picture was that nobody was armed, at least nothing visible. Thankfully, I knew otherwise.

The new man was checking out the room with his eyes while not moving his head or body. *He was good at this game.* I could tell it wasn't his first field assignment. Nor, from the looks of him, did he expect it to be his last. Especially considering the crew he had come with.

I wasn't comforted in any way.

I would guess a full three minutes passed without anyone uttering a word. That *had* to change. I have always hated silence. If you're going to kill me, do it, get it over, and then be finished. Stop jerking us around.

I figured, oh what the hell. "I guess it's time to call this meeting to order or cancel it. Who's going to start? Did anyone bring an agenda, or is this a practice run?"

My attitude at least brought forth a chuckle from the new man; followed by Animal, Eric, Les, and Ben.

Comedy was good; I wasn't laughing.

New Man spoke. "I think the only ones here who don't know me would be you, Eileen, and Ben. The rest of us are *old souls,* so to speak. I'm sorry we're meeting under these circumstances, but it was unavoidable. I'll get right to the meat of my reason for being here.

"Vicky I'm happy to see you're looking so well. Especially for someone I understood was dead. I'll come back to address that in a minute.

"Animal, I'm sorry I blew your cover. It was necessary; I needed you to get this straightened out.

"Eileen, you've taken the brunt of this mess without even knowing what you stepped into. Additionally, it doesn't seem to want to go away.

"Eric, I truly appreciate what you bring to the table.

"Les…forget it, you are not, and have never been retired. I need all of you if this situation is going to be resolved.

"Vicky, the instant I received word of what happened to you, I initiated a silent tracer to verify facts. Everything I received informed me the story I'd received was pure fiction. *However,* with a great back up cover story.

"If you hadn't arrived here, they would have killed you. Of course, in that case, I would've been no use to you. As far as I knew from trusted sources, you were dead.

"Before the smelly stuff hits the fan, I want to tell all of you how sorry I am you're all involved in something you know nothing about. I'm hoping we can stop this here and now.

"The man you shot the other day was someone I'd put great trust in. If you hadn't shot him, Eileen, I never would have found out how deep in the manure pile he really was. I didn't send him on a mission; he created that on his own. Thankfully, you didn't kill him. He's just going to wish he were dead when I'm through with him.

"I've rounded up the group you identified, Eric; they're all in separate cells, in different places. It will be just a matter of time and they'll be singing about each other, and perhaps more outside sources.

"Vicky, I need names of who was involved in this mess with you. Can you ID them?"

At first, she nodded, then after some mental reflection, she spoke in her husky, but much stronger, voice. "It makes no difference now. I'm a dead woman walking, no matter how you dice it. One was a person named Volt, who'd worked on our team. He knew everything we knew with the exception of some new information I'd stumbled into by accident. I was going to pass it along that day until he started acting oddly.

"The other man was Gregg S. and someone they kept referring to as Sue. I never saw or knew who that person was.

"We were standing at the table talking, which wasn't out of the ordinary, when Volt wanted to know where Eric was. I told him I was sure Eric would check in with the unit soon.

"Eric did. Volt told him we had new info and wanted him to come at once. I didn't know of any new info other than what I'd recently learned, but hadn't shared yet. I kept quiet.

"When Eric arrived with Bruno, Volt began acting nuts... first about the dog, then about me. Eric stated it was time for him and me to leave. Volt pulled his weapon and fired at Eric, hitting him. I saw Eric go down. Bruno grabbed Volt while Gregg began pistol-whipping me.

"He was laughing and calling me names. I never had a chance to get my weapon out. The next thing I heard was shooting without a silencer…I passed out.

"I woke up in a hospital. They told me both Eric and Bruno were dead.

"I was done. They patched me up. When they released me, I went away for a few weeks and tried to heal my mind and body.

"When I came back to the unit, I submitted my resignation, cleaned out my cubby, and walked away.

"I got to my car, and stashed my stuff in the trunk. However, before I could get into the car, someone grabbed me and threw me into a van. No one spoke. Someone yanked a hood over my head and we drove off. I can't tell you how long we drove.

"When we arrived, it was dark. I was manhandled into a building and dragged down to the basement. I surmised it was an older house because of the odors.

"Once we got into the basement, they began to strike me. I still had the hood on so I couldn't see them, first one then the other.

"When I fell onto the concrete floor, they kicked and stomped me. I played dead. At that point, it didn't require many acting skills.

"They called each other Carson and Willey.

"They were standing there discussing the fact they were doing trades from their desks at the bureau. They were getting passes for the buyers to come into the building right under your nose.

"Sorry sir…they said you were the most 'fog-bound and inept good-old-boy they'd ever encountered someone who couldn't find his own ass if he had both hands free'. If they'd figured this out sooner, their offshore accounts would be a hell of a lot fatter than they were.

"They talked about how they were going to dispose of me. They decided later would be better because I wasn't going anywhere.

"They also wanted to have a hit of the new *stuff* they'd just gotten.

"As soon as I heard the basement door close and I heard them walking around upstairs. I got the hood off. The basement was full of what looked like cardboard shipping cartons.

"I crawled around looking for an exit. I found what looked like an old coal chute. I kept trying to crawl up inside of it. I finally made it, but when I reached the outside door, I found it locked. I knew they'd return to get rid of me. I needed out. I managed to get one of the windows to open. Then I heard them returning. I hid back in the coal chute.

"I was badly hurt and knew my time was running out. When they got down there, they saw the window and stared yelling at each other.

"Another person, who seemed to be more in charge, stated it didn't make any difference where I'd gone, they could track me. They called him Getchell.

"I don't know how long I stayed inside the chute but I was fading in and out. I knew I had to attempt to get out through the window. I made it out.

"I looked back at the house. It was an old brownstone number eleven sixty-eight on the corner of Colonial and State.

"I made it about two blocks and fell. That was when this angel picked me up and put me into her car. She sent me here. That started the mess for these folks."

The man in the chair seemed impassive. His expression hadn't altered one iota while Vicky talked. She looked drained. It was like watching a chess match while not understanding the game at all.

Not a soul in the room stirred. It was as if time had ceased to be.

I didn't know what to expect. I, also, just stood.

Animal changed the dynamics. "Sir, man on point A is sneaking down from the tree line and signaling to point B. He's on the move also. It looks like they're taking up new positions."

Eric spoke up, "C is on the move. I thought their orders were to stay put unless you personally notified them. Did you, sir?"

This whole situation was strange. Nobody had bothered to introduce either Ben or me. We didn't have any idea about what this person was or whom he represented. Les had told us he was the chief. O*f what?*

How did Animal play into this? Far too many questions, no logical answers, and I never dealt well without logic.

Animal looked at me and patted where he knew I had the .45. I nodded my head slightly so he knew I was aware.

Les spoke up. "Well sir, you have us all in a fish bowl, so you can get us all at once. Then you can take your hangmen and be off to greener pastures. What are you waiting for? You now have the information, if you truly didn't know, everything you need to know. Ball's in your court.

"You worked in the field before you began flying a desk. You were a good operative. I trusted you, but at the moment I think the time has arrived to either buy or fly…the tides have turned."

Without ever looking up, the chief said, "It's done; I have the last pieces of the puzzle. Now we're going to close this final chapter right now. Animal, do it now!"

What in the hell had he meant? Animal took what looked like a small garage door opener out of his pocket. He opened the cover, looked over at the chief and quietly asked, "Are you certain? We can take them, you know."

"Do it now!" was the reply from the chief.

Animal looked from Les to Eric then said, "Ready?" Both nodded and Animal did something with the gadget he held in his hand. There were three small distinct explosions.

Animal, Eric and Les burst out through the doors. Eric went to the shore. Animal went to the cove. Then Les went to the tree line.

Ben had his gun in his hand, guarding the door Eric had gone through. I moved toward the front door then changed my direction when I saw Vicky had a full sight line to the door and she was holding what looked like a 9mm Glock in her hand. I went to the kitchen door.

I couldn't see movement. The dogs were all gone, with the exception of Seaweed. Strange, they'd followed the men without a single growl or bark.

How still the house was. Not a sound from anything or anyone; total silence. We waited.

It was like hunting. I remembered sitting quietly for long periods waiting for the prey to appear so it could be shot and harvested.

Still we waited.

The first movement I saw was from the cove. Two men were walking toward the parking area. Zeus was with them. Animal had the man who was dressed in military gear completely bound with rope from head to foot. He looked like a rolled roast with a noose around his neck. If he moved, he'd strangle himself.

I sidled to the front window and could see two men walking down from the tree line by the ledge. It was the same thing, except Shadow was with Les.

Where was Eric? My heart began to hammer just as Ben said, "Eric is coming around to the front."

Same show, except this time Bruno was with them. They were all standing in groups in the parking area when the gate alarm sounded.

It startled me. *Dear God, help us, who could be coming here now?*

The chief spoke, "It's all right; that should be the transport I ordered for our friends. You can let them in." I pushed the gate release.

A horrid looking Hummer painted flat black lumbered into my parking area. Without an ounce of fanfare, they loaded the trussed prisoners into separate doors resembling individual cells without untying them. The men from the vehicle returned to their seats and drove off.

The chief extracted his phone from his pocket. I would have to say, for a 'fog-bound, inept, etc.,' person, he was precise with his orders. He used a voice accustomed to commanding. "Pull the alarm. Everyone, and I mean *everyone*, is to go to the meeting place and stand down. No one is to leave the area for anything.

"Collect all weapons, cell phones, tablets, pagers, etc. I want no electronics or weapons to leave the space. Place them in bins and leave them there.

"I have the buses ready for the pick-up; they already have their orders as to where to go. It's all prepared. I don't want a soul in the building. Consider it to be on permanent lock-down until I say so.

"Let me make one thing clear and certain to you. If you screw this up in *any* way, you'll be counting paper clips in Leavenworth for the rest of your days. Am I clear? Once everyone is out of the building and boarded on the buses, you are to join them. I'll be in touch."

The men had returned and the dogs were back on the porch. As always, it was *as if nothing ever happened,* all over again.

The chief spoke into his cell once more with the same authoritative manner. "Stop and strip each of them thoroughly, include body cavities. Leave them naked and keep them separate. If you find anything I should know about, call me."

Bruno began to howl a strange keening noise I'd never heard a dog make.

Eric dashed out the door with Animal on his heels. Bruno headed for the cove, fast. The men were in hot pursuit. Bruno stopped. He stood still, yet at total attention, all blocked up, looking at the ground.

What was wrong? Had the dog snapped?

Eric circled around behind to one side and Animal circled to the other side. They just stood there. Eric must have ordered Bruno back. Then both men retreated away from the shoreline.

Still, they seemed to be watching something. Then from about six feet out in the water there came a soft *whump* of a sound then a large spurt of water sprayed up into the air. I could see Eric and Animal laughing like kids as they returned.

The cell that sat on the chief's knee buzzed, "Only two? Did you dispose of them? We found the other one. Carry on and don't stop for anything and I do mean *anything*. Do not refuel, no toilet breaks, nothing. Am I clear?"

The chief took up the conversation. "First I want to address Vicky. What is it you want to do? Do you really want to leave your career? The treatment you received was abysmal. I wouldn't blame you for wanting out.

"Let me offer you a deal. You're a great agent and an asset to the service. I'd like you to take six months leave with full pay and benefits. I'm also going to give you a pain-and-suffering package.

"If it's your decision not to return, you'll never have to be concerned about financial security.

"If you do opt to return, you'll be a trainer-analyst with no fieldwork ever again. Think about it and we'll talk again in a few weeks.

"Les, I know you also resigned. I didn't accept it. Sorry, but you're needed. Especially now, while we regroup. I want you to come to the center as my assistant. All perks, benefits and raises retroactive to when you thought you quit. I have a strong need for people I can trust, totally.

"Eric, I know you don't want full time service, but I'd like you to stay on in the capacity in which you've been serving. However, you change rank, also retroactively to when this started last year with the pay and benefits included.

"Animal, I already know your answer about returning to the bureau and I don't blame you. The lifestyle no longer holds any appeal. However, I will compensate you for your services, for this entire mess. I want to feel, in the future, we can continue to collaborate on special projects, hopefully not in your back yard.

"Ben I personally want to thank you for all of your assistance in this matter. Les will take care of this with you, electronically.

"Now, Eileen, we have used your property yet again and your hospitality. I hope and pray there will be no more difficulties here. Les will also compensate you in the same method as Ben.

"To all of you, this is important; I think I've rounded up all of the main players in this drama. I think you would all do well to keep your guard up, stay armed for a bit, and remain vigilant. We have ruined many big-money sources today.

"Within hours, I'll have cleaned out most of the staff at Central, charged some, imprisoned some, and just plain fired some. There will be fall-out, I'm sure.

"Not too shabby for a fog-bound, inept, good-old-boy, who just for reference, *can* find his own ass with both hands."

Les spoke up, "Sir I'm pleased you asked me to work with you but I need to know why you're replacing your current assistant."

The chief never changed expression. "He lied to me. It was a small matter and didn't or wouldn't make any difference in the grand scheme of things. I believe if you will lie a little then you'll lie a lot. When trust is gone, it's over in this business.

"By the way, Animal, I'll be sending you a new load of dogs next week. Can you handle them? You know what I'm looking for."

Standing slowly, he looked around at the view. "Someday, I would love to come and just sit here and watch the water and listen to the gulls. I've missed so much over the last few years.

"Les, are you ready to leave? I need to get back and sort out the sheep from the goats. This will be a long couple of days. Vicky, get better. Eric, thank you again. Ben and Eileen, so much has been accomplished, all because of your tenacity.

"Oh by the way, Eric, you get to keep the boat you returned with. However, the crew is already gone, so you are on your own to operate it.

"To all of you, remember, *this never happened.*"

They all left, driving out of the yard as if they had been casual visitors.

I noticed Zeus was still here. It seemed odd the dog was still around, but I knew Animal would be back shortly for him.

I wanted to ask either him or Eric about the explosion in the water at the cove. I chose Eric. "What was all the ruckus about down in the cove?"

Eric smiled, "The noise Bruno made let me know it was either an IED or some kind of explosive. We use those when we want to create a diversion, or make it seem as if there are more of us than there really are. They can be radio controlled to move along the ground or you can manually wind them up. When you want an explosion, you either push the control switch or set the timer on them. They're one of our many toys."

Forty-three

We just kind of sat and stood around in stunned silence. It was so quiet in the room I could hear the click of the battery operated clock in the kitchen. *My guess is we were doing what you should do, when you are a player in something that never happened.*

I hated the silence. I broke it with, "Shall I fix us something to eat and drink? I can't remember when we ate last. I'm starved…how about you folks?"

I threw together a bunch of munchies then started to cook dinner.

Just as the snack-tray began making its rounds, Dan returned with Roger. He looked like a kid who'd just had the greatest time in his life.

We all dug into the food and drinks.

I sipped from the wine glass Ben handed me. *I think this is finally over.* Then I took a deep breath and thanked God we were all safe and mostly unharmed.

Vicky would recover. She'd become a healthy, happy and well-loved young woman again.

Roger entered the kitchen as I was setting out the food. He looked somewhat sheepish. "Eileen, is this mess really over or is this just a lull in the action? I'm not as dumb as I appear. I figured out a long time ago Vicky was an agent, but never said anything to her. I was certain if she thought I knew then I'd worry. I've worried more than you can imagine. I raised her to be independent so I can't tell her to stop now. Thank you for taking care of her. I'll always be grateful."

I didn't know what to say, but he deserved an answer. "I don't honestly know if it's done. I think we're much safer now than we were. After all this mess, I don't trust anyone anymore. I never was a very trusting soul; however, Ben and Eric have restored some of my faith in humanity. Let's pray it's over."

I served dinner to the hungriest folks I ever remembered. We just ate and sipped while the fire blazed in the fireplace and darkness fell softly on the cove. The stars were super bright and twinkling, making a subdued light. Peace at last? Perhaps…we would have to wait and see.

Forty-four

The next few days were quiet; Vicky was recovering nicely under Roger's quiet watchfulness.

The day began with a lovely sunrise and the promise of light breezes and ample sunlight. My guests were sitting on the patio enjoying the sun's warmth and ocean views.

Eric arrived for his usual early morning visit, along with Bruno. His arrival always sparked the day. There were laughter and dog yips as the dogs played happily. They were seemingly all over the property playing a game that resembled hide and seek. They were quite a sight to see. Zeus, Shadow, and Bruno bounded over the rocks into the tree line only to emerge, join up, then race across the rocks. Then they ran back to poor old Seaweed while she sat on the settee like a queen. They would check in with her then bound away again.

My hopes for the day were visiting the shop, enjoying Ben's company, and maybe, just maybe, going for a sail.

It had been so long since we'd enjoyed any normal time here.

As I was putting my bag together, the dogs began a chorus of barking, yipping, and tail wagging. I went to check out the new influence and found all of the dogs down at the cove.

Ben had sailed into the cove. He tossed the line to Eric who pulled him ashore. As I stepped out onto the veranda, Ben looked up, smiled, and called, "Is there a lady here who would like to go for a sail and a picnic?"

"That would be me." I grabbed my bag and headed for the cove.

We sailed and talked while enjoying our peace and freedom until we reached the little deserted island where we went ashore for our picnic.

The island was very small with a sandy cove on the inshore side where you could beach a boat. The rest looked to be rocky shoreline.

As we were getting out of the boat, I noticed footprints in the sand. They would've been very recent because of the tides. We looked around, but there were no other boats there.

I leaned into Ben and said, "Whoever was here came in an inflatable and carried it up into the tree-line. Should we call Eric or just leave? Why would they be hiding?"

Ben nodded and told me we needed to leave. He went to the edge of the rocky out-crop to scan the shoreline.

When he returned, we shoved off and sailed around to the end of the island. Ben called Eric on his cell to report.

We sailed off to a location where we could still observe the island without being too obvious.

Shortly we spotted the Zodiac heading out to the area we'd left. Eric was not alone; I could make out Bruno and another man with a dog. Who would that be?

"Ben, can you make out who is with Eric, other than Bruno? It looks like a man with a dog. The animal looks like a big Shepherd."

Ben was watching intently but he shook his head, "Your eyes are better than mine to even notice the breed of dog. I'm going to sail back toward the island, if you don't mind."

We swung around, and I could see who was with Eric. It was Animal. I still couldn't recognize the dog.

We tacked back toward the island, staying some distance off shore.

When Eric beached the boat, all of the dogs hit the sand as if they were on a mission. The men were close behind. There was no barking, just serious trailing. It wasn't long before they re-emerged from the trees with a man in front of them wearing camo-gear. Oh, oh, that didn't look good.

Eric and Bruno had the man while Animal went back into the bushes, returning moments later with an inflatable in tow.

I watched Eric handcuff the man then load him into his own boat accompanied by the new dog on full alert. Eric, Animal, and Bruno boarded their Zodiac while tying a line to the other craft. They headed back to the boat yard.

Ben's cell rang. He put it on speaker, "Okay kids, you can go eat your picnic. The coast is clear. Call me if you need a tow home." As always, Eric enjoyed teasing us.

Ben looked at me and gestured towards the beach. I shrugged my shoulders and nodded. "Who owns this island Ben?"

I got a big grin along with the response, "I do."

I learned something new every day.

When we arrived at the beach and stepped out of the boat I grinned... on the sand, Eric had written '*Kilroy was here.*'

I wondered who the intruder was and what he'd been doing. I was determined to enjoy at least some of the day.

As always, Ben had brought the hamper fully equipped. He had a blanket, sandwiches, cheese, and a bottle of wine. Life doesn't get better than this.

We sailed back in the lengthening shadows of late afternoon. There was just a hint of chill in the air, although the weather was still pleasant. We glided into my cove and Eric pulled us onto the edge of the beach. What a treat, good service! I could get used to this.

Eric informed us the authorities were investigating our visitor from the island. He would keep us informed about who and why. He did take time to admonish us for not carrying. He also made it clear we still needed to be cautious.

Animal was sitting on the patio with the dogs. Seaweed was firmly ensconced in his lap, loving every second. I thought the new dog was a Belgian Shepherd.

He was very large with a nice, almost all black coat. He had a happy expression in his eyes. He was also very attentive to Animal.

The dogs socialized so well you would have thought they'd always known each other.

Animal made the introductions. "This is Bentley. He's a good boy with a checkered past. He's been living with me for a little while. It seems he sometimes forgets his manners and likes to play war-games with folks. It gets him into trouble. He won't bother either of you, as you don't pose what he considers a real *threat*. He's still not good with strangers, but he will be soon, then we'll find him a nice home."

The gate alarm sounded. I checked the screen and saw a familiar face; it was Woodie. He hadn't been here for some time. It would be fun to see him again. He rattled into the yard with his old pickup truck parking down in front of the garage.

As always, the group of dogs went off to do the meet and greet, all but Seaweed.

Animal watched, not saying a word. He never took his eyes off Bentley. He took out his silver dog whistle, blew, and the whole group sat as if suddenly turned to stone.

I was always amazed at that.

Woodie spoke to the dogs, then walked on past them coming up to the patio. I loved the fact he never addressed anyone. He just ambled up, gave a general nod, and then folded his big frame into a chair. It's as if he were attending a lawn party.

He looked around at the shrubs and garden plantings with a big grin of satisfaction.

Animal made a hand gesture, allowing the dogs to join us. They came, checked in with him, and then sat, awaiting further instructions. His move was so subtle, unless you were watching very closely you would've missed it. They all laid down at ease. What a picture of tranquility.

I had to ask, "Woodie, what brings you out this way? I'm delighted to see you for whatever reason you've come."

Woodie looked at Animal. "I came to meet this new fella Animal has. He told me he'd be visiting with you and I should come by, so I did. I like the dog. He's big and rugged and looks as if he would make a great pal to go with me. Does he like to ride? Would he be afraid of the equipment? Other than bad guys, what do you feed him?"

Now this was the Woodie I knew and loved. He was always a 'no nonsense, just the facts' kind of a man.

I never knew if he liked the dogs or not. He always patted them and they seemed to like him. I assumed Woodie lived alone, so perhaps a companion would be nice for him.

Animal was slow to answer, "He loves to ride and I haven't found anything he's shy about around the shop. He needs to have one master who he's certain is in charge, or he *will* take charge.

"He walks well on or off a lead. Let me see how he is with you one-on-one. Walk down toward your truck and I'll send him to you."

Woodie stood and sauntered toward his truck while Animal motioned the dog to come to him.

He bent down and spoke softly to the dog while Bentley maintained constant eye contact with him. With the flick of his hand, he sent Bentley off. The dog caught up with Woodie and walked in lock step with him to the truck.

When Woodie stopped, Bentley sat watching him for orders. Woodie walked up the drive toward the gate with the dog seemingly attached to his leg. What a sight!

When Woodie returned to the patio, he had a big grizzly-bear grin on his face. He sat back in his chair. Bentley sat by his side with Woodie stroking his head. They both looked like they needed each other.

I'd never thought too much about Woodie's home life, although I'd guessed he lived alone. He seemed connected to the new dog that had arrived in our midst.

Woodie and Bentley went home together with the promise he'd bring him to Animal for more training.

Animal shared some of Woodie's history with me later. When Woodie was in the service years earlier, he'd been a dog handler. However, he hadn't had a dog since. Woodie had confided in Animal it'd been too hard to train them, and then give them up. Now, he had his own. Animal seemed happy with his choice for Bentley.

Eric's cell had sounded as he walked out onto the patio with Vicky on his arm. His conversation was short, ending with a huge chuckle. "Well children, it seems our visitor to the island was someone from out of state who'd watched too many survival television stories. He came to Maine thinking it was deserted. He was going to see if he could live *off the land* for six months. They ran him through all of the databases and he showed clean.

"However, being he's from away, they're going to let him stay in the crow bar hotel overnight. We should be nice and go fetch his gear for him, I guess. I'll run out now and retrieve it. Be back in a few. Animal, you up to another boat ride?" Eric, Animal, and Bruno departed for the island leaving Ben, Vicky and me to visit.

Vicky sat enjoying the warmth of the sun. She looked so much better I knew she'd soon be leaving. I wondered if she would move down to the boat yard with Eric.

Roger strolled out to join us. He looked rested, but something was on his mind. He sat, pulling his chair a little closer to Vicky reaching out to touch her hand.

His voice was quiet when he spoke, but what he had to say was for all of us to hear. "I have to leave tomorrow and get back to the clinic.

"Before I leave, I want to set the record straight. Vicky, I always knew what you did for a career. I suspected it long ago, fretted, then hoped you'd get tired of the danger and opt out of the service. I've come to peace with it. You're an adult and what you choose to pursue for a career path is your business. I wonder if you realized how close to dying you were this time. Your body can't withstand this kind of constant trauma. If you're thinking sometime down the road you'd want to have children and a different life, this may be the time to make a change. Perhaps give up the fieldwork, or just retire. I wish you'd at least consider it. Maybe you'd like to come home for a period while you make up your mind."

"Ben, do you think I could impose on you for a ride to the airport tomorrow afternoon? I've booked a flight out at two."

Vicky looked at her dad with tears in her eyes... then she looked away toward the cove where we could see Eric and Animal just rounding the rocky outcrop, arriving at the beach.

The men landed with lots of laughter and bad-boy banter.

When Eric reached the patio he greeted Roger, still grinning, until he looked at Vicky, then his expression sobered. "Vicky what's the matter? Did something happen, while I was gone? Are you okay?"

Vicky nodded then asked Eric to pull up a seat while she explained the recent conversation with her father. Eric looked relieved and smiled, "Well sir, I understand your concern, so I guess now is as good a time as any to discuss it, along with our intentions. Vicky, do I have your approval? I wish you weren't leaving so soon, but we know you have a life and the clinic to take care of.

"Vicky and I are going to be married. We'll live here and make it our home. Our intention is neither of us will be involved with the service again, once this mess is completed. We'll both have to testify and wrap up loose ends; however, we'll use computers and the phone to facilitate most of this. I hope I have your consent to marry your daughter. I'll protect her and make her happy."

Eric turned his attention to Ben. "Dad, do you think we could get the minister from church to marry us this evening so Roger can be here?"

Ben looked at me. We both grinned and dashed off to make phone calls. All they needed was a marriage license and the minister. I called the town office while Ben called the minister.

A wedding; tonight. WOW! What would she wear? Where would they do it? What would I feed them? Easy, I can do this. After all, it is *only* late afternoon.

The wedding went off without a hitch. It was the first time I ever attended, or was part of, a moonlight ceremony on a patio.

The scent of the late blooming flowers had been a perfect complement to the salt air. The bride was lovely. After a great deal of raiding the closets, she was beautifully dressed, including fresh flowers for her hair and bouquet.

Eric was handsome beyond words. I suppose it was because I'd never seen him in a suit and tie.

Ben turned out in suit and tie looking quite dapper.

Animal was the biggest surprise of all…he was dressed in a suit and tie along with a newly trimmed beard and hair.

We all enjoyed a nice, quiet, late wedding dinner jointly prepared by Bea, Eric's cook, and me. She somehow even produced a small, but elegant, wedding cake. An excellent wine accompanied everything. Then most of them went home.

Only Roger, Zeus, Shadow, and Seaweed stayed with me.

After everyone left, I cleaned the kitchen and set the dining room in order. Around here, you never knew what would or could happen next. I needed to be prepared.

I took the dogs for their evening stroll. Even though it was getting chilly, the air was refreshingly clean with the strong scent of pine and salt air while the stars sparkled. It was a perfect evening to end a lovely day.

We would take Roger to the airport while Eric and Vicky would go cruising in the newly acquired boat for a couple of weeks.

Forty-five

The trip to the airport was uneventful, thankfully.

We treated ourselves to dinner on the way home while discussing our boat building business. Even though we'd been in turmoil, it seemed the orders had flooded in. We needed to get a production schedule in the works to fill them.

At a time when we least expected it, we were successful and busier than ever.

The house seemed empty and quiet after all the hubbub. It took me a couple of days to get back to the usual swing and rhythm of life.

We sailed in the afternoons when we had time. I was getting better, and more confident, with Ben teaching me from the other boat. I wasn't ready to sail to Europe yet. I felt I could at least sail solo around the islands, which was all I really wanted to do.

Ben laughed at me because I still fished any chance I could get.

I began to wonder why Animal hadn't taken Zeus home yet. I loved the dog. He seemed to be content to sit on the porch overseeing the property.

When I went to the shop, Shadow always traveled with me while Seaweed would lie on the settee with Zeus sitting or lolling in front of her, guarding the property, although I had caught him napping in the afternoon sun while still looking like a guard dog.

When I returned from the shop late the next day, I met Animal just coming into my driveway. Talk about mental telepathy! I was happy, as always, to see him.

I guessed he'd come to retrieve Zeus.

When he got out of his truck, he reached back onto the seat and retrieved what appeared to be a large cat. Then I realized it was a very small dog.

I'd never seen him with anything but large or very large animals. He had the bundle wrapped in a black and white bath towel. "What on earth do you have there? At first I thought you had a cat."

Animal shook his head, grinning as he offered the bundle to me. "I brought you something. She's in rough shape. I thought if anyone could rehab her, it would be you. Somebody tossed her out on the roadside, leaving her to die. You can see by how thin and malnourished she is as well as beaten nearly to death. I gave her a flea-dip because as you can see she has almost no hair. She's been so flea ridden they nearly finished off the job the humans began."

I took the poor creature from him and looked into the saddest eyes I had ever seen. She was a very tiny old Sheltie. She had almost no hair with the exception of her white ruff. She was shaking all over with terror. I held her and stroked her tiny head. How can people be so cruel to something without any defenses?

Animal was leaning back against his truck, smiling as if he'd gotten away with something. "What will you name her?"

I looked at him with a smile, "I didn't say I would take her...are you trying to fast-close me here? I'll keep her for you until she's well enough for you to find a good home for her. I'll call her Sand Dollar, Sandy for short. I'm not sure how the queen bee will take to a new Sheltie but we'll soon see."

"I guess you're going to swap her out for Zeus, right?" His answer took me aback. "Nope, he belongs here with you...see how happy he is? Here he's free. No one bothers him; he doesn't wander, and he has a job. If you ever have any problems, he'll take care of you. He won't let anyone on the property if you're here or not. I like the security for you. The test will be when cold weather comes. I'm hoping he'll come into the house with you and the rest of the group. He'd never come in for me. I never knew why. Where do you feed him?"

"In the house with the rest of them. It's quite a sight, like feeding time at the zoo. I get all of their dishes out and put the food in them. Then they each have to shake and give me five before I put the dish down.

"They never scrap over food or treats, although I have seen Seaweed filch a kibble out of Zeus' dish by walking up between his front legs and just helping herself. He didn't care, I guess, because the next time I fed them, he reached into his dish, took one piece of kibble and put it into her bowl. Now it's a habit at each feeding time. They all use the same water bowl, or tub, both inside and out. After they eat, he sometimes will just go over and lie on the entryway rug for a bit before I let them back out."

"Aren't you going to miss him?"

Animal shook his head, "Nope, I know where he is and that he's well cared for. I'm in the middle of training a new bunch of dogs for the returning and wounded vets. I have about fifty dogs at the property right this minute, with more due to arrive in about a month. Most of the dogs coming to me have seen combat and, like the vets, they have their own PTSD to deal with. I like what I'm doing."

Animal chatted on. "I stopped by to see how Woodie was making out with Bentley, and you wouldn't recognize him. He got a haircut, shaved off his beard, and trimmed his mustache. That wasn't the only thing…he began going into town to get his supplies. As far as I know, he'd never made the trip once since he came back here years ago. Oh, I also sold him a newer truck. It was a surprise to me. He takes Bentley with him everywhere. I got him a therapy dog jacket, so he can take him anywhere. Bentley has behaved like a champion with not a hint of aggression. That was a win-win for sure."

"He's going to come over and help me with this new batch of dogs and the vets. I guess we all came out of this mess in good order. I gotta go. See you in church Sunday. Say 'Hi' to Ben for me and take good care of your new project. Call me if you need me."

With that, he signaled Zeus to come. He gave him a scratch, a pat, and whispered something into his ear.

Animal got into his truck and left. Zeus moved over and sat at my feet looking up at Sandy.

I hadn't even considered how he would react to another dog in the house. It wasn't a problem. He added her to his harem just like this happened all the time. He'd nuzzle her, washing her face and feet. The oddest thing was when he'd lie down on his side, she would curl up alongside his stomach inside his long legs, and sleep like a baby.

It didn't take long before she was trying to run and play with the rest of them. The heavy romping and running was left to Zeus and Shadow, with the two old-lady dogs watching and joining in when the play quieted down.

I loved watching them enjoying each other. They were great company to me and to each other.

Life was once again peaceful and quiet in the cove. We didn't, at least *I* didn't, hear from either Les or the chief again...*yet*. To me it was a very welcome relief. No news was good news. I felt safe. There didn't seem to be any reason to carry a gun or consider anyone would be trespassing. Thank you, God!

We'd all relaxed our guard returning to our own lifestyles, more or less, while still running the *Survivor* business.

Forty-six

Animal arrived with yet another new friend amid the greetings from my group of dogs.

As always, it was quite a welcoming committee when anyone arrived at my home. Although they are happy to see friends, the dogs can appear equally as unwelcoming to strangers. I enjoyed the mix of attitudes. All of the dogs were well mannered; they would never jump up on a person or a vehicle.

I didn't think it was odd for Animal to come, although it had been awhile since I'd last seen him.

He'd been very busy for the past few weeks rehabilitating dogs from the military. He then matched them with discharged veterans. He enjoyed this task immensely.

First, he loved the animals, and then he had a real heart for what was happening to our men who'd served in the military. He described them as the walking wounded.

When the problems at Haven Cove had erupted several months and two lifetimes ago, we learned a lot about what happened to vets. We learned the fate of some who'd been discharged either honorably or otherwise released from the service.

Many of the men who returned from combat were so impaired by the horrors of war and the carnage they'd witnessed they couldn't overcome the mental anguish.

Some lost their families along with their homes. Some became drifters with no purpose because they couldn't settle back into a society which didn't or couldn't understand them, or relate to their problems. Some were so addicted it was their only interest. Others, due to the combination of issues, theirs, and our society's became victims of unscrupulous entities who wished only to further their own greed.

We were all upset about the smuggling of the weapons and drugs, not to mention the money found still wrapped in waterproof packets. However, when we unearthed the remains of several human remains in the swamp while rebuilding the road we were all shocked. Some of them were still wearing their dog-tags. That discovery changed all of us, in an instant; forever

I recognized Animal had a purpose as soon as he stepped out of his truck.

He didn't open the door for the passenger nor had they attempted to exit the truck.

As always, he came straight to the point. "Eileen, I wonder if you'd consider doing me a favor."

Of course, he *had* to be kidding. I owed my life to this person, in the literal sense, so why would he even ask? I guessed he saw the confusion on my face, so he continued with the request. "Could you billet someone for me for a few weeks?"

I'd known Animal for almost as long as I'd lived there I was still surprised at the request. Although I knew him, had been to his shop several times, I'd no idea of his living accommodations.

I knew he was working with vets who came to get dogs as companions after he re-trained them by helping the dogs adjust to peacetime conditions. So why did he need to find new lodgings for someone now?

He knew I'd housed Vicky when she arrived as an abuse victim, sent by my sister from Virginia.

It was apparent why Animal was asking when he walked back to the truck. He opened the door and escorted the passenger back to me.

Animal introduced us as if he were presenting her to the Queen. I had to admit, my internal snicker machine immediately went into overdrive, although I didn't let it register on my face or in my voice.

"Jaci, I want you to meet the very best person you'll ever get to know…my dear friend, Eileen. You can trust her with anything, including your life, if necessary. Eileen, this is Jaci…she's getting ready to work with one of my dogs in training.

"She'll need to be here for about a month or so. Can I leave the two of you to chat while I run an errand? I'll be about two hours." He almost ran to the truck and left.

The first time I met Jaci I knew here was a remarkable individual… not as you're thinking. She was average height, a little overweight but not pudgy, light brown to dirty-blonde hair pulled back into a very messy bun. She wore no make-up, or fingernail polish on what I'd describe as working hands. She was dressed in jeans and a sweatshirt. She wasn't stylish. I'd never take a second look at this person if I met her on the street or in a store.

When Jaci spoke, she looked me in the eye and used a very soft voice. It should have made me comfortable, especially when meeting a stranger. However, when I made eye contact I knew... her eyes are what I called old eyes meaning they've witnessed it all, most of it very bad. Her handshake was firm and confident. Her stance was the give-a-way, expressing her discomfort from meeting strangers in strange settings.

As we chatted, she relaxed slightly. To me, her attitude was very interesting. She appeared to be knowledgeable, and seemed willing to share her knowledge. However, this only extended to where she would allow individuals to accept her on her terms.

It was apparent from the beginning this was a broken soul. Could I help her? Did I want to go through it again?

Yet, my *check-person* light was instantly on. Something was amiss here.

I invited her into the house out of politeness, along with a feeling of owing Animal.

My life had finally settled into a comfortable pattern again. How would having her here change it?

I showed Jaci the room Vicky had used. She made no comment and, with other than what appeared to be a causal glance, walked only far enough into the room to look into the bathroom, which was en suite.

I showed her the remainder of my home with the exception of my office and my bedroom suite.

When we came to the studio, as I called the spare bedroom, because it was usually full of half-done art projects, her interest seemed to be aroused. I inquired, "Do you paint?"

I got a shoulder shrug, "Some."Jaci obviously wasn't interested in having a conversation.

I showed her the grounds. I had to admit I was proud of the gardens. I hadn't done the planting of the shrubs; my builder had done it to a T. I'd built the flower and vegetable raised beds.

We sat on the patio area while I again tried to engage her into some sort of conversation.

Either she was a lost and troubled soul, or she had an agenda she was unwilling to share. She seemed consumed with whatever was driving her.

I recognized this from years of working with foster children.

I wondered who she really was and what kind of a visitor she would be. The dogs hadn't alerted. She seemed to like them, but only in a cursory manner. This added to my red flag collection.

I hoped she was neat. I hated slobs. I'd no more than had the thought when she asked, "What are the house rules?" I was thunderstruck.

I clearly saw she was waiting for my answer. "I guess as far as rules go, they would be for youngsters not adults. I like my home to be neat. I keep a consistent schedule. I always eat breakfast and dinner here but often take lunch at the shop. I'm sure we can figure out what would work for the two of us."

Her only question was, "The shop?"

I explained to her that Ben and I had a business we ran from his boat yard down the road. I also told her I was usually there for a few hours each day.

Her next question floored me. "What type of security do you have here? Animal told me this was the most secure place in the state."

My first thought was to give her a review of my system. With all the sensors, the gate, cameras etcetera then for some reason, which I couldn't explain, even to myself, I simply stated, "It's more than adequate."

Her reaction was, "We may indeed need all of it; I have some baggage. I don't want to bring you any trouble. Perhaps I should find somewhere else to stay."

Oh, oh, not a good indication of where this was going. I had to ask, "What's the problem?"

Jaci seemed to ponder for a bit before replying, "Before I left the service, I turned in a couple of guys for stealing weapons from the armory. Animal knows about this and he alluded to the fact you were stuck in the cross hairs with the gang last year. He said it was how he met you and why you have the security system here.

"They were both incarcerated and swore when they got out they'd kill me for turning them in. They will. It's only a matter of time. I know that. I really don't want to bring any harm to anyone else."

I heard and understood what she was trying to tell me but I'm a tad stubborn. After weighing all of the options, I want to make my own decisions. "Frankly, I'm less concerned about them than I am about you."

I heard an involuntary intake of breath as I glanced at her out of the corner of my eye; she looked shocked. "I want you, if you decide to stay here, to feel comfortable and relaxed enough to get your feet back under you so you can live your life without hiding."

I saw a tear sliding down her cheek. She wiped it away, seemingly embarrassed by this show of emotion. As always, as many of the wounded ones do, she had a life-story which was hindering her growth. Physical injuries always heal much faster, even leaving scars sometimes. However, emotional ones remain and the shame of being less than perfect emotionally stays hidden.

I knew she was a rough-and-tumble woman who could handle herself in a scrap. She was not only fully educated in combat training, physically fit, and well prepared to fight, as demonstrated by the knife in the holster on her ankle. I was sure she didn't know I'd spotted it.

"What do you want for yourself now that you've been discharged from the service?"

Her answer startled me. "I want not to be scared all the time. I want to find out who I really am, then learn to like myself; at least a little. I've spent almost all of my life trying to be what other people wanted me to be.

"It began with my alcoholic, hateful father. He wanted me to be another son. Then the military, where my commanding officers wanted me to become a killing machine without a conscience. When I was getting ready for my discharge, they sent me to a counselor who told me to 'get over it and get on with it.' He didn't want to be bothered with me. I thought he made it clear. So much for being *all you can be*. Now I need to see if I can figure my next step out on my own."

I knew she was troubled but there was something more— did I really want to get involved?

Jaci's next question stunned me. "Is it safe to run out here on the roads and trails?"

I nodded while pondering my answer. "Sure, we're in a very rural area and the only ones who use this road would be the folks from the boat yard and me."

She stood and stretched. "Then I think I'll take a quick run, if that's okay with you." Without waiting for my response, she was off at a fast trot.

I didn't know why or what, but something was still bothering me. I went into my office and turned on the security cameras on the road.

Jaci ran down to the parking area then up the drive.

When I'd rebuilt the drive, I'd added two slight curves. My intention being when you started down the drive the visitor would approach the gate. A person would then need to ask and get permission to enter.

I wanted to know why I was uncomfortable with her. She ran up the drive while taking careful notice of the surroundings, especially the trees. Odd, I thought. I continued to watch. Was she looking for the security cameras? Unless you were great at detection, you'd never see them; even in the winter when most of the trees were bare of their leaves.

There's a big King's pine tree set back off the drive about twenty feet. We'd saved it when we were doing the excavating.

Jaci spotted it, stopped, turned to her right, and walked into the woods. I knew this wasn't a bathroom break nor was there a scenic overlook.

The hair on the back of my neck stood on end, never a good omen. I haven't had a moment of feeling it since we cleaned up the second mess. On the other hand, was this perhaps a continuation of the first one?

The feeling was back. Now I knew why. The area she entered was where we'd found the second cache of arms. It was also where we'd found the bundles of stolen cash that were stolen from trucks moving it from the mint to a secure location.

This spot was also where we'd found several skeletal remains.

When my security system was installed, we, the Federal Agent and I, decided we would add cameras as well as sensors to the area. We hadn't known if we'd discovered everything buried there. We also didn't know who would come looking for it, or when.

Bingo! I hate it when I'm right about these things. Jaci was walking carefully while it appeared she was counting her paces. She truly *knew* what she was looking for.

Jaci had walked beyond where we'd dug. At that point, she'd begun scanning the trees. I'd guess the trees were marked in some way, which wouldn't have been obvious to a casual observer.

She walked on, still examining the trees, and then stopped. She looked as if she were listening for something. Satisfied, she walked about another ten feet into the bushes.

She removed the knife from her leg holster and began digging at the base of a tree. Suddenly, her head snapped up and she listened again.

She cleaned the knife of the soil on the moss replacing it in the holster as she pushed debris over the dig with her foot, and then began moving out of the woods.

Jaci changed her mind and hid in a group of young alders.

I could hear Animal's truck on the road. When he pulled into the drive and up to the gate, Jaci stayed hidden. The gate opened and he drove through. She remained crouched in the bushes even after he'd passed.

When Animal pulled into the yard, the dogs were all yelping and playing around him. He walked up to the house and entered the kitchen door.

I called out from the office, "I'm in here. Come quickly! I want you to see this, now."

He entered and I showed him the monitor from which we were watching Jaci while she was crouched in the bushes.

He looked but didn't get the impact of what I was trying to show him. I switched to the other monitor and replayed the tape of her journey down the drive and into the woods. "Shit," was his total response.

He started to move toward the door when I stopped him. "We need to know what she's looking for and why. If you confront her now we'll never know. She won't stay there too long because she wants us to think she went for a run.

"Her conversation, when she returns, will be interesting because you can't get out unless you climb the gate or the fence setting off the alarms. Let's just wait and watch for a few minutes."

With a silent nod of his head, Animal agreed we needed more information.

"Did she specifically ask you to bring her here to billet or was it your idea? If it was her idea, I need to know how she knew about me."

Animal looked so distressed I thought he was going to cry. I patted his shoulder. "We have to know what this is all about. We'll have to ride this pony to the finish line. Just be careful because as you can see, she's not who or what you thought she was.

"She may not be in this alone either. You'll need to watch your back with whoever else is at your place.

"Should we call Eric? He needs to know what's going on here. This was not a coincidence.

"By the way, when you told her I had a great security system, thanks for not elaborating on it. I don't think she has a clue we're watching her every move."

Jaci had returned to her last dig site and resumed her efforts.

We'd been able to listen to the digging sounds, thanks to the audio sensors, which were part of the security installation. So far she'd not spoken. The only sound was grunting from the exertion of digging.

Then, as if on cue, Jaci spoke clear as a bell. "Well damn, Eddie, you could've made it clearer which tree. I've seen three with the marks. I could be here for a month before I find the right one, you dumb ass."

Animal pulled his phone out and called Eric. Because Animal would never call him unless it was important and related to what had gone on here, Eric answered quickly. Animal being a man of almost no words said, "Gotta talk now ...be right there."

I wasn't sure Eric had time to hang up before Animal headed for his truck. I stopped Animal with the warning that, if Jaci saw him go to Eric's, she might suspect something.

I called Ben to come with the electric Zodiac to pick him up.

I knew Eric would need his safe room and equipment in order to rally any support they would need.

In the meantime, I continued to monitor and record what was going on in my woods.

Jaci kept digging around the roots and trunks of the trees. I guessed she hadn't found what she was looking for. I was certain she'd have to stop soon. She wouldn't have an explanation for why she'd been gone so long, especially when she knew Animal had returned.

I saw the Zodiac had nosed into the outside of the rocks which shielded the cove. I watched as Animal ducked down, boarding the boat and was hurried away.

Jaci didn't seem deterred in her digging, as she rooted around the base of tree after tree. I could hear from the muttering she was getting disgusted, if not discouraged with the mission.

At one point, she stood and kicked the tree and swore like a pirate. Whoever Eddie was, she was mad at him and taking out her anger and frustration on the poor tree.

Something caught her attention. I watched as she cocked her head as if listening to something. I couldn't pick up anything on the audio. She remained standing and listening for several minutes then walked farther into the woods.

I could still monitor her, but not as well. She was almost at the limit of one camera and not quite within range of the other. She bent over and brushed away some debris with a look of satisfaction.

When I switched over to the other camera, I could see she'd found a piece of the twine we'd discovered on the initial dig.

I recalled vividly the twine was what sent poor old Woodie, the contractor, into an almost total state of shock. He'd served in Nam, returning with PTSD. Back then, they did little to diagnose or treat it. He came home with all of his demons. Over time and by isolation he'd made it through. To him the twine spelled trip-wire. He'd called us instantly. When we arrived, although he'd recovered some, he was still upset.

Eric had investigated it. We found somebody had used the line to mark the path to where there was buried a very large stash of cash all neatly packaged in waterproofing. Was this what she was looking for?

Jaci seemed elated. I called Eric to report the new finding just as she began to dig in earnest with a grin the size of Texas on her face.

Eric instructed me to stay on the surveillance. He didn't want to show up and stop the process. This was just the tip of *another* iceberg.

I thought *here we go again*. I wondered if it would truly ever be *all over* or if my life would have periods of peace and quiet then shift back to mayhem again.

I watched as Jaci dug, seemingly without thought of how much time had lapsed since she'd left. She could have run to the village and back in the same length of time.

At last, she unearthed a small packet of something wrapped in black sheathing. She began to cut away the packaging with her knife. She was sitting on the ground, totally intent with the chore at hand. She seemed pleased with the contents.

I couldn't make out what it was because of the angle. She set it to one side and then dug rapidly with renewed vigor in her efforts.

I called Eric to report. He agreed it was time to take action. We had to figure out what she'd found and who she was connected to.

Damn, is anything ever easy?

I knew from experience, it was beginning again. From the safe, I fished out my .38 Colt with the holster. When I was slipping it on, I remembered how it had saved me before. Better to be safe and look stupid than to be dead with no excuses.

Jaci must have heard Eric's truck approaching because she was quickly burying whatever she'd found. Then, as an afterthought, she pulled something from the packet and stuffed it into her bra. She finished the burial and covered it with debris. She cleaned her knife and returned it to the holster.

She made a great effort to wipe her pants clean. After Eric got through the gate, she paused to listen for when he shut the motor off. She began to run rapidly in place. I watched fascinated. I would have been hyperventilating and passed out cold by this time. Jaci slowly began jogging toward the garage then up to the house.

As she arrived, Eric, Animal and I were standing outside in the patio area. Other than some dirt on her trousers and a minimal smudge on her shirt, if we hadn't known, we would have assumed she'd gone for a run. Her skin was aglow with the sheen of sweat, which would be difficult to fake. Now I knew why she ran in place before heading back. She was no dummy, this kiddo.

She seemed to know who Eric was; perhaps from Animal or someone else, I didn't know.

We'd put a game plan into place before she arrived. Eric turned to me and excused himself with, "Well, I'll be going back to work now."

I offered Jaci and Animal a drink of lemonade. They sat in the patio chairs in silence. I returned with the glasses and pitcher on a tray. There had been no conversation.

Jaci was the first to break the silence with, "Boy this is a nice place to go for a run. It's quiet, no traffic and the weather is cool."

Animal asked quietly, "How far did you go?"

She smiled. Strangely, the smile never went any further than her lips, while her eyes retained a cool, very distant look. There was a total disconnect there.

"I ran quite a distance, first on the road then down some woods trails. It was a nice run. I hope I wasn't gone too long."

It was a great answer; however, you can't get off my property except by boat without setting off the alarms, period. How dumb did she think we were? Little did she know!

I heard Eric's truck returning and thought, *oh, oh, show time*. I was so right.

I would like to have the luxury of being wrong now and then.

Animal walked down to meet Eric while I stayed with Jaci on the patio.

I knew we were all on the monitor. It was recording all of this. I'd switched it on when we decided where we would confront her.

She didn't seem to be alarmed Eric had returned so soon. If someone had asked for my opinion, I would have guessed she was trying to keep herself calm and to appear normal. The fact I could sense she was anxious to contact someone with the news of her discovery seemed to be conflicting with her staying calm.

Eric reached the patio. He had something in his hand. He dropped it onto the table, dirt and all.

Jaci looked like it was a snake. She turned her eyes to Eric and spat out, "They told me you were a son-of-a-bitch and to avoid you at all costs. So, what do you think you're going to do to me?"

God bless Eric…he remained cool, calm, and professional, and stated the facts. "I'm going to arrest you on a Federal Warrant."

I'd never seen anyone move so fast. Jaci yanked the knife from the holster and threw it at Eric before any of us could move. All I saw was a blur of movement.

I hadn't considered the dogs; they were such a constant in my life. No matter where I am, they're always there. They have a keen sense of what people are feeling. They seemed to know before the person doing it did. They reacted instinctively, or as they'd been trained to do.

When Jaci threw the knife, while her arm was still in motion, Zeus had his jaws locked on her forearm mid throw. The knife missed Eric by inches. Animal had Jaci on the ground with Zeus still hanging onto her arm.

I never moved out of my chair. I must be getting old, or been there and seen that too many times in the last few months.

Animal got Zeus to release and sit. Shadow stood by Eric. Sandy sat by me. Jaci was still on the ground pinned by Animal.

What a lawn party. I need to invite better guests in the future, I thought.

"Jaci, I'll take the sheet you have on your person now."

As Eric reached for her, she snarled, "You touch me and I'll scream you sexually assaulted me, smart ass."

Time to get involved, "I'll retrieve it for you, Eric. She's not sexually attractive to me in the least. At my age, they wouldn't believe her anyway." I reached down the front of her shirt and removed the paper we'd seen her stuff down her bra before she left the dig site.

I passed it to Eric. He opened the sheet, nodded and then returned his gaze to Jaci, "This makes you an accomplice to the robbery. You do understand what this means, don't you?"

She fairly spat out, "Go to Hell, they can't stop us. We're much smarter than a bunch of hicks in this stupid state. So how are *you* going to arrest me?"

I'd heard the chopper coming as she was talking, or snarling, I guess seemed like a better word.

The Feds Eric had contacted for back up landed the chopper in the parking area. They were efficient, wasting no time. They cuffed her, read her rights, and she was loaded. There was a short conversation with Eric and they were gone, as always, easy in, easy out.

Eric returned to the patio area to inform me others would be arriving shortly to complete the recovery; damn, more digging.

"Eric, how large of an area do you think they'll dig up this time?" Last time they trashed the whole hillside in the cove then another large area in the alder swamp. The alders grew quickly, so if they confined the dig to there, it would be okay. I also knew I didn't have a choice in the matter.

Animal was downhearted and sad. He looked like he'd lost his last friend in the world. "I'm so sorry to bring misery to you again. I had no idea. I should've guessed. She didn't really seem to have much interest in the dog I'd chosen for her.

"I bet she sucks at poker."

Forty-seven

Life almost returned to normal, if there were such a thing, when Animal came to visit again.

He looked apologetic as he walked up to the house. I could only wonder what was going on. As usual, he came right to the point. Again, he needed to billet someone. "I would understand if you say no, considering the last situation I put you in. Please, meet her first; then make up your mind."

As he walked back to his truck, I wondered if I were running a boarding house for wayward women. I had no qualifications for either mental or medical care. Nor, truthfully, did I wish to get any.

Selfishly, I wanted to live peacefully in the cove with my dogs, work with Ben, sail, fish, paint, and garden. Those were the only things on my agenda.

Animal was escorting a thin young woman into my home. She looked like a waif found abandoned on the steps of an orphanage in some third-world country. She wasn't tall, although it was difficult to tell because she had her shoulders rolled forward. She appeared to be attempting to assume the fetal position while being forced to stand upright.

"This is Willow…she needs some help." His simple sentence was the biggest understatement Animal had *ever* made to me.

She didn't need *some* help... she needed probably more help than I could possibly provide.

We sat at the table in the kitchen while I provided coffee for the three of us. Animal and I chatted. Willow held the coffee mug with both hands as if it were her only lifeline. She had only nodded when he introduced us without making any eye contact with me. Personally, this is never a good or positive sign.

I needed some answers, so I dealt with the problem directly, as is my usual way.

I began with the questions which would provide me with some of the necessary information I wanted answers to. "Willow, what is it you need?"

Dear God in Heaven, I had never looked at someone so totally unplugged from life, *ever*. When she finally lifted her head and I could look into her eyes, I was shocked and saddened.

I've met people, mostly children, whose expressions were *flat*. Willow's expression was *vacant*. It was like looking at a computer screen after it crashed, leaving only a blank, black space. I was lost.

I pondered... without any mental health skills, could I help her? What happened to create this total disconnect? Would she be violent? Could I handle her physically if she were? My mind was on fire with questions. I had no answers.

Finally, Willow answered my question. "I don't know." Her voice was small and the words seemed to require all of her energy to speak. This girl was excessively fragile.

I'm kind of a rough-and-tumble person who isn't afraid to speak her mind, a *git-er-done* type.

I like to believe I'm kind, at least I hope I am. I gave up being nice to folks just to get along a long, long, time ago.

What did I have to offer Willow which would or could assist her in her return voyage to the land of the living?

Would I be harmful to her? This was always a big concern for me. I don't want to make things worse for anyone who doesn't deserve it.

Now if they deserve it, then as far as I'm concerned, they're on their own and fair game.

I looked at Animal; he needed to contribute to this conversation. "Eileen, I can only tell you what they told me. The information I had stated that Willow entered the service after completing a CNA course. They're really short of medical personnel so they fast-tracked her into being an assistant to a medic. When he was shipped to Iraq, he requested Willow to go as his assistant.

"I really believe she was ill prepared for combat medical work. She'd only worked in the hospital doing routine care, while still training, and had excelled.

"She didn't have enough time to transition to the battlefield hospital scene. She worked hard, acquired many new skills, and most likely would have been okay.

"Then the field hospital tent took a direct hit with no warning. The only ones who survived were Willow and the patient she was prepping for transport in the medivac chopper.

"They transferred her and the patient to the regional hospital. When they arrived at the hospital, they took the patient and sent her to the dorm for the nurses. They didn't check on her until the next day. By then she was catatonic. They tried some therapy and meds but nothing seemed to make much difference. They mustered her out on a medical discharge with honors.

"Because of my contacts around the disabled vets regarding the dogs, they sent her to me. *This isn't something I can fix.*

"I will tell you she does like the dogs. I have a special old female dog I'm keeping for her when she's up to it.

"Right now I think you can really help her."

Even though we were discussing her as if she weren't involved, I needed to know some facts. "Where's her family? How do they feel about this? Don't you think she would do better with folks she knows?"

Willow spoke very softly. "I have no family; I was a ward of the state because I was left in a supermarket cart with a note. I lived with several foster families and in group homes. I have nowhere to go, nor anyone who wants me. You don't have to take me in if it's a burden."

That did it. I was almost in tears. Damn, I hate being a mush-pot. I, too, had lived on the street when I was thirteen, after my dad died. I knew what it was like to be unwanted. I would be damned if I'd turn my back on this scrap of humanity.

My anger nearly choked me. This was never good for me because I despise injustice! In our family, we call it *righteous indignation*. It had always gotten us into a whole lot of trouble, and, when acted upon, a whole lot of satisfaction when justice is applied.

At that very moment, I thought I should change her name from Willow to *Wisp*… a strong wind would knock her over

"Animal, bring her things and we'll see how this goes." He grinned as he headed for his truck. The stinker had already brought them.

I showed Willow to the room she would use. When I inquired if she needed anything such as shampoo, lotions or other products I got a slight smile. That was progress!

It took a couple of days to be able to engage Willow in a conversation beyond a few words at a time. I was careful not to push her too far, or too quickly. I didn't want her to shut down. I could see some progress. It was a good sign.

Willow would be an attractive girl when she put on a little weight and began standing taller.

She seemed to enjoy the room and having a private bathroom. I think she only had two pair of pants and a couple of tee shirts. They looked like military issue to me.

I broached the idea of going shopping for some clothes and things she might want. Too soon, I realized, this was a mistake the minute I opened my mouth. It'd taken me most of the remaining day to reassure her we didn't need to do that.

I wanted her to have some pretty things to wear. I'm stubborn to the max, so I went online and ordered them. If they didn't fit or she didn't like them, I could return them. I was smug for the next two days while I waited for my package to arrive.

On the third day, the gate alarm sounded and there was the delivery! When the driver had placed the package in the kitchen and gone, I called Willow to come and see her presents.

To say she was surprised would have been a total understatement. I opened the large box and then started passing out pants, shirts, panties, socks, sandals, sweaters, sweatshirts, and sneakers. You would have thought the kid never had any clothing bought for her.

It was better than Christmas! I sent her to her room to try on clothes.

I was beginning to think I'd misjudged the sizing, as she didn't come out. I waited and then finally the door opened and out stepped a young woman dressed in brightly colored, well-fitting garments. She was so shy it hurt my heart to see her. "They are lovely. Thank you so much."

My mind just stamped the *effort-bill,* "Paid in full."

Willow spent the afternoon putting on her *fashion show,* as she called it. "How did you know what size to order?"

I smiled and thought of my children and grandchildren. "I've bought a lot of clothing for kids in my time. I'm so pleased they fit and you liked them."

Her next question caught me off guard. "Would you cut my hair for me?"

I thought about it for a minute then offered to take her to a beauty parlor for a cut. Wrong again— she looked like I was asking her to leave. Oh, oh, back to the foster kids.

Grinning, I responded, "Sure, I'll cut it if you're brave enough for my skills." Her hair was a dark auburn with a lot of wave and body to it. I could do this.

We gathered an old sheet, some scissors from the sewing box and went to the porch. I trimmed and shaped it to the best of my ability. She thought it looked great. I was pleased it didn't look as if I'd used a bowl.

That evening, as we sat on the patio after dinner, I felt we were making progress. She looked young and was healthier looking each day. I guess I couldn't expect anything more for the moment.

I asked her if she would like to take the dogs and we would go for a walk. So far, in the time she'd been with me, she was always with me in the house or out in the yard. I wanted her to begin to explore our world and make it hers. She seemed to hesitate for a moment, then nodded.

I called the dogs. I knew Zeus wouldn't go farther than the gate. He'd wait there for our return. Shadow and Sandy were happy for an adventure. Sandy had adopted Willow; spending most of her time with the girl. Willow seemed to enjoy having her company, so it was a win-win for both of them.

I really believe when wounded animals and hurt people connect, it forms a special bond. They seem to sense the other's angst, providing comfort to each other.

We walked up to the end of the drive. I was hoping I could encourage her to walk down to the boat yard. We managed to get about halfway there when she asked if we could go home. I was pleased we'd gotten so far.

Willow seemed to like to walk along and chat. Not much, but more than when she first came.

I learned she'd enjoyed the acquired nursing skills. However, when she'd gotten into the combat situation, some of the wounded were so badly damaged it had overwhelmed her. She said she still had nightmares about the bodies just coming and coming and all the blood and the awful smells. The noise had scared her horribly. She said it never ended. Willow told me she'd tried to do a good job and make a difference. When the hospital tent exploded and everyone died except her and her patient, she felt she was a total failure.

She was only a child. It was difficult to get her to understand there had been nothing she could have done to change the outcome of that terrible day.

The next day I asked her if she liked boats. Her answer made me laugh. She told me she didn't know. She'd come from the Midwest and had never been around any boats. I explained I'd grown up on the water and loved boats and fishing. When I asked her if she would like to try boating and fishing, she gave me a very reserved, "Okay."

Because I usually spent most of my days at the shop in the boat yard with Ben, I'd kept *Survivor* there. I told Willow I was going to go get my boat and bring it back to the mooring in the cove so we could use it. She seemed to be in agreement with that.

I asked her if she knew how to drive a car. She smiled and told me she didn't know how to drive because no one had taught her. She'd never had the use of an automobile.

Gee, I guessed I had a lot of teaching to do.

I called Ben and told him I'd like to bring the boat down to the cove. As always, Ben's answer was, "I'll be right down to get you."

I heard the Zodiac coming and asked Willow if she wanted to ride down and sail back with me. I could see she at least thought about it before saying, "No." This was another giant step.

I explained to her I expected her to come to the beach with me to meet Ben. There would be no negotiating this. If something happened here, she had to know Ben, Eric, and Vicky so they could help her.

I knew the meeting with Ben would go well. He was a quiet and kind person. I don't believe anyone would be ill at ease around him. He's just *nice-people,* as we say down here.

After meeting Ben, she was obviously wavering on going with us. When Shadow jumped into the boat, as she always did, leaving Sandy waiting for assistance, Willow shrugged her shoulders, scooped Sandy up into her arms, and decided to climb aboard.

Wow! Leaps and bounds here in the recovery department!

I told Ben this was Willow's maiden voyage. He promised to get us there safely. Willow's only comment was, "I like the way the ocean smells."

We sailed home without incident. I believed I impressed Willow with how well I handled the boat. It was a good day's work. I'd coaxed her away from the house; she met a stranger, and learned she liked the boats.

I needed to get back to working at the shop. We had orders coming in, bills to pay, and business plans to complete. I told Willow I was going to the shop to work for a couple of hours. I invited her to come with me. To my surprise, she agreed. We all piled into the Jeep and went to work.

I showed Willow the boatyard and pointed out the different shops making up the operation. We went into our shop where it was generally quiet because we'd taken over another building for the major production of our sailboats.

Willow's first comment was, "I love the smell in here."

Good start…I loved the wood smell too.

Ben greeted us warmly and we began to go over the paper work for the office.

We were deep in discussions when Eric arrived with Vicky in tow. We greeted each other and I introduced Eric and Vicky to Willow.

At first, she seemed shy around them. Then with a great deal of gusto, Bruno, Eric's Rottie, came into the shop. The dogs greeted each other and clearly, Shadow and Bruno wanted to go out and play. Sandy remained seated at Willow's feet.

I blessed these folks for not being the inquisitive, intrusive type. Willow found a chair and just sat and listened to our chatter about the business.

Eric runs a very different part of the yard with the big-block engines for racing boats. Ben and I laugh and call our part the *mom and pop* end of the yard.

Vicky asked if we would please join them for lunch. I'd taken a quick glance at Willow to see if she was comfortable with that. I received a "Yes" nod. We all walked down to their home on the point.

When Ben and Eric built the home many years before, they had situated it perfectly on the point so the water appeared to surround it. They had installed a lot of glass across the front facing the ocean. The views were breathtaking.. Vicky redecorated it after she and Eric married.

We had enjoyed a great lunch and were leaving when the general alarm for the yard sounded.

It meant big trouble somewhere. Eric's phone rang. The look of horror on the man's face was enough to panic all of us.

Eric began to run, shouting to us to call an ambulance. Ben passed Vicky his phone and we all began to run as fast as we could to the big building where the boatlifts were. I couldn't think about anything except what might have happened and how I might assist.

Ben and I landed there just after Eric. It was not good. Somehow, one of the boats on the hydra-lift had slipped in the straps, pinning Dan. He was badly hurt but still able to talk. Eric and the rest of the crew were busy putting blocking in so it couldn't slip any further. Eric needed to see how they could lift the boat and extract Dan without injuring him more.

Eric got the crane into position and was busy with rigging the boat when I noticed somehow Willow had darted past us and was down next to Dan. I could see she was talking to him very quietly and he seemed to stop struggling. She was holding his hand, crouched on her knees. They seemed oblivious to all the drama going on in the building with the rigging and blocking. I was amazed.

It seemed like hours, but it was only a matter of minutes before Eric could safely raise the boat enough so they could slide Dan free. Willow was asking Eric for something I couldn't hear. Eric nodded and ran to the side of the shop, returning with a large flat board and some strapping. I stood in amazement as Willow helped to move Dan onto the board and strap him down to restrict any movement when they lifted him.

He was badly hurt…that was readily apparent. Dan seemed to take great comfort from Willow holding his hand and talking to him.

We heard the sirens as the ambulance arrived. Those folks were always great when they responded. They were impressed with the backboard and strapping already applied. Dan was lifted, board and all, and carried to the gurney.

I wasn't sure Dan would let go of Willow's hand. She leaned in closer to him, said something, and got a lopsided smile as he released her hand.

There was a short discussion as to who would go with Dan. Eric's assistance was required to complete the stabilization of the boat in the lift, so Ben volunteered to go. I told Ben I'd follow so he would have a ride home.

Most likely, they would take him to the city directly, rather than to the small local clinic. This meant he would have to ride for at least an hour and a half. I prayed he could make it and would be okay.

When we got into the car, I asked Willow if she wanted me to leave her at the house with the dogs or if she wanted to come.

She surprised me with her answer. "I need to go with you. I told Dan I'd come to the hospital to be certain he was all right."

After dropping off the dogs, I drove as fast as possible to catch the ambulance. During our ride, I could sense there was an internal struggle going on with Willow.

I assumed when she got to the point she wanted to talk she would begin the conversation. By the time we arrived at the emergency room, she still hadn't said anything.

I noticed Willow was not only aware, she was actively engaging in a professional manner with the staff. Talk about a changed person! I don't know what happened, but the change was great, as far as I could see.

I knew Dan, but I didn't know anything about his family or anything outside of the boat yard.

The staff determined they needed to keep Dan for testing and to repair his broken leg. The doctors would not release him until the following day, if all the tests came back negative for internal injuries.

I asked Ben, "Has anyone notified Dan's family?"

Ben responded, "Dan doesn't have anyone. He was the product of an abusive home, became a state ward early in his life, then lived in foster and group homes. He is alone other than his connection with Eric and I."

He was another casualty of our throw-away-world. Where would it end? As a society, we just toss everything that's troublesome. People, pets, cars, everything and everybody, it seemed, could be gotten rid of.

As we were talking about Dan's situation, Willow said, "You folks can go along home. I'll stay with him. I know what to do. If there's a problem, I'll contact you directly. He shouldn't be here alone. There're too many things which can, and do, go wrong if there isn't somebody to advocate for him. I'll take good care of him…I promise you."

What had happened to the scared, vacant, and shy girl who had come to my house to heal? I didn't know, but I liked what I was seeing.

We left with the assurance Willow had Dan's cell phone and would call us with any news.

Willow called late in the evening to report the testing had gone well. Other than a broken leg and bruised ribs there'd been no internal damage. I offered to come get her; her refusal was humorous, firm, but polite…Dan wouldn't be alone on her watch. His scheduled release was for the next morning. We would go get both of them. My, how quickly things change.

The next morning Ben and I took his big Expedition and headed off on our mercy mission.

By the time we arrived, Dan was ready to leave. Other than the air-cast on his leg, he looked like the young healthy man I'd always known. He had always been a handsome young man. He had black curly hair, which was always tousled and wind-blown and stuck out from the ever-present ball-cap, in all directions. His eyes were jet black, kind and with the hint of constant laughter just below the surface.

I was so thankful that in spite of his injuries, he looked so well. I knew Ben was relieved; Dan was like a second son to him.

The biggest change for me was Willow. I saw a competent young woman. The slouched shoulders, averted eyes, quiet speech were gone. Instead, there in her place was a person who'd found herself. I knew she'd never let go of her confidence and competence again.

I thought to myself about how, when someone somehow loses their sense of what, and who, he or she is, then regains it, they are much stronger. I was so pleased…good for her!

The return trip was fun, with a stop at McDonalds for food. It seemed Dan hadn't enjoyed the hospital food. He alluded to the fact if you were there for more than three meals you might never be well enough to leave.

Eric insisted Dan stay at his house until he recovered. I knew the accident had shaken Eric to the core. He saw Dan as his younger brother.

Once we got everyone home and settled in, Willow and I walked home. On the way, she explained what happened to her.

When she'd seen Dan injured, all of her past training snapped into gear. She knew what to do, and knowing she could help, she did it. When she was at the hospital, she knew what her future was going to be. She wanted to go into the nursing program at the university. She asked if I would let her use the computer to research and apply for fall classes.

I found it difficult to contain my excitement over the development.

We made the trip to the campus for her first meeting. Our shared experience reminded me of going with my granddaughters for their college searches.

The meeting went well and, a few weeks later, Willow got her letter of acceptance to begin in the fall semester.

The friendship between Dan and Willow grew. They were a nice couple. He taught her to drive in the car Animal had presented to her with a large red bow tied on the grill.

Willow would stay at college and only be coming home for breaks. I told her she would always have a home with me.

Life once more settled into an easy pace with working, sailing, and fishing. There was also great excitement—Vicky was pregnant, so I was busy making baby things.

Forty-eight

Animal came on a cold, wet Saturday morning to request space for another female. I knew he had some trepidation about this person. I agreed to meet her, but didn't commit to taking her. Jaci left a real foul taste in my mouth, which even the success with Willow hadn't lessened.

When they arrived, I *wasn't* impressed. As Animal was trying to introduce us, he'd barely spoken, "Eileen this is Bertha," when she interrupted.

"Call me Bert. You don't have to be concerned; I can take care of you."

To say I was astounded by the total lack of manners, to mention nothing of the statement. *Take care of me,* who in hell did she think she was? Better still, who did she think *I* was? Nope, this wasn't going to work.

She shifted her weight slightly, making me think of a fighter waiting to throw the next punch, much too aggressive for my comfort level.

Even for Animal, I had my limits.

"I'll get my gear." With that, she was out of the door.

I turned to Animal. "I won't take her. Sorry, she's too excessively aggressive for my liking. I don't have a good feeling about this one."

Animal surprised me with his next statement. "Les, our friendly agent, requested I bring her here so you can keep an eye on her. He has a theory about where some of the other contraband is, and who else is still involved. She knows nothing about any of this. It will only be for a very few days. I'm on speed dial for you. Also, if it will give you more comfort, carry your weapon."

Gee, that was reassuring.

I don't want to get involved in another dust-up. I thought…no I *knew* I'd done my part more than once. I just wanted to enjoy what was left of my life.

Animal interrupted my thoughts with, "I've already contacted Eric so he knows. Contact him if you need to. I'll be back shortly."

I saw movement at the cove and wanted a better sight line so I stepped to the kitchen window. Bert was standing on the rocks looking over *Survivor* on the mooring. My hackles stood up straight. The first thought that popped into my head was, *don't even think about it*. If she touched my boat, she would need more than her training to save her sorry ass.

She walked toward the house with her duffle slung over her shoulder. She was tall, rugged in a tough way with short clipped medium brown hair with a perpetual chip attached to both shoulders. I *didn't* like her, nor did I trust her. I'd noticed the dogs hadn't gone to greet Bert; however, they never took their eyes off her either. The dogs' focused attention was a bad omen.

Bert's lack of social graces continued. "Which room is mine? I like a private bath."

What nerve! I showed her to the back bedroom, without a private bath. I smiled to myself as I did so. I could have put her into the guest suite with the private bath. She didn't deserve it. She would use the hall bath.

When I had the house was re-built, I had installed three baths. I was on an old dug well with a good water supply and a new septic system. I still didn't think for one person and a few guests I needed more than three bathrooms. At that time, I didn't know I would become a boarding house for females either.

Bert walked into the room, sweeping it with her eyes, then asked, "Where's the bath?"

I smiled my snarkiest grin and quietly said, "Next door, in the hall."

Bert's reply set my teeth on edge. "This won't do. I told you I needed a private bathroom."

I didn't hesitate even a nano second before I informed her, "This is it, kiddo. Take it or leave it. If this doesn't suit your needs, put your gear back in the truck and find other space. It's your choice. This is *my* home and I won't tolerate bullies or bad manners. Do I make myself clear?"

She seemed surprised I'd spoken to her so harshly. It took her a second to respond. "Yeah, I guess this'll have to do. I won't be here *that* long anyhow."

I didn't like this person at all.

Bert slung her duffel onto the floor with a loud thump.

I made a mental note to check the contents when the opportunity arose.

It wasn't long before the opportunity presented itself.

Bert came out of her room and announced she was going for a walk and didn't know when she'd return.

Here we go again. I wondered if she knew about the security system. If they, the smugglers, keep sending these people, they must communicate.

I watched her walk toward the cove. She stood silently, smoking what looked to be a small cigar, while looking *Survivor* over. She glanced back at the house and saw me watching her from the glass door; she nodded and walked on around the beach.

I went into my office and turned on the security scanners. I wanted to watch this bird.

She climbed the rocks on the far side of the cove until she came to the fence. She stood still, looking around from right to left. I knew she was trying to see if there were cameras in the area.

She was seemingly satisfied she wasn't being observed, and then she moved down onto the rocks so she could get around the fence. She didn't have a clue the move set the security system into screech mode. The alarm wouldn't sound out there, but my system was lit up like a Christmas tree.

I continued to watch Bert as she paced off from the rock back toward the trees. She listened, looked around, and then removed the most vicious looking long knife from a leg holster. While she was removing the knife, I spotted a small gun strapped to her leg. Certainly explained the baggy combat pants she wore tucked into the boot tops.

She began to dig. All I could picture in my mind were Jaci's antics while she was here.

I wondered if the military supplied all women with big knives and leg holsters. It wasn't my idea of a fashion statement.

Bert seemed to have better directions, because it wasn't long before she unearthed a large black parcel. It was a different shape and size than the other ones I'd seen. In a matter of minutes, she was busy inflating a black Zodiac. Wow! What would she do next?

She appeared to be looking for a spot where she could launch the craft. However, in the area where she was, it was too steep to get safely down to the water. She continued to walk along the edge of the bank scanning below her.

I took the opportunity while she was on the far side of the fence line to run into her room and see if I could check out her duffel. I had no problem opening the top after making a careful observation as I memorized how it fastened.

I pulled the top open and nearly fainted. She had a black commando style hood, black long sleeved knit shirt, a bulletproof Kevlar vest, a large nasty machine pistol and a bunch of loaded banana clips.

There was a clear plastic pouch with a grey putty-like material. One other clear baggie contained what looked like unsharpened pencils.

My mind went to a recent article I'd read; I think the stuff is plastic explosives and the other things are pencil-timers.

Dear Lord, I pray I'm wrong.

I'd carefully replaced the stuff into the duffel when the fence alarmed. I knew she was on her way back.

I needed to contact Eric at once. This was beyond anything I was *ever* going to get involved with, even for Animal.

I was unsure if she had a phone tracker so I couldn't call him.

I slipped on my holster, then shrugged into my fleece jacket.

Bert didn't seem to be through with her recon. She walked up the drive to the gate then along the inside of the fence to where it met the rocks on the other side of the property. Again, she went around the fence by dropping down onto the lower rocks. It appeared she was still looking for a launch site for the Zodiac.

The rocks were just as treacherous over there.

How was I going to contact Eric? I didn't want Ben mixed up in this mess.

The gate alarm sounded. Problem solved. It was Animal.

I turned off the surveillance screens and spun the coded lock on the office door closing it securely.

I thanked God as I walked down to meet him in the parking area.

He exited his truck with yet another dog. I'd begun to feel like I was running a kennel along with a boarding house for strange and aggressive women.

The dog was another large mixed breed similar to Zeus. My three dogs arrived in the parking area with me. I looked to see what their reaction was to the newcomer. Nothing… they were all sitting, waiting, and watching.

I had to get him onboard regarding the gear in Bert's duffel and her activities by the fences.

We needed to get Eric involved.

As he always does, Animal began his conversation in the middle, with no introduction to the subject. "Brought you a new friend. I did bring food for all of them."

I needed to get his attention before Bert returned. I was certain she had heard his truck come in. I spoke quietly while pretending to look at the dog. "We've got big trouble and we need to talk with Eric ASAP."

Animal leaned over, showing me the dog's teeth as a cover. "How bad is it? Worse than you thought?"

I look into the dog's mouth saying, "Yes, yes, and yes. Way worse than you or I thought. This is going to happen soon, tonight I think. Body armor, assault pistols with several banana clips and enough plastic explosive and pencil timers to take the town off the map.

"This one is bad to the bone."

Animal's reply was simple. "Shit. I'd hoped it wouldn't be that bad. I'll go speak with Eric. Do you think she has a listening device? Is that why you didn't call him?

"By the way, this big guy's name is Felix. Don't ask, I don't know why, but that's his name. He's well trained, good with people unless you alert him. If you need him to guard or pursue someone, just point and say 'get.' He will only be here with you until I remove the threat. I'll be back in a flash."

"Animal, before I forget, Bert unearthed a Zodiac buried beside the security fence, along with something else I couldn't make out.

"She's armed with a very large knife and has a small automatic pistol strapped to her right leg. God only knows, perhaps a rocket launcher is on the other leg! Be careful, she's roaming the woods. She was on the outside of the right hand fence on the rocks when I came out. She's been looking for the cameras."

Just as I finished speaking, the dogs, all four of them, came to attention without a sound and looked to the rocks where Bert was standing. I wondered if she'd found my cave within the rocks.

Animal nodded and moved toward his truck. "Remember what I told you about Felix. Be right back."

When Animal drove away, Bert walked over the rocks and entered the garden area where she sat on one of the chairs.

I walked up the pathway, with my entourage in tow, to the seating area around the fire pit.

Bert was smoking another one of the small cigars languishing in the chair as if she were at a resort. I was surprised when she spoke. "You don't like me, do you?"

I may not be too smart but I'm honest to a fault. "No, I don't find anything about you that would ever encourage me to like you. I'm certain that doesn't come as a surprise to you. You most likely developed this skill-set over the years and it worked for you."

Bert seemed stunned I'd said this to her. If she thought I was going to become a shrinking violet because she was obnoxious, she'd better rethink the scenario. I don't have any back down in my personality.

It must be catching, because all four dogs were standing around me at attention. The dogs' eyes never wavered for a second; they were riveted on Bert.

The fact Bert didn't like the dogs, even a little bit, was a big warning to me.

Bert shifted in the chair. "I hate dogs, all of them. Tell them to stop staring at me or I'll slit their hairy throats."

"Not here, not now. This is my property, and I won't tolerate that kind of attitude or talk. Am I clear?"

With a big huff, she lifted herself out of the chair and headed for the house with the cigar still stuck in her mouth.

I called after her, "Bert, I don't allow smoking in my home."

She tossed the still lit cigar to the ground and stomped across the porch.

I wanted to grab her by the scruff of her neck and the seat of her pants, throw her to the ground, and stomp all over her.

I restrained myself. I went into the house and entered my office locking the door behind me. I swapped out my .38 for the whopping .45 auto Eric had given me. I didn't trust her at all.

I didn't have security monitors installed for the interior rooms. Now I was regretting my lack of foresight.

The gate alarm sounded and I could see Animal's truck coming in.

I knew Bert had come out of her room while I was swapping out my handguns.

After securing the office, I walked out to the porch to meet Animal. Bert was busily engaging him in an animated conversation. As always, his expression remained the same…unreadable.

Apparently, Bert didn't get the response she had expected. She stomped off up the driveway.

Animal ambled up to where I was standing on the porch with a snarky grin on his face. Chuckling he said, "So you ladies have had words, I take it? Your boarder's unhappy. She's upset with her host, the dog pack, and mostly about your attitude. In addition, what she can and can't do, along with a myriad of other complaints. She wants to leave, now. She told me she would wait at the gate. What do you think of that?"

I smelled a rat. I walked back into the house with Animal on my heels, going directly into Bert's room.

Just as I suspected, the duffel was missing. She didn't have it with her when she stomped up the drive so where had she stashed the thing? I needed to find it ASAP. Had she put it out the window? I looked, not there. When had she removed it?

The only time she'd been in the house alone, as far as I knew, was when she came in from the garden in a huff.

Had she snuck back into the house when I was talking with Animal when he first came with Felix? She could have, then hidden the bag before reappearing on the rocks.

I *had* to find the bag and fast.

Animal saw my concern. "What do you want to do? What do you want me to do to help you?"

"Take her away but keep her with you at all costs while I find this bag. Be careful; she is armed and very loosely wrapped. Are you armed? Do you need to borrow one of mine?"

All I got was a snicker, a grin and a hug. Animal got into his truck and drove off. I watched on the security camera as Bert got into the vehicle and he drove them away.

Eric was the next to arrive with Bruno. I went out to meet him and explained what had just transpired.

He came in so we could review the tapes of Bert finding the Zodiac, then her wandering the rocks on the shore seemingly to find a safe launch site.

He was as concerned about the duffel as I was.

We employed the dogs in our search but to no avail. I searched the cave and the woods line on both sides of the drive, but turned up nothing. We went to where the Zodiac was stashed…still no luck. It was beginning to get dark when we stopped looking.

Eric returned home and the dogs and I began a long vigil. I knew Bert would return here somehow tonight. I changed into dark clothing, sneakers, and a black hoodie. I was still carrying the .45. I did not intend to take it off.

The dogs began to stir just as the night was settling in. I didn't move from my seat on the far edge of the porch; I was alert and ready. All three of the dogs came and sat beside me. Poor old Sandy was in the house on her bed sleeping. I wondered what had bothered them in the first place. Perhaps they'd smelled or heard an animal.

I didn't have long to wait for the answer. There was a muted snuffle and another dog bumped my shoulder. Bruno. Which meant Eric was there somewhere. I felt better already.

The night was so dark even with good night vision I could barely make out the cove. I could just see the silhouette of *Survivor* on her mooring.

Everything was silent, it seemed. The tide was high so there wasn't any wave action on the shore. There wasn't a breeze stirring. It seemed even the night insects had fallen quiet. When insects become silent it means bad news is approaching.

Zeus slipped off the porch; the others remained. I assumed he needed to relieve himself. When he didn't return in a few minutes, I became alarmed. He never left the porch unless there was an issue. I didn't want to call him and break the silence, but I needed to find him.

I touched Shadow and whispered in her ear, "Go find Zeus." She is so clever she knew we needed to be quiet. I put my hand on her collar and walked beside her. Felix and Bruno followed us, all without a sound. Shadow stopped, putting her head down and pulling my hand with her motion. She nosed something. I felt what she had touched. It was Zeus. I knelt. He was breathing but he was unconscious. I felt his head over and couldn't find a bump. The situation was crazy.

Shadow darted away from me with the other dogs in hot pursuit. There wasn't a sound. I couldn't hear them moving but I knew they were. What was going on?

In an instant, Eric touched my shoulder. I nearly fainted from fright. Some night-fighter I'd turned out to be… for shame! Eric had night vision goggles on. He was intent on what he was watching.

He whispered in my ear, "The dogs are okay. She hid the duffel in *Survivor* and retrieved it with the Zodiac. She's paddling out of the cove right now. I don't know if your boat is booby-trapped or not. Don't touch it until I've checked it. The dogs are coming back now. I think she drugged Zeus.

"I'll be back. This may take a bit. Go call Animal so we know he's okay. Don't turn on the house lights. Leave the dogs on the porch. I'll carry Zeus up to the settee."

I entered the house, stood in the corner away from the windows, and called Animal on my cell. No answer. I was panicked…what had happened to him?

I couldn't leave with Eric out chasing a lunatic nor would I call him. Should I call Ben to go see what happened to Animal? I was frightened Ben would be walking into something dangerous.

As I stood there hesitating, my phone vibrated. It was Animal. "What's wrong? Are you okay? Say something! Can you hear me?"

No response. Dear God, he must be really injured. How am I going to help him? Please, God help me!

My phone vibrated again. Animal's ID showed on the screen. No voice but I could hear what sounded like a grunt. "Animal, can you hear me? Are you hurt?"

The line stayed open. I could hear labored breathing. What was going on…I had to find Animal quickly, but how?

A muffled voice came through the phone, "Near you …need help fast …send Zeus."

How could I tell him Zeus was down?

Would Felix know how to find him? I had to try.

I quietly called Felix to me and after telling Shadow to stay with Zeus, I ran up the drive with Felix by my side.

I prayed this would work. I leaned over to Felix's ear and said, "Find Animal, now." He stood looking at me as if waiting for more instructions. Instructions I didn't have.

I ran farther up the drive to the gate and punched the code to open it. We ran through. Felix was ahead of me, and although I could hear him running, I couldn't see him; what if I lost him?

I ran as hard as I could. At my age, I am not a runner. I could barely catch my breath. My side hurt and my lungs burned with the effort. I had to keep going.

When I had all but given up, thinking I was on a wild goose chase, Felix nearly knocked me down. He grabbed my hand and ran forward with me in tow.

Driven far into the woods on a portion of an old tote-road was Animal's truck. I ran to the driver's side and yanked open the door. Animal was sprawled across the seat, his face swathed in duct tape. He wasn't responding. I ran to the passenger side so I could reach him better. I touched his face and one eye opened; he blinked. I had no clue what was wrong with him; I just knew it was dire.

I got into the driver's side and found the keys still in the ignition. I put Felix on the floor of the passenger side while trying to move Animal so I could see if I could drive us out of the woods.

Mission accomplished. The truck started. I reversed it and with some rocking, I managed to get it onto the road and down my drive. I didn't turn on the lights. I got the gate opened and made it to the parking area.

How was I going to get this big man into the house? He needed help. *I* needed help!

I ran into the garden shed and grabbed the big cart I used for mulch. I positioned it beside the open passenger door and as gently as possible, I hauled Animal out of the truck into the cart. I hoped I had enough strength to pull him up to the house.

I tugged and pushed and finally made it to the door. I grabbed the entry rug and tipped the cart so he would slide out. I took hold of the rug and dragged him into the house.

I left him on the floor while I gathered up scissors to cut off the tape. With the tape removed from his mouth and nose, he appeared to breathe better. He was still unresponsive. What should I do?

I was in despair. How could I help my friend and his dog?

It was apparent he'd been drugged, but with what? Would he wake up? Would he die? I know nothing about drugs beyond aspirin, so I wasn't much help.

I remembered in the old days when someone fainted they gave them a sniff of ammonia. I had a bottle under the sink. It was certainly worth a try. I poured a little on a clean cloth and passed it under his nose. The smell almost floored me. How would this help?

He rewarded me with a groan. Should I try again? I did. This time I got a groan and a cough. I waited. Animal opened one eye. It was so bloodshot it almost seemed the blood would run out. The eye closed. I sighed.

I had to get the doctor here, even if it compromised whatever was going on outside.

I had just pulled my cell phone from my pocket when I heard a very large explosion offshore. Then there were sirens out on the bay. I ventured a glance out through the slider and the whole sky was lit up with flares and floodlights.

I prayed Eric was okay.

My phone vibrated. I answered. It was Eric calling to tell me it was okay and he was safe. Had I found Animal yet? I filled him in quickly, telling him I was going to call the doctor because I was afraid both Animal and Zeus would die. He agreed.

Thankfully, even though the doctor was elderly, he came at once. I still had Animal on the floor. The doctor checked his heart and the bloodied eyes, shook his head then reached into his bag for a needle and some medicine. He gave Animal a shot. He never removed his stethoscope from Animal's chest. Dr. Brann looked so serious I just watched and prayed.

In a matter of minutes, which seemed like hours, Animal groaned, then opened his eyes. He was quite a sight. I hadn't removed the duct tape because I wasn't sure how to get it unstuck from his beard.

I told the doctor Zeus was down as well and again I didn't know what had happened to him.

Animal stirred at the information and tried to tell the doctor what to do to help the dog. His speech was so garbled we couldn't understand him. I could see the frustration building in his eyes. He moved his hand slightly and tried to mimic using a hypodermic needle. I asked, "Do you want the doctor to give the dog a shot?"

He nodded for an answer.

The doctor and I went outdoors to the area where I'd left Zeus. He was still there and breathing. His breaths were shallow…not a good sign. Dr. Brann gave him a smaller shot of the same medicine and then between the two of us, we carried the dog into the house and laid him next to Animal.

Animal moved his hand over to touch Zeus. It was like a miracle! The dog lifted his head, sniffed the hand, and gave a slight wag of his tail.

I'd made coffee. Dr. Brann and I sipped a cup and waited to see how our patients would fare, given time.

Animal began to stir. He didn't seem to be agitated, which was a good sign. He reached his hand to his face and touched the duct tape. He sighed in resignation, knowing his beard would be gone when we cut the tape off.

When he was able, we sat him up with his back braced against the wall; I gave him some good news. I thought I could get the tape off without cutting his beard. He grinned and gave me a thumbs-up.

Zeus crawled over to lie beside him putting his head on Animal's leg.

Dr. Brann checked both of them over, and then said his goodbyes. I thanked him for coming.

I wondered why I hadn't heard anything from Ben. I hadn't called him to help find Animal. I was certain he knew Eric was on a mission.

The gate alarm sounded. It was Ben and Eric. They trooped into the house, taking in Animal and Zeus's state of appearance.

Ben asked, "Any coffee left?"

I'd set mugs out along with cream and sugar. We might as well drink coffee; there wouldn't be any sleep here for the rest of the night.

I'd begun the task of getting the tape off Animal. He insisted I trim his beard to get rid of the tape. With Eric's assistance, we got him into the recliner.

Eric filled us in on the off shore events of the evening. Eric had called in the Coastal Marine Patrol along with the Coast Guard. They'd been laying offshore waiting for his signal.

Bert had launched the Zodiac, then paddled into the cove to retrieve the duffel from *Survivor*. She then headed for Ben's small island.

Eric was monitoring the situation from his Zodiac with night vision glasses. She'd gone around to the ocean side of the island and beached the craft. She had signaled with a flashlight to someone waiting offshore.

She'd been busy digging on the side of the bank to unearth bales of drugs. She stacked them while waiting for another boat to come.

Out of the darkness came a small fleet of Zodiacs with electric motors.

The authorities waited until they'd loaded some of the crafts before they surrounded the whole fleet and turned on the spotlights.

The marine patrol had stayed hidden until the small boats had headed for the island, then backtracked to find the vessels which had launched them.

Eric said some of the Zodiacs launched from beach locations monitored by the wardens. Somehow in the ruckus, there was small arms fire with one of them hitting Bert's duffel. It set off the large charge of explosives.

The explosion killed several on the beach and wounded the others. Bert died in the blast.

Eric had left the clean up to the crews gathered.

Ben had been in his Zodiac on the inland side of the island to be certain neither Bert nor any of the others might try to come ashore and harm me.

We drank our coffee and thanked God none of us, other than a groggy Animal and Zeus, was injured.

We wouldn't know the total fall-out from the raid until it was processed.

Somehow, I had a feeling of inner peace…this mess was finally ended.

Epilogue

Eric and Vicky returned from their cruise. They looked happy and rested. Ben was delighted to have them home.

Ben asked if I would go with him to his little house where we picked up the silver Jeep. He was interested in assessing what would be required to re-open the home.

I knew Ben had lived in the big house with Eric; however, I hadn't thought about where he would live now, after Eric and Vicky's wedding.

The house was a cute, small home, which looked to be in good repair. The home was totally void of any human presence. That wasn't unusual, as it had been vacant for a long time. Ben explained how, after his wife died, he'd stayed with Eric until Belle arrived with the children. Then he'd built the apartment over the shop. He felt it was time for him to re-open the house. Ben wondered if perhaps I'd help him make it homier.

I'd give him a dog...always worked for me. I loved projects; this should be easy and fun.

I thought Ben was excited about moving back home.

We all needed some calm and peace in our lives.

I shared Animal's new adventures with Ben and how well Woodie was doing.

He shared his feelings about Eric, saying he seemed happy and content for the first time in forever.

Eric had told his dad he thought there was a buyer for the big boat. I assumed it had been fun to use, but definitely not Eric's style of boating.

Bruno was happy to be home with his family. He liked to come with them to visit my dogs for a romp, but he also loved his home base.

I lost my old Sheltie, Seaweed, during the winter. She had lived, like the queen she was, for a long time. She died in her sleep in my arms with her friends by our side.

Sandy became a welcome addition.

It appeared we'd all found our spaces and places. It was truly peaceful at Haven Cove.

~ * ~

Ben and I sat on the patio enjoying the late day sunshine watching Eric and Vicky's twins, Benjamin and Gale, named after Eric's mother, play on my beach. It was a wonderful sight. The two children were sitting in the sand at the edge of the water with Shadow, Bruno, and Zeus sitting one on either side and one behind guarding them. We would never have to worry that anyone could or would bother the kids. We looked at each other, smiled, and agreed that it doesn't get any better than this.

Willow and Dan began dating, then married in the summer of her graduation from college with her nursing degree. Dan received a partnership agreement in the boat yard. Willow works at the small local hospital. Ben gifted his small home to them and then happily moved into the apartment over the shop.

Ben and I are still working our business and enjoying our friendship.

Animal still trains dogs for retuning vets and builds street-rods.

Meet

H. Wakefield

H. Wakefield is a lifelong resident of the beautiful state of Maine. She shares her home with her dog Miss Joy, a miniature Australian Shepherd. Because of her love for the outdoors, Maine is the ideal environment for the pursuit of her hobbies. She enjoys RV'ing, kayaking, fishing, painting, gardening, and writing. Due to her unlimited energy and boundless curiosity, it has been mentioned she would be the ideal 'poster child' for geriatric ADHD. She enjoys life, being active and engaging with interesting folks and her church. She comes from a family of storytellers with her younger sister being a published author.